THE AFRICAN-AMERICAN BOOK OF DAYS

THE AFRICAN-AMERICAN BOOK OF DAYS

INSPIRATIONAL HISTORY AND THOUGHTS FOR EVERY DAY OF THE YEAR

JULIA STEWART

A CITADEL PRESS BOOK
PUBLISHED BY CAROL PUBLISHING GROUP

A Citadel Press Book
Published by Carol Publishing Group
Citadel Press is a registered trademark of Carol Communications, Inc.
Editorial Offices: 600 Madison Avenue, New York, N.Y. 10022
Sales and Distribution Offices: 120 Enterprise Avenue, Secaucus, N.J. 07094
In Canada: Canadian Manda Group, One Atlantic Avenue, Suite 105, Toronto,
   Ontario M6K 3E7
Queries regarding rights and permissions should be addressed to Carol Publishing Group, 600 Madison Avenue, New York, N.Y. 10022

Carol Publishing Group books are available at special discounts for bulk purchases, sales promotion, fund-raising, or educational purposes. Special editions can be created to specifications. For details, contact: Special Sales Department, Carol Publishing Group, 120 Enterprise Avenue, Secaucus, N.J. 07094

Interior illustrations by Tod H. Schaffer.

Manufactured in the United States of America
10 9 8 7 6 5 4 3 2 1

Library of Congress Cataloging-in-Publication Data

Stewart, Julia
    The African-American book of days : inspirational history and thoughts for every day of the year / Julia Stewart.
        p.   cm.
      ISBN 0-8065-1661-5 (pbk.)
      1. Afro-Americans—History—Chronology.   2. Afro-Americans—History—Miscellanea.   I. Title.
    E185.S8   1995
    973′.0496073—dc20
                                                                    95-19923
                                                                    CIP

DEDICATION

To grandparents—the guardians of our family histories. In particular, this book is dedicated to the memory of Robert Allen, Grace Peoples, Esther Curfman, Lila Gene McKirgan, Edith Darraugh, and Charles "Papa Sol" White.

FOREWORD

If the house is to be set in order, one cannot begin with the present; he must begin with the past.

—John Hope Franklin, African-American historian

For years our myopic and color-biased society has suppressed volumes of information that fill the rich and colorful tapestry that is our country's history. For the better part of this century, history books have glossed over the importance of African-Americans as an essential element of our national character. This one-sided view of history, presented to generation after generation of Americans, has pushed us deeper into the abyss of a divided society.

Fortunately, many attempts are being made to amend such historical oversights. Previously overlooked information is being revived in separate and distinct literature, libraries, museums, courses of study, and even schools. For the time being, it may be necessary to focus on what has been suppressed and to herald it across the land. In turn, the time will arrive when the pendulum swings back toward the middle, and African-American history and culture simply become part and parcel of mainstream American history and culture. Some day young Americans won't be able to distinguish historical figures by the color of their skin, but will recall them instead by their achievements and historical importance.

The sooner we learn to appreciate the entirety of our history and all of our ancestors, the closer we will come to a just and cohesive society.

FOREWORD

Americans must learn to cherish and embrace their own diversity, as the rest of the world has already conceded us. For when an American travels abroad, whether black, white or any other shade, they are one thing before anything else—American. As Swedish scholar Gunner Myrdal remarked in his famous 1940's study of race in America: "America is free to choose whether the Negro shall remain her liability or become her opportunity."

Here on the pulse of this new day
You may have the grace to look up and out
And into your sister's eyes,
And into your brother's face,
Your country,
And say simply
Very simply
With hope—Good morning.

—closing of Maya Angelou's poem "On the Pulse of the Morning," read for
President Clinton's inauguration on January 20, 1993

ACKNOWLEDGMENTS

Thanks are due first and foremost to my eleventh-hour research assistant, manuscript reader, and illustrator Todd Schaffer, who cut short his traipsing about Europe to come to my aid. Appreciation is also due to Georgia Williams for hosting my three-week retreat in Melrose, Florida (gotta love those folks at the Blue Water Bay) and to Mike Cornell for his encouragement and hospitality during visits to the D.C. area. Bongo, once again, sat patiently through the process, but he wasn't such a good dog this time. And lastly, thanks to my editor at Carol Publishing, Allan J. Wilson.

INTRODUCTION

Don't nobody try to tell me to keep quiet and undo my history.

—Nate Shaw, an Alabama tenant farmer who tape-recorded the
history of his life before he died

African-Americans have been an integral part of the unfolding drama of U.S. history since the earliest days of this country, and even well before the United States *became* a country. Records show that a man of African descent navigated Christopher Columbus's flagship to the shores of the New World in 1492. In 1539 the Moor Estevanico led an expedition of Spanish explorers into America's Southwest, becoming the first non–Native American to enter that region and open up what is now New Mexico and Arizona for European expansion.

The first sizable number of Africans to reach American soil were brought on a Dutch ship in 1619. The twenty African captives were taken ashore at Jamestown Colony, Virginia, and exchanged for provisions. By the middle of the seventeenth century, the international slave trade was thriving. Every year thousands of Africans were being stolen from their homes and forcibly transported to European colonies in the West Indies and North America. Soon about one out of every five persons in colonial America was African.

Prior to the full-blown Atlantic slave trade, the British colonists had imported Europeans as indentured servants. Colonists also used Native Americans as forced labor, but found both the natives and Europeans overall more costly and less plentiful than African slaves. Because

European indentured servants and Native Americans fraternized with, and were socially equivalent to, those bound in slavery, intermarriage became quite common. One observer noted that colonial Virginia "swarmed" with mulatto children.

Many of these children grew to be memorable individuals who played important roles in shaping our nation. For example, the part English, part African surveyor and mathematician Benjamin Banneker constructed the first clock made in America. He also wrote several almanacs and helped to design the city of Washington, D.C. The half–Native American, half-African sea captain Paul Cuffe made his fortune in the whaling industry and was an early civil rights advocate who successfully petitioned the Massachusetts courts for the right to vote in 1780.

Both through their sheer numbers and their individual achievements, African-Americans have played a vital role in every military battle this country has ever fought. African "agitator" Crispus Attucks was the first to fall in the Boston Massacre, an incident that kindled the onset of the American Revolution. Beginning with the Battle of Lexington and Concord, some 5,000 black patriots fought in the war of independence from Britain.

An estimated 220,000 African-Americans served with the Union Army during the Civil War, of whom roughly 37,500 died. The bravery of the all-black regiments, particularly the Fifty-fourth Massachusetts Volunteers, is legendary. Following the Civil War, African-American units known as Buffalo Soldiers were stationed primarily on the western frontier, where they performed with exemplary courage. These soldiers also gained praise for their valor during the ten-week Spanish-American War.

Despite mounting racism at home, African-Americans displayed immutable patriotism when nearly a half million were drafted or volunteered to fight in the first World War. World War II followed not long afterwards, and once again African-American patriots demonstrated praiseworthy commitment and courage. More than a million African-Americans fought in the "granddaddy of all wars." One remarkable act of bravery occurred when Dorie Miller, a navy mess attendant with no previous gun training, shot down four enemy planes during the

INTRODUCTION

bombing of Pearl Harbor. African-American soldiers have continued to protect the nation's interests in the frozen hills of Korea, the jungles of Vietnam, and the deserts of the Middle East.

For a long time African-Americans have been overlooked as frontiersmen and pioneers. In fact, African-Americans were as much a part of the western frontier as were banks and brothels. Half of the contestants in a shooting and roping contest on July 4, 1876, in Deadwood, South Dakota were reported to be black men, and African-American broncobuster Nat Love took away the top prize. One cattleman estimated that about one-third of the 35,000 cowboys employed during the golden age of the cattle industry, in the latter part of the nineteenth century, were either of African or Mexican descent.

People of African ancestry were among the first non–Native Americans to settle many points west of the Ohio River. In 1773 "the handsome Negro" Jean Baptiste Pointe DuSable established a trading post at a site the Native Americans called *Shikai-o,* "the place of wild onions," now Chicago, Illinois. Another African-American merchant, George Washington, founded the far west town of Centralia, Washington. The Tumwater Falls area of Oregon's Puget Sound was first settled by a small party of pioneers led by George Bush, a mulatto farmer and cattleman. Los Angeles, California, also records people of African descent among its founding residents.

African-Americans have a history of being pioneers in mechanical and professional fields as well. Norbert Rillieux, an engineer and inventor from New Orleans, forever changed the nature of chemical engineering and revolutionized the sugar industry when he patented the Vacuum-Pan Evaporator in 1843. Similarly, Jan Ernst Matzeliger revolutionized the shoe industry with his 1883 patent for a machine that automatically assembled shoes. In 1893 Dr. Daniel Hale Williams of Chicago performed the first successful open heart surgery on record. More recently, Dr. Ben Carson of Johns Hopkins Hospital led a team of doctors and nurses successfully separating siamese twins joined at the head.

America's creative arenas have also benefitted from decades of African-American innovation. In November 1973 *Ebony* magazine noted that African-Americans "virtually invented" the catering business.

INTRODUCTION

Colored caterers Thomas J. Dorsey, Henry Jones, and Henry Minton reigned as purveyors of the culinary arts in Philadelphia from 1845 to 1875. According to *Ebony*, these caterers "might have been said to rule the social world of Philadelphia through its stomach." Meanwhile, further south in New Orleans, a Mr. Cordovell dominated the fashion world for a good part of the nineteenth century. "The reported fashions of Cordovell are said to have frequently become the leading fashions of Paris," recalled historian Martin Delany.

The Harlem Renaissance of the 1920s spawned an outpouring of African-American literary, artistic, and dramatic achievements. It was a golden era for the Negro and the arts, as African-American writers and artists from across the country rushed to Harlem, in the words of Langston Hughes, "to express their individual dark-skinned selves." Representing the first generation of African-Americans not born into slavery, these artists produced urbane, sophisticated works that broke down many preconceived notions about African-American life. Unlike the outright moralizing of previous generations, the Renaissance artists countered racism in a more subtle and personal manner. A similar creative surge occurred thirty years later, during the Black Arts Movement. But while the Harlem Renaissance embraced "art for art's sake," the Black Arts Movement took a definitive radical and political turn.

African-Americans have repeatedly presented the world with the gift of new and unique forms of music. Ragtime, jazz, blues, gospel, rock 'n' roll, and soul all originated with African-American musicians. It is worth noting that of the personalities profiled in *The Great American Popular Singers*, by inveterate music critic Henry Pleasants, nearly half are African-American. Among the honorees are Ethel Waters, Nat King Cole, Mahalia Jackson, and B. B. King. Pleasants speculates that trumpeter and vocalist Louis Armstrong was "probably, the most famous musician of the century." Numerous popular American dances, including the cakewalk, Charleston, turkey trot, shimmy, black bottom, Lindy hop, and jitterbug, were conceived in black communities as well.

Besides all of the above, African-Americans again and again have beaten the odds and broken through restrictive barriers to become accomplished in virtually every aspect of our country's life. Entrepreneurs like Madame C. J. Walker and John Merrick built up business empires from practically nothing. Countless black athletes figure among America's most legendary sports stars—Joe Louis, Muhammad Ali, Jesse Owens, Hank Aaron, and Michael Jordan, to name a few. African-Americans have stood as key political figures both domestically and internationally. Mayors like Carl Stokes of Cleveland and Thomas Bradley of Los Angeles have spearheaded urban change and growth, while statesmen such as Ralph Bunche and Gen. Colin Powell have left their mark on world affairs.

Perhaps most importantly—from Capt. Paul Cuffe's 1780 petition to the Massachusetts state legislature protesting taxation without representation, to the fearless African-Americans working the Underground Railroad, through the civil rights actions of the 1950s, 1960s, and up to the present day—African-Americans have led the way in assuring that the United States lives up to its democratic, constitutional ideals.

A NOTE FROM THE AUTHOR

It took careful and painstaking research through the annals of our country's history to find all the places where the African has left his or her mark in the making of our country and society. However, there exists now, more than ever before, a great many excellent books on African-American history. Worth special mention is the notable and comprehensive political history by Lerone Bennett Jr., *Before the Mayflower, A History of Black America*, and an excellent collection of historical writings, *Crossing the Danger Water, Three Hundred Years of African-American Writing*, edited by Deirdre Mullane.

The contributions of African-Americans to American history and culture are great and countless, and in no way would it be possible to include them all in one small book. This is not meant to be a comprehensive work, rather it is representative. Presented here are the bulk of the most notable events and people—as much as could fit within the confines of the genre of a day-by-day book.

An inordinate amount of time was required to fit the information into the time-specific format of this book. In several cases exact dates found for certain events varied according to different sources. When it was not possible to verify the accuracy of a date with an original source, the date chosen by the author, of course, was that which accommodated the work at hand. The author apologizes in advance for any errors or omissions. Any corrections or comments are welcomed and may be sent in care of the publisher.

I hope this book surprises and fascinates the reader as much as it did the author and her assistant while doing the research.

JANUARY 1

On the first of January, 1863, President Abraham Lincoln signed the Emancipation Proclamation, bringing it into force on this day. The document declared that slaves in states that had rebelled against the Union were "then, thenceforward, and forever free," and provided for African-American soldiers to enlist in the Union Army and Navy during the Civil War.

Crowds in the North had awaited with anticipation the signing of the Proclamation, which ignited what was known as the Year of Jubilee.

> *Once, the time was that I cried all night. What's the matter? What's the matter? Matter enough. The next morning my child was to be sold, and she was sold; and I never 'pected to see her no more till the day of judgement. Now, no more that! No more that! No more that! With my hands against my breast I was going to my work, when the overseer used to whip me along. Now, no more that! No more that! No more that!...We'se free now, bless the Lord! They can't sell my wife an' child no more, bless the Lord! No more that! No more that! No more that, now!*

—elderly man speaking at a gathering in Washington, D.C. on the eve of the signing of the Emancipation Proclamation

JANUARY 2

On this day in 1990, David Norman Dinkins began his first working day as mayor of New York City with a 7:00 A.M. appearance on NBC-TV's *Today* show. After defeating former mayor Edward Koch in the September Democratic primaries and then, by a small margin, beating Republican Rudolph Guiliani in the general election, Dinkins had become the first African-American mayor of America's largest city.

The 62-year-old Dinkins had been sworn into office the day before in a simple ceremony on the steps of city hall in front of an estimated crowd of 12,000. "The crowd at the inauguration," wrote the *New York Times*, "at least three times as large as those at similar ceremonies over the last two decades, was a testament to the historic nature of Mr. Dinkin's election."

Attending the mayor's inauguration ceremonies were singer and civil rights activist Harry Belafonte, Anglican archbishop Desmond M. Tutu of South Africa, and Reverend Jesse Jackson, among other friends and well-wishers. Archbishop Tutu congratulated the new mayor, saying, "thank you for your victory. Thank you for what you are doing for our struggle. We shall overcome."

In Dinkins's inaugural speech he pledged to be a "mayor of all people," and remarked:

> *Today we mark more than the transfer of power. Today we travel another mile on freedom's road....*
>
> *We are all foot soldiers on the march to freedom, here and everywhere. We all belong to the America that Lincoln called "the last best hope of earth." In advancing that hope, our most powerful weapon is example. And this year, this city has given powerful proof of the proposition that all of us are created equal.*
>
> *I stand before you today as the elected leader of the greatest city of a great nation, to which my ancestors were brought, chained and whipped in the hold of a slave ship. We have not*

finished the journey toward liberty and justice, but surely we have come a long way.

JANUARY 3

On this day in 1985, the first African-American to gain international fame as a star of grand opera gave her farewell performance at the Metropolitan Opera in New York City, playing the title role in Verdi's *Aida*.

Leontyne Price's performance of Aida, which was telecast live from Lincoln Center, is considered the peak of excellence against which all others are compared. Price ranks among the best sopranos of the modern era, often being credited with having the perfect Verdi voice.

Price was the first African-American since Marian Anderson to appear in a major role with the Metropolitan Opera. She debuted at the Met on January 27, 1961, as Leonora in Verdi's *Il Trovatore*. For this performance she received a forty-two-minute standing ovation—the longest salvo in Met history.

Trained at the Juilliard School of Music and inspired as a child by Marian Anderson, Price won thirteen Grammy Awards for her recordings and three Emmys for television appearances. She was awarded the NAACP's Spingarn Medal in 1965 for being "the outstanding soprano of our era."

I'm asked to be booked more and more, but look, I'd like to find out who I am. If I do have some success, I'd like to try to enjoy it, for heaven's sake! What is the point of having it otherwise? Everyone else gets excited but you're the one who's always tired. That's not life. That's not living.

—Price quoted in *Divas: Impressions of Six Opera Superstars*, by Winthrop Sargeant (1959)

JANUARY 4

Archie A. Alexander, architectural engineer and former governor of the Virgin Islands, died on this day in 1958 at the age of 69. He had been appointed governor of the Virgin Islands by President Eisenhower in 1954. His term was short, however, as he was forced to resign from the post in 1955 due to ill health.

This coachman's son earned an engineering degree from the State University of Iowa, where he also played football. He later became coowner of the construction firm Alexander and Repass, with offices in New York and Washington, D.C. Alexander was the designer and engineer of the Tidal Basin Bridge in Washington, D.C. In 1928 he was awarded the NAACP's Spingarn Medal for being an outstanding African-American businessman.

Known for his wit, Alexander once exchanged the "colored" and "white" signs at segregated toilets with signs that read "skilled" and "unskilled."

JANUARY 5

Today is George Washington Carver Day in honor of the brilliant agricultural chemist who died on this day in 1943. Nicknamed the Peanut Man and the Wizard of Tuskegee, Carver headed the agricultural department of the Tuskegee Institute in Alabama and was one of the most prominent scientists of his day. He was renowned for finding new uses for everyday items. Carver discovered 188 ways to use the sweet potato and 300 uses for the peanut, which included peanut milk, dye, a scrubbing powder, sweets, flour, and livestock feed.

Carver's research in improved farming techniques helped to revolutionize farming in America. He was especially concerned with improving the lot of poor southern farmers and organized outreach programs to assist them. He encouraged farmers to diversify from the single cash crop of cotton, which depleted nutrients from the soil, and promoted the planting of peanuts, cowpeas, and sweet potatoes. In addition, he formulated cheaper farm inputs, such as organic fertilizer, to substitute for more costly commercial fertilizers.

Born in Diamond, Missouri, during the Civil War, Carver was raised by a white farm family. As a child he was curious about all things natural. He once wrote, "I wanted to know the name of every stone and flower and insect and bird and beast."

Carver received the NAACP's Spingarn Medal in 1923, the Roosevelt Medal for distinguished service in 1939, and the Thomas A. Edison Foundation Award in 1943. He died at the age of 78. Carver's birthplace is now a national monument.

> *The world of science has lost one of its most eminent figures....The versatility of his genius and his achievements in...the arts and sciences were truly amazing.*
>
> —President Franklin D. Roosevelt speaking at Carver's funeral

> *There is a use for almost everything.*
>
> —George Washington Carver

JANUARY 6

On this day in 1874, Congressman Robert Brown Elliot delivered one of the most eloquent speeches of the times in defense of Charles Sumner's civil rights bill. Elliot's hour-long speech began:

> *I regret, sir, the dark hue of my skin may lend color to the imputation that I am controlled by motives personal to myself in advocacy of this great measure of national justice. Sir, the motive that impels me is restricted to no such narrow bound-*

ary, but is as broad as your Constitution. I advocate it, sir, because it is right.

Elliot was directing his comments toward rival congressman Alexander H. Stephens of Georgia, the elderly former vice president of the Confederacy, in what was dubbed a battle between the "Anglo-Saxon and the undoubted African." With his signature afro hairstyle, the sophisticated representative concluded, "The constitution warrants it; the Supreme Court sanctions it; justice demands it."

A major southern Reconstruction politician, Elliot was elected to the U.S. House of Representatives at the age of 38 and was among the first African-Americans in the U.S. government. Both before and after serving at the national level, he held office in South Carolina's state legislature.

Elliot had studied law in London and ran a successful law practice in South Carolina. Also a linguist and scholar, Elliot owned one of South Carolina's biggest private libraries. His motto was: *I am what I am and I believe in my own nobility.*

JANUARY 7

On this day in 1955, Marian Anderson appeared at the Metropolitan Opera in New York as Ulrica in Verdi's *Masked Ball*, making her the first African-American to perform at the Met. Considered the finest contralto of her time, Anderson was told by famed conductor Arturo Toscanini, "a voice like yours comes once in a century."

Anderson was awarded the NAACP's Spingarn Medal in 1939 for her achievements as "one of the greatest singers of our time." Noting "her magnificent dignity as a human being," the citation continued: "Her unassuming manner, which has not been changed by her phenomenal success, has added to the esteem not only of Marian Anderson as an individual but to the race which she belongs." Anderson also served as U.S. delegate to the United Nations in 1958.

I had gone to Europe...to reach for a place as a serious artist, but I never doubted that I must return. I was—and am—an American.

—Anderson quoted in *Famous American Women*, by Hope Stoddard (1970)

Where there is money, there is fighting.

—Anderson quoted in *Marian Anderson, a Portrait*, by Kosti Vehanen (1941)

Marian Anderson

JANUARY 8

On this day in 1867—the first year of the Reconstruction era—a bill was passed by Congress, despite President Andrew Jackson's veto, which gave African-Americans living in the nation's capital the right to vote. By March, a series of Reconstruction bills were passed by Congress that put army generals in control of Confederate states, ordered constitutional conventions to be held, and gave blacks and poor whites throughout the South suffrage.

Lasting from 1867 to 1877, Reconstruction left a legacy of public school systems and public works, such as roads and dams, in the war-damaged South. Economic conditions and social status were improved for many blacks, poor whites, and women. Charities and penitentiary systems were established and damaged ferries, bridges, and courthouses were rebuilt.

During what W.E.B. DuBois dubbed "the mystic years," African-Americans held public offices in unprecedented numbers. Upon visiting the South Carolina House of Representatives, the first majority black legislative body in the Western world, reporter James S. Pike wrote, "the Speaker is black, the clerk is black, the doorkeepers are black, the little pages are black, the chairman of the Ways and Means is black, and the chaplain is coal black."

Blacks and whites mixed on the social level as well. One Republican reflected on a social event of the era:

> *The colored band was playing "Rally 'Round the Flag."....There was a mixture of white and black, male and female. Supper was announced, and you ought to have seen the scramble for the table. Social equality was at its highest pitch.*

JANUARY 9

Countee Cullen died on this day in 1946 in New York City at the age of 42. This poet and teacher is considered one of the most representative figures of the Harlem Renaissance of the 1920s. His works reflected the social and political mood of the times, and he treated racial and African heritage themes in an urbane and romantic way.

Cullen's first volume of poetry, *Color*, was published in 1925. His other works include *Copper Sun* (1926), *The Ballad of the Brown Girl* (1926), and *My Lives and How I Lost Them* (1942). Cullen also edited a book of verse by African-American poets of the twenties entitled *Caroling Dusk*. In this book he wrote his own biographical sketch, which reads: "As a poet he is a rank conservative, loving the measured line and skillful rhyme; but not blind to the virtues of those poets who will not be circumscribed; and he is thankful indeed for the knowledge that should he ever desire to go adventuring, the world is rife with paths to choose from."

> You have not heard my love's dark throat,
>   Slow-fluted like a reed,
> Release the perfect golden note
>   She caged there for my need.
>
> Her walk is like the replica
>   Of some barbaric dance
> Wherein the soul of Africa
>   Is winged with arrogance.

—first verses of Cullen's poem "A Song of Praise"

JANUARY 10

Edward Brooke was sworn in as the first popularly elected African-American senator on this day in 1966. A Republican from Massachusetts, Brooke served two terms. He was defeated in his bid for a third primarily because of a bitterly and very publicly contested divorce that led to accusations of welfare fraud and other improprieties.

Brooke showed special interest in Africa throughout his career. One of his early actions as a freshman senator was to make a month-long tour of twelve African countries to assess the effects of U.S. reductions in

9

foreign aid. After leaving Congress, as chairman of the Emergency Committee for African Refugees, he wrote a letter to the editor of the *New York Times* to drum up aid for African refugees. Dated December 2, 1981, it read, in part:

> More than 6.3 million refugees—half of the world's total—are struggling for survival across the continent of Africa. The tragic victims of war, famine, the remnants of colonialism, despotic rule or apartheid, they are the forgotten refugees of our times. Until now, the world has failed to heed their desperate pleas for help....
>
> Since 1975, there have been, on the average, one million new refugees each year in Africa. Yet the response of the world community has been negligible, certainly in contrast to the assistance provided to the refugees of Southeast Asia, Eastern Europe and Cuba. The disparity is enough to make one wonder about the Western World's traditional prejudices....
>
> It is vital that all of us personally support the voluntary agencies providing aid in Africa. We must urge our Government to increase our effort to feed, clothe and shelter the homeless and the hungry.

JANUARY 11

An article appearing in the *Washington Post* on this day in 1984 noted that 22-year-old Wynton Marsalis had been nominated for four Grammy awards. Marsalis, an African-American trumpet prodigy, was the first person in the history of the Grammys to win awards in both the jazz and classical categories.

Marsalis was born into a musical family and raised in the quintessential musical city, New Orleans, Louisiana. He received his formal training at the Juilliard School of Music in New York. His first solo album, *Wynton Marsalis*, was released in 1981. The record was a critical success, although some claimed it sounded too much like Miles Davis, to which Marsalis replied, "If you play trumpet and you don't sound like Miles or Dizzy or Clifford [Brown] or Fats [Navarro], you're probably not playing jazz." In 1983, he released his first classical album, *Trumpet Concertos*, recorded with the National Philharmonic Orchestra in London. This, along with his 1983 jazz album *Think of One*, were the two discs for which he won the Grammys in 1984.

Marsalis has helped to elevate the reputation of jazz—which he calls "the ultimate twentieth century music"—as a respectable art form. And he has claimed that jazz is more difficult to play than classical music.

If we had a better sense of art and a stronger sense of history, we wouldn't have to accept the idea that entertainers are artists.

An art form can influence your thinking, your feeling, the way you dress, the way you walk, how you talk, what you do with yourself.

—Marsalis, in *Ebony* magazine, February 1986

JANUARY 12

The first issue of *Opportunity* magazine was published by the National Urban League (NUL) in January 1923. The magazine was described as "a journal of Negro life that would devote itself religiously to an interpretation of the social problems of the Negro population."

The magazine's first editor was Charles S. Johnson. Johnson employed an investigative, scientific style, and promoted international black culture. Examples of article titles include "Columbus Hill—The Study of a Negro Community," "The Negro in Chicago Industries," and "Africa—A Study in Misunderstanding."

Although *Opportunity* was considered a house magazine for the NUL, it also played a significant role in promoting the arts during the

Harlem Renaissance of the 1920s, particularly during the five and one-half years that Johnson served as editor. Johnson was instrumental in helping the "New Negro Movement" gain broader acceptance and brought African-American literati together with white publishers through the magazine's literary contests.

"The importance of the *Crisis* magazine and *Opportunity* magazine," explained Johnson, "was that of providing an outlet for young Negro writers and scholars whose work was not acceptable to other established media because it could not be believed to be of standard quality despite the superior quality of much of it." *Opportunity* magazine ceased publication in the winter of 1949.

> *Droning a drowsy syncopated tune,*
> *Rocking back and forth to a mellow croon,*
>   *I heard a Negro play.*
> *Down on Lenox Avenue the other night*
> *By the pale dull pallor of an old gas light*
>   *He did a lazy sway...*
>   *He did a lazy sway...*
> *To the tune o' those Weary Blues.*

—excerpt from the "The Weary Blues," by Langston Hughes; "The Weary Blues" won first prize for poetry in the *Opportunity*'s first literary contest in May 1925

JANUARY 13

On this day in 1966, Dr. Robert Weaver was appointed by President Lyndon B. Johnson to head the newly created Department of Housing and Urban Development (HUD). Weaver was the first African-American in history to serve in a presidential cabinet. "I want the job," Weaver was known to have said to insiders, "but damn if I'll ask for it!" As the director of HUD, Weaver oversaw 9,000 employees and approximately $4.5 billion in annual expenditures.

Before his HUD post, Weaver served as administrator of the Housing and Home Finance Agency in the Kennedy Administration—the highest federal position held by an African-American up to that time. A former NAACP board chairman and chairman of the National Committee Against Discrimination in Housing, he was awarded the NAACP's Spingarn Medal in 1962 for his leadership in housing issues and human and civil rights. Weaver held a Ph.D. in economics from Harvard and was also formerly a college professor.

Bob Weaver's performance as administrator of the Housing and Home Finance Agency has been marked by the highest level of integrity and ability to stimulate a genuine team spirit. I have found him to be a deep thinker, but a quiet and articulate man of action. He is well versed in the urban needs of America as any man I know. Bob Weaver now has a charge. It is to build our cities anew. Maybe that is too much to put on the shoulder of one single man. But we shall never know until we try.

—President Lyndon B. Johnson at Weaver's swearing-in ceremony at the White House

JANUARY 14

At noon on this day in 1868, South Carolina's constitutional convention got underway. This was the era of Reconstruction, and throughout the South constitutional conventions were being held under the supervision of Union military commanders.

It took the delegates to South Carolina's convention fifty-three painstaking days to create a constitution which would be readily approved by the electorate. The new constitution extended rights to blacks, women, and poor whites, as well as established the first state public school system that "shall be free and open to all children...without regard to race or color."

While some of the delegates were well-to-do and freemen, most were former slaves and poor whites. Of the 124 delegates to the convention, 76—or 61 percent—were colored, reflecting the majority African population of the state. This was the first and last official state assembly with an African-American majority.

As one white reporter described the scene, white representatives were "sandwiched between delegates in every stage of nigritude." And the *New York Times* correspondent wrote: "...the colored men in the convention possess by long odds the largest share of mental calibre. They are the best debaters; some of them are particularly apt in raising and sustaining points of order."

Convention president Alber Gallatin Mackey, a white man, opened the convention with the following remarks:

> ...in the call for this body, every true man who could labor for the support or fight for the defense of commonwealth has been invited to a representation. Manhood suffrage has for the first time been invoked to convene a body which is to make the fundamental law for all. This is, then, truly and emphatically a people's Convention—a Convention by the representatives of all who have minds to think—and to think for themselves, or muscles to work—and work for themselves.

JANUARY 15

Today in 1929, Martin Luther King Jr. was born in Atlanta, Georgia. The son of a Baptist minister and grandson of a slave, King became America's most revered civil rights leader. A Nobel Peace Prize recipient, King was a wise and moving orator whose words are often quoted, as below.

> The ultimate measure of a man is not where he stands in moments of comfort and convenience, but where he stands at times of challenge and controversy.

Don't hate, it's too big a burden to bear.

Human salvation lies in the hands of the creatively maladjusted.

If a man is called to be a street sweeper, he should sweep streets even as Michelangelo painted or Beethoven composed music or Shakespeare wrote poetry.

Martin Luther King Jr.

King's birthday is honored as a national holiday every third Monday in January.

JANUARY 16

Hiram R. Revels died on this day in 1901 in Aberdeen, Mississippi, at the age of 78. Revels became the first African-American in the U.S. Senate when, in 1870, the Mississippi legislature elected him to complete the term of Jefferson Davis, the former Confederate president. Revels served only one year in the Senate before leaving to become the first president of Alcorn University, America's first land-grant college. Revels also taught theology at Shaw University and was an African Methodist Episcopal Church (AME) superintendent.

Born a freeman in North Carolina, Revels began his career as a missionary in Tennessee, Kentucky, Kansas, Illinois, and Indiana. In 1860 he moved to Baltimore, where he was a minister of an AME church. Revels served as chaplain for two all-black regiments in the Union Army during the Civil War. He founded a school for free Africans in St. Louis, Missouri, and moved to Mississippi in 1866, where he was selected to represent that state as senator four years later.

The U.S. Senate discussed the credentials of Revels for three days before confirming his seat. During the debate Republican James Nye of Nevada—who once said "color never made a man; color never unmade a man"—remarked:

> In 1861 from this Hall departed two Senators who were representing here the State of Mississippi; one of them who went defiantly was Jefferson Davis. He went out to establish a government whose cornerstone should be oppression and the perpetual enslavement of a race because their skin differed in color from his. Sir, what a magnificent spectacle of retributive justice is witnessed here today! In the place of that proud, defiant man, who marched out to trample under foot the Constitution and the laws of the country he had sworn to support, comes back one of that humble race whom he would have enslaved forever to take and occupy his seat upon this floor.

JANUARY 17

On January 17, 1882, U.S. Patent No. 252,386 was assigned to Lewis Howard Latimer for the Process of Manufacturing Carbons. This process greatly improved the quality of carbon filaments used in electric lamps. Latimer had earlier patented an electric lamp, commonly referred to as the Latimer lamp, which was widely used in his day, as well as a pivoted bottom for train bathrooms and water closets that opened and closed automatically.

A draftsman, inventor, and expert of the U.S. electrical industry, Latimer was a member of the Edison Pioneers, a group of scientists who had assisted Thomas Edison during his pioneering work in inventing the electric light. Latimer also prepared the drawings for Alexander Graham Bell's 1876 patent application for the telephone.

In addition to his technical skills, Latimer was an amateur poet. He wrote the following poem on the occasion of his wedding.

EBON VENUS

Let others boast of maidens fair,
Of eyes of blue and golden hair;
My heart like needles ever true
Turns to the maid of ebon hue.

I love her form of matchless grace,
The dark brown beauty of her face,
Her lips that speak of love's delight,
Her eyes that gleam as stars at night.

O'er marble Venus let them rage,
Who set the fashions of the age;
Each to his taste, but as for me,
My Venus shall be ebony.

JANUARY 18

On this day in 1830, David Walker, a used-clothes dealer in Boston and the son a free mother and slave father, caused a stir in America by publishing a militant antislavery pamphlet. *Walker's Appeal, in Four Articles,* excerpted below, warned of slave revolt.

...Remember, Americans, that we must and shall be free and enlightened as you are. Will you wait until we shall, under God, obtain our liberty, by the crushing arm of power? Will it not be dreadful for you? I speak Americans for your good. We

must and shall be free I say, in spite of you. You may do your best to keep us in wretchedness and misery, to enrich you and your children, but God will deliver us from under you. And woe, woe, will be to you if we have to obtain our freedom by fighting. Throw away your fears and prejudices then, and enlighten us and treat us like men, and we will like you more than we do now hate you, and tell us no more about coloniza-tion [the movement to return free blacks to Africa], for Amer-ica is as much our country, as it is yours. Treat us like men, and there is no danger but we will all live in peace and happiness together. For we are not like you, hard hearted, unmerciful, and unforgiving. What a happy country this will be, if the whites will listen...

Three editions of the controversial pamphlet were printed. *Walker's Appeal* was widely distributed in the North and secretly made its way into the South, to the vexation of slaveholders and exuberance of African-Americans.

Southerners reacted by arming themselves in preparation for a slave insurrection, making it illegal to teach slaves to read and write, and deeming it a capital offense to possess treatises calling for a slave insurrection. On June 28, 1830, not long after a reward had been offered for Walker, his dead body was found near his clothing store, possibly having been poisoned.

JANUARY 19

In 1918, John H. Johnson was born on this day in Arkansas City, Arkansas. Johnson is founder and publisher of the leading African-American magazines *Negro Digest* (1942), *Ebony* (1945), *Tan* (1950), and *Jet* (1951). Founded at the dawn of the mass-media age that emerged after World War II, these magazines provided positive role models for African-Americans, and, in the words of Johnson, made "*Ebony* and the Negro consumer market integral parts of the marketing and advertising agendas of corporate America."

Johnson's first magazine, *Negro Digest*, was modelled on the pocket-size format of *Reader's Digest*, and was "dedicated to the development of interracial understanding and the promotion of national unity." A popular feature of the magazine was "If I Were A Negro"—essays written by prominent white Americans, such as Eleanor Roosevelt. *Ebony*, a monthly photo magazine of which the first issue sold 25,000 copies, focused on promoting positive images of African-Americans.

In addition to publishing magazines and books, Johnson—among America's 400 richest people—founded Fashion Fair Cosmetics, the *Ebony/Jet Showcase* television show, the Supreme Life Insurance Company, and a radio station.

> *Very often when you try to see things in their largest form, you get discouraged, and you feel that it's impossible....I never thought I would be rich. Never in my wildest dreams did I believe that* Negro Digest *would lead to the Johnson Publishing Company of today. If I'd dreamed then of the conglomerate of today, I probably would have been so intimidated, with my meager resources, that I wouldn't have had the courage to take the first step.*
>
> —from Johnson's autobiography (written with Lerone Bennett Jr.)
> *Succeeding Against the Odds* (1989)

JANUARY 20

On January 20, 1986, America celebrated Dr. Martin Luther King Jr.'s birthday as a national holiday for the first time. On November 2, 1983, President Ronald Reagan signed the bill making the third Monday of January a federal holiday in honor of King. King is the first and only African-American to be honored by a national holiday.

King's actual date of birth is January 15. He was born in 1929 in

Atlanta, Georgia. At the age of 19 he graduated from Morehouse College with a bachelor of divinity degree and was working as a pastor by the time he was 25.

He earned his Ph.D. in theology in 1955—the same year he was propelled to the forefront of the civil rights movement when, as pastor of Dexter Avenue Baptist Church, he led the year-long Montgomery, Alabama, bus boycott. In 1957 he was elected first president of the Southern Christian Leadership Conference (SCLC), an organization that promoted nonviolent action to secure full civil rights for African-Americans. In 1963 he led the March on Washington, at which he delivered his famous "I Have a Dream" speech from the steps of the Lincoln Memorial to some 250,000 civil rights demonstrators.

King wrote several books, including *Stride to Freedom* (1958) and *Strength to Love* (1963). In 1964 he was awarded the Nobel Peace Prize, and four years later, on April 4, 1968, he was assassinated.

His memory is engraved in the hearts and minds of his fellow Americans, and it is appropriate...to remember and honor the principles for which he stood.

—Coretta Scott King's response to President Reagan signing the bill which made Martin Luther King Jr.'s birthday a national holiday

JANUARY 21

On this day in 1984, the "Mr. Nice Guy" of soul music died at the age of 49. Nine years earlier, while on stage at the Latin Casino in Camden, New Jersey, Jackie Wilson had suffered a heart attack, fell and hit his head, which resulted in brain damage from which he never recovered. "Mr. Wilson was not the most famous or the most far-reaching figure in rock 'n' roll," wrote the *New Republic* a week after his death, "He was...merely perfect."

Wilson's wide-ranging voice has been called "almost operatic." His first solo release in 1957, "Reet Petite," was an instant success. Over the years he recorded many *Billboard* top-forty songs, including "Talk That Talk," "I'll Be Satisfied," "Am I the Man," and his first million-seller, "Lonely Teardrops." He also topped the rhythm-and-blues charts with the songs "Doggin' Around" and "A Woman, A Lover, A Friend," among others.

Born in Detroit, Michigan, Wilson won boxing's Golden Gloves competition at the age of 16, but with his mother's encouragement turned to music after finishing high school. Nicknamed Mr. Excitement, he has been likened to James Brown because of his high-energy stage perform- ances, during which he danced madly and sweated profusely. Wilson was inducted into the Rock and Roll Hall of Fame in 1987.

JANUARY 22

On January 22, 1971, twelve African-American congressmen boycotted President Richard Nixon's State of the Union address because of his "consistent refusal to hear the pleas and concerns of black Americans." For a year Nixon had rejected requests to meet with the African- American representatives, with whom he differed on several issues, such as the Vietnam War, voting rights, and school integration through busing.

In a letter to the Republican president, the congressmen—all Demo- crats in the House of Representatives—wrote: "In view of the fact that the opinions of black Americans have not been heard or considered by you, as they relate to the 'State of the Union' for blacks, we only conclude that your views on the state of black affairs cannot possibly be accurate, relative or germane."

However, by March 25 of that year, President Nixon met with the group, by then formally organized into the Congressional Black Caucus. Representative Charles C. Diggs of Michigan noted that this was an important step for the country because the president had acknowledged "that there is a group in the Congress that is uniquely sensitive to a very large section of this country."

President Nixon accepted a list of recommendations from the Congressional Black Caucus that pointed out the major needs of African-Americans and assigned a White House staff panel to examine it. The thirty-two-page document explained:

> *Our people are no longer asking for equality as a rhetorical promise. They are demanding from the national Administration, and from elected officials without regard to party affiliation, the only kind of equality that ultimately has any real meaning, equality of results.*

JANUARY 23

On this night in 1977, the first episode of the twelve-hour miniseries *Roots* aired on television. An estimated 130 million Americans stayed glued to their television sets for eight nights watching this drama about the experience of slavery in America from the slaves' point of view. This captivating television program was based on Alex Haley's bestselling novel *Roots: The Saga of an American Family.* The story begins in a village in Gambia in West Africa with Haley's own forefather, Kunta Kinte, who was captured and brought to Maryland as a slave, and traces the lives of Kunta Kinte's offspring.

Roots was considered innovative for covering such a huge sweep of history and for bringing to light the universal cruelties of the eighteenth and nineteenth centuries. The miniseries also served to showcase America's black acting talents, such as John Amos, Leslie Uggams, Ben Vereen, Maya Angelou, and Louis Gossett Jr. It was a true cultural phenomenon and ignited a trend in America of charting genealogy.

> *Roots' success was unprecedented. Approximately 100 million viewers saw the concluding installment, and it must be considered an event of considerable magnitude when nearly*

half the entire population of the U.S. can be assembled in front of its TV sets to watch a single dramatic presentation.

—TV Guide's *The Complete Dictionary to Prime Time Network TV Shows 1946–Present*

JANUARY 24

On this day in 1972, just days before he died of a heart attack, Jackie Robinson was inducted into the Baseball Hall of Fame. Robinson was the first African-American to play modern* major league baseball, paving the way for the integration of all professional sports in America.

Robinson generated excitement in African-American communities when he signed on with the Montreal Royals, the Brooklyn Dodgers' minor-league team, in October 1945. He broke baseball's color barrier when he began playing with the Dodgers in April 1947. In 1949 this versatile ballplayer and bold base runner was selected Most Valuable Player in the National League. In his career, Robinson stole 197 bases, including home eleven times.

In 1956, the year he retired from baseball, Robinson was awarded the NAACP's Spingarn Medal for his conduct "on and off" the field. Robinson was also known for being opinionated and outspoken.

I had to fight hard against loneliness, abuse and the knowledge that any mistake I made would be magnified because I was the only black man out there. Many people resented my impatience and honesty, but I never cared about acceptance as much as I cared about respect.

—from Robinson's autobiography *I Never Had It Made*

---

*Moses Fleetwood Walker played in the American Association for Toledo in 1884.

JANUARY 25

Constance Baker Motley became the first female African-American federal judge when she was appointed to the U.S. District Court for southern New York by President Lyndon B. Johnson on this day in 1966. Motley chalked up other firsts, including first African-American woman to win a seat in the New York State Senate, in 1964, and first woman to become Manhattan borough president, in 1965.

Born in Connecticut of West Indian parents, Motley received her law degree from Columbia University. She worked as a civil rights lawyer for the NAACP from 1954 to 1964, successfully arguing nine NAACP cases before the U.S. Supreme Court. One was that of James Meredith, an African-American air force veteran who sued to be admitted to the University of Mississippi.

It is important for women, and especially African-American women, to become involved and to hold public office.

—Constance Baker Motley

JANUARY 26

On this day in 1863, the first all-black regiment in the Union Army, the Fifty-fourth Massachusetts Volunteers, was established after the War Department authorized the governor of Massachusetts to recruit African-American troops.

Since the Civil War began, on April 12, 1861, African-Americans had pressed for the right to serve as soldiers. Or, as one pundit phrased it, they fought for two years for the right "to be kilt." In total, during the Civil War some 220,000 African-Americans served in the Union Army in various regiments, the majority coming from southern slave states. The United States Colored Troops (USCT) were commanded by 7,000 white officers who volunteered for these positions "despite ridicule and abuse." The black troops quickly proved their worth and valor, engaging in the Battle of Port Hudson in May 1863, and two weeks later repelling a Confederate assault at Milliken's Bend, Louisiana. Perhaps the most famous USCT engagement was the heroic Battle of Fort Wagner, on July 18, 1863.

The historian pen cannot fail to locate us somewhere among the good and the great, who have fought and bled upon the alter of their country.

—Garland H. White, African-American chaplain of the Twenty-eighth U.S. Colored Infantry

~~~~~~

JANUARY 27

Today in 1972 the "Queen of Gospel Song" died in Evergreen Park, Illinois, at the age of 60. Mahalia Jackson—who once said "blues are the songs of despair, but gospel songs are the songs of hope"—was the first gospel singer to become internationally famous.

Raised in New Orleans, Louisiana, in the early 1900s, Jackson began singing gospel in the church choir. Her 1945 record *Move on Up a Little Higher* sold almost two million copies, propelling her to instant fame. Soon she was performing in Carnegie Hall, appearing on *The Ed Sullivan Show*, and touring Europe. Toward the end of her life she became a civil rights activist. She also wrote a cookbook titled *Mahalia Jackson Cooks Soul* (1970), which includes the following recipe.

SAUSAGE-CORN BREAD SKILLET

1 pound sausage links	*1 teaspoon salt*
4 apple rings, one inch thick	*1/4 cup sausage fat*
2 cups corn meal	*2 cups buttermilk*
1 tablespoon sugar	*2 eggs well-beaten*
1/4 teaspoon soda	*2 teaspoons baking powder*

Brown sausages on all sides and remove from skillet. Pour off excess fat and reserve. Arrange apple rings and half of the sausage links in the bottom of the skillet. Cut remaining sausages a half inch long. Sift together meal, sugar, soda, and salt. Add fat and buttermilk with vigorous beating. Fold in eggs. Add baking powder and cut sausages, blending well. Pour into skillet and bake at 450 (degrees) F twenty to thirty minutes. Immediately turn out of skillet after cooking. Serve with butter and syrup or jelly. Makes five or six servings.

It's easy to be independent when you've got money. But to be independent when you haven't got a thing—that's the Lord's test.

—Mahalia Jackson

JANUARY 28

The most prominent and prolific female African-American writer of the 1920s, '30s, and '40s died this day in 1960 on welfare in Fort Pierce, Florida. Zora Neale Hurston's grave went unmarked until Alice Walker, who edited a collection of Hurston's works called *I Love Myself When I Am Laughing...And Then Again When I'm Looking Mean and Impressive* (1979), placed a headstone at the plot.

A Harlem Renaissance veteran and folklorist, Hurston wrote about the everyday struggles of the common person trying to make their way in the world. Hurston's numerous works include *Jonah's Gourd Vine* (1934), *Mules and Men* (1935), *Their Eyes Were Watching God* (1937), *Moses, Man of the Mountain* (1939), and *Seraph on the Suwanee* (1948). In 1942 she published her autobiography *Dust Tracks on a Road*. The Zora Neale Hurston Festival of the Arts and Humanities is held each year in the all-black town of Eatonville, Florida.

You love like a coward. Don't take no steps at all. Just stand around and hope for things to happen outright. Unthankful and unknowing like a hog under an acorn tree. Eating and grunting with your ears hanging over your eyes, and never even looking up to see where the acorns are coming from.

—from Chapter 23 of *Seraph on the Suwanee*

Ships at a distance have every man's wish on board. For some they come in with the tide. For others they sail forever on the horizon, never out of sight, never landing until the watcher turns his eyes away in resignation, his dreams mocked to death by Time. That is the life of men. Now, women forget all those things they don't want to remember, and remember everything they don't want to forget. The dream is the truth. Then they act and do things accordingly.

—from Chapter 1 of *Their Eyes Were Watching God*

JANUARY 29

On this day in 1926, Violette Neatly Anderson, a Chicago lawyer, became the first African-American woman to practice law before the U.S. Supreme Court.

Anderson graduated from the University of Chicago Law School in 1920, when she was nearly 40 years old. She was the first African-American woman to practice law in the state of Illinois. An active member of the community, Anderson served on the executive board of the Chicago Council of Social Agencies and was presi-

Violet Neatly Anderson

dent of the Friendly Big Sister's League of Chicago. She died in 1937 in her mid-fifties.

> *It may be true that the law cannot make a man love me, but it can keep him from lynching me, and I think that's pretty important.*

> —Martin Luther King Jr.

JANUARY 30

On January 30, 1970, Joseph L. Searles III became the first African-American proposed as a seat holder on the New York Stock Exchange. The 178-year-old stock exchange has 1,366 seats and is the country's top securities market. Only seat holders can buy and sell on the floor. Searles took one of the three seats belonging to Newburger, Loeb and Co., as well as became a general partner of the firm.

The 30-year-old former college football player said of his posting on the Big Board, "It's a personal challenge to me as a black man to become part of the economic mainstream of this country." Heading off potential criticism from more radical African-Americans, he added, "I'm not giving up the movement. I'm simply attacking from a different direction."

By the 1990s, African-Americans on Wall Street have become a routine matter, despite being under-represented by percentage. According to a 1991 Bureau of Labor Statistics report, 5 percent of workers in the financial services industry, or 77,000 people, were African-American. African-Americans have risen to the top levels of some of Wall Street's most prestigious firms, and there are numerous African-American—owned investment companies operating in this competitive industry.

> *There's a saying in the business: The higher up you go, the bigger the target on your back.*

> —James F. Haddon, African-American manager on Wall Street

Wall Street is still a very macho environment. In the work environment being black was usually an issue. But on Wall Street being a woman became a critical concern. Once I understood the system, I knew how to operate. As a woman, there are certain doors you're never going to go through. You're never going to be in the locker room where whatever little magic between men happens. I just tried to make sure that one of the men who was in that room was looking out for my interests.

—Marianne Spraggins, the first African-American female managing-director on Wall Street, in *Black Enterprise*, October 1992

JANUARY 31

In 1865, the House of Representatives passed the Thirteenth Amendment to the U.S. Constitution by a narrow margin, with eleven Democrats defecting to the Republican side to vote yes. The amendment had already passed in the Senate, on April 8, 1864. The Thirteenth Amendment reads:

Neither slavery nor involuntary servitude, except as punishment for crime whereof the party shall have been duly convicted, shall exist within the United States, or any place subject to their jurisdiction.

Despite the Emancipation Proclamation, issued two years before, the Thirteenth Amendment was still required because the proclamation was a war statement that used limited language and wielded questionable legal power. It is estimated that only one of every three slaves was freed under the Emancipation Proclamation.

Reporter Noah Brooks described the scene in the House on January 31, 1865:

...there was a pause of utter silence, then a burst, a storm of cheers, the like of which no congress of the United States ever saw. Strong men embraced each other with tears. The galleries and spaces stood bristling with cheering crowds; the air was stirred with a cloud of women's handkerchiefs and cheer after cheer, burst after burst followed....

The *New York Tribune* reporter called it "the most august and important event in American Legislation and American History since the Declaration of Independence," adding, "God Bless the XXXVIIITH Congress!"

FEBRUARY 1

On Monday, February 1, 1960, at four-thirty in the afternoon, four freshmen from North Carolina Agricultural and Technological College, Ezell Blair Jr., David Richmond, Joseph McNeil, and Franklin McCain, sat down at the lunch counter at the local F. W. Woolworth store and ordered coffee and cherry pie. This simple act was extremely bold for the times. These African-American students were acting in defiance of Jim Crow laws that permitted blacks to shop in the store but not to eat a meal there.

After being refused service, the students opened their textbooks to study, making it clear that they weren't going to move until they were either served or the store closed. Called the Greensboro Four, the young men returned the next morning, this time with more A&T students. On Wednesday, seventy students joined the protest, including women from Bennett College and some white women from nearby schools. By this time, the Greensboro sit-in became national news.

Thursday's UPI story read, "The demonstration—in its third day—spread. Some of the 150 North Carolina A&T students moved to the S. H. Kress & Co. store down the street to launch a similar sitdown." The sit-ins spread not only down the street, but throughout the South to chain stores, beaches, libraries, movie theaters and supermarkets. Demonstrations were also held in the North at franchises of the violating stores and at universities.

The Greensboro sit-in is credited with re-igniting the civil rights movement in America, transforming the older generation's don't-rock-the-boat tactics to a more militant, protest-based platform.

Don't strike back or curse if abused.
Don't laugh out.
Don't hold conversations with floor workers.
Don't block entrances to the store and aisles.
Show yourself courteous and friendly at all times.
Sit straight and always face the counter.
Remember love and non-violence.
May God bless each of you.

—the Nashville Student Organization's code of conduct, which
reflects the philosophy of the sit-in movement

FEBRUARY 2

Jefferson H. Long

Georgia representative Jefferson Long delivered his first speech to Congress on this day in 1871. Long was among the first African-Americans to serve in the national legislature. Speaking in favor of retaining the test-oath that required voters to obey the Constitution, Long said:

...sir, we propose here today to modify the test-oath, and to give to those men in the rebel States who are disloyal today to the government this favor. We propose, sir, to remove political disabilities from the very men who were the

leaders of the Ku Klux Klan and who have committed midnight outrages....Why, Mr. Speaker, in my State since emancipation there have been over five hundred loyal men shot down by the disloyal men there, and not one of those who took part in committing those outrages has ever been brought to justice. Do we, then, really propose here today, when the country is not ready for it, when those disloyal people still hate this Government, when loyal men dare not carry the "stars and stripes" through our streets, for if they do they will be turned out of employment, to relieve from political disability the very men who have committed these Ku Klux outrages?

Long's plea was unsuccessful, and soon afterwards Congress defeated upholding of the test-oath. Long had experienced the violence of the "disloyals" firsthand. On election day in 1869, mobs in Georgia attacked African-American voters, killing seven. Long, then a candidate for Congress, barely escaped a mob by hiding in a sewer.

FEBRUARY 3

On this day in 1870 the Fifteenth Amendment to the U.S. Constitution was ratified, giving African-American men the right to vote. The amendment states:

The right of citizens of the United States to vote shall not be denied or abridged by the United States or by any State on account of race, color, or previous condition of servitude.

Despite being granted the constitutional right to vote, African-Americans and other minorities were prohibited from voting by local practices such as poll taxes, literacy tests, property requirements, and outright intimidation. It wasn't until a century later that the right to vote was fully assured by the government. The Voting Rights Act of 1965 specifically outlawed poll taxes and literacy tests. The act also required states to obtain preclearance at the national level before making changes in their voting laws and stiffened the penalties against those interfering with a person's right to vote.

Human law may know no distinction among men in respect to rights, but human practice may.

—Frederick Douglass

If colored men get their rights, and not colored women theirs, you see the colored men will be masters over the women, and it will be just as bad as it was before.... I am glad to see that men are getting their rights, but I want woman to get theirs, and while the water is stirring I will step into the pool.

—Sojourner Truth on the Fifteenth Amendment

FEBRUARY 4

On Tuesday, February 4, 1975, the National Women's Political Caucus honored the eighteen female members of the new U.S. Congress. One of these congresswomen was Yvonne Braithwaite Burke, a California Democrat in her second term.

Burke, an attorney and politician, holds several firsts. She was the first African-American woman to represent California in the national government; the first African-American woman to be elected to the California General Assembly; and the first woman on the Los Angeles County Board of Supervisors.

Burke was also the first woman in the U.S. Congress to be granted maternity leave, and in 1973 she became the first member of Congress to give birth while holding office. She was 40 years old when her daughter Autumn Roxanne was born. The March 27, 1995 issue of *Time* magazine reported that Burke gave this advice to Utah Republican Enid Greene Waldholtz, the second woman to carry a child while in Congress:

"Introduce all the bills you want now, because everyone will be afraid to debate you."

~~~~~~

FEBRUARY 5

On this day in 1956, L. R. Lautier became the first African-American admitted to the National Press Club. For years the journalism profession had been a bastion of white male domination, discriminating against minorities and women. In a 1968 report, President Johnson's National Advisory Commission on Civil Disorders wrote that "the journalistic profession has been shockingly backward in seeking out, hiring, training and promoting Negroes." Twenty years later, in 1988, only 7 percent of the employees in America's newsrooms were minorities, while minorities composed 25 percent of the general population.

Today it is commonplace for minorities and women to appear on local and national nightly television news shows and for their bylines to appear in newspapers. One news conglomerate, Gannett Co. Inc., publisher of *USA Today* and many dailies, is known for its excellent affirmative action record. "When others were talking about a desire to launch training programs for minorities in management," said the editor of the *Philadelphia Daily News* in a *Time* magazine article, "Gannett was naming editors and publishers."

> *It is our responsibility to let Black youth and the world know that strong voices in history, such as W. E. B. DuBois, Marcus Garvey and Frederick Douglass, were publishers who used their presses to make a mighty impression on the world... [we] must always acknowledge the crusading editors who challenged the status quo, and we must illustrate that until racism is gone from the face of the planet we must develop news editors to combat it.*

—Robert W. Bogle, president of the National Newspaper Publishers Association

FEBRUARY 6

On February 6, 1865, Dr. Martin Robinson Delany arrived in Washington, D.C. to arrange a meeting with President Abraham Lincoln. Three days later he sat with the president and presented his case. Delany urged the commander in chief of the armed forces to permit African-American soldiers to attain higher positions in the Union Army through the creation of more all-black regiments led by black officers. This, argued Delany, would allow African-Americans to hold superior positions without inducing racial antagonisms. Lincoln agreed. Immediately thereafter, Delany was sworn in as a major in the Union Army and charged with mustering African-American troops.

Writer, physician, army major, and African explorer, Delany has been called "the black renaissance man of the mid-nineteenth century." He partook in charitable causes and in the 1840s coedited the *North Star* with Frederick Douglass. A Harvard-educated physician, he practiced medicine in Pittsburgh, Chicago, and Chatham, Canada, where many of his patients were refugee American slaves. While in Chatham, on the behest of John Brown, he recruited colored men to attend the Canada Convention prior to Brown's attack on Harpers Ferry.

Delany spent one year exploring the Niger Valley in Africa. His findings, published upon his return, were well received by England's scientific community, and Delany was made a member of the prestigious International Statistical Congress. He also wrote the book *Blake, or the Huts of America* (1859), the second novel by an African-American to be published in America. Delany died in 1885 in Xenia, Ohio.

> *No living man is better able to write the history of the race, to whom it has been a constant study, than he...Few, if any...have so entirely consecrated themselves to the idea of race as his career shows. His religion, his writings, every step in life, is based upon this idea. His creed begins and ends with it—that the colored race can only obtain their true status as men, by relying on their own identity; that they must prove, by*

merit, all that white men claim; then color would cease to be an objection in their progress—that the blacks must take pride in being black, and show their claims to superior qualities, before the whites would be willing to concede them equality. This he claims is the foundation of manhood. Upon this point Mr. Frederick Douglass once wittily remarked, "Delany stands so straight that he leans a little backward."

—from Frances Rollin's *Life and Public Service of Martin R. Delany* (1868)

FEBRUARY 7

The Exodus of 1879 is generally said to have begun in February of that year and continued for several years thereafter. This wave of African-American migration to the western United States was prompted by political and social oppression in the southern states, represented by Black Codes, limited educational opportunities, and out-and-out violence, such as lynchings and violations of black women.

Spurred on by "Exoduster" leaders such as Benjamin "Pap" Singleton and Henry Adams, hundreds of thousands of ordinary black citizens, mostly from Louisiana, Alabama, and South Carolina, moved to the promised lands of the West. Pap Singleton, a 69-year-old ex-slave and modern Moses figure, led about 7,500 African-Americans from Tennessee to Kansas, where he established a settlement in Baxter Springs. One of the most famous black communities in the West, Nicodemus, was founded in 1877 in northwest Kansas. While the majority of Exodusters settled in Kansas, numerous other African-American colonies sprouted in Missouri, Arkansas, Nebraska, Iowa, Colorado, Oklahoma, the Dakotas, and into Mexico, helping to fuel the country's westward expansion.

In only a few years about 20,000 African-Americans are believed to have made the trek west. Many others were physically prevented from doing so by armed patrols because southern businessmen were loath to lose their source of cheap labor.

> We cross the prairie as of old
>   The pilgrims crossed the sea,
> To make the West, as they the East,
>   The homestead of the free!
>
> We go to rear a wall of men
>   On Freedom's Southern line,
> And plant beside the cotton-tree
>   The rugged Northern pine!

—the first two verses of a poem written in 1854 to encourage freemen to move west

FEBRUARY 8

On this day in 1986, 18-year-old Debi Thomas won the women's Senior Singles U.S. Figure Skating Championship, becoming the first African-American to win this title. Thomas went on to win the women's World Figure Skating Championship in March of the same year—another African-American first—defeating East Germany's Katarina Witt. She regained the U.S. national title in early 1988. A few months later she won a bronze medal at the Olympic Games in Calgary, Canada, becoming the first black athlete to win a medal in the Winter Olympics.

Thomas was raised by her mother, a computer programmer and analyst. As a youth, Thomas practiced ice skating six hours a day with Scottish coach Alex McGowan, at a cost of about $25,000 a year. Her mother recalled, "Debi comes from several generations of people who refused to think in black-and-white terms. But I communicated my lunch-counter experiences to her, and she's had a few of her own. When Debi was eleven, we came home from a competition to a cross burning in the front yard."

Maybe I have different values, I don't know. But I think my outlook on life has been my advantage. Things like the importance of education and being whatever you can be give me an inner strength to pull things off on the ice.

—Thomas in an article in *Time* magazine, February 15, 1988

FEBRUARY 9

Today in 1780, Capt. Paul Cuffe and six other African-American residents of Massachusetts petitioned the state legislature for the right to vote. Claiming "no taxation without representation," the residents had earlier refused to pay taxes. The courts agreed and awarded Cuffe and the six other defendants full civil rights.

The son of a freed slave and a Native American mother, Captain Cuffe made his fortune as a shipowner in the whaling industry. Cuffe was one of many African-American sailors and whalers. In fact, over 50 percent of American seamen before the Civil War were of African ancestry.

This Quaker merchant also supported the back-to-Africa movement and personally transported African-Americans to Sierra Leone on his ship. The Cuffe Farm, located at 1504 Drift Farm in Wesport, Massachusetts, was designated a national historic landmark on May 30, 1974.

I swear to the Lord
I still can't see
Why Democracy means
Everybody but me.

—from Langston Hughes's poem "Jim Crow's Last Stand"

~~~~~~

FEBRUARY 10

On this day in 1869, Nat Love, a former slave from Tennessee, bought some new clothes and set out to make his fortune in the Wild West. He headed for Dodge City, Kansas, "the cowboy capital," where he put his bareback horse-riding and horse-breaking skills to test in his first job as a cowpuncher. Working in the Duval outfit with Bronco Jim, another Negro cowpuncher, he made $30 a month and was given the name Red River Dick, after one of the greatest cowpunchers the owner had ever known. In the three years he worked for Duval he learned to speak Spanish, fought renegades, rustlers, and Indians, and became a skilled marksman.

On July 4, 1876, while passing through Deadwood, South Dakota, Love entered a roping and shooting contest, competing against what observers called eleven of the best cowboys in the West—six of whom were colored. It is said that in the shooting contest he shot his Winchester rifle from the hip, putting all fourteen shots in the bull's-eye. Love won the $200 purse and earned the nickname Deadwood Dick.

In the same spirit as the famous black mountain man Jim Beckwourth, Love was prone to "wanton exaggeration." In 1907 Love published his bestselling autobiography *The Life and Adventures of Nat Love: Better Known in the Cattle Country as "Deadwood Dick"*. Love tells how, in October of the same year that he won the Deadwood contest, he was captured by Indians after single-handedly holding off a large number of attackers in a fierce gun battle. He lived among the red men for about one month before escaping. Another story relates the time Love lost his horse on the prairie and walked into a fierce winter storm; he was reportedly found with one hand frozen to his rifle and the other to his saddle.

As the West began to be tamed, Love quit cowboy life. Like many other former cowboys, he took a job on the "iron horses" as a Pullman porter. In his later years he worked as a bank guard. He died in Los Angeles, California, in 1921, at the age of 67.

> Imagine...riding your horse at the top of his speed through torrents of rain and hail, and the darkness so black we could not see our horses' head. We were chasing an immense heard of maddened cattle which we could hear but could not see, except during the vivid flashes of lightening, which furnished our only light....Late the next morning we had the herd rounded up 30 miles from where they started the night before.

—from *The Life and Adventures of Nat Love*

FEBRUARY 11

In 1989, a 58-year-old African-American woman, the Reverend Barbara C. Harris, was ordained as bishop of the Episcopal Diocese of Massachusetts. Before a crowd of 8,000 at the Hynes Convention Center in Boston, Massachusetts, Harris become the first female bishop of the Episcopal Church, a worldwide religious organization originating from the Church of England. Harris was quoted after her consecration as saying, "If the Diocese of Massachusetts had decided to play it safe, I would not be here wearing a broche and a chimere and a pectoral cross." She noted that the church's move to break color and sex barriers had brought "new hope...and new vision to hundreds of thousands."

Harris became an Episcopal priest late in life, serving in Philadelphia parishes. In 1984 she was appointed executive director of the Episcopal Church's publishing company that produces *The Witness*, a journal known for its liberal outlook.

FEBRUARY 12

On this day in 1909, six African-Americans, most of them former members of the short-lived Niagara Movement, and forty-seven liberal whites founded the National Association for the Advancement of Colored People.

W. E. B. DuBois, who served the organization for two decades, was the NAACP's only African-American officeholder in the early years. It wasn't until 1920 that James Weldon Johnson became the first African-American executive secretary.

The NAACP's stated purpose was to attain nothing less than full citizenship rights for African-Americans. Methods for reaching this goal have included political lobbying, mass pressure tactics, propaganda, and legal action. The NAACP has recorded several Supreme Court victories to this end. According to the 1995 *Encyclopedia of Associations*, the NAACP currently has 400,000 members, 132 staff, and 1,802 local branches.

The NAACP annually awards the prestigious Spingarn Medal to "the man or woman of African descent who shall have made the highest achievement during the preceding year, or years, in an honorable field of human endeavor." The first Spingarn Medal—named after the chairman of the board at the time, Joel E. Spingarn—was awarded in 1915 to scientist Ernest E. Just for his work in the field of biology.

If the unemployed could eat plans and promises, they would all be able to spend the winter on the Riviera.

—W. E. B. DuBois, from "As the Crow Flies," in the January 1931 issue of the *Crisis*, the NAACP journal

FEBRUARY 13

On February 13 and 14, 1957, a meeting was held in New Orleans which established the Southern Christian Leadership Conference (SCLC). The meeting was presided over by Martin Luther King Jr., who became its first president.

Along with the National Urban League and the National Association for the Advancement of Colored People, the Atlanta-based SCLC is one of the triumvirate of major civil rights organizations in America. Like its fellow organizations, SCLC peaked during the 1960's civil rights era and went through a slump in the early 1970s. During this low point, singer Harry Belafonte donated the money to pay the organization's salaries for one month. "Don't get discouraged because we're broke," said then SCLC leader Reverend Ralph D. Abernathy, "When did black folks let white folks upset us because we're broke?"

Today, the organization that has been charged with having "too many preachers and not enough other professionals" is occupied with addressing many social challenges. The SCLC has undertaken AIDS information projects, engages in voter registration drives, and has sponsored gun buy-back programs, to name a few. In a June 14, 1993 article in *Jet* magazine, SCLC president Dr. Joseph Lowery said of the gun buy-back efforts, "The National SCLC organization's campaign must do more than removing guns from the nation's homes and streets. We must dissolve the romance we have in this country with guns."

> *When evil men plot, good men must plan. When evil men burn and bomb, good men must build and bind. When evil men shout ugly words of hatred, good men must commit themselves to the glories of love.*
>
> —Martin Luther King Jr.

FEBRUARY 14

The boxer who is often called "pound for pound, the greatest fighter of all time," won the world middleweight championship for his first time on this day in 1951, hammering Jake La Motta in thirteen rounds. Sugar Ray Robinson, with his "matador" style, went on to win the 160-pound middleweight title four more times and the world welterweight title once.

Robinson was a skillful fighter who was never knocked out, though he knocked his opponents to the canvas 109 times. "For most of his 25 years as a professional boxer," wrote one author, "the slim, handsome fighter had everything—all the punches and all the moves, plus speed, hair-trigger timing, and a supreme will to win."

Born Walker Smith Jr. in Detroit, Michigan, Robinson was raised in a rough neighborhood in New York City. He picked up his professional name after he began fighting in the Amateur Athletic Union using the card of another teenager named Raymond Robinson, who had quit boxing.

With his big ego and flamboyant life-style, Robinson caused a sensation outside of the ring as well as in. He spent much of his $4 million in earnings on pink Cadillacs, fancy suits, and several small businesses in Harlem, including a nightclub, barber shop, lingerie store, and dry cleaners. After retiring from boxing in 1965, Robinson established the Sugar Ray Youth Foundation. He died in 1989 of Alzheimer's disease and diabetes.

You are the king, the master, my idol.

    —Muhammad Ali's often repeated praise for Robinson

I am a blessed man. A chosen man.

    —Robinson's often repeated words about himself

FEBRUARY 15

On this day in 1965, the most successful post–World War II African-American pop singer died of lung cancer in Santa Monica, California, at the age of 45. The deep voice of Nat King Cole made hits of many romantic ballads such as "Mona Lisa," "Unforgettable," "Too Young," and "Time and the River."

Born Nathanial Adams Cole in Alabama in 1919, he began his recording career in the 1930s with the King Cole Trio as front man and keyboard player. He only began to sing, in his words, "to break the monotony." Cole's smooth voice soon became the main attraction of the band.

In 1956 he hosted *The Nat King Cole Show*, becoming the first African-American to host a regular network television program. The show lasted only one year due to a lack of sponsors. Although fellow jazzmen of his era accused him of selling out to mainstream commercialism, more recent compilations of Cole's work and his daughter's 1991 revival of his song "Unforgettable" have secured his place in music history as a superb artist and one of the top vocalists of the 1950s.

FEBRUARY 16

Joe Frazier solidly pounded Jimmy Ellis in four rounds on this day in 1970, to become boxing's world heavyweight champion, succeeding Muhammad Ali. "Man, you can't hit," taunted the challenger as he smiled at Ellis during the fourth round, "I'm takin' everything you got man and you ain't hurtin' me." Before a crowd of 18,000, Frazier twice sent Ellis to the canvas with a wicked left hook, prompting Ellis's trainer to stop the bout. When the referee called the fight an overjoyed Frazier leaped into the arms of his trainer.

Immediately afterward, Frazier—who up to that point had won

twenty-five fights with twenty-two knockouts—said, "I'm gonna retire. I'm gonna wait until that other fella, the one who was gonna give me that belt, until he can fight me. I'm gonna sing rock 'n' roll until that Muhammad Ali or Cassius Clay or whatever his name is can fight me."

The new heavyweight champ, who had already recorded four LPs, did go on to sing rock music. Two months after winning the Ellis fight he broke his right ankle while dancing on stage at Las Vegas's Ceasar's Palace during a performance with his rock band The Knockouts. He finally got his opportunity to fight Muhammad Ali in the fight dubbed The Thrilla In Manila, held on October 1, 1975, in the Philippines. Frazier lost to Ali in fourteen rounds.

FEBRUARY 17

"It is a great shock," said James Baldwin in a speech on February 17, 1965, "at the age of five or six to find that in a world of Gary Coopers you are the Indian."

Taken literally, Baldwin's metaphor may have been more accurate than he intended. The proportion of Native American blood in African-Americans is believed to be quite high. In the early days of this country the two races frequently intermingled as fellow slaves and as allies in the fight against white domination. In some cases Native Americans owned African slaves, while in others Native American nations welcomed Africans as free members.

Anthropologist Melville J. Herskovits found that of the African-Americans questioned at Howard University and in Harlem, 33 percent claimed partial Native American ancestry. Historian Kenneth W. Porter used the term *Aframerindian* for this mixed race.

Dr. Reuter, another historian, explains African-Native American mixing in the early days of slavery:

> With these enslaved Indians the Negro slaves came into close
> and intimate contact. The social status was the same and as
> slaves they met on terms of equality. Intermarriage followed

and, as the body of Negro slaves increased and Indian slavery declined, the Indian slaves were gradually absorbed into the larger black population.

~~~~~~

FEBRUARY 18

The first formal protest against slavery in the Western world was signed this day in 1688 by four Mennonite men in Germantown, Pennsylvania. Francis Daniel Pastorius, Gerhard Hendericks, and Dirck and Abraham Op den Graeff wrote:

...There is a saying, that we should do to all men like as we will be done for ourselves....Here is liberty of conscience, which is right and reasonable; here ought to be likewise liberty of the body....But to bring men hither, or to rob and sell them against their will, we stand against....Pray, what thing in the world could be done worse towards us, that if men should rob or steal us away, and sell us for slaves to strange countries; separating husbands from their wives and children....

Perhaps referring to their own experiences during a sea voyage, the men added:

How fearful and fainthearted are many on sea when they see a strange vessel, being afraid it should be a Turk, and they should be taken and sold for slaves in Turkey.

Throughout the next few centuries the Mennonites and Quakers continued to be a primary force in the antislavery movement in America, establishing the first abolitionist society in Philadelphia in 1775 with Benjamin Franklin as president.

To sell souls for money seemeth to me a dangerous merchandize.

—John Eliot, Englishman, 1675

FEBRUARY 19

From February 19 through 21, 1919, the Pan-African Congress was held at the Grand Hotel in Paris. According to the *New York Times*, the purpose of the conference was "the protection of the natives of Africa and the people of African descent in other countries." The organizers felt it was time for Africans around the world to speak for themselves rather than relying on "philanthropic effort," and they wanted to ensure that the "negro's interests [were] safeguarded" within the League of Nations.

The meeting was organized by the brilliant American sociologist W. E. B. DuBois, Blaise Diagna, the French Deputy from Senegal, and I. F. Fredricks, from New Guinea. Fifty-seven delegates attended, representing sixteen countries or colonies, including the United States, Liberia, Abyssinia (now Ethiopia), Portugal, France, the West Indies, and Cuba. The American delegates were nearly prohibited from attending because the U.S. State Department had at first refused to issue their passports, claiming "the French Government...does not consider this a favorable time to hold such a conference." DuBois was awarded the NAACP's Spingarn Medal for his role in this effort.

The problem of the twentieth century is the problem of the colour line—the relation of darker to the lighter races of men in Asia and Africa, in America and the islands of the sea.

—DuBois, Chapter 2, *The Souls of Black Folk*

FEBRUARY 20

On this day in 1895, Frederick A. Douglass died of heart failure in Anacostia Heights, Washington, D.C. With his impressive appearance and eloquent manner of speech, Frederick Douglass had been the main intellectual voice of black America for nearly fifty years. He was a primary figure in the abolitionist movement and continued to demand full rights for freedmen after slavery was abolished. He also actively supported the women's rights movement.

Douglass published the newspaper the *North Star* from 1847 to 1864. In 1872 he moved to Washington, D.C., where he held government posts under several Republican administrations. He was a U.S. marshall in 1877, recorder of deeds in 1881, and U.S. minister to Haiti and Santo Domingo.

Born a slave of mixed European, African, and Native American blood, he escaped slavery at the age of 21. He wrote three autobiographies, which were popular both in American and Europe.

> *It was not color, but crime, not God, but man, that afforded the true explanation of the existence of slavery…what man can make, man can unmake.*
>
> —from *Narrative of the Life of Frederick Douglass* (1845)

〰〰〰〰〰〰〰〰〰〰〰〰〰〰〰〰〰〰〰〰〰〰〰〰〰〰〰

FEBRUARY 21

On this day in 1965, Malcolm X was assassinated while speaking at a rally of the Organization of Afro-American Unity (OAAU) at the Audubon Ballroom in New York City. Malcolm X was a charismatic speaker and disciplined leader who quickly rose to prominence through his association with the Nation of Islam. He severed relations with the Nation and formed the OAAU only one year before his death. Malcolm X wrote his autobiography with the assistance of African-American author Alex Haley, and—convinced that he would die young and violently—he correctly prophesied that he would never see the book in print.

> *If you knew him you would know why we must honor him: Malcolm was our manhood, our living, black manhood! This was his meaning to his people. And, in honoring him, we honor the best in ourselves....However much we may have differed with him—or with each other about him and his value as a man, let his going from us serve only to bring us together, now. Consigning these mortal remains to earth, the common mother of all, secure in the knowledge that what we place in the ground is no more now a man—but a seed— which, after the winter of our discontent will come forth again to meet us. And we will know him then for what he was and*

is—a Prince—our own black shining Prince!—who didn't hesitate to die, because he loved us so.

—Ossie Davis's eulogy for Malcolm X

Among the Negroes there was mass mourning for Malcolm X. Nobody talked much for days.

—in his book *Soul on Ice*, Etheridge Cleaver described the mood at Fulsom Prison, California

FEBRUARY 22

On this day in 1911, the "Bronze Muse" died in Philadelphia, Pennsylvania. Frances Ellen Watkins Harper wrote more than a dozen books, including *Poems on Miscellaneous Subjects* (1854), *Moses, A Story of the Nile* (1869), and *Sketches of Southern Life* (1872). Harper was the most famous female poet of her day and the most famous African-American poet of the nineteenth century. Also a well-known orator, she spoke frequently in public—sometimes twice in one day—promoting equal rights for women and African-Americans. She was a worker for the Underground Railroad, and in 1896 she helped establish the National Association of Colored Women.

Frances E. W. Harper

Make me a grave where'er you will,
In a lowly plain, or a lofty hill;
Make it among earth's humblest
    graves,
But not in a land where men are slaves.

I could not rest if around my grave
I heard the steps of a trembling slave;
His shadow above my silent tomb
Would make it a place of fearful gloom.

—from "Bury Me in a Free Land" (1854)

Light! more light! the shadows deepen,
    And my life is ebbing low,
Throw the windows widely open:
    Light! more light! before I go....
Not for greater gifts of genius;
    Not for thoughts more grandly bright,
All the dying poet whispers
    Is a prayer for light, more light.

—from "Let the Light Enter (the Dying Words of Goethe)"

FEBRUARY 23

On this day in 1868, William Edward Burghardt DuBois was born in Barrington, Massachusetts. DuBois was a leading figure in African-American protest for most of his adult life. He emerged at the turn of the century as an opposing voice to Booker T. Washington, who appeared to have accepted segregation, or—in DuBois's eyes—defeat. His book *The Souls of Black Folk*, written in 1903, presented an alternative to Booker T. Washington's "accommodation" platform and is considered a classic work of the civil rights movement.

DuBois was instrumental in the formation of both the Niagara Movement and the organization which the Niagara Movement helped spawn, the NAACP. DuBois was the NAACP's only African-American officeholder when it was chartered. He continued to work for the organization for two decades, including serving as editor of the NAACP's journal the *Crisis*.

A true Renaissance man, DuBois was a professor, sociologist, novelist, and nonfiction writer who made contributions in politics, social issues, and the arts. In 1895 DuBois became the first African-American to receive a doctorate degree from Harvard University. He was tried as anti-American during the McCarthy era and won the Lenin International Peace Prize in 1958. DuBois died in 1963 in Ghana, where he had taken up citizenship.

> *Herein lies the tragedy of the age; not that men are poor...not that men are wicked...but that men know so little of men.*
>
> —from Chapter 12 of *The Souls of Black Folk*

> *We stand again to look America fully in the face, it lynches, it disenfranchises, it insults us. We return fighting. Make way for Democracy. We saved it in France, and by great Jehovah, we will save it in the USA.*
>
> —DuBois commenting about African-American soldiers returning home after World War I

FEBRUARY 24

In 1973 Roberta Flack's single "Killing Me Softly With His Song" hit number one on *Billboard*'s chart for the week beginning February 24 and remained number one for four more weeks. The following year, her song "Feel Like Makin' Love" went to the number one spot on the week of August 19. Other Roberta Flack hits include "The First Time Ever I

Saw Your Face" and duos with Donny Hathaway, "Where Is the Love" and "You've Got a Friend."

This 1970's soul star is noted for her exceptional and unusual voice. In an interview with the *New York Times* on March 29, 1970, she said:

> *I've been told I sound like Nina Simone, Nancy Wilson, Dionne Warwick, even Mahalia Jackson. If everybody said I sounded like one person, I'd worry. But when they say I sound like them all, I know I've got my own style.*

FEBRUARY 25

"One-Man Show of Art by Negro, First of Kind Here, Opens Today," read the headline of a front-page article in the *New York Times* on this day in 1928. The article announced the opening of Archibald J. Motley Jr.'s show at the New Gallery on Madison Avenue. This was the first time in history that an artist had made the front page of the *New York Times* and it was the second one-person show by an African-American artist (the first being Henry O. Tanner).

African scenes, voodoo dances, and African-Americans at leisure were themes presented by the artist who Edward Jewell of the *New York Times* claimed "plumbs the Negro soul." Motley's major works include *Black Belt* (1934), *Chicken Shack* (1936), *The Jockey Club* (1929), and *Parisian Scene* (1929). At the Chicago Art Institute Exhibition in 1925, his painting *The Mulattress* won the Frank G. Logan Medal and *Syncopation* took the Joseph N. Eisendrath Prize.

Born in 1891 in New Orleans, Louisiana, of mixed East African pygmy, French, and Native American blood, he was raised in Chicago, where he studied at the Art Institute. The determined Motley was proud of being self-supportive. He held various manual labor jobs to put himself through college and keep his head above water during his early years as an artist. He heaved coal, worked as a steamfitter, and plumber, and waited tables in a train dining car.

I have found that, try as I will, I cannot escape the nemesis of my color....I am not complaining. I am satisfied to go quietly along, doing what I can, painting the things that suggest themselves to me. In fact, I believe, deep in my heart, that the dark tinge of my skin is the thing that has been my making. For, you see, I have had to work 100 per cent harder to realize my ambition.

—Motley in a March 25, 1928 article by Edward Jewell in the *New York Times Magazine*

FEBRUARY 26

At the Grammy Award's ceremony on this day in 1985, African-American musicians won awards in several categories. Lionel Richie's *Can't Slow Down* won best album of 1984. Tina Turner's "What's Love Got to Do With It" took the best record slot and earned her the title Best Female Pop Vocalist. The Pointer Sisters won best pop group for *Jump*.

Dad had a wonderful habit of talking to everybody the same way. A briefcase and a three-piece suit didn't impress him. "The guy with the mop may have the answer you need," my father told me, "but if you're holding your head too high, you're going to miss what he's saying."

—Lionel Richie in "Words of the Week" in the February 23, 1987 issue of *Jet* magazine

In a strange kind of way I've always been embarrassed about sex. I guess no one would ever think of me as shy. I rarely use profanity. Sometimes I'm shocked by what people say. I don't want to say raunchy things because I think, psychologically, I really don't want that as an image. Raunchiness is what I do best, I suppose, and enjoy it, but I have limitations.

—Tina Turner in an article in *Ebony*, November 1989

So who's going to challenge the ladies Pointer as the best female R&B group of the '80s? Nobody with any sense would after hearing this album [Serious Slammin' (1988)], which is full of fun funk, romance and just about everything on earth that's admirable except glazed doughnuts....Just work up the Best of Their Era trophy and tell the engraver to get started putting Anita's, June's, and Ruth's names on it.

—review in *People Weekly*, May 2, 1988

FEBRUARY 27

On this day in 1833, Maria W. Stewart delivered one of the four speeches which confirmed her place in history as the first American-born woman to give public lectures. (In 1829 Fanny Wright of Scotland was the first woman to speak publicly in America.) Stewart's lectures focused on encouraging African-Americans to attain education, political rights, and public recognition for their achievements. Her speech on this day, delivered at the African Masonic Hall in Boston, Massachusetts, was titled "On African Rights and Liberty."

Individuals have been distinguished according to their genius and talents ever since the formation of man, and will continue to be while the world stands. The different grades rise to honor and respectability as their merits may deserve. History informs us that we sprung from one of the most learned nations of the whole earth; from the seat, if not the parent, of science. Yes, poor despised Africa was once the resort of sages and legislators of other nations, was esteemed the school for learning, and the most illustrious men in Greece flocked thither for instruction.

Sixty-seven years later in Boston on this same day, African-American teacher and poet Angelina Weld Grimké was born. Grimké was a descendant of the famous white abolitionist and feminist sisters Angelina and Sarah Grimké. This "colored aristocrat" debuted as a writer during the Harlem Renaissance of the 1920s. The following is the first verse from her poem "A Mona Lisa."

I should like to creep
Through the long brown grasses
That are your lashes;
I should like to poise
On the very brink
Of the leaf-brown pools
That are your shadowed eyes;
I should like to cleave
Without sound,
Their glimmering waters,
Their unrippled waters,
I should like to sink down
And down
And down...
And deeply drown.

FEBRUARY 28

Michael Jackson swept the Grammy Awards on this day in 1984. His *Thriller* LP won best album of 1983. "Beat It" took best single record, and Michael was awarded Best Male Pop Vocalist. One of the best-selling LPs in rock history, *Thriller* includes seven top-ten hits—a first in pop music—and sold over thirty million copies.

Arguably the greatest entertainer of the twentieth century, Michael Jackson is a true musical genius who has enjoyed unprecedented success as a commercial artist. Jackson began his career at age 10 as the youngest brother of the popular group out of Gary, Indiana, the Jackson Five. In the early 1970s, teenagers across America danced to Jackson Five hits like

"ABC" and "Never Can Say Goodbye." Michael's first solo single to reach number one on the *Billboard* chart was "Ben," in October 1972.

> *I always joked that I didn't ask to sing and dance, but it's true. When I open my mouth, music comes out. I'm honored that I have this ability. I thank God for it every day. I feel I'm compelled to do what I do.*

> —from Jackson's 1988 biography *Moonwalk*

FEBRUARY 29

On February 29, 1692, arrest warrants were issued for three women accused of witchcraft in Salem Village, Massachusetts. Tituba Indian and two elderly women—the first of twenty "witches" to be sentenced to hang in a year-long hysteria—were hauled off to Ipswich Prison.

It all began in the winter of 1691–92, when several teenage girls began to have convulsive fits. Finding no medical explanation for the fits, the village doctor proclaimed, "the evil hand is on them." The young women began to point the finger at likely suspects, such as Sarah Good, who failed to attend church and was considered something of a tramp, Sarah Osburne, and Tituba Indian, a slave from the West Indies of African and Indian descent. Earlier Tituba had recounted voodoo stories and shown tricks and spells to some of these teenagers, leading to their claim that they had been bewitched by her.

The preliminary hearing for the three accused witches was a major community event. Tituba kept the court spellbound for days telling elaborate stories and spilling out her "confession." Fortunately for Tituba, she was pardoned in May of the same year. Most of the other twenty witches were hung on Gallows Hill. It wasn't until 265 years later, in August 1957, that the witchcraft convictions of six of these women were reversed by Massachusetts governor Foster Furcolo.

MARCH 1

On March 1, 1925, *Survey Graphic* published a special issue titled "Harlem, Mecca of the New Negro." By the end of the year, editor Alain Locke had reprinted and expanded upon the writings from this issue, producing a full-length anthology of African-American writing called *The New Negro*. This anthology, known as the Manifesto of the Harlem Renaissance, included works by established figures such as James Weldon Johnson, William Stanley Braithwaite, W. E. B. DuBois, and Claude McKay, and introduced rising stars like Countee Cullen, Langston Hughes, Jean Toomer, and Zora Neale Hurston.

Harlem in the 1920s was a thriving African-American, middle-class community that gave birth to a creative outpouring, not only from African-American writers, but also from musicians like Duke Ellington, Louis Armstrong, Ethel Waters, Bessie Smith, and "Bojangles" Robinson, and visual artists such as Aaron Douglas and Palmer Hayden. Harlem was also a magnet for political personages, including Mary McCleod Bethune, Walter White, and Marcus Garvey. It attracted wealthy patrons as well, most notably A'Lelia Walker.

This age of unprecedented artistic and intellectual activity in the African-American community—with Harlem as its heart and soul—was dubbed the Harlem Renaissance, and lasted approximately from 1919 to 1929.

The onset of the Great Depression coincided with the end of the gilded days of the Renaissance. Being a largely nonpolitical movement, the Harlem Renaissance hadn't greatly affected the African-American masses anyway. Most "hadn't heard of the Negro Renaissance," according to Langston Hughes, "and if they had, it hadn't raised their wages any."

MARCH 2

On this day in 1962, "Wilt the Stilt" Chamberlain scored 100 points in a single basketball game—a professional record that still stands today. He sunk thirty-six field goals and twenty-eight foul shots.

Chamberlain, who played for the Philadelphia Warriors and 76'ers and then the Los Angeles Lakers, was the best scorer and rebounder in the history of the sport, and the first player to score 30,000 points. Although some have since been broken, at one time he held or shared forty-three NBA records. He was also voted the NBA's Most Valuable Player four times.

At seven-feet-one-inch tall, Chamberlain was the first professional player over seven feet, changing basketball into a tall man's game. Chamberlain retired from basketball in October 1974 and was inducted into the Basketball Hall of Fame in 1979.

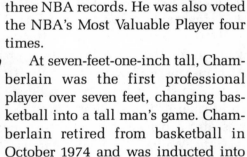

Wilt Chamberlain

One summer before junior high school, I grew four inches over the vacation on my uncle's farm in Virginia, and I came back to Philadelphia about 6 feet tall and a big jumble of wristbones and long legs. My mother refused to believe it. 'You're not my boy,' she said.

—Chamberlain quoted in *The Lincoln Library of Sports Champions*

You ever hear of cycles? Basketball is now in its black cycle.

—Wilt Chamberlain in *Inside Sports* (1980)

MARCH 3

On this day in 1865, Congress created the Freedmen's Bureau to aid destitute ex-slaves and impoverished whites in the South following the Civil War. The bureau provided medical services and helped establish schools, hospitals, and social service agencies during Reconstruction. Union general Oliver O. Howard, who founded Howard University the following year, was appointed its commissioner. Many of the major African-American colleges were established during this period, both with the bureau's assistance and through large combined contributions from the African-American community, sometimes coming in the form of hard-earned nickels and dimes.

It was at this time that Thaddeus Stevens, a 74-year-old white congressman from Pennsylvania, suggested that each freedman be given "forty acres and a mule" in compensation for their years of servitude. Former slaves did not receive forty acres and a mule, however, and the bureau began to run into a rising tide of racism. Southern states adopted discriminatory laws, violence against African-Americans increased, and the Ku Klux Klan and other white supremacy societies sprang up.

Congressman Stevens—once called "the best white friend black people have ever had"—went to his grave fighting for equal rights. Stevens requested to be buried in an African-American cemetery,

Schreiner's Cemetery in Lancaster, Pennsylvania, and had the following epitaph engraved on his headstone.

> *I repose in this quiet and secluded spot,*
> *not from any natural preference for solitude,*
> *but finding other cemeteries*
> *limited by charter rules as to race,*
> *I have chosen this that I might illustrate in my death*
> *the principles which I advocated through a long life:*
> *Equality of Man before his Creator.*

MARCH 4

The first session of the Forty-second U.S. Congress opened on this day in 1871. Among the legislators was Republican Joseph H. Rainey. Rainey had been elected to his second term of office with a solid victory of 20,221 votes received from South Carolina's First Congressional District.

Rainey had earlier become the first African-American to be seated in the House of Representatives when he was sworn in on December 12, 1870, after being chosen to fill a vacancy. He was joined by Jefferson Long of Georgia, Robert C. DeLarge and Robert B. Elliot of South Carolina, Benjamin S. Turner of Alabama, and Josiah T. Walls of Florida as the first African-Americans to serve in the House of Representatives. Republican leader James G. Blaine described these pioneer legislators as "studious, earnest, ambitious men, whose public conduct...would be honorable to any race."

Rainey was born in South Carolina in 1832 to mulatto slave parents. His father bought the family's freedom, and father and son supported their families by working as barbers. Rainey was drafted by the Confederate Army, from which he escaped and fled to Bermuda with his wife. Upon hearing of the end of the Civil War, harboring political ambitions, he returned to South Carolina. Rainey served in the state senate before being elected to the U.S. Congress for five terms. After his defeat for a sixth term, he was appointed South Carolina's internal revenue agent. Later he worked as a banker, rather unsuccessfully, in Washington, D.C. Rainey died in 1887 at the age of 55.

> *I say to you, gentleman, that you are making a mistake. Public opinion is aroused on this question. I tell you that the Negro will never rest until he gets his rights. We ask them because we know it is proper, not because we want to deprive any other class of the rights and immunities they enjoy, but because they are granted to us by the law of the land.*
>
> —Rainey speaking to the House of Representatives on December 19, 1873

MARCH 5

Around nine o'clock on the evening of March 5, 1770, a mob of about sixty rioters marched against a British garrison on King Street in Boston, Massachusetts. They were led by a huge, knock-kneed mulatto who lived in Boston under the fictitious name Michael Johnson—the man's real name was Crispus Attucks. According to contemporary accounts, Attucks was carrying a wooden club and taunted the Redcoats. When he grabbed a bayonet, aiming to strike a soldier, the cornered and frightened British infantrymen fired at him and into the crowd.

Attucks and four other men were killed in what became known as the Boston Massacre. The event was successfully propagandized by patriots to garner support from the colonies for the upcoming war against the British. Some historians contend that the British soldiers were entirely provoked by the mob, led by the "agitator" Attucks. It has even been speculated that American Revolutionary leader Samuel Adams orchestrated the entire event for the purpose of deepening anti-British sentiment in America.

Provoked or not, the Boston Massacre marks the beginning of America's struggle for independence. And Attucks—a runaway slave from Framingham, Massachusetts, likely of mixed African and Native American blood—was the first to fall, making him "the first martyr of the American Revolution." The Crispus Attucks monument in Boston, dedicated in 1888, commemorates the victims of the Boston Massacre.

On that night the foundation of American independence was laid.

—John Adams, second U.S. president (1797–1801)

MARCH 6

On March 6, 1857, the decision was handed down in the infamous *Dred Scott v. John F. A. Sandford* Supreme Court case. Dred Scott, a part-Native American slave, had lived for four years with his owner in Illinois and Minnesota, where slavery was prohibited under the terms of the Missouri Compromise. After returning to Missouri, Scott sued for his liberty in 1847 on the basis that he had *de facto* become free by living in free territory.

Although the St. Louis court agreed with Scott, the Missouri Supreme Court ruled against him. So his master's widow, in attempts to assist Scott, sold him to her brother John A. Sanford, who lived in New York. (Sanford's name was erroneously written in court records.) This maneuver took Scott's case to the federal level, since it now involved citizens of two different states.

The case met a wall of racism at the U.S. Supreme Court. The highest court in the land denied Scott his freedom based on the logic that slaves were property, and that the right to property was protected under the Constitution. The Court also ruled, in effect, that the Missouri Compromise was unconstitutional.

There were three important outcomes of this case: slaves and their descendants were denied full citizenship in the United States; slavery was permitted in federal territories; and the Supreme Court asserted its right to review acts of Congress to rule on their constitutionality. Called the "most ill-considered decision in Supreme Court history," the Scott decision heightened regional tensions in America, fueling the onset of the Civil War.

Upon Sanford's death in 1857—just a few months after the unfavorable court decision had been handed down—Scott and his family were freed. Dred Scott lived only a short time as a free man, dying of tuberculosis some sixteen months later.

We owe no allegiance to a country that grinds us under its iron hoof and treats us like dogs.

—from an article in the *Liberator* dated April 10, 1857, in response to the Dred Scott decision

MARCH 7

Today in 1539, an expedition left Mexico for what is now the southwest United States in search of the Kingdom of Quivira, a legendary city paved in gold. The expedition was initially led by a Catholic priest, Father Marcos de Niza. When de Niza decided to remain behind to celebrate Easter at a settlement, his "Moorish" scout, Estevanico, also known as Esteban or Stephan Dorantez, took over the advance party. Father de Niza wrote of Estavanico's adventure:

...Stephan departed from mee on Passion-sunday after dinner: and within foure dayes after the messengers of Stephan returned unto me with a great Crosse as high as a man, and they brought me word from Stephan, that I should forthwith come away after him, for hee had found people which gave him information of a very mighty Province....It was thirtie dayes journey from the Towne where Stephan was, unto the first Citie of the sayde Province, which is called Ceuola. Hee affirmed also that there are seven great Cities in this Province, all under one Lord, the houses whereof are made of Lyme and

*Stone, and are very great...and that in the gates of the
principall houses there are many Turques-stones cunningly
wrought....*

Moving northeast along what is today U.S. 666, or the Coronado
Trail, Estevanico was the first non–Native American on record to reach
America's Southwest. By the time Estevanico arrived in Zuni land, he
had with him a retinue of beautiful women and Native American
followers, and the party was loaded down with turquoise. Estevanico
himself was a memorable sight, sporting a beard and dressed in
medicine man garb with bells and feathers tied to his arms and legs.

Unfortunately for Estevanico, the Zuni looked upon him sus-
piciously, doubting that white men would send a black ambassador. They
refused his demands for a tribute of women and turquoise and denied
him a meeting with their chief. Instead, he was shot to death by arrows
while attempting to escape. His corpse was cut in pieces and passed
around the village as a curiosity. Later they killed his dog. To this day,
the Zuni tell the tale of the black Mexican whom they describe as "a
large man, with chili lips" (meaning they were swollen as if he had eaten
chili peppers).

MARCH 8

On this night in 1982, Sammy Davis Jr. was among the stars who
appeared on ABC's "Night of 100 Stars," a benefit for the Actor's Fund
taped at Radio City Music Hall. Davis was a comedian, singer, dancer,
and actor who worked in stage, television, films, and nightclubs, and
who frequently made special appearances at benefits and balls.

Davis's road to stardom began as a child vaudeville performer. He
landed his first movie role in 1933 in *Rufus Jones for President*. He
served in the army during World War II, mainly functioning as an
entertainer of troops. Davis starred in his own television variety show in
1966. The show was short-lived, however, due to poor ratings resulting
from its unfavorable time slot. Several of his renditions of songs, like

"The Candy Man," "That Old Black Magic," and "I've Gotta Be Me," became national favorites.

In April 1966 Davis was called the "busiest man in show business" by *Ebony* magazine. "Some people think Davis has a God complex," wrote Dick Schaap of the New York *Herald Tribune*, "but this is absurd. On the seventh day he works." Another critic remarked, "Davis comes on so strong, so terribly eager to please that he forces the onlooker into a quick decision—You either buy him or you don't."

Davis, a convert to Judaism, wrote two autobiographies. He was a supporter of the civil rights movement in the 1960s and was awarded the NAACP's Spingarn Medal in 1968. This all-around performer died of cancer in 1990 in Beverly Hills, California, at the age of 64. Upon his death, Benjamin Hooks, executive director of the NAACP, called Davis "an American treasure that the whole world loved."

MARCH 9

Today in 1841, the U.S. Supreme Court declared Joseph Cinquez and his fellow mutineers free. In August 1839, in the most famous slave ship revolt in history, Cinquez, the son of an African king, and his Mendi followers had killed the captain and taken over the Spanish slaver the *Amistad*. The rebels were captured off Long Island, where they had been discovered floating in a "mysterious long black schooner" with tattered sails before trying to sail the *Amistad* back to Africa.

At the age of 73, former president John Quincy Adams came out of retirement to successfully argue the Amistad case before the Supreme Court. None of the mutineers could speak a language intelligible to anyone who received them, pointing to their recent capture from Africa. The Court ruled, therefore, that the men had been kidnapped from Africa in violation of the 1808 ban on the international slave trade. The Court refused to honor claims that the Africans were property of the ship's Spanish owners, and stated that the "United States are bound to respect their rights as much as those of Spanish subjects."

On November 27, 1841, thirty-five of the fifty-four *Amistad* mutineers sailed back to Africa aboard the *Gentleman*. The First Church of Christ in Farmington, Connecticut, which had been the focus of the *Amistad* insurrectionists' lives while awaiting the court's decision, was declared a national historic landmark in December 1976.

> *Brothers...our hands are now clean for we have striven to regain the precious heritage we received from our fathers....I am resolved that it is better to die than be a white man's slave, and I will not complain if by dying I save you.*
>
> —Joseph Cinquez

MARCH 10

In 1913, Harriet Tubman, the most famous conductor of the Underground Railroad, died in Auburn, New York. With a $40,000 reward on her head, Tubman personally rescued over 300 slaves in nineteen trips to the South. She was known to say, "I never ran a train off the track, and I never lost a passenger."

The woman who became known as the Moses of Her People was born a slave in Maryland around 1820. She escaped and fled north at the age of 28. Tubman served for three years as a spy, scout, and nurse in the Union Army during the Civil War. She was the only female to successfully undertake operations in enemy territory and was the first, and probably only female to ever lead American troops into battle.

> *Long 'go when de Lord tole me to go free my people I said "No, Lord! I can't go—don't ask me." But he came anoder time. I saw him jes as plain. Den I said again, "Lord, go away—get some better edicated person—get a person wid more cultur dan I have; go way, Lord." But he came back de third time, and speaks to me jess as he did to Moses, and he says, "Harriet, I wants YOU," and I knew den I must do what he bid me. Now do*

you s'pose he wanted me to do dis jess for a day, or a week? No! de Lord who tole me to take care of my people meant me to do it jess so long as I live, and so I do what he told me.

—Harriet Tubman

~~~~~~

MARCH 11

On March 11, 1959, Lorraine Hansberry's *A Raisin in the Sun* opened at the Ethel Barrymore Theater in New York City with Sidney Poitier and Claudia McNeil in the lead roles. The play ran for 530 performances, becoming the longest running Broadway play written by an African-American. This was also the first Broadway drama written and directed by an African-American woman.

A Raisin in the Sun won the New York Drama Critic's Award for the best play of 1959. The 29-year-old Hansberry was the youngest playwright to win this award, as well as being the first African-American recipient. Hansberry took the title of her signature piece from a well-known line in the Langston Hughes poem "Harlem" that goes: "What happens to a dream deferred: Does it dry up like a raisin in the sun?"

In 1961 *A Raisin in the Sun* was made into a movie, again starring Sidney Poitier as the chauffeur Walter Younger. Hansberry's landmark career was cut short when she died of cancer in 1965 at the age of 34. The following are excerpts from *A Raisin in the Sun*.

WALTER: *Baby, don't nothing happen for you in this world 'less you pay somebody off!*

* * *

BENEATHA: *While I was sleeping in my bed in there, things were happening in this world that directly concerned me— and nobody asked me, consulted me—they just went out and did things—and changed my life.*

* * *

ASAGAI: *Ah, I like the look of packing crates! A house-hold in preparation for a journey!...Something full of the flow of life....Movement, progress...*

~~~~~~

MARCH 12

While serving at Fort William, Alexander Henry Jr. recorded in his journal on March 12, 1801, that Pierre Bonza's Native American wife had given birth to a baby girl. "The first fruit of this fort," wrote Henry, "and

Stephen Bonza

a very black one." The French-speaking Bonza was employed by the North West Company as Henry's personal assistant.

It was not unusual to find African men among the fur traders of the Old West. Colonel James Stevenson of the Bureau of American Ethnology wrote that fur traders preferred to employ African-Americans as negotiators with the Native Americans "because of their 'pacifying effect'...they could manage them better than white men, with less friction."

Pierre Bonza (also written Bonga) hailed from a prominent fur trading family that prospered in the Middle West from the late 1700s into the 1800s. The family was especially well-known among the Ojibway and Chippewa Indians of Minnesota. All of the Bonzas were noted for their remarkable physical strength and large stature.

George Bonza, Pierre's son, learned to speak English and became an interpreter and trader. It is believed that George Bonza was the interpreter at Fort Snelling in 1837 during the Chippewa treaty negotiations. An early account described George as "quite a prominent trader and a man of wealth and consequence...he was a thorough gentleman in both feeling and deportment." Although George was clearly of African descent, one account claims:

> Never having heard of any distinction between the people but that of Indians and white men, he would frequently paralyze his hearers when reminiscing by saying, "Gentleman, I assure you that John Banfil and myself were the first two white men that ever came into this country."

In 1900 there were still around 100 descendants of the Bonza family reported to be living around Lake Leech, Minnesota.

~~~~~~

MARCH 13

On this day in 1773, Jean Baptiste Point du Sable established the first permanent settlement at *Shikai-o*, meaning "the place of wild onions," and is now known as Chicago, Illinois. This African-American merchant also established trading posts at present-day Peoria, Illinois, Port Huron, Michigan, and Michigan City, Indiana.

Du Sable was probably either a West Indian or a mulatto from the du Sable family of New France. This Paris-educated pioneer was described as "tall, handsome, cultured." He enjoyed good relations with both whites and Native Americans and was married to a Potawatamie woman named Catherine.

Du Sable's log cabin home, located at 401 North Michigan Avenue, became a national historic landmark in 1976. The Native Americans of the area have been known to say "the first white man who settled here was a Negro."

MARCH 14

In an editorial in *Freedom's Journal* dated March 14, 1829, African-American editor John Russworm made his case in favor of the colonization of Africa by African-Americans. He wrote:

> We feel proud in announcing to our distant readers, that many of our brethren in this city, who have lately taken this subject into consideration, have like ourselves, come out from examination advocates of the Colony, and ready to embrace the first convenient opportunity to embark for the shores of Africa....
>
> Our wiseacres may talk as much as they please upon amalgamations, and our future standing in society, but it does not alter the case in the least; it does not improve our situation in the least; but it is calculated rather to stay the exertions of those who are really willing to make some efforts to improve their own present conditions. We are considered distinct people, in the midst of millions around us, and in the most favorable parts of the country; and it matters not from what cause this sentence has been passed upon us; the fiat has gone forth and should each of us live to the age of Methuselah, at the

end of the thousand years, we should be exactly in our present situation: a proscribed race, however unjustly....

However, the majority of African-Americans opposed the colonization movement, which some viewed as a white plot to force blacks back to an uncivilized land where they were sure to face hardships and perhaps even death. Prominent African-Americans such as the orator Frederick Douglass and Bishop Richard Allen expressed determination to remain in the land of their nativity. Douglass remarked, "Our minds are made up to live here if we can, or die here if we must; so every attempt to remove us, will be as it ought to be, labor lost." Bishop Allen wrote in the November 1827 issue of *Freedom's Journal*: "This land which we have watered with our *tears* and our *blood*, is now our *mother country* and we are well satisfied to stay where wisdom abounds and the gospel is free."

MARCH 15

On March 15, 1965, an angry President Lyndon B. Johnson addressed a joint session of Congress after voting rights demonstrations in Selma, Alabama, resulted in police-led violence. President Johnson took advantage of his prestige and position to drum up support for the Voting Rights Act of 1965. The president titled his speech "We Shall Overcome." In it he declared:

There is no Negro problem. There is no Southern problem. There is no Northern problem. There is only an American problem...

A century has passed since the day of promise, and the promise is unkept. The time of justice has now come, and I can tell you that I believe sincerely that no force can hold it back. It is right in the eyes of man and God that it should come, and when it does, I think that day will brighten the lives of every American.

The real hero of this struggle is the American Negro. His actions and protests, his courage to risk safety, and even to risk his life, have awakened the conscience of this nation...

~~~~~~

MARCH 16

In the first issue of *Freedom's Journal*, dated March 16, 1827, John B. Russworm and Reverend Samuel E. Cornish explained their reasons for founding the first African-American newspaper:

We wish to plead our own cause. Too long have others spoken for us. Too long has the publick been deceived by misrepresentations, in things which concern us dearly, though in the estimation of some mere trifles...

The civil rights of a people being of the greatest value, it shall ever be our duty to vindicate our brethren, when oppressed; and to lay the case before the publick.

The interesting fact that there are FIVE HUNDRED THOUSAND free persons of colour, one half of whom might peruse, and the whole be benefitted by the publication of the Journal; that no publication, as yet, has been devoted exclusively to their improvement....

Published in New York City, the paper was widely distributed in Boston, Washington, D.C., Baltimore, and even as far away as Haiti. The cover page slogan was "RIGHTEOUSNESS EXALTETH A NATION." The paper did not last long, however, as editors Russworm and Cornish disagreed on the issue of colonization of Africa. This conflict culminated with Russworm migrating to Liberia in 1829; the same year Cornish revived the newspaper under a new name, the *Rights of All*.

~~~~~~

MARCH 17

Blanche Kelso Bruce, a major Reconstruction politician, died in Washington, D.C. on this day in 1898. In 1875, Bruce had become the first African-American to serve a full six-year term in the U.S. Senate.*

During his tenure Bruce defended minority rights, including those of Chinese-Americans and Native Americans. He chaired the Select Committee that investigated the failed Freedman's Savings and Trust Company. In this capacity he uncovered gross incompetence, fraud, and scandal, and was successful in recovering all or at least part of the investments of 61,000 African-American depositors.

Bruce was a former slave who established a school for African-Americans in Hannibal, Missouri, in 1864, the first such school in the state. After moving to Mississippi he became a wealthy planter and held offices as sheriff, tax collector, levee board member, superintendent of schools, and Mississippi state senator. After serving one term as Republican senator from Mississippi, Bruce went on to hold various government posts, including registrar of the U.S. Treasury. He had also been suggested as a vice presidential candidate. Bruce's home, located at 909 M Street, N.W., Washington, D.C., was designated a national historic landmark in 1975.

I have confidence, not only in my country and her institutions but in the endurance, capacity, and destiny of my people.

—Bruce speech to the U.S. Senate on March 31, 1876

---

*Hiram Revels had been the first African-American elected to the Senate in 1870, but he served only one year before quitting to become the first president of Alcorn University. It wasn't until 1966 that Edward W. Brooke of Massachusetts became the third African-American in the U.S. Senate.

MARCH 18

On this day in 1895, 200 African-Americans set sail from Savannah, Georgia, to make a new home in Monrovia, Liberia, a west African colony founded by freed slaves.

Henrietta Fullor, an ex-slave who had made the transition to Liberia several years earlier, wrote the following in a letter, dated October 24, 1849, to her former master in Louisiana.

> ...Liberia is the home of our race and as good a country as they [our colored friends] can find. Industry and perseverance is only required to make a man happy and wealthy in this our adopted country. Its soil yields abundant harvest to the husbandman, its climate is healthy, its laws founded upon justice and equity. Here we sit under our own vine and Palm Tree, we all enjoy the same rights and privileges that our white brethren does in America.

While the back-to-Africa movement had a number of supporters, the majority of African-Americans opposed the idea. James Forten, a wealthy African-American from Philadelphia, wrote in a letter dated January 25, 1817:

> ...We had a large meeting of Males at the Reverend R. Allen's Church the other evening. Three thousand at least attended, and there was not one sole that was in favour of going to Africa. They think that the slave holders want to get rid of them so as to make their property more secure....

~~~~~~

MARCH 19

On March 19, 1831, the following poem—possibly a hymn—appeared in the *Liberator*.

> *Forc'd from home and all its pleasures,*
> *Afric's coast I left forlorn;*
> *To increase a stranger's treasures,*
> *O'er the raging billows borne.*
> *Men from England bought and sold me,*
> *Paid my price in paltry gold;*
> *But though slave they have enroll'd me,*
> *Minds are never to be sold.*

The *Liberator* newspaper was founded only three months earlier by white abolitionist William Lloyd Garrison, who said, "I have a system to destroy, and I have no time to waste." The *Liberator* was the most popular abolitionist paper in America. Three-quarters of the readers were African-Americans, and the paper was supported by African-American patrons, such as wealthy Philadelphia businessman James Forten. In an editorial in the first issue of The *Liberator*, the outspoken Garrison wrote:

> *I am aware, that many object to the severity of my language; but is there not cause for severity? I will be as harsh as truth, and as uncompromising as justice. On this subject, I do not wish to think, or speak, or write, with moderation. No! No! Tell a man whose house is on fire, to give a moderate alarm; tell him to moderately rescue his wife from the hands of the ravisher; tell the mother to gradually extricate her babe from the fire into which it has fallen;—but urge me not to use moderation in a cause like the present. I am in earnest—I will not equivocate—I will not excuse—I will not retreat a single inch-AND I WILL BE HEARD.*

77

MARCH 20

On March 20, 1883, Jan Ernst Matzeliger did what others said couldn't be done—he patented an automatic Shoe Lasting Machine. The application for U.S. Patent No. 274,207 reads:

> *My invention relates to the lasting of boots and shoes. The object of it is to perform by machinery and in a more expeditious and economical manner the operations which have heretofore been performed by hand. Heretofore devices have been contrived for performing u part of the operation, such as holding the last in proper position and drawing the leather over the last, while the nailing was done by hand. In my machine, I perform all the operations by machine, and automatically, requiring only the service of a boy or girl or other unskilled labor to attend the machine.*

Matzeliger's Shoe Lasting Machine changed the nature of the shoe industry. Production output increased dramatically, the price of shoes decreased by half, and quality improved immensely. Although initially many workers lost their jobs, in the long run mechanized shoe production benefitted laborers by resulting in reduced hours and higher wages.

Matzeliger, an emigre from the Dutch East Indies, spent most of his

brief adult life in Lynn, Massachusetts, the center of the shoe manufacturing industry in America. This ingenious mechanic died from tuberculosis at the age of 37. He willed most of his stock in the Consolidated Lasting Machine Company, which had bought his patents, to the North Congregational Church of Lynn. Now called the First Church of Christ, the church's bulletin of September 8, 1968, read:

We are taking a few minutes this morning to honor the life of Jan Ernst Matzeliger. Jan Matzeliger's invention of the shoe lasting machine was perhaps the most important invention for New England. His invention was the greatest step forward in the shoe industry. Yet, because of the color of his skin, he was not mentioned in the major history books of the United States....We are not honoring Matzeliger because he gave the church money, but because he is a hero with whom the American people can identify.

MARCH 21

On this day in 1964, Reverend Dr. Martin Luther King Jr., Under Secretary of the United Nations Ralph Bunche, and Reverend Ralph David Abernathy led 3,200 protestors in a second effort to march from Selma to Montgomery, Alabama, the state capital. Two weeks earlier the first attempt had gone sour when state police, under orders from

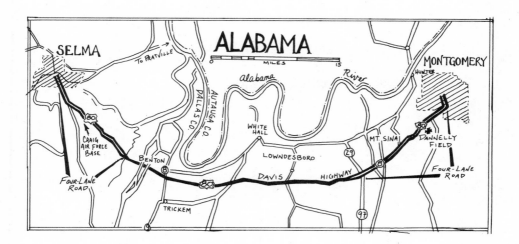

Governor George Wallace, used violent means to disperse the demonstrators.

Television images of peaceful demonstrators being choked by tear gas and set upon by police wielding clubs and whips shocked the nation and the world. President Lyndon B. Johnson reacted by securing a federal order allowing the march to proceed, and mobilizing thousands of troops to protect the marchers. Despite several attacks on participants, the taunts of hecklers, the "unpleasant" attitude of state troopers, and reports of numerous bomb scares in the African-American community in nearby Birmingham, the activists completed their fifty-four-mile journey along U.S. 80. On March 25, some 25,000 black and white demonstrators joined the marchers in front of the capitol building in Montgomery.

The Selma to Montgomery march was one of the most significant acts of the 1960s civil rights movement. Reverend King compared the event in historical importance to Ghandi's march to the sea. One year later the Voting Rights Act was passed, which secured federal protection of voting rights for all citizens in all states. Upon signing the act, President Johnson evoked the theme song of the 1960s civil rights movement, "We Shall Overcome."

> We shall overcome.
> We shall overcome.
> We shall overcome,
> Someday.
> Oh, deep in my heart,
> I do believe, that
> We shall overcome,
> Someday.

MARCH 22

On this day in 1931, Richard B. Harrison was awarded the NAACP's Spingarn Medal for his "fine and reverent characterization of the Lord in Marc Connelly's play, *The Green Pastures* [which] has made that play the outstanding dramatic accomplishment in the year 1931." The citation continues, "The Medal is given to Mr. Harrison not simply for his crowning accomplishment, but for the long years of his work as dramatic reader and entertainer, interpreting to the mass of colored people in church and school the finest specimens of English drama from Shakespeare down. It is fitting that in the sixty-seventh year of his life he should receive wide-spread acclaim for a role that typifies and completes his life work."

On February 26, 1930, *The Green Pastures* had opened on Broadway with Harrison playing De Lawd. For cultural critic Alain Locke, this drama marked the end of an era. Explained Locke in *Opportunity* magazine:

> *That spring for me was the end of the Harlem Renaissance. Sophisticated New Yorkers turned to Noel Coward. Colored actors began to go hungry, publishers politely rejected new manuscripts, and patrons found other uses for their money. The cycle that had charlestoned into being on the dancing heels of* Shuffle Along *now ended in* Green Pastures *and de Lawd. The generous 1920s were over.*

MARCH 23

Today in 1971, comedian and television star Flip Wilson received International Broadcasting's Man of the Year award. The following year he appeared on the cover of *Time* magazine.

Flip Wilson's television comedy program, *The Flip Wilson Show*, aired from 1970 to 1974 and received consistently high ratings. Wilson's originality and his knack for creating memorable characters earned him four Television Champion awards. His signature phrases, "The Devil made me do it!" and "What you see is what you get!" became part of the national vocabulary, while his characters Geraldine Jones (along with her jealous boyfriend "Killer") and Reverend Leroy of the What's Happening Now Church became household names.

Flip Wilson was the first African-American to become a bona fide television superstar. Born Clerow Wilson, he was dubbed Flip by his air force buddies whom he "flipped out" with his humor.

Violence is a tool of the ignorant.

—Wilson in an *Ebony* interview, April 1968

Being your own man does not mean taking advantage of anyone else.

—Wilson in an interview in *Black Stars*, February 1973

MARCH 24

Based on his belief that the Vietnam War was an obstacle to the civil rights movement, Dr. Martin Luther King Jr. publicly announced his strong opposition to the war on this day in 1967. Several other prominent African-Americans joined the voices of dissent.

Cultural critic and author Eldridge Cleaver challenged the war as an expression of solidarity with the world's disadvantaged and oppressed. "The black man's interest lies in seeing a free and independent Vietnam," claimed Cleaver, "a strong Vietnam which is not the puppet of international white supremacy. If the nations of Asia, Latin America, and Africa are strong and free, the black man in America will be safe and secure and free to live in dignity and self-respect."

Malcolm X opposed the protracted military conflict for purely ethical reasons. Malcolm explained: "We are not anti-American. We are anti or against what America is doing wrong in other parts of the world as well as here. And what she did in the Congo in 1964 is wrong. It's criminal, criminal. And what she did to the American public, to get the American public to go along with it, is criminal. What she's doing in South Vietnam is criminal. She's causing American soldiers to be murdered every day, killed every day, die every day, for no reason at all. That's wrong. Now, you're not supposed to be so blind with patriotism that you can't face reality. Wrong is wrong, no matter who does it or says it."

In addition, the African-American boxer Muhammad Ali was stripped of his first heavyweight title because he had refused to enlist in the draft because of his religious convictions. (The title was later restored.)

This is not to say that African-Americans did not contribute dearly to the war effort. Whereas African-Americans constituted only 11 percent of the American population at the time, they accounted for 23 percent of the fatalities of the Vietnam War.

MARCH 25

Ida B. Wells died at the age of 78 in Chicago, Illinois, on this day in 1931. This turn-of-the-century antilynching crusader was also a civil rights and black women's rights activist. A founding member of the NAACP, Wells was viewed as even more militant than the DuBois camp.

Wells published a newspaper called *Free Speech and Headlight* in Memphis, Tennessee, until 1892. She was forced to close the paper down after an angry mob attacked her press because she had printed a story about white businessmen who had three black competitors lynched. It was at this juncture—with threats against her life—that Wells moved to Chicago. Three years later she published *Red Record: Tabulated Statistics and Alleged Causes of Lynching in the United States*, the first statistical study of lynching in America. The cover read: "Respectfully submitted to the Nineteenth Century civilization in 'the Land of the Free and Home of the Brave.'" In it she wrote:

> ...Surely the humanitarian spirit of this country which reaches out to denounce the treatment of Russian Jews, the Armenian Christians, the laboring poor of Europe, the Siberian exiles, and the native women of India—will not longer refuse to lift its voice on this subject. If it were known that the cannibals or the savage Indians had burned three human beings alive in the past two years, the whole of Christendom would be aroused, to devise ways and means to put a stop to it. Can you remain silent and inactive when such things are done in our own community and country? Is your duty to humanity in the United States less binding?

Wells became a lifelong authority on lynching, finding that between the years of 1878 and 1898 about 10,000 Americans were lynched. The following excerpt from an article in the June 1910 issue of *Original Rights* magazine provides an example of her investigative-style reporting:

> On the morning of November 11th last year, a double lynching was reported from Cairo, Ill.—a white man and a Negro. A white girl had been found murdered two days before. The bloodhounds which were brought led to a Negro's house three blocks away....

Wells's house in Chicago, at 3624 South Dr. Martin Luther King Jr. Drive, was designated a National Historic Landmark in 1974.

MARCH 26

On this day in 1944, the "First Lady of Soul" was born in Detroit, Michigan. At the age of 16, Diana Earle joined the singing group the Supremes, which later became Diana Ross and the Supremes. Between

1964 and 1969, the group recorded sixteen top-ten hits on the Motown label.

After going solo in 1969, Ross became a '70s superstar both in the United States and England. Her numerous hits included "Reach Out And Touch," "Ain't No Mountain High Enough," "Touch Me In the Morning," and "It's My Turn." She also starred in the movies *Lady Sings the Blues*, *Mahogany*, and *The Wiz*.

> *I never considered it a disadvantage to be a Black woman. I never wanted to be anything else. We have brains. We are beautiful. We can do anything we set our minds to....*
>
> *Instead of always looking at the past, I put myself ahead twenty years and try to look at what I need to do now in order to get there then....*
>
> *You can't just sit there and wait for people to give you that golden dream, you've got to get out there and make it happen for yourself.*

—Ross quotes from an October 1989 article in *Essence*

MARCH 27

The woman who, according to author Barry McRae, has "the most wholly beautiful voice in all jazz history" was born in Newark, New Jersey, on this day in 1924. Sarah Vaughn began her musical career as a child, singing in church and playing piano and organ. "I learned to take music apart and analyze the notes and put it back together again," explained Vaughn.

Her break came when she won first prize in the famous Wednesday night talent contest at Harlem's Apollo Theater in New York. In addition to being paid ten dollars, she performed for a week at the theater. Her three-octave voice caught the attention of Billy Eckstine, a jazz vocalist with Earl Hines's big band. Eckstine recommended the 19 year old to Hines, who hired her as a pianist and vocalist in 1943.

The "Divine Sarah," with help from colleagues Dizzie Gillespie and Charlie Parker, recorded her first solo hit, "Lover Man," in 1945. Soon she began to sell an average of three million records per year, and for six years in a row was selected best female singer by *Downbeat* magazine. In 1959 she released "Broken-Hearted Melody," her first record to sell a million copies. Other Vaughn hits included "Misty," "Smooth Operator," and "Send In the Clowns."

Four times married and divorced, Vaughn was a fairly private person who was known to enjoy the company of her musicians. Her long and impressive career included appearances in movies and on television, international tours, and performances at the White House.

MARCH 28

A report on the front page of the *New York Times* dated March 28, 1909, began, "More than a hundred, possibly several hundred Creek Indians, outlaw negroes, and half-breeds, who have defied State authority, are being sought by five companies of militia and hundreds of citizens, forming Sheriff's posses."

The Crazy Snake Uprising of late March 1909 was a last-ditch effort by Creek Indians and Seminole Negroes to hold off white dominance over their lands in Kansas. The new state of Kansas, formed by combining Oklahoma and Indian Territories, had just been admitted to the Union, and Creek lands were being opened up to settlers. Neither the Creeks nor the Negroes were keen to live under a white-led government, with its discriminatory laws and racist society.

According to the newspaper account, the "first real Indian uprising" in years began, when "several deputy sheriffs went to Henryetta to arrest negro cattle thieves. They were fired on by negro and half-breed friends of the criminals and forced to retreat." The sheriffs returned with reinforcements and the violence escalated. During the initial battle three

Negroes were killed, several Negroes and Indians were wounded, and forty-one people were arrested. A few days later, when authorities tried to capture the Creek leader Crazy Snake, the rebels shot and killed two deputies. Crazy Snake escaped.

~~~~~~

MARCH 29

The Black Community Survival Conference, organized by the Black Panther Party, was held in Oakland and Berkeley, California, from March 29 through 31, 1972. Conference advertisements announced that 10,000 free bags of groceries (with chickens in every bag) would be given away. "They've been voting for a chicken in every pot for the last thirty to forty years," explained party chairman Bobby Seale, "but, now, we've got the food: A chicken in every pot; and, if necessary, if you don't have a pot to cook it in, we'll open up a Free Pot Program."

In 1966 Bobby Seale and Huey P. Newton founded the Black Panther Party as a revolutionary political movement, drawing support largely from disenfranchised ghetto youth. Originally their platform centered around uniting urban blacks to protect their rights, specifically to protect themselves against police brutality. Early Panthers wore identifying black berets and black leather jackets. They espoused radical terminology like "pigs" for police, "fascists" for establishment figures, and "comrade" for fellow party members. In 1966 party rules included incendiary statements such as, "If we ever have to take captives do not ill-treat them."

The militant, "urban warfare" phase of the party was rather short-lived. The party's leaders—much maligned and harassed—soon shifted toward a less radical ideology, converting the movement from a race struggle to more of a class struggle. "Having come away from arrogance, cultism," stated the April 1, 1972 issue of the party paper *The Black Panther Intercommunal News Service*, "we have returned to our original aims, producing what we call the Survival Programs...." According to the paper, these programs were aimed at African-Americans and other oppressed peoples and included free screening for sickle-cell anemia, the Angela Davis free food program, and free bussing of family and friends to visit prisoners.

~~~~~~

MARCH 30

The Fifteenth Amendment to the U.S. Constitution, which had been ratified on February 3, went into effect on this day in 1870. The amendment extended the right to vote to all males, regardless of "race, color, or previous condition of servitude". The next day Thomas Peterson became the first African-American to exercise his new constitutional right.

However, many African-Americans remained disenfranchised by both trickery and treachery until many years later. One method of screening out blacks was to require voters to pass literacy tests. On one such occasion, as the story goes, an African-American teacher educated at Harvard and Eton went to the Mississippi registrar to vote. He was shown a text in Latin, which he read easily. He was then asked to read Greek, which he did without difficulty, and then German and Spanish, both of which he could read. Finally he was shown Chinese writing and the registrar asked him what it meant. The teacher replied, "It means you don't want me to vote."

~~~~~~

MARCH 31

Today in 1988, the Pulitzer Prize for fiction was awarded to Toni Morrison for her 1987 novel *Beloved*. In 1993 Morrison became the first African-American woman to win a Nobel Prize for literature. Morrison has written several celebrated novels, including *The Bluest Eye* (1970), *Sula* (1974), *Song of Solomon* (1977), *Tar Baby* (1981), and *Jazz* (1992). *Song of Solomon* won the National Book Critics Award and was a main selection in the Book-of-the-Month Club, only the second book by an African-American to earn this honor since Richard Wright's *Native Son* in 1941.

Born in Lorain, Ohio, Morrison's stories of black life in America have made her one of today's internationally acclaimed authors. About her own writing, this teacher, editor, and author says:

> *I have always tried to establish a voice in the work of the narrator which worked like a chorus, like what I think is going on in the black church, or in jazz, where people respond, where the reader is participating. So the problem is always how do you get that feeling, which I call Black writing, which is not dropping 'g's, it's much more subtle than that—the way people do it in churches, the way you do it in jazz concerts, the way you say "yes", "amen", get up and move, so whoever is up there is not working alone.*

*   *   *

> *Macon Dead's Packard rolled slowly down Not Doctor Street, through the rough part of town (later known as the Blood Bank because blood flowed so freely there), over the bypass downtown, and headed for the wealthy white neighborhoods. Some of the black people who saw the car passing by sighed with good-humored envy at the classiness, the dignity of it. In 1936 there were very few among them who lived as well as Macon Dead.*

> —from Chapter 2 of *Song of Solomon*

APRIL 1

Lott Carey, the first missionary to the West African country of Liberia, died on this day in 1828. Carey had first sailed for Liberia in January 1821, soon after the country was founded as a republic for freed American slaves by the American Colonization Society.

Established by white statesmen John C. Calhoun and Henry Clay in 1817, the American Colonization Society was not welcomed by the majority of African-Americans. In January of that same year, free blacks in major U.S. cities organized protest meetings against the attempt, in their words, "to exile us from the land of our nativity."

By the 1850s, however, the movement had gained support from several notable African-Americans, including Martin Delany, Alexander Crummell, Henry Highland Garnet, and AME bishop Henry McNeal Turner. Nearly 12,000 African-Americans emigrated to Liberia by the turn of the century. The American Colonization Society dissolved in 1892, at which time Bishop Turner took up the colonization banner by forming the International Immigration Society.

The concept of returning to Africa gained broad support again during the 1920s with the arrival in New York City of Jamaican black nationalist Marcus Garvey, whose Universal Negro Improvement Association espoused a back-to-Africa platform.

The making of an American begins at that point where he himself rejects all other ties, any other history, and himself adopts the vesture of his adopted land.

—James Baldwin from his book *Notes of a Native Son*

APRIL 2

Today in 1939, the "Lover Man of Soul" was born. Marvin Gaye, the master of soul-based rock, recorded many Motown hits and soul classics, such as "Sexual Healing," "How Sweet It Is to Be Loved by You," "Ain't

No Mountain High Enough" (with Tammi Terrell), and *Billboard's* number one hit for 1973, "Let's Get It On." Gaye scored one of Motown's biggest hits ever with "I Heard It Through the Grapevine."

This son of a Pentecostal minister grew up in Washington, D.C., where he began playing the organ and singing in church at the age of five. Gaye, who pleaded in song "Brother, brother, there are too many of us dying," was shot and killed by his father following an argument on April 1, 1984, in Los Angeles. He was one day shy of 45 years old.

An estimated 8,000 people jammed Forest Lawn Memorial Park to mourn the soul star. Dick Gregory, African-American comedian and social activist, eulogized Gaye, saying, "Marvin told me, 'I like to raise people's consciousness....I want to give them hope.' Well, brother Marvin, you did that—with class and warmth and love. You left us too soon, but any time would have been too soon."

Most fear stems from sin: To limit one's sins must assuredly limit one's fears, thereby bringing more peace to one's spirit.

—Gaye quoted in the November 1974 issue of *Ebony*

APRIL 3

THE BIRMINGHAM MANIFESTO

We have always been a peaceful people, bearing our oppression with superhuman effort. Yet we have been the victims of repeated violence, not only that inflicted by the hoodlum element but also that inflicted by the blatant misuse of police power....For years, while our homes and churches were being bombed, we heard nothing but the rantings and ravings of racist city officials.

The Negro protest for equality and justice has been a voice crying in the wilderness. Most of Birmingham has remained silent, probably out of fear. In the meanwhile, our city has acquired the dubious reputation of being the worst big city in race relations in the United States.

Dated April 3, 1963, *The Birmingham Manifesto* marked the beginning of a direct-action civil rights drive in Alabama. Demonstrations and boycotts were organized in several cities to protest widespread discrimination in the state who's governor vowed "segregation forever."

The shocking events that took place in the city of Birmingham following the release of the manifesto awakened the American public to the struggles faced by African-Americans. Americans who tuned in to television news were horrified by scenes of police dogs and high-pressure water hoses being turned on demonstrators. More than two thousand activists, including Martin Luther King Jr., were arrested during Birmingham's antisegregation campaign.

We have waited for more than 340 years for our constitutional and God-given rights. The nations of Asia and Africa are moving with jet-like speed toward the goal of political independence, and we still creep at horse-and-buggy pace toward the gaining of a cup of coffee at a lunch counter. I guess it is easy for those who have never felt the stinging dart of segregation to say "wait."

—excerpt from King's "Letter From the Birmingham Jail"

APRIL 4

On this day in 1968, Martin Luther King Jr. was shot outside of his room at the Lorraine Motel in Memphis, Tennessee. King's assassination precipitated marches and rallies across America and riots erupted in over 100 cities. In the melee, forty-six people were killed and 20,000 arrested. From April 5 to 11, 50,000 federal and state troops were called in to keep order. President Lyndon B. Johnson declared April 7 an official day of mourning. King was 38 years old at the time of his death.

> *There is nothing more tragic than to find an individual bogged down in the length of life, devoid of breadth.*
>
> —Martin Luther King Jr.

> *How many must die before we can really have a free and true and peaceful society?*
>
> —Coretta Scott King, speaking four day's after her husband's death

> *You are no longer innocent, you are condemned to awareness.*
>
> —African-American author and cultural theorist Michael Eric Dyson reflecting on his thoughts as a nine-year-old boy upon learning of King's death

APRIL 5

On a small farm in Franklin County, Virginia, Booker Taliaferro Washington was born into slavery on this day in 1856. Booker T. Washington went from slavery to become one of the most famous Americans of his day. Washington, whose father was believed to be white, was freed at the age of nine. As a youth he labored in the salt furnaces and coal mines of West Virginia. In 1881 he founded the all-black Tuskegee Normal and Industrial Institute in Alabama.

In 1895, at the Cotton States Exposition in Atlanta, Georgia, Washington delivered a speech that became known as the "Atlanta Compromise." In this landmark speech Washington promoted vocational rather than academic education for African-Americans, and during the emergence of Jim Crow laws appeared to be endorsing separate-but-equal policies. Following the Atlanta Exposition, Washington became the most prominent, and for a while the only, spokesperson for African-American interests, as well as the darling of white Americans. Soon detractors appeared on the scene, however, best represented by W. E. B. DuBois, who believed Washington condoned second-class citizenship for blacks.

Washington wrote several books, including *Up From Slavery* (1901) and the *Life of Frederick Douglass* (1907). He died on November 14, 1915, at Tuskegee, Alabama.

After the coming of freedom there were two points upon which practically all the people on our place were agreed...that they must change their names, and that they must leave the old plantation for at least a few days or weeks in order that they might really feel sure that they were free. In some way a feeling got among the coloured people that it was far from proper for them to bear the surnames of their former owners, and a great many of them took other surnames. This was one of the first signs of freedom...and so in many cases "John Hatcher" was changed to "John S. Lincoln" or "John S. Sherman," the initial "S" standing for no name, it being simply a part of what the coloured man proudly called his "entitles."

—from "Boyhood Days" in *Up From Slavery*

APRIL 6

On this day in 1909, Matthew Henson became the first man to reach the North Pole. Adm. Robert E. Peary, the expedition's commander, arrived about forty-five minutes after Henson. The temperature was −29 degrees when Henson planted the American flag at 90 degrees north— the only place on the planet where the only way you can go is south.

Upon his return to the United States, Henson lectured and wrote the book *A Negro Explorer at the North Pole*. Overall, though, he remained obscure in the annals of history, while Admiral Peary was credited with discovering the North Pole.

In April 1988 Henson's remains were transferred to Arlington National Cemetery and laid next to Peary's in belated recognition of his achievement.

> *A tragic wrong has been righted. Welcome home, Matthew Henson, to a new day in America. May your presence here inspire generations of explorers.*
>
> —eulogy at Henson's reburial at Arlington given by Dr. S. Allen Counter, Harvard history professor

APRIL 7

South Pacific opened on this day in 1949 at the Majestic Theater in New York City with African-American actress Juanita Hall playing Bloody Mary. Hall's renditions of "Happy Talk" and "Bali H'ai" quickly turned the songs into national hits. The Juilliard-trained performer became the first African-American to win a Tony Award for her role in this Broadway show.

In addition to stage acting, Hall made club appearances, was a choir singer and director, and worked in such films as *Miracle in Harlem* (1948) and *Flower Drum Song* (1961). Hall died in 1968 in Bayshore, Long Island.

> *...you will find high standards of characterization and acting throughout. Take Juanita Hall, for example. She plays a brassy, greedy, ugly Tonkonese woman with harsh, vigorous, authentic accuracy; and she sings one of Mr. Rodgers' finest songs, "Bali H'ai" with rousing artistry.*
>
> —review of *South Pacific*, the *New York Times*, April 8, 1949

APRIL 8

At 9:07 P.M. on this day in 1974, in Atlanta Stadium, Atlanta Braves baseball player Hank Aaron sent a fastball served up by Al Downing of the Los Angeles Dodgers over the left field fence hitting his 715th home run and breaking Babe Ruth's record. A fellow Braves player ensured that Aaron stepped on home plate, where a welcoming party of fans, players, and his mother awaited him. The ball game stopped while 53,775 fans showered the "The Hammer" with a fifteen-minute ovation. "Downing stood on the mound offering his own tribute," wrote the *Washington Post*, "he quietly applauded Aaron as the Atlanta slugger rushed into the arms of his teammates."

Aaron seemed unfazed by the barrage of media attention leading up to this record-breaking feat. Wrote one *Sports Illustrated* correspondent, "Aaron had labored for most of his twenty-one-year career in shadows cast by more flamboyant superstars, and if he was enjoying his newfound celebrity, he gave no hint of it. He seemed to be nothing more than a man trying to do his job and live a normal life in the presence of incessant chaos." After walloping his 715th home run, commercial endorsement contracts, fund-raising requests, and fan mail poured in.

By the end of his career, in 1976, Aaron had broken numerous baseball records, including most runs batted in, with 2,297, and a total of 755 home runs. The "Home Run King" was awarded the NAACP's Spingarn Medal in 1976 and was inducted into the Baseball Hall of Fame in 1982.

APRIL 9

On Easter Sunday in 1939, Marian Anderson, one of the world's best contralto opera singers, performed a concert on the steps of the Lincoln Memorial in Washington, D.C., before an admiring crowd of 75,000 people. The concert wasn't originally planned to be open-air, but in deference to the local customs of the segregated capital, Anderson had been denied the use of Constitution Hall by the Daughters of the American Revolution.

The event blossomed into a major political affair, with First Lady Eleanor Roosevelt quitting the Daughters of the American Revolution in disgust. Washington, D.C. desegregated many public sites immediately following the concert.

> I could see that my significance as an individual was small....I had become, whether I liked it or not, a symbol, representing my people.
>
> —Anderson quoted in Hope Stoddard's *Famous American Women*

> As long as you keep a person down, some part of you has to be down there to hold him down, so it means you cannot soar as you otherwise might.
>
> —Anderson in a CBS-TV interview on December 30, 1957

~~~~~~

APRIL 10

On this day in 1816, Richard Allen was elected first bishop of the African Methodist Episcopal Church. The church had broken away from the white-dominated Methodist Church earlier in the same year. Today, the AME is one of the largest black religious organizations in America.

Allen was born a slave in Philadelphia in 1760. He bought his own freedom and became a strolling preacher in Philadelphia. Together with Absalom Jones, he organized the Free African Society, one of the first black organizations in America. In July 1794, Allen founded the Bethel African Methodist Episcopal Church of Philadelphia, the first African-American controlled church in America and believed to be the oldest property continually owned by African-Americans.

Known to be industrious and thrifty, Allen managed a successful boot and shoe store, becoming one of the richest and most prominent African-Americans of his day. A colleague, Reverend Walter Proctor, described Allen as "a man of mixed blood, his mother being a mulatto and his father a pure African; this gave his complexion a soft chestnut tint....The expansive forehead and the fullness of the lower eyelids [showed] expansiveness of intellect and a ready command of language."

Richard Allen

Richard Allen was also the main force behind the first African-American national convention held only five months before his death in 1831.

APRIL 11

The "Soybean Chemist" was born on this day in 1899 in Montgomery, Alabama. Percy Lavon Julian, who received his Ph.D. in organic chemistry from the University of Vienna, used soya beans for several of his important discoveries.

For example, from soya beans Julian developed a synthetic form of the pain killer cortisone, a drug widely prescribed to arthritis sufferers, and his discovery made the drug more affordable for patients. Julian used soybeans to make a fire-smothering foam that was employed during World War II to extinguish fires on board navy vessels and at airplane crash sites. Its brand name was Aero-Foam, but American sailors called it "bean soup."

The innovative chemist also improved methods of extracting the hormones testosterone and progesterone from soya beans. And he was the first to synthetically reproduce the drug physostigmine, used for treating the eye disease glaucoma.

"I have had one goal in my life," said Julian, "that of playing some role in making life a little easier for the persons who come after me."

APRIL 12

The Civil War began on April 12, 1861, when Confederate troops attacked Fort Sumter in Charleston Harbor in South Carolina. "This, boys," said future Union Navy pilot Robert Smalls, upon observing the Union Army preparing for the attack, "is the dawn of freedom for our race." Frederick Douglass, famed African-American abolitionist and orator, exclaimed, "God be praised!"

In the earliest months of the Civil War, free African-Americans in northern cities who came forward to volunteer for the Union Army were refused admission, and slaves who escaped to the Union lines were sent back to their owners. It wasn't long, however, before President Lincoln declared escaped slaves to be "contraband" of war, and ordered his commanders to retain the men. By July 1862, Congress officially legalized the recruitment of African-American troops, which had already been taking place in practice for over a year.

The best known of the all-black regiments were the Fifty-fourth Massachusetts Volunteers, commanded by Robert Gould Shaw, and Thomas Wentworth Higginson's First South Carolina Volunteers. In total, about 385,000 African-Americans served in some capacity during the Civil War. A little less than half were soldiers and the other half worked in support roles, such as cooks, stevedores, mechanics, and manual laborers.

Thomas Long, a soldier in the First South Carolina Volunteers, expressed his view on the importance of African-Americans fighting in this war:

If we hadn't become sojers, all might have gone back as it was before...suppose you kept your freedom without enlisting in dis army; your chilen might have grown up free and been well cultivated so as to be equal in any business, but would always have been flung in dere faces—"Your fader never fought for he own freedom"—and what could dey answer? Neber can say that to dis African Race any more.

~~~~~~

APRIL 13

On this day in 1964 Sidney Poitier won an Oscar for Best Actor of the Year for his role in *Lilies of the Field*, becoming the first African-American to win an Oscar. Poitier's successful forty-year career changed the way black men were portrayed in film. Poitier was cast as an intelligent, articulate, charming, proud, and attractive man. Although other actors before him, such as Paul Robeson, had played similar dignified roles, Poitier's presence in the industry was more consistent.

Of his many films, some of the most memorable are *To Sir With Love*, *In the Heat of the Night*, and *Guess Who's Coming to Dinner*. Poitier was also popularly acclaimed as Walter Younger, a chauffeur, in both the Broadway production and film version of *A Raisin in the Sun*.

If Paul Robeson had not been there, I would not be here. And so it is with the youth of today. The stand you took will help us with a stand in the days, weeks, months, and years ahead, for peace, for the rights and needs of people.

—Poitier speech at the tribute to Paul Robeson, Carnegie Hall, New York City, April 15, 1973

APRIL 14

The Motown Record Corporation was incorporated on this day in 1960 in Detroit, Michigan. Originally called Hitsville, USA, owner Berry Gordy Jr. started the company in his own home with an $800 loan. Motown's *Shop Around* by the Miracles went gold only a few years later. A former factory worker, Gordy drew the company's second and now-famous name from the African-American slang for Detroit—the Motor Town—reflecting the city's importance as a center of automobile manufacturing.

Calling itself "the sound of young America," Motown launched the careers of numerous superstars. Among them were Diana Ross and the Supremes, the Temptations, Marvin Gaye, the Jackson Five and a nine-year-old blind boy named Stevie Morris, or Little Stevie Wonder. Other early Motown talents included the Marvelettes, Smokey Robinson and the Miracles, the Four Tops, and Martha and the Vandellas.

When asked to define the Motown sound, Gordy replied that he, Smokey Robinson, and some others pondered the question and concluded, "We thought of the neighborhoods we were raised in and came up with a six-word definition: rats, roaches, struggle, talent, guts, love."

Motown moved its offices to Los Angeles in 1969, which many claimed ripped the heart out of Detroit.

APRIL 15

On April 15, 1962, Diahann Carroll starred in Richard Rodgers's *No Strings*, becoming the first African-American in the romantic lead of a white Broadway musical.

Carroll chalked up another first in September 1968 with the airing of her television program *Julia*. She became the first African-American in the lead role of a television program. "It is time to present the black character primarily as a human being," she said of her ground-breaking show, "I want to do something that deals with a black person in the everyday situation of ups and downs, good and bad."

In 1976 Carroll had her own variety show, *The Diahann Carroll Show*. Over the years, she appeared in other television shows and several movies, including *Porgy and Bess*, *Paris Blue*, and *Claudine*, the last of which she was nominated for an Oscar. In 1984 Carroll took the role of Dominique Deveraux on the popular nighttime soap opera *Dynasty*, calling herself television's "first black bitch."

I've learned to enjoy my life. I'm not divided and guilty about the fact that I want to work. The guilt is gone. I won't allow that word in my life, and I've forgotten how to spell it.

—Carroll in a 1984 article in *Time* magazine

APRIL 16

For Africa to me...is more than a glamorous fact. It is a historical truth. No man can know where he is going unless he knows exactly where he has been and exactly how he arrived at his present place.

—Maya Angelou quoted in the *New York Times* on April 16, 1972

Maya Angelou—feminist, writer, poet, playwright, actress, dancer, and director—is probably best known for her five autobiographies. The most famous of these was her first, *I Know Why the Caged Bird Sings*, published in 1970. *I Know Why the Caged Bird Sings* is a classic of twentieth-century feminist literature and was the first book written by an African-American to appear on the national bestseller lists.

Angelou has certainly led an interesting life. At the age of 15 she became the first African-American streetcar conductor in San Francisco. She appeared in the opera *Porgy and Bess* in 1954, and taught at the University of Ghana from 1963 until 1967. She was nominated for an

Emmy for her role in the TV miniseries *Roots*, and in 1975 the *Ladies' Home Journal* named her the Woman of the Year in Communications.

More recently, this eloquent speaker was invited by President Bill Clinton to read poetry at his inauguration in January 1993. She wrote a poem specifically for the occasion titled "On the Pulse of Morning."

She said that I must always be intolerant of ignorance but understanding of illiteracy. That some people, unable to go to school, were more educated and even more intelligent than college professors. She encouraged me to listen carefully to what country people called mother wit. That in these homely sayings was couched the collective wisdom of generations.

—from Chapter 15 of *I Know Why the Caged Bird Sings*

APRIL 17

Today in 1971, Sam Napier, circulation manager for the *Black Panther* newspaper, was shot and killed in the basement of the New York City circulation office. The Black Panther Party claims the perpetrators were police agents working under COINTELPRO, an FBI conspiracy to destroy the organization.

According to accounts in the April 6, 1980 issue of the party paper the *Black Panther*, the FBI hired *agent provocateurs*—such as one "Othello"—to spy on the organization. The newspaper also accused the FBI of planning counterintelligence tactics to undermine the group's main public voice—the *Black Panther*. These included "a vigorous inquiry by the Internal Revenue Service" into newspaper sales, sending hate mail, fixing a powder in the newspaper production premises that let off a noxious odor, and forcing an airline to increase mail delivery rates for the paper.

An editorial in the April 6 issue of the *Black Panther* declared, "In the 203 years of the history of this country, no American political group has been more consistently, illegally and viciously brutalized by the

United States government than the Black Panther Party." The Black Panther Party believes that since 1968 at least twenty-eight of their members had been killed as a consequence of the COINTELPRO conspiracy.

~~~~~~

APRIL 18

On this day in 1966, Bill Russell was named coach of the Boston Celtics, making him the first African-American head coach of a major professional sports team. Russell succeeded sixteen-year veteran Arnold "Red" Auerbach to become the basketball team's fourth coach. This six-foot-ten-inch sports icon was a star center for the Celtics at the time of his appointment, and continued to play during his first season at the helm. He became the highest paid coach or manager in professional sports at the time, earning an estimated $125,001 per year.

William Felton Russell was born in Monroe, Louisiana, on February 12, 1934. When Russell was eight years old his family moved to Oakland, California, where he grew up. At school in Oakland, Russell suffered from poor grades, and in the ninth grade he didn't even make the basketball team. Soon enough, the youth grew to six-foot-five-inches tall and became a successful varsity basketball player. At the University of San Francisco he led his team to two national championships. Russell was the star center of the gold medal—winning U.S. basketball squad at the 1972 Olympic games in Australia.

Off-court achievements for Russell have included publishing his autobiography *Go Up for Glory*, meeting two U.S. Presidents, and owning an African rubber plantation and a New England restaurant.

> One of the all-time dominant figures in professional basket-ball, both as a player and a coach, Big Bill Russell, in just seven years of coaching with the Celtics and Supersonics, established a record of 324–249 and won two NBA champion-ships as a player/coach. In 1980, the PBWA chose Russell as

the "Greatest Player in the History of the NBA." He is also one of its greatest coaches.

—Michael D. Koehler in his book *America's Greatest Coaches*
(1990)

APRIL 19

"The Shot Heard Round the World" was fired on this day in 1775, marking the beginning of the American Revolution. Among the farmers holding off the British at the Battle of Lexington and Concord was the slave Prince Estabrook. Estabrook was wounded in this first skirmish, but carried on fighting throughout the Revolutionary War as a soldier in Gen. George Washington's Continental Army.

Constituting 20 percent of the country's population in 1776, African-Americans—such as Estabrook—took part in the Revolutionary War in large numbers. Approximately 5,000 African-Americans had served in the Continental Army by the end of the war. An observer of Washington's army noted, "a quarter of them were negroes, merry, confident, and sturdy." The First Rhode Island Regiment was composed entirely of African-American volunteers. African-Americans fought in the Continental Army both for the independence of their adopted country and in hopes of gaining their own freedom; many slave soldiers were freed upon enlisting in the service or when the war ended.

Meanwhile, many African-Americans in the South saw the British army as their ticket to freedom. The majority of northern blacks born in America and fairly well integrated into their local communities, identified with their neighbors in the fight against the invading English. Many southern blacks, on the other hand, lived in separate and distinct slave communities, and therefore viewed the British as potential allies against their oppressive masters. More than 50,000 slaves escaped to British camps during the war. Several military units serving under the British flag were composed entirely of fugitive slaves; some were even commanded by black officers. However, after the war, most of the black

Redcoats were abandoned by their British allies. Many died of diseases rampant in makeshift camps or of exposure and starvation. Others were betrayed and resold into slavery in the Caribbean. Only about 5,000 were protected by the Royal Army, who took them to Nova Scotia, Canada, Britain, and Sierra Leone, a British colony in West Africa for former slaves.

APRIL 20

Today in 1982, international opera star Leontyne Price gave a concert for the opening of the Daughters of the American Revolution convention at Constitutional Hall in Washington, D.C. The concert was in honor of Marian Anderson, who had been prohibited from performing at the same venue in 1939 by the Daughters of the American Revolution because of racist practices.

> All token blacks have the same experience. I have been pointed at as a solution to things that have not begun to be solved, because pointing at us token blacks eases the conscience of millions, and I think this is dreadfully wrong.
>
> —Leontyne Price in *Divas: Impressions of Six Opera Superstars,*
> by Winthrop Sargeant (1959)

APRIL 21

On this day in 1932, the 72-year-old African-American cowboy Bill Pickett died after being kicked while roping a bronco. Called the Dusky Demon, Pickett was one of the most talented and loved cowboys of the 101 Ranch Wild West Show that toured throughout America and Europe.

Pickett invented—and was the master of—the rodeo event called bulldogging. Still a rodeo favorite, bulldogging requires a cowboy to

Bill Pickett

wrestle a longhorn steer to the ground using his bare hands in a race against the clock. Pickett's former assistant, famed cowboy and comedian Will Rogers, once told the *New York Times*, "Even the steers won't hurt old Bill."

In 1971 Pickett was inducted into the Cowboy Hall of Fame in Oklahoma City, becoming the first African-American to receive this honor. The 101 Ranch was designated a national historic landmark in 1975.

If they check his brand, and I think they will,
It's a runnin' hoss they'll give to Bill.
And some good wild steers till he gets his fill,
With a great big crowd for him to thrill.

—poem written after Pickett's death by Zack Miller

~~~~~~

APRIL 22

To be sold at Public Vendue on Tuesday, 22nd April 1740, at 2
o'clock in the afternoon at the house where the late Mr. Caleb
Copeland lived, one weaver's loom and sundry appurtenances,
two bedsteads, chairs, tables, a Turkey carpet, various articles
of tin and pewter ware, and one likely Negro, in good health,
thirty years of age.

This notice in a local paper put the slave Amos Fortune up for sale. Fortune had been born a prince of the Atmunshi tribe of the Gold Coast (now Ghana) in 1710. He arrived in Boston in July 1725 on the slave ship *White Falcon.* Although Caleb Copeland, a Quaker, opposed slavery, he purchased the African boy while in town one Monday, took him home, and treated him as a member of the family. Copeland offered to free Fortune whenever he was ready. Unfortunately, Copeland died before the agreement was formalized, and the "slave" was sold to pay Copeland's debts.

Fortune's new owner, Ichabod Richardson, eventually allowed Fortune to purchase his own freedom. In 1769, at the age of 59, he became a free man. Fortune established a tannery business and bought freedom for three wives—the first two of whom died. His third wife, Violet Baldwin, and her daughter accompanied the 71-year-old Amos to Jaffrey, New Hampshire. There he again established a tannery business and became one of Jaffrey's most respected citizens. At 80 years of age, Fortune bought his first plot of land—twenty-five acres. Fortune died on November 17, 1801, and willed part of his fortune to the local church and school. His headstone reads:

> *Sacred to the memory of Amos Fortune, who was born free in Africa, a slave in America, he purchased liberty, professed Christianity, lived reputably, and died hopefully.*

APRIL 23

On this day in 1872, Charlotte E. Ray became the first female African-American lawyer. She was also the first female law student at Howard University Law School, from which she graduated.

Now over a century later, the number of African-American lawyers remains low. According to the U.S. Bureau of Labor Statistics, in 1983, of the 651,000 employed lawyers and judges in America only 2.7 percent were black. In 1993 that percentage had risen to just 2.8 percent.

Most of these African-American lawyers belong to the National Bar Association, headquartered in Washington, D.C. The NBA was established on August 1, 1925, at a time when African-Americans were excluded from the American Bar Association (ABA). Although black lawyers are now admitted to the ABA, the National Bar Association still thrives, addressing problems unique to the African-American community. "Because somebody else decides to let you in their house," noted John Crump of the NBA, "you don't burn yours down." Since its inception, the National Bar Association has been involved in civil rights actions, monitored legislation affecting minorities, and taken stands on issues related to Africa.

There is a new sense of commitment, dedication on the part of the black lawyer to return and advocate a cause. And I think a motivating force behind that has been the organized black bar.

—Bob Harris, National Bar Association president, in *Sepia* magazine, January 1980

APRIL 24

The United Negro College Fund was incorporated on this day in 1944. Dr. Frederick Patterson, President of Tuskegee Institute, founded the UNCF to help raise funds for America's historically black colleges and universities, which were facing severe financial crises at the time.

With the birth of the UNCF came the slogan that has become part of our national vocabulary—A Mind Is a Terrible Thing to Waste. Since its founding in 1944, the UNCF has raised over $1 billion for some forty-four institutes of higher learning.

There are two ways of exerting one's strength: one is pushing down, the other is pulling up.

—Booker T. Washington

APRIL 25

In April 1776 the *Pennsylvania Magazine* published a poem written by slave and poet Phillis Wheatley in honor of Gen. George Washington. Wheatley was the first African-American and the second American woman to publish a volume of poetry. Earlier Wheatley had sent a copy of the poem to General Washington, who wrote the following letter to Wheatley in reply.

Miss. Phillis: Your favor of the 26th of October did not reach my hands 'till the middle of December. Time enough, you will say, to have given an answer, ere this. Granted...

I thank you most sincerely for your polite notice of me, in the elegant lines you enclosed; and however undeserving I may be of such encomium and panegyrick, the style and manner exhibit a striking proof of your great poetical Talents. In honour of which, and in tribute justly due you, I would have published the Poem, had I not been apprehensive, that, while I only meant to give the World this new instance of your genius, I might have incurred the imputation of Vanity. This and nothing else, determined me not to give it place in the public prints.

If you should ever come to Cambridge, or near Headquarters, I shall be happy to see a person so favoured by the Muses, and to who Nature has been so liberal and beneficent in her dispensations. I am with great Respect, etc.

Wheatley did in fact meet with the general at his headquarters in Cambridge, Massachusetts, soon after receiving his letter.

~~~~~~

APRIL 26

On April 26, 1844, Jim Beckwourth discovered a path through the Sierra Nevada Mountains that now bears his name. Beckwourth Pass, located on U.S. Alt. 40, between Reno, Nevada, and Sacramento, California, made overland travel to the gold fields of California possible. In the passage below Beckwourth describes his discovery:

We proceeded in an easterly direction, and all busied themselves in searching for gold; but my errand was of a different character; I had come to discover what I suspected to be a pass.

It was the latter end of April when we entered upon an

extensive valley at the northwest extremity of the Sierra range....Swarms of wild geese and ducks were swimming on the surface of the cool crystal stream, which was the central fork of the Rio del las Plumas, or sailed the air in clouds over our heads. Deer and antelope filled the plains, and their boldness was conclusive that the hunter's rifle was to them unknown. Nowhere visible were any traces of the white man's approach, and it is probable that our steps were the first that ever marked the spot. We struck across this beautiful valley to the waters of the Yuba, from thence to the waters of the Truchy....This, I at once saw, would afford the best waggon-road into the American Valley approaching from the eastward, and I imparted my views to three of my companions in whose judgement I placed the most confidence. They thought highly of the discovery, and even proposed to associate with me in opening the road....

Born a slave in 1798 on April 26—the same day of the year that he discovered the pass—Beckwourth was believed to be the son of a slave and a Revolutionary War officer, although historians disagree on his parentage. Beckwourth escaped from slavery at the age of 19 and went on to become one of the most notable figures in the early history of America's western frontier.

In 1824 Beckwourth was adopted by Crow Indians, with whom he lived for several years, leading them into war and attaining the rank of Crow chief. Renowned for his toughness, he was in turns a trapper, trader, frontiersman, Indian fighter, army scout, and gold prospector, as well as cofounder of Pueblo, Colorado. Beckwourth was also known for spinning tall tales, prompting historian Kenneth W. Porter to call him an "immortal liar."

APRIL 27

"It is not easy being Ronald H. Brown," began an article in the *New York Times* on April 27, 1989. The paper was referring to Brown's endorsement of Chicago's new Democratic mayor Richard Daley over an African-American independent candidate who was supported by Jesse Jackson and most of Chicago's black community. "He finds himself jumping from one high wire to another," continued the article, "barely steadying himself before he has to leap again."

Why was Brown in this precarious position? On February 10, 1989, Brown, an influential Washington, D.C. lawyer, had became chairman of the Democratic National Committee. Brown was the first African-American to head a major political party. As one of America's most influential politicians, Brown represented a new breed of African-American whose success in predominantly white institutions meant juggling loyalty to the organization with loyalty and commitment to race. Forseeing the need for this balancing act, upon accepting the post of national chairman Brown stated:

> *I accept the responsibility beholden to no individual, afraid of no faction, and pledged to no institution except the Democratic Party and its members....I did not run on the basis of race, but I will not run away from it. I am proud of who I am and I am proud of this Party, for we are truly America's last best hope to bridge the division of race, region, religion, and ethnicity.*

In 1993 Brown was appointed secretary of commerce in the Clinton Administration. During the opening ceremonies of an African business organization in Washington, D.C. in that same year, Brown remarked:

> *Unless we start to believe in ourselves, we will never convince anyone to believe in us. It is time to believe in ourselves, it is time to start believing in Africa.*

APRIL 28

Asa Philip Randolph, civil rights pioneer and a major figure in American labor relations, was quoted on this day in 1944 in the *Call* as follows:

> *In politics, as in other things, there is no such thing as one getting something for nothing. The payoff may involve compromises of various types that may strike at the ideals and principles one has held dear all his life.*

Randolph organized, and for many years was president of, the Brotherhood of Sleeping Car Porters. On the first of May, 1941, this union organizer called for African-Americans to march on the nation's capital to protest discrimination in war industries and the U.S. military. The threat of 100,000 potential protestors was taken seriously by President Franklin D. Roosevelt. The following month Roosevelt issued Executive Order No. 8802, which banned racial discrimination in defense industries and the national government, and established the U.S. Fair Employment Practices Commission.

Again, with positive results, Randolph also used nonviolent pressure tactics on President Harry Truman. Historian Lerone Bennett Jr. calls Randolph "one of the most remarkable leaders in American history." Others in his day called him "the most dangerous Negro in America."

Randolph was awarded the NAACP's Spingarn Medal in 1942 for his "unparalleled record of leadership in the field of labor organization and national affairs for a period of more than three decades...in recognition of the dramatic culmination of his years of effort in the mobilization of Negro mass opinion in 1941 in a March on Washington to exercise the constitutional right of citizens of a democracy to petition their government peaceably for the redress of grievances..."

APRIL 29

From April 29 through May 1, 1992, rioting rocked the predominantly African-American neighborhood of South Central Los Angeles. Fifty-three people were killed, making it the deadliest riot in U.S. history. President George Bush called in federal troops to restore calm. By the end of the three days of chaos, district suffered more than $550 million in property damage.

The immediate cause: Four white officers of the Los Angeles Police Department were acquitted by an all-white jury in Alameda County, California, in the brutal beating of African-American motorist Rodney King. The beating, which occurred on March 3, 1991, after King had been pulled over for speeding, was videotaped by a witness at a nearby apartment building. To the horror of the viewing public, the videotape was repeatedly aired on news stations in America and throughout the world. Having been "at the scene of the crime," Americans showed their disagreement with the jury's verdict by rioting in several other major cities as well, including San Francisco, Seattle, Atlanta, and Las Vegas.

Congresswoman Maxine Waters, representing South Central Los Angeles at the state and national levels for some twenty years, testified before the Senate Banking Committee on May 14, 1992. Waters explained the underlying causes of the riots, which she said included: hesitancy on the part of banks to lend to inner-city communities and African-Americans; high unemployment in black communities while jobs are exported to other countries that have cheap labor; federal cuts in job training programs; a largely white-dominated legal system; and longer jail sentences for blacks than for whites. "The verdict in the Rodney King case did not cause what happened in Los Angeles," claimed Waters. "It was only the most recent injustice—piled upon many other injustices—suffered by the poor, minorities and the hopeless people living in the nation's cities. For years they have been crying out for help. For years, their cries have not been heard."

The riots in South Central harkened back to August 1965, when Watts erupted after white police mistreated an African-American motorist who was pulled over for drunk driving.

APRIL 30

Wallace Saunders, an African-American engine wiper, always admired train conductor Casey Jones. So on April 30, 1900, when Saunders heard that Casey Jones had crashed the Cannonball Express of the Illinois Central Line into a stationary train after rounding a curve near Vaughan, Mississippi, he wrote a song in Jones's honor. His epic ditty was sung in vaudeville houses across the country and became one of America's classic folk tunes. Saunders accepted a bottle of gin in return for the song's copyright.

Whereas train accidents were relatively common in those days, with 7,856 deaths caused by rail accidents in 1900 alone, this particular accident lives in infamy thanks to Wallace Saunders.

> *Come all you rounders listen here,*
> *I'll tell you the story of a brave engineer.*
> *Casey Jones was the hogger's name.*
> *On a six-eight wheeler, boys, he won his fame.*
> *Caller called Casey at half-past four,*
> *he kissed his wife at the station door.*
> *Mounted to the cabin with his orders in his hand*
> *and took his farewell trip to the Promised Land.*
>
> *Put in your water and shovel in your coal,*
> *Put your head out the window,*

Watch the drivers roll.
'I'll run her till she leaves the rail
'Cause we're eight hours late with the Western Mail.'
He looked at his watch and his watch was slow,
Looked at the water and the water was low,
Turned to his fireboy, then he said,
'We're bound to reach 'Frisco
But we'll all be dead.'

—the first two verses of "Casey Jones," from Donald Mitchell and Roderick Biss's *The Children's Songbook* (1970)

MAY 1

Today in 1950, Gwendolyn Brooks was awarded a Pulitzer Prize for her second collection of poetry, titled *Annie Allen*. A Chicago native, Brooks was the first African-American to win a Pulitzer. This prolific writer has produced over fifteen volumes of poetry, and wrote the novel *Maud Martha* in 1953 and her autobiography *Report from Part One* in 1972. She was designated poet laureate of Illinois in 1968. In 1985 she became the first African-American woman to be appointed to the coveted position of poetry consultant at the Library of Congress.

> *Does man love Art? Man visits Art, but squirms.*
> *Art hurts. Art urges voyages—*
> *and it is easier to stay at home,*
> *the nice beer ready.*

—the first stanza of "The Chicago Picasso," from *In the Mecca* (1968)

> *The ballad of Edie Barrow:*
> * I fell in love with a Gentile boy.*
> *All creamy-and-golden fair.*
> *He looked deep and long in my long black eyes.*
> *And he played with my long black hair.*
> *He took me away to his summertime house.*
> *He was wondrous wealthy, was he.*
> *And there in the hot black drapes of night*
> *he whispered, "Good lovers are we."*

Close was our flesh through the winking hours,
closely and sweetly entwined.
Love did not guess in the tight-packed dark
it was flesh of a varying kind.

—excerpt from "In the Mecca," *In the Mecca*

MAY 2

Elijah McCoy was born on this day in 1844, to fugitive slave parents in Ontario, Canada. McCoy later moved to Michigan, where he worked as a mechanical engineer. This mechanical genius was awarded fifty-seven patents for devices ranging from a lawn sprinkler, to an ironing table, to his most important invention—the lubricating oil cup.

McCoy's Lubricating Oil Cup automatically oiled heavy machinery. Previously, oiling of trains and other machines was done by hand during periodic shutdowns. From 1872 until 1915, the McCoy oil cup was used in most train engines in the United States and overseas. Because the McCoy lubrication system was considered the best available, people would ask when inspecting a new machine, "Is this the real McCoy?" This expression remains with us today as a way of asking if something is authentic.

Elijah McCoy

~~~~~~

MAY 3

The "Godfather of Soul" was born into a poor South Carolinian family on this day in 1933. By the time he was a teenager, James Brown had become, in some ways, a present-day Robin Hood who reportedly shoplifted for other needy kids. His penchant for petty theft landed him in jail, though within a matter of years Brown ascended from juvenile delinquent to American musical celebrity.

In 1956 the street-smart Brown recorded the song "Please, Please, Please." This one-lyric hit secured his reputation as a superstar in the African-American community. By the mid-1960s his tunes "Think," "Papa's Got a Brand New Bag," and "Cold Sweat" propelled him into the music mainstream in both the United States and Europe. His biggest hit in America was "I Got You (I Feel Good)," released in 1966. In total, he has recorded eighty-three songs that have sold one million or more copies.

Brown has mastered several genres of contemporary music. During the 1950s he produced rhythm and blues, in the 1960s he concentrated on soul, and in the 1970s he was a pioneer of funk. Also known as The King of Rhythm and Blues and Soul Brother Number One, he was one of the first ten musicians inducted into the Rock and Roll Hall of Fame in 1986, its inaugural year.

Called "the world's greatest authority on feeling good" by *Ebony* magazine, Brown is a tireless and outrageous stage performer. He has led a comparably spirited private life, spending many of his millions on fancy clothes, cars, and homes, as well as being a generous philanthropist. And his much-publicized scrapes with the law prompted one legal authority to call him a "rascal."

Chuck Berry? Elvis? The Beatles?
When it comes down to who has the most profound and lasting influence on pop music, no one can touch the godfather of soul.

—*People Weekly*, June 10, 1991

MAY 4

Thirteen members of the Congress of Racial Equality (CORE) set off on a bus ride from Washington, D.C. to New Orleans on this day in 1961. These civil rights activists were testing a 1960 Supreme Court ruling that expanded antidiscrimination laws covering interstate travel to include facilities used by travelers. The Freedom Riders bravely entered segregated terminals, waiting rooms, restrooms, and restaurants. They were met with harassment, violence, and even arrest.

On May 15, an article appeared in national newspapers showing the charred remains of a bus that Freedom Riders had scrambled out of after a white mob set it on fire near Anniston, Alabama. Freedom Riders were later beaten by a mob in Birmingham, Alabama. By the time they were arrested in Jackson, Mississippi, the Student Non-Violent Coordinating Committee, Southern Christian Leadership Conference, and Nashville Student Movement had recruited and prepared over 300 Freedom Riders to fill the Mississippi jails. The NAACP joined the effort by assisting with legal defense for the activists.

> *The whites in the South know how to handle violence—they are used to it. But if we just sit there and smile, he doesn't know how to react. And if you sit there and love him—I hope you would love him or at least be sympathetic—well, he doesn't know how to react, and maybe eventually he will forget he is white and you're a Negro and start smiling with you— just men.*
>
> —a CORE member's understanding of the theory of nonviolence, from Inge Powell Bell's book *CORE and the Strategy of Nonviolence*

MAY 5

On this day in 1918, William Stanley Braithwaite was awarded the NAACP's Spingarn Medal for his literary achievements as a critic, editor, and poet. W. E. B. DuBois called Braithwaite "the most prominent critic of poetry in America."

Braithwaite was born in Boston on December 6, 1878, of part West Indian and part British ancestry. Braithwaite wrote over twenty books, and from 1913 to 1929 published an annual anthology of the best poetry printed in American magazines. His own poetry was traditional, reflecting late nineteenth-century style. Nonetheless, Braithwaite gave full support to more progressive poets, especially during the Harlem Renaissance, by which time Braithwaite was already established as a man of letters. Braithwaite died in 1962.

> *Father John's bread was made of rye,*
> *Felicite's bread was white;*
> *Father John loved the sun noon-high,*
> *Felicite the moon at night.*
>
> *Father John drank wine with his bread;*
> *Felicite drank sweet milk;*
> *Father John loved flowers, pungent and red;*
> *Felicite, lilies soft as silk.*
>
> —from Braithwaite's "Rye Bread"

MAY 6

African Lodge No. 459 in Boston, Massachusetts, was chartered on this day in 1787 by England's Grand Lodge. Prince Hall had established this self-help organization eleven years earlier, after being denied membership in white Masonic lodges. In addition to being a pioneer in institution building, Hall was a Revolutionary War veteran, soap maker, landowner, and voter. In 1800 he founded a school for African-American children in his own home in Boston. Hall died of pneumonia in 1807.

On June 24, 1797, Hall delivered a speech on discrimination to African-American Masons at the African Lodge in which he said:

> ...Patience I say, for were we not possessed of a great measure of it you could not bear up under the daily insults you meet with in the streets of Boston; much more on public days of recreation, how are you shamefully abus'd, and that at such a degree, that you may be truly said to carry your lives in your hands...[since many have been attacked] by a mob of shameless, low-lived, envious, spiteful persons, some of them not long since, servants in gentlemen's kitchens....
>
> My brethren, let us not be cast down under these and many abuses we at present labour under; for the darkest is before the break of day....
>
> Although you are deprived of the means of education; yet you are not deprived of the means of meditation....
>
> Live and act as Masons, that you may die as Masons; let those despisers see, altho' many of us cannot read, yet by our searches and researches into men and things, we have supplied that defect...[and] give the right hand of affection and fellowship to whom it justly belongs [and] let their colour and complexion be what it will: their nation be what it may, for they are your brethren.

MAY 7

"Campaigning in Free Verse," an article about Jesse Jackson's bid for the 1984 Democratic presidential nomination, appeared in the May 7, 1984 issue of Time magazine. It included the following excerpt from a sermon that Jackson had recently delivered in Baltimore, Maryland:

Yesterday was a day of mixed emotions for me. Jesus was crucified on Friday, resurrected on Sunday. That's great joy because the stone was rolled away. But for the poor of Baltimore, for the malnourished of our nation, for the poor mothers who cannot get a breakfast program or lunch programs, for the youth who can't get a skill, they were crucified on Sunday, crucified on Monday. The hands are still bleeding, the thorns are still in their heads. I say it's time for the poor to realize resurrection, to stop the hammers, stop the nails, wheel away the stone.

Jackson was the first African-American to be taken seriously as a contender for a major political party nomination. (Eldridge Cleaver ran for president in 1968, and Shirley Chisholm vied for the office in 1972.) His campaign has been called "one of the most dramatic developments in modern American political history." The charismatic black leader proposed the creation of a new political alliance—the Rainbow Coalition. Based on the concept of economic justice, the coalition was to be composed of peoples traditionally marginalized by the American system—African-Americans, Hispanics, Native Americans, Arab-Americans, Asian-Americans, elderly, women, the poor, disabled, and small-scale farmers. His campaign workers were charged with the gargantuan task of not only running a campaign, but also building up this grass roots organization.

In the 1984 primary elections, Jackson received 2.5 million black votes and 800,000 nonblack votes, which included 10 percent of the total white primary vote. He ran again in 1988, this time garnering 20 percent of the white primary vote. Presidential scholar James Barber said (in the words of author Robert C. Smith): "while the other candidates were making news, Jackson was making history."

MAY 8

On this day in 1915, Henry McNeal Turner died at the age of 82. Turner was an outspoken bishop of the African Methodist Episcopal Church and served as the first African-American chaplain in the U.S. Army.

A strong supporter of the African colonization movement, Turner called for a separate black empire and encouraged African-Americans to return "to the land of our ancestors" and to "give the world, like other race varieties, the benefit of our individuality." He founded AME churches in both of the African colonies for former slaves—Sierra Leone and Liberia—and established the International Immigration Society.

During Reconstruction, Turner had been elected to the Georgia House of Representatives but was denied admission. The following is an excerpt from his speech delivered to the Georgia legislature on November 3, 1868, after being refused his seat:

You may expel us, gentlemen, but I firmly believe that you will someday repent it. The black man cannot protect a country, if the country doesn't protect him; and if, tomorrow, a war should arise, I would not raise a musket to defend a country where my manhood was denied. The fashionable way in Georgia when hard work is to be done, is, for the white man to sit at his ease, while the black man does the work; but sir, I will say this much to the colored men of Georgia, as if I should be killed in this campaign, I may have no opportunity of telling them at any other time: Never lift a finger nor raise a hand in defense of Georgia, unless Georgia acknowledges that you are men, and invests you with the rights pertaining to manhood....

You may expel us, gentlemen, by your votes, today; but while you do it, remember that there is a just God in Heaven....

MAY 9

Today in 1930, defending world welterweight champion Jackie Fields "was thrashed as soundly as ever a ring champion has been beaten" by African-American boxer Jack Thompson. This 147-pound title upset was witnessed by a crowd of about 14,000 fans at the Olympia Arena in Detroit, Michigan, and brought in a total of $70,000 dollars in receipts.

Thompson, from Oakland, California, defeated Chicago's Fields in fifteen "torrid" rounds. *The New York Times* described the final round of the fight: "Fields electrified the crowd with a closing rally which was more surprising than painful to Thompson at a time when each boxer had difficulty in raising his hands, they were so weary." It had been about fifteen years since an African-American had taken the welterweight title.

MAY 10

On this day in 1919, race riots broke out in Charleston, South Carolina, beginning the Red Summer of 1919. During this bloody episode in U.S. history, twenty-six violent riots took place across the country. In Washington, D.C., from July 19 to 21, 6 people were killed and 100 were injured. On July 27, in Chicago, 15 whites and 23 blacks were killed, and over 500 people were wounded. As late as October, 5 whites were killed and 25 to 50 African-Americans were murdered by a white posse in Elaine, Arkansas.

These white-on-black riots occurred at the height of post–World War I racial tensions in America, driven by the recent mass migration of African-Americans into both northern and southern cities. Whereas in 1900 there were 30,000 African-American residents of Chicago, by 1925 this number had risen to 120,000. In 1925 the black population in Detroit was 80,000, up from 8,000 only ten years earlier. Accommodations in urban centers—in particular the housing supply—simply couldn't keep pace with the rapid population increases, and white residents were bound and determined to prevent blacks from taking over their neighborhoods.

> *The Summer of 1919 was a terrifying period for the American Negro. There were race riots in Chicago and in Washington and in Omaha and in Phillips County, Arkansas; and in Longview, Texas; and in Knoxville, Tennessee; and in Norfolk, Virginia; and in other communities. Colored men and women, by dozens and by scores, were chased and beaten and killed in the streets.*
>
> —James Weldon Johnson quoted in The Black 100

> *The Washington riot gave me the thrill that comes once in a life time, I...read between the lines of our morning paper that at last our men had stood like men, struck back, were no longer dumb driven cattle. When I could no longer read for my streaming tears, I stood up, alone in my room, held both hands high over my head and exclaimed aloud: "Oh I thank God, thank God."*
>
> —a letter to the editor, printed in the November 1919 issue of the Crisis, written by a southern African-American woman

MAY 11

On May 11, 1976, the Villa Lewaro in Greenburgh, New York, was designated a national historic landmark. Villa Lewaro had been the home of African-American millionaire Madame C. J. Walker. The thirty-two-room Italianate-style mansion, located on the Hudson River in Irvington, was built before World War I at a cost of $250,000—enormously expensive for the time. The home was designed and built by

Vertner Woodson Tandy, the first African-American architect to be registered in the state of New York.

Madame C. J. Walker's fortune was inherited by her daughter A'Lelia Walker. A'Lelia—whom Langston Hughes described as a "gorgeous dark Amazon, in a silver turban"—was a notable patron of the Harlem Renaissance. Like her mother, A'Lelia threw lavish parties for artists, European royalty, and the New York elite at her elegant brownstone on West 136th street in Harlem. Villa Lewaro was auctioned off after A'Lelia's death on August 17, 1931, and her town home was leased to the city.

A night club quartette that had often performed at A'Lelia's parties arose and sang for her. They sang Noel Coward's "I'll See You Again," and they swung it slightly, as she might have liked it. It was a grand funeral and very much like a party. Mrs. Mary McLeod Bethune spoke in that great deep voice of hers, as only she can speak. She recalled the poor mother of A'Lelia Walker in old clothes, who had labored to bring the gift of beauty to Negro womanhood, and had brought them the care of their skin and their hair, and had built up a great business and a great fortune to the pride and joy of the Negro race—and then had given it all to her daughter, A'Lelia.

—Langston Hughes's recollection of A'Lelia's invitation-only funeral

MAY 12

On this day in 1968, Coretta Scott King was one of the leaders of the Mother's Day March on Washington, D.C. King and 5,000 other protestors joined welfare mothers in this demonstration at the nation's capital.

After the death of her husband, civil rights leader Martin Luther King Jr., Coretta Scott was dubbed The Keeper of the Flame. She was a prominent civil rights leader and peace activist in her own right. King addressed 35,000 Vietnam War protestors at the White House on November 27, 1965, and spoke to a crowd of 87,000 people at an antiwar demonstration in New York City on April 27, 1968. She was the main force behind establishment of the Martin Luther King Jr. Center for Non-Violent Social Change in Atlanta, Georgia, which opened in June 1982.

> *We are concerned not only about the Negro poor, but the poor all over American and all over the world. Every man deserves a right to a job or an income so that he can pursue liberty, life, and happiness. Our great nation, as he often said, has the resources, but his question was: Do we have the will?*
>
> —Coretta Scott speaking at Memphis City Hall on April 8, 1968

MAY 13

Just before dawn on the morning of May 13, 1862, while their white commanding officers were still ashore, seaman Robert Smalls, his wife, children, and a crew of twelve African-American men set sail in the *Planter*—a cotton steamer that had been converted into a Confederate battleship. Smalls piloted the gunboat straight into the Union lines that surrounded Charleston Harbor and presented the ship to the U.S. Navy.

Smalls became a national hero and was awarded a considerable sum of money for delivering this contraband of war. The U.S. Navy retained him as a pilot on the *Planter*. A year later—after the previous captain panicked when his vessel was fired upon, leaving Smalls in control—Smalls was promoted to captain.

This Civil War hero was elected to South Carolina's state senate in 1868 and represented South Carolina in the U.S. Congress in 1875, serving five terms.

On this same day three years later, the last battle of the Civil War was fought at White's Ranch, Texas. Sergeant Crocker of the all-black Sixty-

An 1857 gunboat at sea

second United States Colored Troops is believed to have been the "last man to shed blood" in the Civil War.

> *Your country? How come it's yours? Before the pilgrims landed we were here....Actively we have woven ourselves with the very warp and woof of this nation....Could America have been America without her Negro people?*
>
> —W. E. B. DuBois, 1903

MAY 14

On this day in 1949, the following letter to the editor (excerpted) appeared in the *Washington Post*. It was written by Mary Church Terrell, an antidiscrimination activist and one of the founders of the NAACP.

I am urging the Post and others willing to advance our interests and deal justly with our group to stop using the word "Negro". The word is a misnomer from every point of view. It does not represent a country or anything else....

To be sure the complexion of the Chinese and Japanese is yellow. But nobody refers to an individual in either group as a colored man....They say he is Chinese....When I studied abroad and was introduced as an "American"...occasionally somebody would say, "You are rather dark to be an American, aren't you?" "Yes," I would reply, "I am dark, because some of my ancestors were Africans." I was proud of having the continent of Africa part of my ancestral background. "I am an African- American," I would explain. I am not ashamed of my African descent. Africa had great universities before there were any in England and the African was the first man industrious and skillful enough to work in iron. If our group must have a special name setting it apart, the sensible way to settle it would be to refer to our ancestors, the Africans, from whom our swarthy complexions come.

MAY 15

Today in 1785, John Marrant of New York was ordained a Methodist minister in London, England. Marrant was the first African-American missionary to work among the Native Americans, converting a Cherokee chief and his daughter. In 1785 his *Narrative of the Lord's Wonderful Dealings with John Marrant* was published, and in 1790 Marrant published a journal of his four years preaching in Nova Scotia.

Unhappily, too many Christians, so called, take their religion not from the declarations of Christ, but from the writings of those they esteem learned....

* * *

Envy and pride are the leading lines to all the misery that mankind has suffered from the beginning of the world to this present day.

—excerpts from a sermon delivered by Marrant at the African Lodge in Boston, Massachusetts, on June 24, 1789

~~~~~~

MAY 16

Isaac Burns Murphy won the Kentucky Derby on this day in 1884, riding the horse Buchanan. He won riding Riley in 1890 and Kingman in 1891, becoming the first jockey to win the Kentucky Derby three times. Murphy also won the American Derby and Latonia Derby five times each; these races were considered even more illustrious than the Kentucky Derby at the time. Out of 1,412 races, Murphy came in first 628 times, earning recognition as "the greatest horse jockey of the nineteenth century."

The fact that he was African-American was not unusual in his era. Horse racing in the late 1800s was dominated by African-American jockeys, who had won fifteen of the first twenty-eight Kentucky Derby runnings. Murphy died of pneumonia in 1896 at the age of 35. His gravesite is found in the Man O' War Park in Lexington, Kentucky. Known for his honesty, Murphy gave the following advice to a young jockey (as quoted in the *Thoroughbred Record*):

You just ride to win. They get you to pull a horse in a selling race, but when it comes to a stake race they get Isaac to ride. A jockey that'll sell out to one man will sell out to another. Just be honest. You may only become rich in reputation but they will record you as a success.

MAY 17

On this day in 1954, the U.S. Supreme Court handed down its decision in the historical case of *Brown v. Board of Education of Topeka*. Chief Justice Earl B. Warren read the Court's decision:

> *Does segregation of children in public schools solely on the base of race, even though the physical facilities and other "tangible" factors may be equal, deprive the children of the minority group of equal education opportunities? We believe that it does....*

The case began when Reverend Oliver Brown of Topeka, Kansas, attempted to enroll his daughter Linda in Sumner Elementary School, which was closer to his home than the black schools. The case was taken up by the NAACP, with Thurgood Marshall acting as the NAACP's chief counsel.

> *We conclude* [continued Justice Warren] *that in the field of public education the doctrine of "separate but equal" has no place. Separate educational facilities are inherently unequal. Therefore, we hold that the plaintiffs and others similarly situated for whom the actions have been brought are, by reason of the segregation complained of, deprived of equal protection of the laws guaranteed by the Fourteenth Amendment.*

The court's ruling that "separate but equal" was not possible in public schools in America reversed the outcome of the earlier *Plessy v. Ferguson* case, putting a legal end to segregation in America. However, for the following decade, southern states resisted integration by creating "freedom of choice" programs, publicly funding private segregated schools, and even closing public schools. By 1964 less than 2 percent of African-Americans in the South were enrolled in desegregated schools.

MAY 18

On this day in 1896, the U.S. Supreme Court handed down the decision in *Plessy v. Ferguson*. The Court's decision upheld "separate but equal" doctrines and signaled the beginning of full-blown Jim Crow days in America. *Plessy v. Ferguson* gave rise to racial segregation throughout all facets of American life, which lasted for over fifty years. The Court ruling claimed:

> *The object of the [Fourteenth] Amendment was undoubtedly to enforce the absolute equality of the two races before the law, but in the nature of things it would not have been intended to abolish distinctions based upon color, or to enforce social, as distinguished from political equality, or a commingling of the two races upon terms unsatisfactory to either. Laws permitting, and even requiring, their separation in places where they are liable to be brought into contact do not necessarily imply the inferiority of either race to the other and have been generally, if not universally, recognized as within the competency of the state legislatures in the exercise of their police power....*

In the dissenting opinion, Justice John Marshall Harlan wrote:

> *...in the view of the Constitution, in the eye of the law, there is in this country no superior, dominant, ruling class of citizens. There is no caster here. Our Constitution is color-blind, and neither knows nor tolerates classes among citizens....It is, therefore, to be regretted that this high tribunal, the final expositor of the fundamental law of the land, has reached the conclusion that it is competent for a state to regulate the enjoyment by citizens of their civil rights solely upon the basis of race. In my opinion, the judgement this day rendered will, in time, prove to be quite as pernicious as the decision made by this tribunal in the Dred Scott case.*

MAY 19

On this day in 1925, the man who was nicknamed Red as a young street hustler and later called himself El Hajj Malik El-Shabazz after making a pilgrimage to Mecca, was born in Omaha, Nebraska. Best known as Malcolm X, this captivating speaker became a leader of great stature who preached self-sufficiency and self-discipline to African-Americans. However, he experienced a stormy relationship with other African-American leaders of his era, and the press branded him a "black supremacist" and "messenger of hate." Malcolm's radical statements—such as calling the historic 1963 March on Washington the "Farce on Washington," organized by "integration-mad Negroes"—fueled these tensions.

Malcolm X rose to prominence through his association with the Nation of Islam. In 1964 he broke with the Nation after conflicting with its spiritual leader, Elijah Muhammad, over Muhammad's questionable morals and unorthodox form of Islam. Malcolm X formed his own nonreligious political organization, the Organization of Afro-American Unity (OAAU), in June 1964. Shortly thereafter, he was assassinated while speaking at an OAAU rally in New York.

My hobby is stirring up Negroes.

—a frequent statement by Malcolm X

For twelve long years I lived within the narrow-minded confines of the "strait-jacket" world created by my strong belief that Elijah Muhammad was a messenger direct from God....If Western society had not gone to such extremes to block out the knowledge of True Islam there would not be such a religious "vacuum" among American Negroes today into which any religious faker can bring all forms of distorted religious concoctions and represent it to our unsuspecting people as True Islam.

—from Malcolm X's "Letter From Mecca," September 22, 1964

I remember one night at Muzdalifah....I lay awake amid sleeping Muslim brothers and I learned that pilgrims from every land—every color and class and rank—all snored in the same language.

—from Malcolm X's autobiography

~~~~~~

MAY 20

On May 20, 1991, the *Washington Post* announced that legendary blues guitarist B. B. King was among sixteen master folk artists to win a $5,000 fellowship from the National Endowment for the Arts (NEA). The chairman of the NEA called the winners "our living national treasures...keepers of seasoned and mature artistic traditions that speak to us across hundreds of years."

B. B. King, who refers to his guitar as Lucille, has recorded countless blues favorites, such as "Sweet Sixteen," "Everyday I Have the Blues," "The Thrill Is Gone," and "Ain't Nobody Home." This blues master has cut over fifty-five albums, performed in fifty-seven countries, and won numerous awards, including five Grammys, *Record World Magazine*'s Artist of the Decade in 1974, and NATRA's award for Best Blues Singer, also in 1974.

Born Riley B. King on September 16, 1925, in Ita Bena, Mississippi, his simple but strong style represents the Delta blues tradition. He is considered by many to be the greatest living blues man, and is certainly the most successful.

"More than anything else," said B. B. (Blues Boy) King in a February 1992 interview in *Ebony* magazine, "it is important to study history, to know history. To be a Black person and sing the blues, you are Black twice. I've heard it said, 'If we don't know from whence we came, we don't know how to go where we are trying to go.'"

Maybe our forefathers couldn't keep their language together when they were taken away from Africa, but this—the blues—

*was a language we invented to let people know we had
something to say.*

And we've been saying it pretty strong ever since.

—B. B. King quoted in Valerie Wilmer's *The Face of Black Music*
(1976)

~~~~~~

MAY 21

Captain William Clark wrote in his diary on May 21, 1804, "...set out
from St. Charles at three o'clock after getting every matter arranged..."
Louis and Clark were embarking on their historic expedition into the
Northwest to explore the source of the Missouri River and find the best
passage to the Pacific Ocean. Ben York, Clark's servant, was no doubt
instrumental in "getting every matter arranged" for the great trek that lay
ahead.

York proved an invaluable member of the expedition. He was an
expert huntsman and swimmer, was good with languages, and exhibited
superior strength. He was also a source of curiosity and appeasement for
the Native Americans that the team encountered along the way. They
called him "good medicine," and would come from far away to see and
touch him.

"These people (the Arikaras)," wrote Clark, "are much pleased with
my black Servent. Their womin verry fond of carressing our men..."
While among the Mandans, Clark wrote, "I ordered my black Servent to
Dance which amused the crowd verry much, and Somewhat astonished
them, that So large a man should be active...."

Charles Mackenzie of the North West Company described a transac-
tion with the expedition party: "A mulatto," he wrote, "who spoke bad
French and worse English, served as interpreter to the Captains [Lewis
and Clark], so that a single word to be understood by the party required
to pass from the Natives to the women [Sacajawea], from the woman to
the husband [Charbonneau], from the husband to the mulatto, from the
mulatto to the captains."

MAY 22

On this day in 1967, the masterful and prolific writer Langston Hughes died in New York City. His career spanned from the Harlem Renaissance of the 1920s through the new black Renaissance of the 1960s. His first volume of poetry, *The Weary Blues*, was published in 1926 and his first book of short stories, *The Ways of White Folks*, was published in 1934.

Hughes's poetry, novels, plays, and short stories were central to the transition of black writing from the "plantation tradition" to contemporary, urbane forms which exuded racial pride. A household name in America, he is considered one of the most important African-American writers of the twentieth century. In 1960 Hughes was awarded the NAACP's Spingarn Medal, at which time he was dubbed the poet, laureate of the Negro race.

"Bread and meat come first," said Simple. "Gentlemens of the Summit, I want you-all to think how you can provide everybody in the world with bread and meat. Civil rights comes next. Let everybody have civil rights, white, black, yellow, brown, gray, grizzle, or green. No Jim-Crow-take-low can't go for anybody! Let Arabs go to Isreal and Isreals go to Egypt, Chinese come to America and Negroes live in Australia, if any be so foolish as to want to. Let Willie Mays live in Levittown and Casey Stengel live in Ghana if he so desires. And let me drink at the Stork Club if I get tired of Small's Paradise. Open house before open skies. After which comes peace, which you can't have nohow as long as peoples and nations is snatching and grabbing over pork chops and payola so as not to starve to death. No peace could be had nohow with white nations against dark."

—from Lanston Hughes's *Tales of Simple* (1961)

MAY 23

The musical review *Shuffle Along* opened on Broadway on this day in 1921. Written, produced, directed, and performed by African-Americans, *Shuffle Along* received rave reviews and played on Broadway for 504 performances before embarking on a year-long nationwide tour. This musical comedy featured exceptional singing, dancing, and comedy routines. It was also renowned for its gorgeous chorus girls and launched the careers of entertainers Florence Mills and Josephine Baker. Noble Sissle and Eubie Blake composed the musical score, which included such favorites as "Love Will Find A Way," "In Honeysuckle Time," and the song that was used years later for Harry Truman's presidential campaign, "I'm Just Wild About Harry."

Some historians cite *Shuffle Along* as the beginning of the Harlem Renaissance. However, other landmark events have been cited as well, such as the publication of Claude McKay's poem "If We Must Die" in the *Liberator* in 1919. At any rate, the wider public may not have been aware of the Renaissance until about March 1925, when a special issue of *Survey Graphic* titled "Harlem, Mecca of the New Negro" was published.

It began with Shuffle Along, Running Wild, *and the Charleston. Perhaps some people would say even with* The Emperor Jones, *Charles Gilpin, and tom-toms at Provincetown. But certainly it was the musical review,* Shuffle Along, *that gave a scintillating send-off to that Negro vogue in Manhattan, which reached its peak just before the crash of 1929.*

—Langston Hughes from his autobiography *The Big Sea* (1963)

MAY 24

On this day in 1974, legendary big-band leader Duke Ellington died of lung cancer in New York City. One of the most creative composers of the twentieth century, Ellington influenced American music from the swing era of the 1930s until his death in the 1970s.

For over fifty years Ellington led what some critics consider the best jazz orchestra of all time—the Duke Ellington Orchestra, also known as the Jungle Band. His early recordings include "Creole Love Call," "Jubilee Stomp," "Black and Tan Fantasy," and "Hot and Bothered." The orchestra's signature piece in later years was "Take the A Train." Ellington composed the scores for, and appeared in, several movies, including *A Day at the Races* (1937) and *Cabin in the Sky* (1943).

> *If "jazz" means anything at all, which is questionable, it means the same thing it meant to musicians fifty years ago— freedom of expression. I used to have a definition, but I don't think I have one anymore, unless it is that it is a music with an African foundation which came out of an American environment.*
>
> —Duke Ellington, from Stanley Dance's *The World of Duke Ellington* (1972)

MAY 25

On this day in 1878 in Richmond, Virginia, Luther Bill Robinson was born, and along with him was born a new word in the English language. Best known as Bill "Bojangles" Robinson, he coined the term *copacetic*, which means okay, or fine.

Bojangles began his entertainment career on the vaudeville circuit. His exceptional tap dancing—considered an original African-American art—took him to Broadway and Hollywood in the 1920s. He starred in many films, including three with Shirley Temple, *The Little Colonel* (1935), *The Littlest Rebel* (1936), and *Rebecca of Sunnybrook Farm* (1938). With these films he became an American dance legend and inspired a younger generation of dancers that included Fred Astaire.

Bojangles, who said his nickname means "easygoing and happy-go-lucky," died in 1949 in New York. Sammy Davis Jr. revived the Bojangles legacy with his 1969 hit song "Mr. Bojangles."

MAY 26

Aaron Douglas was born this day in 1899 in Topeka, Kansas. Known for his style of "geometric symbolism", Douglas was one of the principal visual artists of the Harlem Renaissance. African-American writers during the 1920s often called upon Douglas to illustrate their works, for which he gained the title "official artist" of the Harlem Renaissance.

Douglas's illustrations appeared in many magazines, including the NAACP's *The Crisis*, the National Urban League's *Opportunity*, *Harper's*, and *Vanity Fair*. He also illustrated numerous books, such as James Weldon Johnson's *God's Trombones* and Claude McKay's *Home to Harlem*.

Douglas produced epic murals depicting scenes from African-American history, one of which is found in the Harlem Branch of the New York Public Library. From 1937 to 1966, Douglas taught fine arts at Fisk University, where he was professor emeritus. He died of a pulmonary embolism in Nashville, Tennessee, on February 2, 1979.

Sometimes referred to as the father of African-American Art, Douglas once told fellow African-American artist Romare Bearden: "Technique in itself is not enough. It is important for the artist to develop the power to convey emotion....The artist's technique, no matter how brilliant it is, should never obscure his vision."

By eliminating details and reducing forms to silhouettes, he lifted everything above mere observation of the visual world.

The unveiling of Aspects of Negro Life had a dramatic influence on the next generation, my generation, of black artists. The scale, the unique blend of history, religion, myth, politics, and social issues, made a lasting impression. By clearly telling us, that in order to perceive the future, we must understand the past, Douglas has brought us full circle.

—artist David C. Driskell, from the film *Hidden Heritage: The Roots of Black American Painting*

MAY 27

The first of three Seminole Wars ended on this day in 1818 with Gen. Andrew Jackson's capture of Pensacola, Florida, then under Spanish control. This first Seminole War had begun in 1816, when General Jackson attacked a Creek and Seminole fort in western Florida, where hundreds of runaway slaves were living. Florida settlers also attacked the Seminole Indians. The Seminoles counterattacked in November 1817 by raiding Georgia homesteads and carrying slaves back with them.

By 1819 the United States' claims against Spain for restitution of runaway slaves had reached $5 million, causing Spain to cede Florida to the United States. With the Adams-Onìs treaty, signed on February 22, 1819, Spain also surrendered Florida and parts of Alabama, Louisiana, and Mississippi.

Florida's new government did not respect Seminole territorial claims. In hopes of solving their "Indian problem," the U.S. government attempted to forcibly remove the Seminoles from Florida to Indian territory west of the Mississippi. The Seminoles fiercely resisted in two more wars.

At the time of the Adams-Onìs treaty there were about 5,000 Seminoles living in Florida. The Seminole tribe included a large number of ethnic Africans—or "Indian" Negroes—who were nominally slaves. The Africans were quite free among the Indians, only being required to pay an annual tribute of agricultural produce. Because of their superior understanding of whites, the Africans often served as interpreters and go-betweens. Some historians contend the blacks were de facto rulers of the Seminole nation. Indian Negroes were an essential element in all of the Seminole Wars.

> *The negroes exercised a wonderful control. They openly refused to follow their masters, if they moved to Arkansas. Many of them would have been reclaimed by the Creeks, to whom some belonged. Others would have been taken possession of by the whites, who for years had been urging their claims through the government and its agents. In Arkansas, hard labor was necessary for the means of support, while Florida assured them of every means to indulge in idleness, and enjoy an independence corresponding with their masters. In preparing for hostilities they were active, and in the prosecution bloodthirsty and cruel. It was not until the negroes capitulated, that the Seminoles ever thought of emigrating.*

—words of a Seminole War army officer

MAY 28

A review in the *New York Times* dated May 28, 1943, read:

> Cabin in the Sky *is a bountiful entertainment. The Metro picturization of the Negro fantasy, which settled down at Loew's Criterion yesterday for what should prove to be a long tenancy, is every inch as sparkling and completely satisfying as the original stage production.*

Cabin in the Sky's star-studded cast included Ethel Waters as Petunia, Eddie "Rochester" Anderson as the gambler Little Joe, Lena Horne as Georgia Brown, and Rex Ingram as both Lucifer Jr. and Lucius. It also featured appearances by Louis Armstrong and Duke Ellington. Directed by Vincente Minnelli, the film cost $600,000 to produce.

MAY 29

On this day in 1973, Thomas Bradley won the Los Angeles mayoral election against three-term mayor Sam Yorty. Bradley became the first African-American mayor of Los Angeles and one of America's most powerful elected officials.

The son of poor Texas sharecroppers, Bradley was a former Los Angeles policeman. He fought against discrimination in the police force, personally breaking the color barrier by rising to the rank of sergeant. Bradley became active in local politics as early as 1946, and at one point was a member of more than 100 clubs and organizations in the city. Upon retiring from the LAPD in 1961, he began practicing law, having earned a law degree while working on the force. In 1963 he became the first African-American elected to the Los Angeles City Council.

At the time Bradley was elected mayor the population of Los Angeles was only 15 to 18 percent African-American, which reflected his wide range of support. Bradley effected some notable changes in the sprawling metropolis during his years as mayor. In his first term he secured federal funds to begin constructing mass transit lines. In his second and third terms he gained international recognition for successfully bringing the 1984 Olympic Games to his city. Bradley stepped down from the mayorship in 1992 after serving five terms—or two decades—as mayor.

In a great city, City Hall must be a beacon to the people's aspirations, not a barrier.

—from Bradley's book *The Impossible Dream* (1986)

MAY 30

Every year on Memorial Day weekend, the Black Rodeo is held in Boley, Oklahoma. This annual event highlights the fact that African-Americans had a much larger presence in the cattle country of the Old West than popular culture would have us believe.

Of the trail drivers moving cattle herds from southern Texas to grazing lands and railheads for delivery to markets, about one-quarter were black cowboys. George W. Saunders of the Texas Trail Drivers Association estimated that during the golden age of the cattle industry (1866–1895) "about one-third of the 35,000 men trail driving were Negroes and Mexicans."

African-Americans worked for cattle outfits mainly as cooks, horse-breakers, and ropers, and sometimes as bodyguards to cattle owners. Cooks played an essential role in cow country. They not only supplied the vittles, but often having musical skills, they provided the gaiety as well. Cooks were higher paid than cowhands and were considered second in importance to trail bosses. Few African-Americans, however, became bosses or foremen. Jim Perry, cook and cowboy at XIT Ranch, lamented, "If it weren't for my damned old black face I'd have been boss of one of these divisions long ago."

There are several legendary black cowboys, such as Bill Pickett of 101 Ranch Wild West Show fame, and Nat Love—better known as Dead-wood Dick—as well as a host of more obscure names. For instance, there was Matthew "Bones" Hooks, a train porter and former professional horsebreaker who, once when his train stopped at a station, reportedly peeled off his uniform and broke a horse no one else could break. "Nigger" Jim Kelly, according to historian Kenneth W. Porter, was a cowboy that the "old-time cowboys considered the peer of any rider they had seen in the United States, Canada or the Argentine." Isham Dart of Brown's Hole was said to be among "the top bronc stompers of the Old West." One white Texan claimed, "there was no better cowman on earth than the Negro."

MAY 31

"An exceptionally good book and in parts an extremely funny one," said a review in the *New Yorker* dated May 31, 1952, in reference to the novel *Invisible Man*. An "impassioned first novel of a Negro rebel in the modern world," wrote the *New York Times*, adding that the book embraced a "major literary awareness which the class-conscious novel of the Thirties often lacked."

The release of *Invisible Man* propelled first-time author Ralph Ellison into the limelight. Critics praised the work and compared Ellison to such other prominent postwar authors as William Faulkner and Ellison's friend Richard Wright. According to *Barron's Book Notes*, "readers on both sides of the Atlantic viewed Invisible Man as a work to be read alongside the popular plays and novels of Jean-Paul Sartre and Albert Camus."

Although he never wrote another novel, Ellison became an established man of letters. He taught at several universities, published short stories, and released two collections of essays—*Shadow and Act* (1964) and *Going to the Territory* (1986). "It may be all right being a one-novel man," maintains *Barron's Book Notes*, "if the novel is as good as *Invisible Man*."

He was an odd old guy, my grandfather, and I am told I take after him. It was he who caused the trouble. On his deathbed he called my father to him and said, "Son, after I'm gone I want you to keep up the good fight. I never told you, but our life is a war and I have been a traitor all my born days, a spy in the enemy's country ever since I gave up my gun back in the Reconstruction. Live with your head in the lion's mouth. I want you to overcome 'em with yeses, undermine 'em with grins, agree 'em to death and destruction, let 'em swoller you till they vomit or bust wide open." They thought the old man had gone out of his mind.

—from Chapter 1 of *Invisible Man*

I don't recognize any white culture. I recognize no American culture which is not the partial creation of black people. I recognize no American style in literature, in dance, in music, even in assembly-line processes, which does not bear the mark of the American Negro.

—Ralph Ellison

JUNE 1

On the first day of June, 1843, Sojourner Truth set out from New York on an historic journey across America. She traveled far and wide preaching about the evils of slavery and promoting women's rights. She claimed the Lord gave her the name Sojourner Truth, as he had called upon her "to travel up and down the land" declaring the truth to people.

Truth was born a slave, originally bearing the name Isabella Baumfree. She gained her freedom when the New York State Emancipation Act was passed in 1827. An impressive sight, she stood six-feet tall and wore a satin banner that said, "Proclaim liberty throughout the land unto all the inhabitants thereof." Truth was the guest of President Lincoln at the White House on several occasions and was one of the voices that influenced Lincoln to recruit African-American soldiers for the Union Army during the Civil War.

> *I come from another field—the country of the slave. They have got their liberty—so much good luck to have slavery partly destroyed; not entirely. I want it root and branch destroyed. Then we will all be free indeed. I feel that if I have to answer for the deeds done in my body just as much as a man, I have a right to have just as much as a man. There is a great stir about colored men getting their rights, but not a word about the colored women; and if colored men get their rights, and not colored women theirs, you see the colored men will be masters over the women, and it will be just as bad as it was before.*

> —Sojourner Truth's speech delivered at the Convention of the American Equal Rights Association, New York City, 1867

JUNE 2

The week of June 2, 1962, Ray Charles's all-time bestselling single "I Can't Stop Loving You" hit number one on the *Billboard* chart and remained there for four weeks. Charles had two previous *Billboard* number one hits, "Georgia On My Mind" in 1960 and "Hit the Road Jack" in 1961.

The career of this blind superstar has spanned more than forty years. Charles began recording rhythm-and-blues and pop tunes in the 1950s. He and Sam Cooke were leading figures in the development of soul music, a fusion of gospel and blues with a touch of country influence. Charles also successfully performed rock 'n' roll and jazz, and led the way for African-American performers in country music. Author Ralph Tee in *The Best of Soul* called him "black America's great gift to world culture and entertainment."

In the '60s, I did a lot of country songs, but I always made them sound contemporary. I'd add strings, give them a pop feel, so that way I got a lot of people into country for the first time.

—from a 1980s
Billboard interview

Soul is a way of life, but it is always the hard way.

—Ray Charles

Ray Charles

149

JUNE 3

On this day in 1906, one of the most legendary American expatriates was born in St. Louis, Missouri. Josephine Baker sang and danced her way into the hearts of the French, earning the title the Toast of Paris in the 1920s. Her trademark role was "Dark Star" in the Folies Bergère, in which she appeared topless, wearing only a skirt of rubber bananas. Baker was called "a complete artist, the perfect master of her tools" by critics of her day.

During her Folies Bergère days, it is believed she received 2,000 offers of marriage and 40,000 love letters. As flamboyant offstage as on, Baker owned pet leopards that she took for strolls down the Champs-Elysées, the main thoroughfare of Paris. During World War II she worked as a spy, for which she was later awarded the French Legion of Honor.

In the 1950s Baker adopted fourteen children of many nationalities, which she called her rainbow tribe. Unfortunately, her rainbow tribe caused her considerable financial difficulties. Authorities forcibly evicted Baker from her $2 million fifteenth-century French chateau and auctioned it off to pay her debts. In order to raise funds for the care and schooling of her children, Baker continued to perform well into her twilight years.

Baker died in 1975 while attending a show in Paris honoring her fifty years in entertainment. A twenty-one-gun salute was fired at her funeral—a first for an African-American female.

I really didn't do some of the things that people reported, but then there were some others that they didn't know about.

—Baker in an article in *Ebony* magazine, December 1973

JUNE 4

On June 4, 1972, Angela Davis was acquitted of complicity in a plot to free three San Quentin prisoners from a Marin County, California, courthouse. During the escape attempt, four people had been killed. Because the guns used were registered to Davis, the FBI put her on its Ten Most Wanted list. The FBI tracked her down and charged her with conspiracy, kidnapping, and murder. Davis sat in jail for sixteen months awaiting trial. The Angela Davis trial was one of the most infamous courtroom dramas in contemporary American history.

This tall and politically outspoken "black militant" and self-avowed communist had earlier been fired from her job as a professor of philosophy at UCLA. She twice ran for vice president as the Communist Party candidate and was a recipient of the Lenin Peace Prize. Today Davis is a teacher and writer.

> Many people are unaware of the fact that jail and prison are two entirely different institutions. People in prison have already been convicted. Jails are primarily for pretrial confinement, holding places until prisoners are either convicted or found innocent. More than half of the jail population have never been convicted of anything, yet they languish in these cells. Because the bail system is inherently biased in the favor of the relatively well-off, jails are disproportionally inhabited by the poor, who cannot afford the fee. The O.R. program— which allows one to be released without posting bond, on one's own recognizance—is heavily tainted with racism. At least ninety-five percent of the women in the [House of Detention] were either Black or Puerto Rican.
>
> —from Angela Davis: An Autobiography (1974)

151

JUNE 5

Senator Robert Kennedy was leaving his victory rally after defeating Eugene McCarthy in the California Democratic primary when he was assassinated by Sirhan Sirhan on this day in 1968. Roosevelt Grier immediately disarmed the gunman. "Grier banged the man's hand repeatedly on the table until the gun was loosed," explained an article in the *Baltimore Sun*.

Grier, a former defensive tackle for the New York Giants and the Los Angeles Rams, was one of three African-American bodyguards protecting Kennedy that day. The others were Olympic decathlon champion Rafer Johnson and another former Los Angeles Rams player, Deacon Jones.

In Washington, D.C., the Reverend Ralph David Abernathy, leader of the Poor People's Campaign, addressed an emotional prayer service held in front of the Lincoln Memorial. He likened Senator Kennedy to slain civil rights leaders such as Martin Luther King Jr. and told the crowd, "He has come to our help so many times and heard our prayers so many times." Abernathy had earlier called Kennedy "one of the precious few leaders of national stature who have worked effectively to end the violence, the hatred, the oppression and the war mentality that have been poisoning America."

JUNE 6

On this day in 1943, attorney and educator William Henry Hastie was awarded the NAACP's Spingarn Medal for a "distinguished career as a jurist and as an uncompromising champion of equal justice." Hastie was the first African-American judge on the U.S. Circuit Court of Appeals and was a member of President Franklin D. Roosevelt's "Black Cabinet." He resigned his post as civilian aide to the secretary of war in protest of continued racial bigotry in the U.S. Army.

The treatment accorded the Negro during the Second World War marks, for me, a turning point in the Negro's relation to America. To put it briefly, and somewhat too simply, a certain hope died, a certain respect for white Americans faded. One began to pity them, or to hate them. You must put yourself in the skin of a man who is wearing the uniform of his country, is a candidate for death in its defense, and who is called a "nigger" by his comrades-in-arms and his officer; who is almost always given the hardest, ugliest, most menial work to do; who knows the white G.I. has informed the Europeans that he is subhuman (so much for the American male's sexual security); who does not dance at the U.S.O. the night white soldiers dance there, and does not drink in the same bars white soldiers drink in; and who watches German prisoners of war being treated by Americans with more human dignity than he has ever received at their hands. And who, at the same time, as a human being, is far freer in a strange land than he has ever been at home.

> —James Baldwin, in his celebrated essay *The Fire Next Time*, explaining the African-American point of view on racial discrimination in the U.S. Army during World War II

~~~~~~

JUNE 7

The "Princess of Black Poetry" was born on this day in 1943 in Knoxville, Tennessee. Nikki Giovanni's first volume of poetry, *Black Feeling, Black Talk*, was published in the mid-1960s during what has been called the African-American Literary Awakening, or the Black Arts Movement. At that time her trademark style was mixing slang and cuss words with elegant speech and poetry, with the intention of consciousness-raising.

> *So the great white prince*
> *Was shot like a nigger in Texas*

And our Black shining prince was murdered
like a thug in his cathedral
While our nigger in Memphis
Was shot like their prince in Dallas
    and my Lord
ain't we never gonna see the light.

—from "The Great Pax Whitie"

Giovanni—a prolific writer to this day—has moved away from her angry, bitter style of the 1960s. As she explained in a newspaper interview, "One winds down. We've touched on every sore that anybody in the world ever had and I think we ought to do some healing. I'm not downgrading anger, but how long can you stay angry?"

Mistakes are a fact of life
It is the response to the error that counts.

—from Giovanni's poem "Of Liberation"

JUNE 8

On June 8, 1953, the refusal to serve African-Americans in Washington, D.C. restaurants was unanimously outlawed by the U.S. Supreme Court. The Court upheld an 1873 law that prohibited owners of eating establishments from refusing service because of a person's race or color.

Mary Church Terrell, at the time in her late 80s, filed the complaint, called the "Thompson Restaurant Case," and was one of the key plaintiffs in the suit. The case began in 1950 when the John R. Thompson restaurant refused to serve three African-Americans.

The NAACP's board issued a statement praising the ruling and said "We urge the people of this country, both white and Negro, North and South, to follow the example of the Supreme Court and to consider the question of the validity of racial segregation on the basis of facts, the law and their moral responsibility rather than upon the irrational rantings and ravings of biased, die-hard 'white supremacist' demagogues."

I will always protest against the double standard of morals.

—from Mary Church Terrell's *Confessions of a Colored Woman in a White World* (1940)

~~~~~~

JUNE 9

The sculptress Meta Vaux Warrick Fuller was born on this day in 1877 in Philadelphia, Pennsylvania. Fuller was one of the principal visual artists during the Harlem Renaissance of the 1920s. She was the first African-American artist to draw themes for her work largely from African-American folktales. Her best known works are a bronze sculpture called *Ethiopia Awakening* (1914) and *Mary Turner* (1919).

As a young artist, Fuller received a scholarship to study at the Pennsylvania Museum and School for Industrial Arts. By the turn of the century she was studying with the French sculptor Rodin in Paris. Fuller was well established in both the United States and Paris at the onset of the Harlem Renaissance. She never actually lived in Harlem—preferring Boston and Framingham, Massachusetts, which to her more closely resembled a European life-style—but she nonetheless embodied the ideals of the Harlem Renaissance. Fuller died on March 13, 1968.

The culminating statement of the artist's career is found in her celebrated work "Talking Skull," executed in 1937. An African male kneels gently in front of a skull silently communication his thoughts, undisturbed by the gulf that separates life from death. Dramatic in its appeal to have us reason with ourselves to see our final end, the work, like "Go Down Death" by Aaron Douglas, executed about ten years earlier, is convincing in its

symbolic, traditional means of communicating the mysteries
of life and death.

—from The Studio Museum in Harlem's book *Harlem*
Renaissance, Art of Black America (1987)

〰〰〰〰〰〰〰〰〰〰〰〰〰〰〰〰〰〰〰〰〰〰〰

JUNE 10

On this day in 1854, at Notre Dame cathedral in Paris, James Augustine Healy was ordained as the first African-American Roman Catholic priest. Later, upon his consecration by Pope Pius IX in 1875, Healy became the first African-American bishop.

Healy was assigned jurisdiction over Portland, Maine, where he became known as the "children's bishop." Upon arrival in Portland, one of Bishop Healy's first self-appointed tasks was to oversee the construction of a new Catholic parochial school. During the winter months Bishop Healy was often spotted in Portland's Munjoy Hill Park with children's sleds attached to his horse-drawn sleigh, pulling them through the snow. This much-loved bishop also paid doctor bills and taxes for the poor and kept in touch with his parishioners.

There is a story of one young girl who admitted to uttering something bad about the bishop. While in confession, she confided to Healy that she had called him "as black as the devil." Healy replied, "Oh, my child, don't say the bishop is black as the devil. You can say he's as black as coal, or as black as the ace of spades, but don't say he's as black as the *devil*."

Healy was born in Macon, Georgia, to an Irish father and mulatto slave mother. His father married his mother in violation of Georgia laws at the time. He was the brother of Patrick Francis Healy, the first African-American to receive a Ph.D. and the first African-American president of Georgetown University.

He moved about among the poor of the North end parish of St. John's quietly and unobtrusively. He courageously visited the cholera victims to administer the last Sacraments, and comfort them in their dying moments. There were no questions asked when Father Healy rushed to their homes to answer their desperate call for a priest....He was warmly received by the immigrant poor, themselves wayfarers and outcasts in a strange and foreign land.

—Albert S. Foley, S.J., describing Healy's days as a priest in Boston in his book *Bishop Healy: Beloved Outcast*

JUNE 11

On June 11, 1875, Senator Brownlow of Tennessee wrote the following in a letter to Col. William M. Cockrum, author of *History of the Underground Railroad* (1915) and a member of the Anti-Slavery League:

...I think that Mrs. Stowe's "Uncle Tom's Cabin" made the southern fire eaters madder than anything that was done to them before....The slave holding elements were very careful to have destroyed every copy of "Uncle Tom's Cabin" that they could hear of. I got a chance and sent to Cincinnati for a copy, which I got in due time. I kept it hid and every time I had an opportunity I read it. The book was interesting to a high degree. It told about one-half the truth. Mrs. Stowe had not a chance to see the worst part of slavery—that could only be seen in the black district of Louisiana, or in some parts of South Carolina....

The white abolitionist Harriet Beech Stowe had published her book *Uncle Tom's Cabin* in 1852 in Boston. Stowe modeled her fictional hero Uncle Tom after the real-life Josiah Henson.

Henson had been born into slavery in 1789. For a long time Henson was a very devoted slave, but his master's plan to sell his children in 1830 was too much for even him to bear. Henson escaped with his family on the Underground Railroad. He established a settlement for runaway slaves near the Canadian town of Dresden and returned south many times to liberate others still in bondage. Henson also travelled to Britain to raise funds for a vocational school for former slaves called Uncle Tom's British Institute, which became the first vocational school in Canada. He died in 1883 at the age of 94. His headstone simply reads "Uncle Tom."

Stowe's book sold 300,000 copies in its first year of publication, helping to convert many northerners to an antislavery position while further antagonizing southerners. *Uncle Tom's Cabin* was dramatized in theaters across America nearly continually from its release in 1852 until 1931.

"Uncle Tom" has become ingrained in modern American English as both a noun and a verb, meaning a black person who is subservient or deferential to whites.

JUNE 12

Today in 1963, 37-year-old Medgar W. Evers was shot in the back by a segregation fanatic while in front of his house in Jackson, Mississippi.

As the NAACP's field secretary in Mississippi, Evers was a central figure in desegregation efforts taking place in the state and was involved in investigating the murders of African-Americans. This World War II veteran had been enlightened to the plight of poor African-Americans while working as an insurance salesman. He quit his successful career to devote himself full-time to the NAACP.

Evers was the first major civil rights leader to be murdered. No conviction was reached until 1994. One month after his death, in July 1963, his wife accepted the NAACP's Spingarn Medal in his honor.

If I die, it will be in a good cause. I've been fighting for America as much as soldiers in Vietnam.

—Ever speaking to a reporter shortly
before his death

You can kill a man, but you can't kill an idea.

—Medgar W. Evers

Medgar Evers

JUNE 13

On this day in 1967, Thurgood Marshall became the first African-American U.S. Supreme Court justice, appointed by President Lyndon B. Johnson. At the time he was solicitor general of the United States.

Many years earlier, in 1946, Marshall had been awarded the NAACP's Spingarn Medal for his work as a lawyer before the Court. During his law career he argued thirty-two U.S. Supreme Court cases and won twenty-nine. Several of these were landmark cases, the most famous being *Brown v. the Board of Education*. He served as director of the NAACP Legal Defense and Educational Fund for twenty years. Marshall died in 1993 at the age of 84.

Why of all the multitudinous groups of people in this country,
[do] you have to single out the Negroes and give them this

separate treatment? It can't be because of slavery in the past, because there are very few groups in this country that haven't had slavery some place back in the history of their group. It can't be color, because there are Negroes as white as drifted snow, with blue eyes, and they are just as segregated as the colored man. The only thing it can be is an inherent determination that the people who were formerly in slavery, regardless of anything else, shall be kept as near that state as possible.

——Marshall, arguing *Brown v. Board of Education* (1953)

The only way to get equality is for two people to get the same thing at the same time at the same place.

——Marshall, the Murray case (1934)

JUNE 14

On this day in 1967, police barricaded a four-block area in a Detroit suburb around the home of Mr. and Mrs. Corado Bailey. For three days angry white neighbors had demonstrated in front of the Bailey's home. Why? Because Corado Bailey was black and Ruby Bailey was white.

The barricading of the Bailey home occurred only two days after the Supreme Court ruled unanimously that states could not prevent interracial marriages. In the aptly named case, *Loving v. the Commonwealth of Virginia*, the Supreme Court wrote, "Under our constitution the freedom to marry or not to marry a person of another race resides with the individual and cannot be infringed by the state." Furthermore, the Court stated that laws involving racial classification were "inherently suspect" of denying people equal protection under the law.

Loving v. the Commonwealth of Virginia had been brought before the Supreme Court by a black woman and white man from Virginia who had married in Washington, D.C. They were convicted of violating Virginia's antiamalgamation law after returning to their home state. On August 12, 1967, two months after the Supreme Court handed down its decision in this case, the *New York Times* reported that a white woman and a black man wedded in Norfolk, in the first mixed marriage to take place in Virginia since the new ruling.

JUNE 15

Today in 1917, Fort Des Moines Provisional Army Officer Training School was established in Des Moines, Iowa, to train African-American officers for World War I. Called the black West Point, the school was disbanded after the war ended. It was designated a national historic landmark in 1974.

The closing of this officer's training school is symbolic of the post–World War I era of broken promises for the African-American. Black soldiers came home from fighting the war that was supposed to "make the world safe for democracy" only to be insulted and attacked, and to find racial tensions in America at a climax. The *Baltimore Afro-American* wrote that a "Negro in military uniform" was like "the flaunting of a red flag in the face of an enraged bull."

Not only did African-American soldiers have to deal with discrimination from the general public, they had faced it in the armed services itself. A secret French army directive dated August 7, 1918, intended for the French military mission stationed with the American army, warned that the French public's tendency to treat Negroes with "familiarity and indulgence" would not be well received by white American troops. "White Americans become greatly incensed," noted the document, "at any public expression of intimacy between white women and black men." The directive concluded that French officers "must prevent the rise of any pronounced degree of intimacy" between themselves and black officers; that the French should "not commend too highly the black American troops, particularly in the presence of white Americans;" and the officers should "make a point of keeping the native cantonment population from 'spoiling' the Negroes."

~~~~~~

JUNE 16

A pictorial essay on Flavio da Silva, an impoverished and sickly boy living in the *favela*, or slums, of Rio de Janeiro, Brazil, appeared in the June 16, 1961 issue of *Life* magazine. Award-winning photojournalist Gordon Parks Sr. had spent three months with Flavio and his family, taking thousands of photos and keeping a heart-wrenching diary.

> *March 24*
>
> *Flavio was daydreaming when I arrived today—looking out over the shacks, past the football field, the lake, and the great white buildings. Though he is 12 he has never been across the small lake to downtown Rio. None of the kids has—not even to Rio's famous Copacabana Beach, which is only 10 minutes from the bottom of their miserable world.*

America's heart went out to Flavio and the da Silva's. Within a month after the story appeared in print nearly $30,000 dollars had been donated, most of which went toward the purchase of a new home for the family. The rest helped to bring Flavio to America for a two-year treatment for severe asthma.

A year before presenting Flavio's story to the world, Parks had been chosen Photographer of the Year by the American Society of Magazines. By the 1970s Parks had signed with Paramount Pictures as the first African-American filmmaker to work for a major motion picture studio. In his films *Shaft* and *Shaft's Big Score*, Parks introduced American audiences to the character John Shaft—a "handsome, brave, intelligent, confident and cool charmer." The Shaft films brought a new image of black males to the big screen. The films also brought to light the potential for large box-office receipts from movies directed at African-American audiences; *Shaft* grossed $12 million in its first year.

Parks was awarded the NAACP's Spingarn Medal in July 1972 for his "multi-faceted creative achievements." He was inducted into the Black Filmmakers Hall of Fame in 1973. His son, Gordon Parks Jr., also directed films, including *Super Fly* in 1972 and *Three the Hard Way* in 1974.

JUNE 17

On this night in 1972, Frank Wills, a 24-year-old African-American security guard, embarked on his usual rounds of the Watergate housing and office complex in Washington, D.C. Little did he know he would open up a Pandora's box of political scandal and intrigue.

Wills discovered intruders installing spy equipment in the suite of the Democratic National Party Headquarters. After allegedly refusing to accept bribes from the burglars, Wills alerted city police. This led to the infamous Watergate scandal, which shook the Nixon Administration at its highest levels, ultimately leading to President Nixon's resignation in 1974.

Wills himself was shaken by the incident, causing him to quit his job at the Watergate complex despite a $5 per week raise. A year later, however, he was again working as a security guard at another building in Washington.

> *There is a breakdown in the political system. The American people are not aware of what is really happening. I've seen it firsthand, and it's opened my eyes real wide. I feel sorry for the people who look at Washington and say it's just politics.*

> —Wills in *Time* magazine, May 7, 1973

JUNE 18

On this day in 1954, Eldridge Cleaver took his first trip to Soledad Prison on a charge of possession of marijuana. This ex-con went on to become a major civil rights activist and leader of the Black Panther movement as its minister of information. Cleaver's book of memoirs from prison, *Soul on Ice*, earned him credit as "one of the best cultural critics" of the 1960s.

Cleaver revealed many nasty truths about contemporary America. For example, in the essay "The White Race and Its Heroes," he wrote:

> *What has suddenly happened is that the white race has lost its heroes. Worse, its heroes have been revealed as villains and its greatest heroes as the arch-villains. The new generation of whites, appalled by the sanguine and despicable record carved over the face of the globe by their race in the last five hundred years, are rejecting the panoply of white heroes....They recoil in shame from the spectacle of cowboys and pioneers—their heroic forefathers whose exploits filled earlier generations with pride—galloping across a movie screen shooting down Indians like Coke bottles.*

At one point Cleaver fled to Cuba to avoid another prison term. He spent several years in exile there, as well as in Algeria and France. Upon returning to the United States, he adopted capitalism and became a Republican and a fundamentalist preacher. He also designed clothing that accentuates the penis and founded a church that worships the male reproductive organs. His second book, *Soul on Fire*, was about his conversion to Christianity and was largely ignored.

The price of hating other human beings is loving oneself less.

—Eldridge Cleaver

JUNE 19

R. T. Miller Jr. of Chicago presented a gift of $50,000 to Oberlin College on this day in 1933, on the hundredth anniversary of the founding of the college. Taking its name from a French pastor, John Frederick Oberlin, the college was chartered in Oberlin, Ohio, in 1833. The following year this progressive school became the first institute of higher learning in America to admit both women and African-Americans.

According to the *New York Times*, Oberlin was meant to be "a pronouncedly Christian, radically conscientious educational centre for the Middle West." Oberlin's first catalogue stated: "The object of Oberlin College shall be the diffusion of useful science, sound morality, and pure religion among the growing multitudes of the Mississippi Valley. It aims also at bearing an important part in extending these blessings to the destitute millions which overspread the earth."

Between 1835 and 1865, 140 African-American women attended the college, most hailing from well-to-do free families. One early graduate was Anna Julia Cooper, a pioneer African-American feminist, writer, and educator.

> *Only the BLACK WOMAN can say "when and where I enter, in the quiet, undisputed dignity of my womanhood, without violence and without suing or special patronage, then and there the whole Negro race enters with me."*
>
> —from Anna Julia Cooper's *A Voice from the South by a Black Woman of the South* (1892)

JUNE 20

Today in 1926, Mordecai Wyatt Johnson became the first African-American president of Howard University. Remaining president for more than thirty years, Johnson oversaw a major expansion of the university.

During his tenure twenty new buildings were added to the campus and the library holdings increased twofold.

On July 2, 1929, Johnson was awarded the NAACP's Spingarn Medal "for his successful administration as first Black president of the leading Black university in America, and especially for his leadership in securing, during the past year, legal authority for appropriations to Howard University by the government of the United States."

The son of a Baptist minister, Johnson held three bachelor's degrees, a master's degree in theology, and two doctor of divinity degrees. His mother's death—when Johnson was just 27 years old and was already working as a university professor—had a profound effect on his life. After her death, Johnson's philosophical search took a new turn. In an excerpt from Mary White Ovington's 1927 book *Portraits of Color*, Johnson explains this transformation:

Always I started with my death. Before, I had looked forward, now I looked back. If I were lying dead, as I had seen my mother lie, what in life would be worth while? What, of the many things that I had done, would justify my existence? What would have meaning? One night, as I rocked in my familiar seat, I had a vision. I was lying on my death-bed in a rough cabin, quite alone. The place was very still. Then, silently, the door opened and people came in, poorly dressed, plain people, who moved in line past my bed. And as they passed, each had something to say in affection and gratitude. I had helped one who was in trouble. I had comforted another. I had given wise counsel to a third. I saw the line distinctly, coming in and passing out, while I lay there, dying, on the coarse bed. Before I went to sleep that night, I knew that I had found the meaning of life. It was service, service to the poor and afflicted. And I felt that I could best render this service by leaving my scholastic work and entering the ministry.

JUNE 21

On this day in 1964, in Philadelphia, Mississippi, three civil rights campaigners were killed by the Ku Klux Klan, with local police and a preacher's involvement. Two Jewish men from New York, Michael Schwerner and Andrew Goodman, and a local African-American recruit, James Earl Chaney, were taking part in the Freedom Summer, a cross-country campaign to register black voters. Every bone in Chaney's body was crushed in the murder. This vile episode in American history was recounted in the 1988 movie *Mississippi Burning*.

A murder conviction was never reached. However, on the twenty-fifth anniversary of their deaths, Dick Molpus, Mississippi secretary of state, said to the victims' families, "We deeply regret what happened here twenty-five years ago. We wish we could undo it. We are profoundly sorry that they are gone. We wish we could bring them back. Every decent person in Philadelphia and Neshoba County and Mississippi feels that way."

> *Wherever Negro and white stand up together, there will be the spirit of these three young men. And it's got to happen to every one of us personally.*
>
> —Dr. Algernon D. Black at the close of the combined funeral service in New York as the mothers of the slain men linked arms

JUNE 22

In Chicago on this day in 1937, the "Brown Bomber" knocked out James J. Braddock in eight rounds, becoming boxing's heavyweight champion and providing black America with a healthy dose of pride. Joe Louis—one of America's greatest sports legends—was the longest holder of the heavyweight title. Louis never lost a fight during his tenure, from 1937 to 1949, as heavyweight champion of the world.

During his entire career Louis fought seventy-one professional fights, of which he lost only three. His first defeat took place on June 19, 1936, when he was beaten by Max Schmeling, a German boxer who was hailed as proof of the superiority of the Arian race. "I figure in my own mind," said a determined Louis, "I ain't a real champ until I get that Schmeling." And he did. During a rematch at Yankee Stadium on June 22, 1938, Louis beat Schmeling in two minutes and four seconds of the first round.

After coming out of retirement in 1950, Louis lost a professional match for the second time, fighting against Ezzard Charles. And in 1951, at the age of 37, he was knocked out by Rocky Marciano in a bout at Madison Square Garden, after which his stalwart fans wept. Louis died of a heart attack in 1981.

I don't like money actually, but it quiets my nerves.

Every man got a right to his own mistakes. Ain't no man that ain't made any.

—Joe Louis

~~~~~~

JUNE 23

Every June 23, on St. John's Eve, voodoo followers visit the grave of Marie Laveau at St. Louis Cemetery Number One in New Orleans, Louisiana. Believers in the "Voodoo Queen" make a red cross on her tomb with a piece of brick and say a prayer in the belief that Laveau will make their wishes come true. Others carry away pieces of dirt as symbols of Laveau's supernatural powers. Some believe, however, that she is really buried in St. Louis Cemetery Number Two. "They hadda move 'er," claimed one local, "too many prayin' and hollerin', huntin' luck."

Following the emancipation of slaves, Laveau had been a powerful figure in the African-American community in New Orleans, helping to reestablish the previously banned tribal beliefs of the former slaves. The Voodoo Queen professed to be able to see into the future and read minds. Her love potions were sought after, and she was believed to have the power to cure the sick.

The most celebrated "conjure woman" of her day, Laveau was born in New Orleans on February 2, 1827. As the daughter of a Frenchman named Christophe Glapion, she was technically a Creole quadroon (meaning one-quarter African ancestry). She practiced her craft at her homes on Saint Anne Street and Bayou Saint Johns for over fifty years.

JUNE 24

The June 24, 1929 edition of the *New York Times* contained two articles about organizations that had praised President and Mrs. Hoover for their hospitality to the wife of African-American congressman Oscar De Priest of Chicago. The Women's International League for Peace and Freedom made public a letter written to Mrs. Hoover in which they wrote, "We believe that your hospitality to Mrs. De Priest adheres to the best American tradition of democracy." The Nazarene Congregational Church of Brooklyn had adopted a resolution stating that "President and Mrs. Herbert Hoover be commended for their true spirit of democracy in the conduct of the social affairs of the White House, and that they be encouraged to continue to exercise the right of social freedom despite petty criticism."

Mrs. Hoover had invited Mrs. De Priest to a tea at the White House two weeks earlier, causing a huge flap between progressive and conservative sectors of American society. Washington's society types from the south were reportedly "agog" upon learning of the guest. The Mississippi State Senate drafted a resolution "unreservedly condemning" the social occasion. A southern Methodist bishop, W. N. Ainsworth, was disgusted by all the furor over the social engagement, calling it "a tempest in a teapot." The bishop added, "it is about time for every body to quit seeing black only and having these blatant outbreaks about it." In an attempt to quell the uproar over this supposedly "unprecedented" act of the Hoovers, the secretary of labor compiled a list of every African-American who had been entertained at the White House by previous presidents.

Meanwhile, De Priest went on with his business of being the first African-American congressman from a northern state. On June 24, 1929, the Illinois Representative arrived in Knoxville, Tennessee, where he spoke to an audience of 1,500 African-Americans who met him at the train, advising them to organize themselves politically to ensure they received full political and civil rights.

JUNE 25

On this day in 1876, General Custer of the Seventh U.S. Calvary made his ill-fated charge against Sioux and Cheyenne Indians along the banks of the Little Bighorn River in Montana Territory. An interpreter named Isaiah Dorman was among the 253 men lost in the battle known as Custer's Last Stand.

Dorman was formerly a woodcutter employed by Durfee and Peck on the Missouri River near Fort Sully. He also carried the mail 200 miles between Fort Rice and Fort Wadsworth. Married to a Santee Sioux woman, he learned the Sioux language and befriended other Native Americans. In the winter of 1876, Dorman assisted Chief Sitting Bull with food, an act for which the Sioux chief would return his gratitude only months later.

> As he [Sitting Bull] approached the end of the brush near the prairie-dog town, he came upon the Negro, 'Teat' Isaiah. Two Bulls, Shots-Walking, and several others rode up at the same time. 'Teat' was badly wounded, but still able to talk. He spoke Sioux, and was well liked by the Indians. He had joined the

troops as scout because, he said, he wanted to see the western country once more before he died. And now, when he saw the Sioux all around him, he pleaded with them, "My friends, you have already killed me; don't count coup on me." He had been shot early in the fight. Sitting Bull arrived just then, recognized 'Teat' and said, "Don't kill that man; he is a friend of mine." The Negro asked for water, and Sitting Bull took his cup of polished black buffalo horn, got some water, and gave him a drink. Immediately after, Isaiah died.

—from Walter Stanley Campbell's *Sitting Bull* (1932)

JUNE 26

Today in 1953, Paul R. Williams was awarded the NAACP's Spingarn Medal for his work in the field of architecture. In the 1930s Williams designed the Saks Fifth Avenue department store in Beverly Hills, California, and in the 1940s executed alterations and additions to the elegant Beverly Wilshire Hotel. This landmark building, located at 9500 Wilshire Boulevard, is considered one of the world's finest hotels.

Williams also created many plush Hollywood residences in Bel Air and Beverly Hills, including homes for Lon Chaney, Lucille Ball, Danny Thomas, Cary Grant, and Frank Sinatra. He designed the Los Angeles County Courthouse, the Golden State Mutual Life Building, and the Tudor mansion in Pasadena used in the television series *Batman*.

A pioneer of the "environmentalist" school, Williams employed a utilitarian style that melded physical structures with natural surroundings. Called the Architect to the Stars, he was the first African-American member of the American Institute of Architects.

One thing alone I charge you. As you live, believe in life! Always human beings will live and progress to greater, broader and fuller life.

—W. E. B. DuBois's last message, written on June 26, 1957

171

JUNE 27

On this day in 1872, Paul Laurence Dunbar was born in Dayton, Ohio. This son of former slaves became a popular and prolific turn-of-the-century writer. Booker T. Washington dubbed him Poet Laureate of the Negro Race. Dunbar was most widely known for dialect poetry, although he personally favored his standard English writings. The following excerpt from "The Party" (1896) is an example of his dialect poetry:

> Dey had a gread big pahty down at Tom's de othah night;
> Was I dah? You bet! I nevah in my life see sich a sight;
> All de folks f'om fou' plantations was invited, an' dey come,
> Dey come troopin' thick ez chillun when dey hyeahs a fife an'
> drum.

Dunbar's first volume of poetry, *Oak and Ivory*, was published in 1892 with the help of friends Orville and Wilbur Wright. His 1896 collection *Majors and Minors* won critical acclaim, and in 1901 his novel *Sport of the Gods* was published. This latter book represented Dunbar's transition to the naturalist tradition embraced by writers in the early 1900s. Naturalist novels presented a more scientific view of life and may be considered predecessors to the "Harlem novel" of the 1920s.

> The subtle, insidious wine of New York will begin to intoxicate him. Then, if he be wise, he will go away, anyplace—yes, he will even go over to Jersey. But if he be a fool, he will stay and stay on until the town becomes all in all to him; until the very streets are his chums and certain buildings and corners his best friends. Then he is hopeless, and to live elsewhere would be death.

> —Chapter 7 from *The Sport of the Gods*

Dunbar died of tuberculosis at the age of 34. His home, located at 219 Summit Street in Dayton, remains very much the same as it was at his death in 1906.

~~~~~~

JUNE 28

On June 28, 1935, Mary McLeod Bethune was awarded the NAACP's Spingarn Medal because "in the face of almost insuperable difficulties she has, almost single-handedly, established and built up Bethune-Cookman College.... Both the institution's and Mrs. Bethune's influence have been nationwide."

With only $1.50 to invest, Bethune built Daytona Normal and Industrial School for African-American girls in 1904. The original four-room schoolhouse was built on a garbage dump. After merging in 1923 with the Cookman Institute for men, it grew into one of America's finest universities.

Bethune—called black America's first lady—served as regular counsel to presidents. She worked with Herbert Hoover on child health issues, with Franklin D. Roosevelt on youth and minority affairs, and she was Harry Truman's personal representative at the inauguration ceremony for the president of Liberia. President Roosevelt used to greet her, "I'm always glad to see you, Mrs. Bethune, for you always come asking help for others—never for yourself."

In 1935 Bethune founded, and was the first president of, the National Council of Negro Women. In 1955 after completing a full day's work, she died of a heart attack. In 1974 the $400,000 Mary McLeod Bethune Memorial was unveiled in Washington, D.C.'s Lincoln Park. The inscription was taken from an article that Bethune wrote for *Ebony* magazine in 1955 titled "My Last Will and Testament." It reads:

I leave you love, I leave you hope. I leave you the challenge of developing confidence in one another. I leave you a thirst for education. I leave you respect for the uses of power. I leave you faith. I leave you racial dignity.

JUNE 29

On this day in 1926 Carter G. Woodson won the NAACP's Spingarn Medal for his pioneer work in African-American history. Woodson had founded the Association for the Study of Negro Life and History.

Carter Woodson

On this same day in 1951, the Spingarn Medal was awarded to Mable Keaton Staupers who "spearheaded the successful movement to integrate Black nurses into American life as equals." According to the award citation, her work was "characterized by wisdom, vision, courage, and refusal to equivocate." Proof of Staupers' success was the disbanding in January 1951 of the National Association of Colored Graduate Nurses. The organization was no longer considered necessary because the nursing profession had been successfully integrated.

People are trapped in history and history is trapped in them.

—James Baldwin

~~~~~~

JUNE 30

On this day in 1917, the woman who has often been called "the most beautiful woman in the world" was born in Brooklyn, New York. Lena Horne began her career at the age of 16 as a chorus girl at the whites-only Cotton Club in Harlem. She then toured with Noble Sissle's orchestra and later became the first African-American to front a white band when she sang with Charlie Barnet's orchestra. Her hit tunes included "Stormy Weather," "Blues in the Night," "The Lady Is a Tramp," and "Mad About the Boy."

In the 1940s Horne was transformed from dancer and nightclub singer to Hollywood glamour girl. She was the second black female, after Madame Sul-Te-Wan, to sign with a major Hollywood film studio. Her credits include *Panama Hattie* (1942), *Cabin in the Sky* (1943), *Meet Me In Las Vegas* (1956), and *Death of a Gunfighter* (1969). Horne was also the pin-up girl for African-American soldiers during World War II.

Exhibiting longevity, Horne won a Tony Award in 1981 for her Broadway show *Lena Horne—The Lady and Her Music*, the longest running one-woman show on Broadway. Horne is a recipient of the Kennedy Center's Lifetime Contribution to the Arts award.

In my early days I was a sepia Hedy Lamarr. Now I'm black and a woman, singing my own way.

—Lena Horne

JULY 1

On this day in 1933, Max Yergan won the NAACP's Spingarn Medal for being "a missionary of intelligence, tact and self-sacrifice, representing the gift of cooperation and culture which American Negroes may send back to their Motherland; and he inaugurated last year an unusual local movement for interracial understanding among black and white students."

Yergan first engaged in missionary work in East Africa. In addition to his religious duties, he helped train hospital orderlies and showed motion pictures to villagers. Unfortunately, ill health forced him to return to the United States. He later returned to the African continent as a missionary to South Africa. In this capacity he served as the American secretary of a YMCA for ten years, again keeping a full schedule of religious and social duties.

"Everybody has confidence in him," explained a representative of the South African government, "He can go anywhere. The white people use him increasingly at public meetings, especially among students....His appeal is to the leader and he helps promote liberal feeling. No one can listen to him and say that the Negro is not capable of development. Why, we have so much confidence in him that we are willing to hear his criticism."

> Why is it that we, who better than any others can understand the native African, have done so little for him? Why have we given in other mission fields and left this neglected?
>
> —Yergan query to his fellow African-Americans

JULY 2

Denmark Vesey, a tall, strong carpenter of West Indian origin, along with five coconspirators, were hanged this day in 1822 for planning a slave rebellion. For four years Vesey, a free black, had been organizing over 1,000 slaves and stockpiling weapons and ammunition to take over Charleston, South Carolina, on the second Sunday in July 1822. Authorities learned in advance of the plot from two house slaves. In the end thirty-six people were executed, and many others were kicked out of the state.

The Vesey conspiracy disproved existing theories about slaves being contented with their lot. Had anyone cared to look, there was plenty of previous evidence of discontent. For instance:

- In 1800 Gabriel Prosser planned to lead thousands of other slaves in an attack on Richmond, Virginia, for which he and others were hung.
- In 1773 slaves in Massachusetts petitioned the state legislature for freedom and in 1779 twenty slaves petitioned the New Hampshire legislature to abolish slavery.
- In 1741 a slave revolt took place in New York City for which eighteen African-Americans were hung.
- In 1663, during the colonial period, a major slave rebellion took place in Gloucester, Virginia.

> *There were about forty thousand negroes in the province [of South Carolina], a fierce, hardy, and strong race, whose constitutions were adapted to the warm climate, whose nerves were braced with constant labour, and who could scarcely be supposed to be contented with that oppressive yoke under which they groaned.*

> —memoirs of a resident of South Carolina in the 1730s

~~~~~~

JULY 3

Today in 1928, Charles W. Chesnutt won the NAACP's Spingarn Medal for his "pioneer work as a literary artist depicting the life and struggle of Americans of Negro descent, and for his long and useful career as a scholar, worker and freeman in one of America's greatest cities." Chesnutt was a master short story writer who, like Paul Laurence Dunbar, employed Negro dialect and folklore in his works. The son of free mulatto parents, he worked variously as a schoolteacher, school principal, reporter, and court stenographer, all the while hoping to become a writer. Chesnutt gained national recognition when Houghton Mifflin published his collection of seven short stories, *The Conjure Woman*, in March 1899. He also wrote nine novels, three of which were published—*The House Behind the Cedars* (1900), *The Marrow of Tradition* (1901), and *The Colonel's Dream* (1905).

"Ugh! but dat des do cuddle my blood!"

"What's the matter, Uncle Julius?" inquired my wife, who is of a very sympathetic turn of mind. "Does the noise affect your nerves?"

"No, Mis' Annie," replied the old man, with emotion, "I ain' narvous; but dat saw, a-cuttin' en grindin' thoo dat stick er timber, en moanin', en groanin', en sweekin', kyars my 'memb'ance back ter ole times, en 'min's me er po' Sandy." The pathetic intonation with which he lengthened out the "po' Sandy" touched a responsive chord in our own hearts.

"And who was poor Sandy?" asked my wife, who takes a deep interest in the stories of plantation life which she hears from the lips of the older colored people. Some of these stories are quaintly humorous; others wildly extravagant, revealing the Oriental cast of the negro's imagination; while others poured freely into the sympathetic ear of a Northern-bred

woman, disclose many a tragic incident of the darker side of slavery.

—excerpt from Chesnutt's short story "Po' Sandy"

JULY 4

In 1910, in Reno, Nevada, was a backwater frontier town with a population of just 10,000. But in July of that year a *Chicago Tribune* headline blared, "Reno Now Center of Universe." On Monday, July 4, the population of Reno doubled, filled to the brim with spectators who had come to witness The Fight of the Century. Jack Johnson and James J. Jeffries met in a heavyweight boxing match that had become an international political happening as much as a sporting event. In the British press there was more coverage of this fight than of the Boer War.

The supposedly invincible Jeffries had come out of retirement as the "great white hope" who could take down the first black heavyweight champ. But Johnson was a crafty boxer, able to "block a punch and hit you with the same hand," claimed one contemporary. When he disrobed for the fight, reported the *New York Times*, "there was a sigh of involuntary admiration as his naked body stood in the white sunlight." Johnson won the match with a knockout in the fifteenth round.

White America went into a state of mourning, while black America erupted in frenzied celebration. This led to a backlash of white-on-black rioting in which eleven African-Americans were reported killed.

It was a good deal better for Johnson to win and a few Negroes to have been killed in body for it, than for Johnson to have lost and all Negroes to have been killed in spirit by the preachments of inferiority from the combined white press. It is better for us to succeed, though some die, than for us to fail, though all live.

—Talladega University professor William Pickens in a *Chicago Defender* article

JULY 5

On July 5, 1975, Arthur Ashe defeated Jimmy Conners to win the men's single title at Wimbledon, England. This was the first time an African-American male won the prestigious match. Ashe chalked up several other African-American male firsts: In 1963 he joined the American Davis Cup team; in September 1968 he defeated Tom Okker of the Netherlands in the U.S. Open; and in 1985 he was inducted into the International Tennis Hall of Fame.

Besides his tennis achievements, Ashe devoted time to helping young African-American athletes to develop their skills and wrote *A Hard Road to Glory*, a book which profiled African-American athletes. He was also a civil rights and antiapartheid activist.

In his final years he became a spokesman in the fight against AIDS. Ashe had contracted the disease AIDS from a blood transfusion during open heart surgery. He died in 1993 at the age of 49. David Dinkins, mayor of New York City, said upon his death, "Words cannot suffice to capture a career as glorious, a life so fully lived, or a commitment to justice as firm and fair as was his."

JULY 6

On this day in 1957, Althea Gibson won both the women's singles and doubles titles at Wimbledon, England, becoming the first African-American both to play for, and win, these coveted titles. Gibson won them again in 1958.

In 1950 Gibson was the first African-American to play in a U.S. Lawn Tennis Association tournament. She was the first African-American female to win the national clay-court singles championship in Forest Hills, New York, in both 1957 and 1958. In the same years she also won the women's singles competition at the U.S. Open. In 1963 Gibson traded in her tennis racket and embarked on a career in professional golf.

Gibson was born in South Carolina but was raised in New York, in Harlem. Her street, 143rd, was designated a play street by the Police Athletic League—meaning that during the day it was closed to traffic to serve as a children's playground.

No matter what accomplishments you make, somebody helps you.

> —Gibson quoted in *Time* magazine, August 26, 1957

Most of us who aspire to be tops in our field don't really consider the amount of work required to stay tops.

> —Gibson quote from the book *So Much to Live for* (1968)

JULY 7

For Colored Girls Who Have Considered Suicide/When the Rainbow is Enuf opened at the Studio Rivbea in New York City on this day in 1975. Written by dancer and poet Ntozake Shange, this "choreopoem" was performed by seven African-American women. It is a compilation of twenty poems about African-American females who had been repeatedly hurt or abused in relationships, but survived.

Despite criticism of its negative portrayal of African-American men, the show was enormously popular. It won several awards—the Obie, the Outer Critics Circle Award, the Audelco Award, the *Mademoiselle* Award—besides being nominated for Tony, Grammy, and Emmy awards.

bein alive & bein a woman & bein colored is a metaphysical dilemma I haven't yet conquered.

> —Ntozake Shange

~~~~~~

JULY 8

On this day in 1902, Gwendolyn Bennett was born in Giddings, Texas. This respected poet, writer, and graphic artist came onto the arts scene during the Harlem Renaissance of the 1920s. In 1927 she and Aaron Douglas were the first African-Americans to receive Barnes Foundation Fellowships.

As a high school student in Brooklyn, New York, Bennett won a poster contest with the slogan "Fresh Air Prevents Tuberculosis." She studied fine arts at Columbia University and the Pratt Institute in Brooklyn, graduating from Pratt in June 1924. Bennett studied in France from 1925–26, and taught fine arts at Howard University in Washington, D.C.

> *Something of old forgotten queens*
> *Lurks in the lithe abandon of your walk,*
> *And something of the shackled slave*
> *Sobs in the rhythm of your talk.*

—from Bennett's poem "To a Dark Girl"

~~~~~~

JULY 9

The Fourteenth Amendment to the U.S. Constitution was ratified on this day in 1868. The Amendment gave full civil rights to former slaves, offered equal protection under the law, and extended federal guarantees of civil rights to the states. Section 1 reads:

> *No state shall make or enforce any law which shall abridge the privileges or immunities of citizens of the United States; nor shall any state deprive person of life, liberty, or property, without due process of law; nor deny to any person within its jurisdiction the equal protection of the laws.*

Despite the Fourteenth Amendment, America remained steeped in Jim Crow laws that systematically discriminated against black Americans well into the twentieth century.

While the Union survived the Civil War, the Constitution did not. In its place arose a new, more promising basis for justice and equality, the 14th Amendment, ensuring protection of the life, liberty, and property of all persons against deprivations without due process, and guaranteeing equal protection under the laws. And yet another century would pass before...black Americans [obtained the right] to share equally...and have their votes counted, and counted equally.

—Thurgood Marshall, *Ebony* magazine, September 1987

JULY 10

The following article appeared on July 10, 1863, in the Boston *Commonwealth*.

HARRIET TUBMAN

Col. Montgomery and his gallant band of 300 black soldiers, under the guidance of a black woman, dashed into the enemy's country, struck a bold and effective blow, destroying millions of dollars worth of commissary stores, cotton and lordly dwellings, and striking terror into the

Harriet Tubman

heart of rebeldom, brought off near 800 slaves and thousands of dollars worth of property, without losing a man or receiving a scratch. It was a glorious consummation.

After they were fairly well disposed of in the Beaufort charge, they were addressed in strains of thrilling eloquence by their gallant deliverer, to which they responded in a song "There is a white robe for thee," a song so appropriate and so heartfelt and cordial as to bring unbidden tears.

The colonel was followed by a speech from the black woman who led the raid, and under whose inspiration it was organized and conducted. For sound sense and real native eloquence, her address would do honor to any man, and it created a sensation....

JULY 11

The Niagara Movement developed out of a civil rights meeting held from July 11–13, 1905, on the Canadian side of Niagara Falls. During those three days, twenty-nine African-American intellectuals and activists representing fourteen states gathered to discuss an agenda for ensuring first-class citizenship for African-Americans.

The Niagara group—many of whom opposed the views of Booker T. Washington—called for the abolition of race-based distinctions in America. They proposed increased access to higher education, freedom of speech, freedom of the press, and improved voter rights. Their method for promoting "the colored man's declaration of independence" would be distribution of pamphlets, litigation, and as W. E. B. DuBois, one of the main organizers, said, "plain, blunt complaint, ceaseless agitation, unfailing exposure of dishonesty and wrong—this is the ancient, unerring way to liberty, and we must follow it."

The Niagara Movement was not intended to be a mass movement. Rather, it was targeted toward African-American leaders. One of its representatives, Jesse Max Barber, called it "the tiny piece of leaven which we expect to leaven the whole lump." Although detractors called the Niagara group grumblers and whiners, the movement gained support in following years. It is considered the forerunner to the National Association for the Advancement of Colored People.

~~~~~~

JULY 12

Frederick Jones's patent application for a Removable Cooling Device, dated July 12, 1949, reads:

> *My invention relates to a removable cooling unit for compart-ments of trucks, railroad cars and the like employed in transporting perishables and to a method of cooling such compartments and has for its object to provide a simple and compact self-contained cooling unit positioned at the top of said compartment and combined with air flow passages which produce a vortex of cold air flowing about the walls of the compartment and returning from the center of the compartment.*

Jones had designed the first shock-proof refrigeration unit. This could be fitted into trucks, allowing long-distance trucking of perish-able foods. Jones and his former boss founded the Thermo King company in Minneapolis, Minnesota, and manufactured the truck refrigeration units, forever changing the food industry.

This remarkable African-American engineer registered over sixty patents during his lifetime. He designed refrigeration storage units for blood serum and medicines which were used during World War II and also invented a portable X-ray machine. Jones received his first patent in 1939 for a machine that automatically dispensed movie theater tickets.

~~~~~~

JULY 13

On this day in 1787, the Congress of the Confederation approved the Northwest Ordinance as a guideline for governing the territory north of the Ohio River. At the last minute a provision was attached to the ordinance that read: "There shall be neither slavery nor involuntary servitude."

However, the antislavery provision included no enforcement measures and was written in vague terms. Because the national government proved unwilling to decisively interpret the ordinance, French settlers, primarily living in what is now Indiana and Illinois, continued to enslave some 2,000–3,000 African-Americans from 1787 to 1848. Many other Franco-Americans, fearful that the new government would force them to give up their slaves and indentured servants, accepted the king of Spain's invitation to resettle west of the Mississippi in Spanish territory.

"The legacy of the Ordinance is...a mixed one," wrote professor Paul Finkleman in *The Northwest Ordinance* (1988). "The Ordinance certainly helped put slavery on the road to ultimate extinction in the Northwest, but that road proved to be an extraordinarily long one."

JULY 14

A *Washington Post* editorial dated July 14, 1976, said:

> The Texas delegation was on its feet cheering wildly, and so was just about everyone else in the hall—Florida and South Carolina making a particular ruckus. The lone-star flag was being brandished with almost aggressive enthusiasm, and there on the platform stood two Texans taking the cheers: the son of a Jewish small businessman and the daughter of a black preacher. If the women's movement hadn't made it something of an offense to repeat, we know what we'd say to the Democrats: You've come a long way, baby.

What was all the ruckus about? Two days earlier Barbara Jordan, a congresswoman from Texas, had delivered an unforgettable keynote speech at the Democratic National Convention—the first by an African-

American at a major party's national convention. An estimated seventy-five million television viewers watched the event, which secured Jordan's place in the Orators Hall of Fame. The speech began:

> There is something special about tonight. What is different? What is special? I, Barbara Jordan, am a keynote speaker. A lot of years have passed since 1832 [the first Democratic Party convention], and during that time it would have been most unusual for any national political party to ask that a Barbara Jordan deliver a keynote address...but tonight here I am. And I feel, notwithstanding the past, that my presence here is one additional bit of evidence that the American Dream need not forever be deferred.

JULY 15

Thursday, July 15, 1993, Stonebridge Country Club, Aurora, Illinois.

> The last time any competition made me this nervous was my first pick-up game at North Carolina. Back then, I was trying to show a few of my future teammates that I could play on their level. But golfing with Arnold Palmer in a pro-am with thousands of people watching made me so hyped that I basically missed the ball on my first drive off the practice tee.

—Michael Jordan from Chapter 18 of Mitchell Krugel's biography,
Jordan (1994)

Michael Jordan gained fame as a sports icon not in golf, but playing basketball for the Chicago Bulls. Called basketball's high priest, Jordan is a three-time recipient of the NBA's Most Valuable Player award and holds numerous NBA records. For seven consecutive years (1987–1993), he led the NBA in most points scored per game. He also boasts most consecutive points scored (23 against the Atlanta Hawks on April 16,

1987) and highest average points scored per game in a career (32.3, surpassing Wilt Chamberlain's record of 30.1).

Jordan retired from basketball in 1993 after the Bulls won their third consecutive NBA championship. He then played baseball on the Chicago White Sox's farm team. In March 1995, he quit baseball due to an ongoing players' strike and returned to the Chicago Bulls. Jordan's exceptional skills and his many major commercial endorsements have solidified his image as one of the world's most famous contemporary athletes.

You know the commercial I made for Nike about what if I was just another basketball player? Well, that wasn't done just to sell shoes. That's how I really felt. There came a time when I just wanted to be another basketball player. And you know, I couldn't.

—Jordan in Krugel's book *Jordan*

JULY 16

Today in 1944, Dr. Charles R. Drew was awarded the NAACP's Spingarn Medal "for his outstanding work in blood plasma. Dr. Drew's research in his field led to the establishment of a blood plasma bank which served as one of the models for the widespread system of blood banks used by the American Red Cross."

As noted in the award citation, Dr. Drew developed the first blood banks in the United States, as well as set up England's national blood bank system during World War II. This brilliant clinical scientist won numerous awards and honors during the 1940s for his medical contributions.

As professor of surgery at Howard University in Washington, D.C., he was very devoted to his medical students. "Charlie never made over five thousand dollars a year in his life," explained a colleague, "but he was always taking money out of his own pocket to help needy medical students or residents." Drew died in an automobile accident in 1950.

Handsome, modest, well-endowed both physically and mentally, he is a living refutation of the myth of white supremacy. He has fought his way up through the dense mass of discrimination that only a Negro knows. He is all-American caliber, a man deserving homage from all, black and white.

—journalist Albert Deutsch

JULY 17

African-American inventor Miriam E. Benjamin was awarded a patent on this day in 1888 for the Gong and Signal Chair for hotels. Using a rod-activated signal, this chair was designed to summon waiters to a patron's table. Benjamin's innovative chairs were installed in the U.S. House of Representatives for calling pages. Previously, congressmen had signaled pages by the disruptive method of clapping their hands.

Many other African-American women have registered patents at the U.S. Patent Office. In 1892 Sarah Boone patented an ironing board with "edges curved to correspond to the outside and inside seams of a sleeve." This padded board featured collapsible legs, offering an alternative to the existing method of ironing that involved placing a board across chairs or tables. In 1898 Lyda D. Newman obtained a patent for a hairbrush with detachable bristles for easier cleaning. Sarah E. Goode patented the Folding Cabinet Bed, a forerunner of the sofa bed, in 1885. In 1916, Madeline Turner invented a fruit press for making fruit juices, and in 1919 Alice H. Parker patented a central heating system that had temperature controls in every room and air ducts leading to each room from a central furnace.

Do a common thing in an uncommon way.

—Booker T. Washington

JULY 18

On this day in 1863, the all-black Fifty-fourth Massachusetts Volunteers led the Union attack on Fort Wagner, a Confederate stronghold at the entrance to Charleston Harbor. The battle was a horrible defeat for the Union Army, over half of the soldiers in the Fifty-fourth were killed. "The ocean beach was crowded with the dead, the dying and the wounded," wrote the New York *Tribune*. One of the fatalities was the Fifty-fourth's white colonel, Robert Gould Shaw.

Civil War soldier

Twice-wounded, Sgt. William H. Carney held the regimental flag high in the final, unsuccessful assault on the fort. "That old flag never touched the ground, boys," swore Carney. Carney was awarded the Congressional Medal of Honor for his courage, the first African-American soldier to receive this honor.

Following the heroic display of the Fifty-fourth at Ft. Wagner, Congress finally authorized the recruitment of African-American troops throughout the North. In spite of a Confederate proclamation that all captured Negro soldiers would be returned to slavery and their white commanding offiers would be killed, more than 180,000 African-Americans volunteered. These troops were credited by President Lincoln with changing the momentum of the war.

This historic Civil War battle was depicted in the 1988 Academy Award–winning film *Glory*. A monument to the Fifty-fourth regiment, sculpted in 1897 by Augustus Saint-Gaudens, is found in Boston, Massachusetts.

"The Old Flag never touched the ground!" 'twas thus brave
  Carney spoke,
A Negro soldier: words renowned, that Honor will invoke
Upon the records of the Race whose heroes many are,
Records that Time cannot efface, and Hate can never mar.
Those words were stamped with Carney's blood upon our
  Country's scroll,
And though dislike, deep as a flood, against his Race may
  roll,
It cannot dim, nor wash away, its crimson-written fate
Which history wrote on Wagner's day without a tinge of shame.
Not only Carney did she view, when with immortal pen
She stood to write the honors due one thousand Colored men
Who laughed at death, who felt no fear, and followed Colonel
  Shaw
Where none but heroes dared to go, with cheer and loud
  hurrah.

July the eighteenth, of the year eighteen-and-sixty-three,
To Negroes always will be dear, as any one could be,
For bloody cost of honors won, for loss of noble life,
For valor that no risk would shun in fiercest battle strife.

—"The Old Flag Never Touched the Ground,"
a poem written in honor of Carney and the Fifty-fourth

JULY 19

Today in 1979, Patricia Roberts Harris was appointed secretary of Health, Education and Welfare by President Jimmy Carter. Previously she was secretary of Housing and Urban Development, also in the Carter Administration. Harris was the first African-American female member of a presidential Cabinet.

Upon her appointment in 1965 as ambassador to Luxembourg under the Johnson Administration, Harris became the first African-American female ambassador. She was elected permanent chairman of the Democratic National Convention in the early 1970s.

Harris's remarkable career in politics paralleled an impressive career as an educator. She taught law at George Washington University and served as the first African-American female dean of Howard University Law School. In 1970 she was the youngest person to ever be appointed to the board of directors of Georgetown University.

Harris died of cancer in 1985 in Washington, D.C., at the age of 60.

We defeat oppression with liberty. We cure indifference with compassion. We remedy social injustice with justice. And if our journey embodies these lasting principles, we find peace.

—Patricia Roberts Harris, 1985

JULY 20

From July 20–23, 1967, the first Black Power Conference was held in Newark, New Jersey. "Black Power is a call for black people of this country to unite, to recognize their heritage, to build a sense of community," wrote Stokely Carmichael in his 1967 book *Black Power: The Politics of Liberation in America.*

Carmichael is credited with coining the slogan Black Power during a civil rights campaign in Mississippi in the 1960s. Elected chairman of the Student Non-Violent Coordinating Committee in 1966, Carmichael was a leading figure in the civil rights movement and voter registration drives in the South during the 1960s.

Carmichael quickly became disillusioned with the limited progress achieved through nonviolent methods and moved toward a more militant position. In 1967 he joined the Black Panther Party, which espoused urban violence to force change. He left the Black Panthers in 1969, going into self-imposed exile in Guinea, West Africa. There he adopted the African name Kwame Toure, and immersed himself in the pan-African movement.

One does not fight to influence change and then leave the change to someone else to bring about.

Violence is as American as cherry pie.

—Stokely Carmichael

JULY 21

On this day in 1896, at the 19th Street Baptist Church in Washington, D.C., the National Association of Colored Women was formed by a merger of the National Federation of Afro-American Women and the Colored Women's League. Mary Church Terrell, a D.C. school board member at the time, was elected its first president, and the organization adopted the slogan Lift As We Climb.

Mary Church Terrell was a pioneer women's and civil rights activist. Along with Ida B. Wells, she was one of the female founders of the Niagara Movement in 1909, which gave rise to the NAACP. Terrell continued to work on civil rights campaigns into her 90s, such as the effort in the early 1950s to desegregate restaurants and businesses in

Washington, D.C. She had the following to say about women's right to vote:

> Even if I believed that women should be denied the right of suffrage, wild horses could not drag such an admission from my pen or my lips....What could be more absurd and ridiculous than that one group of individuals who are trying to throw off the yoke of oppression themselves, so as to get relief from conditions which handicap and injure them, should favor laws and customs which impede the progress of another unfortunate group and hinder them in every conceivable way. For the sake of consistency, therefore, if my sense of justice were not developed at all, and I could not reason intelligently, as a colored woman I should not tell my dearest friend that I opposed woman suffrage.

JULY 22

On Saturday, July 22, 1939, J. Matilda Bolin was sworn in as the first African-American female judge in the United States. Mayor Fiorello La Guardia summoned her to his office and appointed her—on the spot— judge of the Court of Domestic Relations in New York City. Bolin, who at the time was an assistant corporation counsel for the Domestic Relations and Children's Courts, said the appointment was "a big surprise."

The *New York Times* reported on the female judge's first day on the bench, writing, "Justice Bolin was led through a crowd of spectators by Justice Jacob Panken of the same court, who commended her for her qualifications of 'decency, righteousness, capability and unfailing efforts to obtain good results in her work.'"

Born in 1908 in Poughkeepsie, New York, Bolin's father and brother ran a law practice in New York City. She graduated from Wellesley College with honors in 1928 and in 1931 was the first African-American woman to graduate from Yale Law School. She was a member of the

NAACP, the New York Urban League, the New York County Lawyers Association, and the Harlem Lawyers Association.

I don't think I short-changed anybody but myself. I didn't get all the sleep I needed, and I didn't get to travel as much as I would have liked, because I felt my first obligation was to my child. But professionally, I've never had any disappointments. I've always done the kind of work I like. I don't want to sound trite, but families and children are so important to our society, and dedicating your life to trying to improve their lives is completely satisfying.

—Bolin discusses the problems of combining motherhood with a high-power career in Stephanie Bernardo's *The Ethnic Almanac* (1981)

JULY 23

The July 1929 issue of the *Crisis* called Mahatma Gandhi, the Hindu nationalist and spiritual leader from India, "the greatest colored man in the world, perhaps the greatest man in the world." The magazine printed the following message from Gandhi to African-Americans:

A young Mahatma Gandhi

Let not the 12 million Negroes be ashamed of the fact that they are the grandchildren of slaves. There is no dis-

honour in being slaves. There is dishonour in being slave-owners. But let us not think of honour or dishonour in connection with the past. Let us realize that the future is with those who would be truthful, pure and loving. For, as the old wise men have said, truth ever is, untruth never was. Love alone binds and truth and love accrue only to the truly humble.

~~~~~~

JULY 24

The president of the Harlem Lawyers Association, Wallace L. Ford II, in a tongue-in-cheek letter to the editor of *New York* magazine dated July 24, 1978, had this to say about the recurrent debate over terminology for the African race in America:

> *...Since Mr. Coombs and New York magazine saw fit to write and publish an article dealing with an important and out-spoken minority [mulattos] within the black community, it is only fitting that other minorities within our community also be given similar recognition, including quadroons, octoroons, macaroons (the descendants of black-Irish unions) and kangaroons (the descendants of black-Australian unions).*

Terminology for referring to Africans in America (as with all ethnic groups) differs from era to era. Likewise, the prevailing tastes of the African-American community regarding nomenclature for themselves has altered over the years.

Negro—an English word derived from the Spanish and Portuguese word for black—was the principal word used by the dominant white culture in the early days of slavery. However, based on the names of African-American organizations of the 1700s, within black communities *African* was probably the preferred title. Prominent individuals in the eighteenth century were also known to refer to themselves as *Ethio-*

pians, in classical studies the generic term for an African. For example, Phillis Wheatley was praised as the Ethiopian Poetess by fellow poet Jupiter Hammon. A century later, popular minstrel performer James Bland (1854–1911), referred to himself as an Ethiopian Songwriter.

Throughout most of the 1800s, the terms *colored* and *free persons of color* predominated, while the term *black* was associated with slavery. By the turn of the century, *Negro* began to reappear as an acceptable term, as evidenced by new organizations such as the National Negro Business League and the American Negro Academy. In 1919 *The Negro Year Book* noted, "the word Negro is more and more acquiring a dignity that it did not have in the past."

By the 1960s the debate reignited, and the term *Black* reigned victorious as a symbol of racial pride, as in, Black is beautiful. Along with *black*, *Afro-American* was also popular in the post-1960s. In the 1990s *African-American* is considered the most politically-correct term, based on the logic that it is consistent with other ethnic group titles, such as Chinese-American, Japanese-American, Irish-American, and so on. Yet some quarters feel the trend toward "Africanization" of the subculture is unnecessary and in some ways obscures the separate and unique history of Africans in America. And so the debate goes on.

JULY 25

On July 25, 1967, President Lyndon B. Johnson sent in 4,700 army paratroopers to restore calm in Detroit after race riots erupted the day before. Forty-three people were killed in the uprising—even more than had died in the infamous Watts riots two years earlier.

The Detroit riots occurred at the height of what became known as the long, hot summer of 1967. Since the beginning of the year, violent protests had been erupting across the nation. Inner-city America was growing impatient with the moderate tone of the civil rights movement, taking the cause to a new level—violence in the streets.

On July 27, recognizing that there were deep-seated problems behind these violent outbursts, President Johnson addressed an increasingly concerned America. "We should attack these conditions not because we are frightened by conflict," explained the president, "but because we are fired by conscience. We should attack them because there is simply no other way to achieve a decent and orderly society in America."

The following day the president established the Advisory Commission on Civil Disorders to look into the causes of the rioting and recommend measures to prevent future disturbances. The commission was led by Governor Otto Kerner of Illinois and included Roy Wilkins of the NAACP and African-American senator Edward W. Brooke of Massachusetts. The Kerner Commission report concluded, "Our nation is moving toward two societies, one black, one white—separate and unequal."

> *Where justice is denied, where poverty is enforced, where ignorance prevails, and where any one class is made to feel that society is in an organized conspiracy to oppress, rob, and degrade them, neither persons nor property will be safe.*
>
> —Frederick Douglass in an April 1886 speech delivered in Washington, D.C. on the twenty-fourth anniversary of the Emancipation Proclamation

JULY 26

This day in 1865, after passing his final exams at the University of Louvain in Belgium, Patrick Francis Healy became the first African-American to earn a Ph.D.

Healy began his career as a teacher at St. Joseph's College in Philadelphia and later was a professor of philosophy at Georgetown University in Washington, D.C. Healy served as president of Georgetown from 1874 to 1882, becoming the first African-American to run a predominantly white university. He is often referred to as the second founder of Georgetown.

Born in Macon, Georgia, Healey was the son of an Irish landowner and a mulatto slave mother. Patrick's brother was James Augustine Healy, the first African-American Roman Catholic priest and bishop. Patrick was himself trained as a Jesuit priest. In Patrick's later years he preached at St. Ignatius Church in New York and at St. Joseph's College. He died in 1910 at Georgetown.

To his sisters in Montreal, Father James had dispatched Patrick in early September, being unable to make the trip himself. Patrick was commissioned to look into their business affairs and their health and happiness at their boarding school. He also was to secure their consent to James's plans for rectifying the incongruous situation in which he found himself, his brothers, and his sisters in reference to the Georgia Negroes. James had sensed the inappropriateness of slave-owning on the part of a priest, a seminarian, a Jesuit scholastic, and a nun.

—This passage from Albert S. Foley, S.J.'s book *Bishop Healy: Beloved Outcast*, refers to Michael Morris Healy's estate, which included over fifty slaves. At the time the Healy children inherited the estate, Georgia law forbade manumission of slaves, leaving them little choice but to sell their father's slaves.

JULY 27

In July 1853 the first novel by an African-American, *Clotel; or, the President's Daughter: A Narrative of Slave Life in the United States*, was published in London, England by author and historian William Wells Brown. He told the story of President Thomas Jefferson' daughter borne by his African housekeeper. When the book was published in the United States in 1864 the title was changed to *Clotelle: A Tale of the Southern States*, and references to the father of Clotelle had been removed.

Brown was born to a slave owner and a slave mother in Lexington, Kentucky. He escaped to Canada in 1834, taking the name of the Quaker man who assisted him, Wells Brown. A freeman, Brown traveled in the United States and Europe lecturing against slavery. In 1847 the Anti-Slavery Society published the story of Brown's escape.

A prolific man of letters, Brown was not only the first African-American novelist but also the first to write a drama, and upon publication of his book *Three Years in Europe* in 1852, became the first African-American travel writer. After the Civil War, despite having no formal training, Brown practiced medicine. He died in 1884 in Chelsea, Massachusetts.

> *Dick Jennings the slave-speculator, was one of the few Northern men, who go to the South and throw aside their honest mode of obtaining a living and resort to trading in human beings. A more repulsive-looking person could scarcely be found in any community of bad looking men. Tall, lean and lank, with high cheek-bones, face much pitted with the small-pox, gray eyes with red eyebrows, and sandy whiskers, he indeed stood alone without mate or fellow in looks. Jennings prided himself upon what he called his goodness of heart, and was always speaking of his humanity. As many of the slaves whom he intended taking to the New Orleans market had been raised in Richmond, and had relations there, he determined to leave the city early in the morning, so as not to witness any of the scenes so common on the departure of the slave-gang to the far South....*

—excerpt from the third edition of Brown's novel, this one titled
Clotelle, or The Colored Heroine (1867)

JULY 28

The Booker T. Washington National Monument was founded on this day in 1957, though it wasn't opened to the public until 1963. The monument, in honor of one of America's most notable educators, is located on

Virginia Rte. 122, sixteen miles northeast of Rocky Mount, Virginia. This was the second national monument dedicated to an African-American.

The first, dedicated on July 14, 1951, in Joplin, Missouri, was the George Washington Carver National Monument. Carver was a brilliant botanist and agricultural chemist. Carver and Washington were longtime associates at the Tuskegee Institute in Alabama.

You were born with all that the great have had
With your equipment they all began
Get hold of yourself, and say: "I can."

—This anonymous poem was one of George Washington Carver's favorites, which he used frequently to conclude his speeches.

JULY 29

On this day in 1918, the National Liberty Congress of Colored Americans petitioned Congress to make lynching a federal crime.

The following year there were eighty-three reported lynchings, twenty-five major race riots, and the Ku Klux Klan held over 200 public meetings. In 1921 there were sixty-four mob murders, four of the victims being burned at the stake.

It wasn't until January 26, 1922, that Congress passed the Dyer Anti-Lynching Bill. Up to that point, African-Americans in the northern and border states could be relied upon to vote en masse for Republican candidates. But because the Republicans delayed their pledge that the Harding Administration would make lynching a federal crime, many northern urban blacks soured on the party. The Dyer Anti-Lynching Bill became a major contributing factor in the shift of African-American loyalties from the Republican to the Democratic party.

The bill should pass...as a Republican Party measure. The
brutal and savage treatment of the negro in many Southern
States is causing much alarm among the negroes in all parts of

the country. They are very much stirred and they are charging it to the sins of omission on the part of the party leaders, whom they have so loyally supported in the past.

—an African-American resident of Brooklyn interviewed in the *New York Times*

Conditions in the South regarding lynching have been so steadily growing "no better very fast" that I am decidedly in favor of the Dyer Anti-Lynching bill. I would be akin to inhuman to feel otherwise.

—head of the Catholic colored missions of the United States, also in the *New York Times*

JULY 30

In New Orleans on July 30, 1866, white mobs led by ex-Confederate soldiers and the police attacked both blacks and whites attending a convention that had been called to consider an amendment to the Louisiana Constitution giving African-Americans the right to vote. In the rioting that followed, thirty-four blacks and four whites were killed, and some 200 persons were injured. General Sheridan called it "an absolute massacre by the police."

The North had won the Civil War, but many southerners were not yet willing to yield on certain issues, such as the African-American right to vote and hold government offices. To the aggravation of conservative southerners, African-Americans organized rallies and conventions in protest of Black Codes. Recalcitrant southern whites were further antagonized by the requirement that southern states ratify the Fourteenth Amendment in order to be readmitted to the Union; this amendment afforded full civil rights and equal protection under the law to former slaves.

A similar riot occurred in May of the same year in Memphis, Tennessee. This riot was also a police-led assault that involved three days of burning, pillaging, and rape in which forty-six African-Americans lost their lives.

> When they got to the Mechanics' Institute they found the door fastened and they could not get in; then they backed out and fired several times through the windows....The policemen then succeeded in bursting open the doors and went inside. What they did inside I do not know, but in about a quarter of an hour after there were a good many came out wounded, cut up, shot in the face and head, and there were police taking them to the calaboose. As they passed with them the crowd would knock them down and kill them, and some of the police were helping them kill them on the street. I spoke to the lieutenant of police, with whom I am acquainted...and I begged him "For God's sake, stop your men from killing these men so."

> —the testimony of a 34-year-old African-American describing the police raid on the Mechanics' Institute in New Orleans, delivered before the U.S. Congress during investigations of the New Orleans and Memphis riots

JULY 31

Whitney Moore Young Jr., a civil rights leader, and for a decade, head of the National Urban League, was born on this day in 1921 in Lincoln Ridge, Kentucky. The son of a preparatory school headmaster and a teacher, Young earned a master of arts degree in social work from the University of Minnesota. He served as dean of the school of social work at Atlanta University from 1954 to 1961. Young is best known for his ten years as executive director of the National Urban League, from 1961 to 1971.

An articulate spokesman for the civil rights movement, Young often found himself mediating between the radical elements in the African-American community who pressed for rapid change and the white business community and white liberals, who helped finance the cause. He wrote the books *To Be Equal* (1964) and *Beyond Racism: Building an Open Society* (1969). Young's success at fund-raising helped the National Urban League expand, adding thirty-five affiliates and increasing the budget tenfold during his tenure. Young also chalked up successes in promoting workplace integration, particularly in large corporations such as AT&T, RCA, and General Electric.

In 1969 President Lyndon B. Johnson awarded him with America's highest civilian honor, the Medal of Freedom. This advisor of executives and politicians died of a heart attack on March 11, 1971, while swimming in the ocean off Lagos, Nigeria.

> *I think to myself, should I . . . stand on 125th Street cussing out Whitey to show I am tough? Or should I go downtown and talk to an executive of General Motors about 2,000 jobs for unemployed Negroes.*
>
> —Young in a *New York Times* article

AUGUST 1

Today in 1944, Adam Clayton Powell Jr. was elected to the U.S. Congress for the first of thirteen consecutive terms. He eventually lost his seat in 1970, after being charged with misuse of position and public funds.

Powell began his career as a minister at Harlem's Abyssinian Baptist Church. During this time he fought for fair hiring practices—par-

Adam Clayton Powell Jr.

ticularly at public utilities, transit companies, and the World's Fair. A key civil rights activist in the 1960s, Powell was often steeped in controversy, propelled by his flamboyant lifestyle.

There is no future for a people who deny their past.

—Adam Clayton Powell Jr.

A man's respect for law and order exists in precise relationship to the size of his paycheck.

—Powell from *Keep the Faith, Baby!*

AUGUST 2

On this day in 1924, a boy was born in Harlem, New York, who was to become one of America's most talented writers of the 1950s and 1960s. As an artist, activist and intellectual, James Baldwin was a leading voice of the African-America community. His brilliant essays on race and gender issues launched his career as a writer and social commentator.

Baldwin moved to Paris in 1948, from where he wrote his successful first novel, the autobiographical *Go Tell It On the Mountain* (1953). Two years later he wrote *Notes of a Native Son*, a collection of essays reflecting on the black experience in America and Europe. After returning from France in 1956, his novel *Giovanni's Room*, which dealt with homosexuality, was published. Baldwin's best-known work was *The Fire Next Time*, an essay that delivered a loud message to America about the importance of dealing with race issues to prevent further destruction of society.

"Whatever happens," wrote biographer Fern Eckman, "Baldwin will be remembered as the writer who forced upon the consciousness of white America the terror and wrath of being Negro in the United States." This prolific writer spent his later years in France, where he was awarded the Legion of Honor, the country's highest civilian honor.

I imagine one of the reasons people cling to their hates so stubbornly is because they sense, once the hate is gone, they will be forced to deal with pain.

—Baldwin from *Notes of a Native Son* (1955)

AUGUST 3

On August 3, 1936, at the Olympic Games in Berlin, Germany, Jesse Owens won the 100-meter sprint, capturing his first of four gold medals. Over the next six days, Owens also won Olympic gold in the 200-meter dash, the broad jump, and the 400-meter relay.

The African-American's success was seen as an affront to Nazi claims of Aryan racial superiority. Therefore, rather than present the medals himself, Adolph Hitler watched the presentation of the medals from the stands.

Owens's name at birth was James Cleveland Owens, or J. C. He became Jesse when a Cleveland high school teacher misunderstood the pronunciation of J. C., and began calling him Jesse. Later he became an Ohio State University track star and was nicknamed the Buckeye Bullet. Owens died of lung cancer in 1980 at the age of 66.

Any black who strives to achieve in this country should think in terms of not only himself but also how he can reach down and grab another black child and pull him to the top of the mountain where he is. This is what a gold medal does to you.

—Jesse Owens, from a public lecture

AUGUST 4

On this day in 1931, Dr. Daniel Hale Williams died at the age of 75. Williams, affectionately called Dr. Dan, founded Chicago's Provident Hospital in 1891. For the first time, provident offered African-American women the opportunity to formally train to become nurses, and was America's first interracial hospital.

Dr. Dan made headlines—and a place in history—on July 9, 1893, when he performed the first successful open heart surgery on record. The patient had been stabbed in the heart, and, as a Chicago newspaper exclaimed, Dr. Dan "sewed up his heart." The patient lived for fifty more years.

> 'Tis no time for things unsightly
> Life's the day and life goes lightly
> Science lays aside her sway
> Love rules Dr. Dan today
> Diagnosis, cease your squalling
> Check that scalpel's senseless bawling
> Put that ugly knife away
> Doctor Dan doth wed today

—written by Dr. Dan's friend, the poet Paul Lawrence Dunbar, on the
occasion of his wedding

AUGUST 5

On August 5, 1922, the *New York Times* reported that an African-American outlaw who had shot three men in Iowa in the previous two days had held off 800 armed men until finally being killed by a bullet. The man went unidentified, not unlike many earlier African-American villains of the Old West. However, through thievery and treachery, several colored renegades like Ben Hodges, Ned Huddleston, and Cherokee Bill secured places for themselves in history.

Judge Isaac Parker, the "hanging judge," considered Cherokee Bill the worst desperado in the West. Born of an African-American father and a half-white, half-Native American mother, Cherokee Bill engaged in his first gunfight at the age of 18. He killed many men in the years that followed, including shopkeepers, policemen, railway agents, and anyone else who crossed him. Cherokee Bill's luck soon ran out; a cousin of one of his girlfriends captured the outlaw and turned him in. Judge Parker told the young gunslinger he was "the most ferocious monster" and that he had a record "more atrocious than all the criminals that have hitherto stood before this bar." When Cherokee Bill was sent to the gallows he was only 21 years old.

Ned Huddleston, better known as Isom Dart, was a horse rustler and card shark. Born a slave in 1849 in Arkansas, he eventually settled in Brown's Park, Colorado. Believed to be a kind man, Huddleston attempted to "go straight" on several occasions, during which time he was employed as a construction worker and bronco buster. In his final year, he owned a ranch and led a peaceful life. However, when Huddleston was 51 years old a bounty-hunter named Tom Horn tracked him down and killed him.

The son of an African-American father and Mexican mother, Ben Hodges worked his trickery as a cattle thief, card shark, and con man out of Dodge City, Kansas. In 1929, at the age of 73, this well-known swindler died of natural causes. He was buried in Dodge City's Maple Grove Cemetery beside other more respectable cowboys and cattlemen, according to a pallbearer, because they "wanted him where they could keep a good eye on him."

AUGUST 6

In August 1847, the *Star* newspaper reported that in June of that year there were 459 residents of San Francisco, ten of whom were of African ancestry. One of these African residents was wealthy merchant and politician William Alexander Leidesdorff. Originally from the Virgin Islands, Leidesdorff lived for some time in New Orleans, Louisiana. He departed New Orleans in protest against southern racial prejudice after his proposed marriage to Hortense, a white aristocrat, was prohibited by her family.

By the time Leidesdorff arrived in San Francisco in 1841 he was already a rich man. Leidesdorff had boundless faith that the small bayside village would one day become a world-class port city. In 1846 he opened one of the first two hotels in the city. He also built the first warehouse and wharf. In 1847 he put the first steamboat, the *Sitka*, in San Francisco Bay, and introduced horse racing to California.

His political career was as distinguished as his commercial life. In 1845 he was named U.S. vice consul to Yerba Buena, as San Francisco was called under Mexican control. In 1847 he was elected to the city council, becoming one of the first black elected officials in the United States. He served as town treasurer in 1848 and sat on the first school board.

Leidesdorff died of "brain fever" in 1848 at the age of 38. He left behind an estate worth over one $1 million, including a 35,000-acre ranch along the American River. Soon after his unexpected death, a small street along the waterfront in San Francisco was named in his honor. He died—one might say luckily—before racist legislation was enacted locally barring African-Americans from public office.

He had lived a lonely life and died a lonely man, even though surrounded by friends. His death was an occasion of deep sorrow. All business in the city closed its doors....The day after his burial men walked sadly through the streets of the city he had helped build, shook their heads, and said a great man had gone from their midst. And then, as was ever the way, they entered their favorite grogshop and talked about the first whisperings of the discovery of gold, and William Alexander Leidesdorff was forgotten.

—from Samuel Dickson's book *Tales of San Francisco* (1957)

AUGUST 7

On this day, Alice Coachman of Albany, Georgia won a gold medal in the high jump in 1948 at the Olympic Games in London, England. Coachman was the only American woman to take first place in track and field events during those Games and was also the first African-American woman to win a gold medal in the Olympics. "I was the country's best prospect, and I couldn't let my country down," explained Coachman of her victory.

The following year the *Chicago Defender* named Coachman, along with twenty-six other individuals and organizations, to its Honor Roll of Democracy for their "historic contributions to democracy and national unity." Coachman was the first in a long line of African-American females to excel in track and field at the Olympic Games.

In Rome in 1960, Wilma Rudolph became the first female athlete to win three gold medals in one Olympiad. Wyomia Tyus won a gold medal for the 100-meter dash in the 1964 Tokyo Olympics, and again in 1968 in Mexico City, becoming the first woman to win back-to-back gold medals.

More recent track and field wonders are sisters-in-law Jackie Joyner-Kersee and Florence Griffith Joyner. In the 1988 Olympics in Seoul, Korea, Joyner-Kersee won three gold medals, one silver, and one bronze, tying the record for second-most medals won by a female. Because of her versatility—exemplified by winning the gold in the seven-event heptathlon—Joyner-Kersee has been called "the world's greatest female athlete." Joyner-Kersee won gold in the heptathlon for a second time in the 1992 Olympics. The East St. Louis–born athlete was named Jacqueline, after Jacqueline Kennedy, by her grandmother, who said, "Someday this girl will be the first lady of something."

In the Seoul Olympics, Joyner won three gold and one silver medal in track events. Wearing Day-Glo track suits and heavy makeup, sporting long black locks and two-inch-long painted fingernails, FloJo's trademark femininity prompted one reporter to call her "a Maybelline advertisement waiting to happen." She herself has said, "Looking good is almost as important as running well."

AUGUST 8

In early August, 1929, *Publisher's Weekly* announced Guy Benton Johnson's upcoming book *John Henry: Tracking Down a Negro Legend*.

Johnson's book was the culmination of his search into the validity of a real-life John Henry. "All questions of the authenticity of the John Henry tradition," wrote Johnson, from the Institute for Research in Social Science at the University of North Carolina, "fade into insignificance before the incontrovertible fact that for his countless admirers John Henry is a reality. To them he will always be a hero, an idol, a symbol of the 'natural' man."

Called the black Paul Bunyan, John Henry represents the struggle between man and machines at the dawn of the industrial age. There are over fifty variations of the John Henry legend, which has remained popular as a ballad, work song, and folk story for over 100 years. Most versions maintain that John Henry was a steel driver who won a competition against a steam drill using only his hammer—and dropped dead immediately afterwards. Some claim that this happened while he was constructing the Big Bend Tunnel on the C&O railway line in 1873; still others contend that it took place while he worked in a quarry.

One of the earliest written versions was Roark Bradford's novel *John Henry*, published in 1931. Bradford alleges that John Henry was born weighing forty-four pounds. In Bradford's version, John Henry's demise came when he competed against a steam winch for rolling cotton:

> *And befo' he'd let dat steam winch burn him down,*
> *He'd die wid the hook in his hand, Lawd, Lawd,*
> *'Cause he's rollin' like a natchal man.*

AUGUST 9

In August 1974, Beverly Johnson became the first African-American to appear on the cover of *Vogue* magazine. The five-foot-nine-inch beauty was asked on a radio show if she was "the biggest black model in the business." She replied, "No, I'm not. I'm the biggest model—period."

Having appeared on hundreds of magazine covers and making a fortune in the high-fashion industry, Johnson branched into acting, appearing in the films *Meteor Man* and *Loaded Weapon I* in 1993. Johnson's daughter, Anansa, is also trying her hand at modelling.

In an interview in the January 11, 1993, *People Weekly*, Johnson discussed the damaging effects of being pressured to stay thin in the modelling business. "In our profession," explained Johnson, "clothes look better on a hanger, so you have to look like a hanger. It will never change. I personally took extreme methods to lose weight and as a result ended up bulimic and, at one time, when I was 27 or 28, anorexic. One day I was visiting my mom, and I had taken a shower, and my mother dragged me out of the bathroom. I said, 'What are you doing?' She stood me in front of her three-way mirror, and I looked like a Biafran. My ribs were poking out and I started to cry."

You have to be insightful. Prepare yourself for the transitions you will have to undertake in life.

—Beverly Johnson in *Right On* magazine, May 1979

AUGUST 10

On this muggy August day in New York in 1992, thousands of mourners passed through the lobby of Harlem's Apollo Theater to view the body of Ralph W. Cooper. For over 50 years Cooper was master of ceremonies of the famous Amateur Night at the Apollo. Cooper first introduced

Amateur Night in 1934, and it remains a Harlem tradition to this day.

Amateur Night's merciless audiences are as legendary as the performers that have graced the Apollo's stage. "This is the place to do or die," fretted one anxious singer interviewed in the *New York Times* on an Amateur Night in 1990. Many music greats—such as Ella Fitzgerald, Sarah Vaughn, Billy Holiday, Diana Ross, and James Brown—went through similar nerve-wracking experiences to get their start at the Apollo Theater.

Located on West 125th Street, this resplendent building was originally constructed in 1913 as an Irish music hall, then it became a whites-only burlesque hall. By the 1930s it was established for what it is best renowned—a showplace for African-American talent. A National Historic Landmark, it has survived some tough financial times. It was shut down in 1977 but later underwent a $16 million renovation and reopened in a gala ceremony in 1985.

> *Small and unprepossessing as it might have been, Harlem's Apollo Theatre was undoubtedly the most prestigious venue of all for black acts over many decades—both established stars and hopeful newcomers. Its infamous amateur nights have passed into legend, with unforgiving audiences likely to pelt unimpressive performers, and stagehands waiting in the wings to hook the no-hopers off the stage with a long pole. But if you conquered the Apollo crowd the world of black music was your oyster.*

—author Ralph Tee in *The Best of Soul: The Essential CD Guide*
(1993)

~~~~~~

AUGUST 11

Today in 1965, rioting broke out in the Watts section of Los Angeles, California, lasted for a week, and turned the neighborhood into a disaster area. Burn, baby, burn was the extremist slogan of these devastating riots. The spark that set off this inferno was the mistreatment by white police officers of an African-American youth under arrest for drunk driving. By week's end, Watts had suffered $175 million in fire damage and $46 million in property damage. The human toll—35 dead, 883 injured, and 3,598 arrested.

> *Baby, they walking in fours and kicking in doors; dropping Reds and busting heads; drinking wine and committing crime, shooting and looting; high-siding and low-riding, setting fires and slashing tires; turning over cars and burning down bars; making Parker mad and making me glad; putting an end to that 'go slow' crap and putting sweet Watts on the map—my black ass is in Folsom this morning but my black heart is in Watts!*

—an inmate of Folsom Prison sharing his thoughts on the Watts riots with other prisoners, from Eldridge Cleaver's *Soul on Ice* (1968)

AUGUST 12

During the second day of the 1965 Watts riots, comedian and civil rights activist Dick Gregory was shot in the leg while attempting, along with other African-American leaders, to help calm crowds on Central Avenue.

Gregory supported most of the major civil rights marches and protests in the 1960s and 1970s, both financially and with his physical presence. He ran for mayor of Chicago in 1966 and for president of the United States in 1968, both unsuccessfully. In the summer of 1968 he fasted for six weeks in solidarity with another American minority, the Native Americans. When told that he could achieve more with his comedy than with political activism, Gregory replied, "They didn't laugh Hitler out of existence, did they?"

A brilliant satirical comic, Gregory dealt with race issues and promoted black pride. He began as a comedian working in Chicago nightclubs, including the Playboy Club. An appearance on Jack Paar's late night talk show boosted his career, and soon he was a national success.

Gregory has also concerned himself with America's diet. In 1973 he wrote *Natural Diet for Folks Who Eat: Cookin' With Mother Nature.* He is also the creator of the *Slim Safe Bahamian Diet,* which has gained international popularity and annually grosses millions of dollars.

> *Personally, I've never seen much difference between the South and the North. Down South folks don't care how close I get as long as I don't get too big. Up North folks don't care how big I get as long as I don't get too close.*
>
> —Dick Gregory

AUGUST 13

An article in the *New York Times* dated August 13, 1962, read:

> *Elijah Muhammad, a 64-year-old Georgia Negro, told a crowd at Kiel Auditorium [that] the United States should say: "I'll give you a nice place to live and I will help you get started."*

By 1962 Elijah Muhammad was well established as the leader of the Black Muslims. Known as The Messenger of Allah, he called for a separate African-American nation within the United States. This powerful and controversial figure attacked the bedrock beliefs of the African-American Christian community by claiming that Christianity was the religion of slavery and was an instrument of oppression controlled by "white devils."

Muhammad began his climb up the ranks of the Nation of Islam after he founded Temple Number Two in Chicago in 1932. He became the Supreme Minister following the mysterious disappearance of Nation of Islam founder W. D. Fard, for which Muhammad had been accused of foul play. Under Elijah Muhammad's leadership, the Nation of Islam gained several hundred thousand black adherents. One hundred and fifty temples were opened in the United States and the Caribbean, and some fifty Islamic universities were established.

The "Lost-Found Nation of Islam here in this wilderness of North America" required strict discipline in personal conduct and encouraged inner-city African-Americans to open businesses. The Nation also instructed blacks to drop their names of bondage and replace them with Islamic names. Or they could simply adopt X, as did Malcolm X, to await the day that "God Himself returned and gave us a Holy name from His own mouth."

Elijah Muhammad died in Chicago on February 25, 1975, at the age of 77. Upon his death, his son Wallace D. Muhammad assumed leadership of the Nation. Wallace ushered in notable changes, such as opening up membership to whites, changing the name to the World Community of Islam, and divorcing the organization from the notion of a separate black nation with the United States.

He went down in the mud and got the brother that nobody else wanted. He got the brother from prison, the brother from the alley, the brother from the poolroom, the sister from the corner and he polished us up.

—Louis Farrakhan on Elijah Muhammad

AUGUST 14

On this day in 1883, in Charleston, South Carolina, Ernest Everett Just was born. Just is known for his pioneering work in cell research, doing much of his early research at the Woods Hole Marine Biology Lab in Massachusetts. He also taught at Harvard University, although his heart was really in research; it was "like putting an eagle in a chicken coop," explained colleague Benjamin Karpman.

Just was the first American to be invited to the prestigious Kaiser

Wilhelm Institute in Berlin, Germany, as a visiting professor. He spent most of his later years doing research in Europe, where he was better known in scientific circles and where he felt less discriminated against. In 1939, Just published *The Biology of the Cell Surface*, a highly-respected scientific work. The following year he was briefly held as a prisoner of war in France. Just returned to the United States only one year before he died.

Charles R. Drew called him, "a biologist of unusual skill and the greatest of our original thinkers in the field." Just was awarded the NAACP's Spingarn Medal in 1915 for his scientific research.

> *Living substance is such because it possesses this organization—something more than the sum of its minute parts. Life is exquisitely a time-thing like music.*
>
> —from *The Biology of the Cell Surface*

AUGUST 15

Today in 1843, at the National Convention of Colored Men, held in Buffalo, New York, a young Presbyterian preacher named Henry Highland Garnet delivered a speech urging slaves to strike and revolt. Below is an excerpt from this classic speech made by the "Thomas Paine of the abolitionist movement":

> *Brethren, the time has come when you must act for yourselves....Look around you, and behold the bosoms of your loving wives heaving with untold agonies! Hear the cries of your poor children! Remember the stripes your fathers bore. Think of the torture and disgrace of your noble mothers. Think of your wretched sisters, loving virtue and purity, as they are driven to concubinage and are exposed to the unbridled lusts of incarnate devils. Think of the undying glory that hangs around the ancient name of African—and forget not that you*

are native born American citizens, and as such, you are justly entitled to all the rights that are granted to the freest. Think how many tears you have poured out upon the soil which you have cultivated with unrequited toil and enriched with your blood; and then go to your lordly enslavers and tell them plainly, that you are determined to be free...*rather* die freemen, than live to be slaves.

Garnet delivered the above "Call to Rebellion" speech to over seventy delegates from twelve states attending the convention. His speech generated much discussion among delegates and later sparked a lively national debate. However, this revolutionary platform—which was defeated by a single vote—was not adopted by the Buffalo convention. Frederick Douglass, for one, opposed taking physical action.

AUGUST 16

Peter Salem, a Revolutionary War veteran and a hero of the Battle of Bunker Hill, died on this day in 1816. During the Battle of Bunker Hill (which actually took place on Breed's Hill) fought in June 1775, Salem shot down British royal marine Maj. John Pitcairn in the final assault. This famous battle rallied the colonies around the fight against the British.

A free black from Framingham, Massachusetts, Peter Salem belonged to the prestigious ranks of the Minutemen. These skilled fighters possessed weapons and were ready to defend the colony on short notice—they were the "rapid-deployment troops" of colonial days. Salem and fellow Minuteman Lemuel Haynes, the first African-American minister of a white congregation, were present at the defense of Concord Bridge. In this battle, which took place on April 19, 1775, the colonialists successfully forced the British back to Boston. Salem also saw action at Saratoga and Stony Point. After the war Salem lived near Leicester, Massachusetts, where he earned a living making woven cane.

AUGUST 17

On this day in 1833 an article by a wealthy Philadelphia merchant James Forten, appeared in the two-year-old abolitionist newspaper the *Liberator*. It read:

> *Has the God who made the white man and the black left any record declaring us a different species? Are we not sustained by the same power, supported by the same food, hurt by the same wounds, wounded by the same wrongs, pleased with the same delights, and propagated by the same means? And should we not then enjoy the same liberty, and be protected by the laws?*

This respected citizen promoted both African-American and women's rights. He owned a sail-making shop that employed forty workers, both black and white. He had been a sailor in the American navy during the Revolutionary War. During the War of 1812 he helped recruit 2,000 African-American volunteers to protect the city of Philadelphia from a potential British attack, which fortunately never took place.

Having rescued seven men from drowning in the Delaware River, Forten became something of a local hero. "On several occasions," wrote Polly Longsworth in *I, Charlotte Forten, Black and Free*, "all during the winter months, he jumped into the river fully clothed to rescue men from drowning. He never could understand why sailors and dockhands undertook their vocation without first learning how to swim."

AUGUST 18

August 18, 1906, was John Brown Day at the first convention held by the Niagara Movement. "We made pilgrimage at dawn barefooted to the scene of Brown's martyrdom," recalled W. E. B. DuBois, "and we talked

John Brown's Fort at Harper's Ferry

some of the plainest English that has been given voice to by black men in America."

Over 100 men and women had gathered at Harpers Ferry—where forty-seven years earlier John Brown made his historic stand against slavery—to discuss an agenda of African-American demands on their country. The conferees called for the right to vote, an end to discrimination in public accommodation, free speech, equal protection before the law, and proper education for black children.

Twenty-eight years later, conference participant J. B. Watson reminisced about the historic meeting:

What a mixture in one family of thought. I recall very well Priest Waller's red and sweaty face as he emerged from a committee room exclaiming with unction, 'How that fellow does swear.' DuBois was in the committee room. In the whole meeting DuBois insisted on having his way and had it as usual. Monroe Trotter was there snorting and gnashing. John Hope took to the meeting a cruse of oil in case of troubled water, but found he needed a tank of heavy viscosity. Though he, himself, at times forgot his oil, I believe Hope would go down as the pacifier of the meeting if there was one. Mary Church Terrell was there in her prime. Sutton E. Griggs strode about the grounds with a large book on abstruse philosophy under his arm. Hershaw, Tom Johnson and who-all. It would take all night to name and evaluate them all. All those, who, in the last twenty-five years, have employed, organized, legitimate protest, more or less have followed in the wake of the Niagaras.

The Niagara Movement was short-lived. It faded during the years following the Harpers Ferry Convention, reemerging in 1909 within the newly formed NAACP. Meanwhile, the "accommodation" camp, represented by Booker T. Washington, also lost steam, and the modern protest movement began to take shape.

~~~~~~

AUGUST 19

On this day in 1859, John Brown met with Frederick Douglass at an old stone quarry in Chambersburg, Pennsylvania, only one month before his famous attack on Harpers Ferry, Virginia. Douglass declined to join what he thought was a futile adventure and tried to dissuade Brown from going through with his plans. However, a runaway slave staying with Douglass, Shields Green, decided to join Brown's company of rebels.

Brown met with several famous African-Americans while planning his ill-fated attack. For instance, he sought out Maj. M. R. Delany at his home in Canada to discuss his strategy for insurrection. During this urgent and secretive meeting, Brown requested Delany's assistance in recruiting men for the rebellion and for Brown's Canada Convention. Delany gathered sixty or seventy colored men to join Brown, his son, and eleven or twelve young white men. "His scheme was nothing more than this," said Delany of Brown's plans, "to make Kansas, instead of Canada, the terminus of the Underground Railroad." For reasons unbeknownst to Delany, Brown changed his point of attack from Kansas to Harpers Ferry at the last minute.

AUGUST 20

On August 20, 1619, the first twenty African settlers arrived in the United States as indentured servants, landing in Jamestown Colony, Virginia, on a Dutch ship under the command of Captain Jope and an English pilot named Marmaduke. The ship was heading for the West Indies, but had been thrown off course when it was robbed by pirates. It was a momentous event, but at the time merited only passing mention in the journal of colonist John Rolfe, who wrote, "...there came a Dutch man-of-warre that sold us 20 Negars." The African arrivals bore Spanish names, such as Antoney, Isabella and Pedro. Four or five years later, Antoney and Isabella, gave birth to the first African-American child, William Tucker.

During the colonial era indentured servitude was legal and quite common among both blacks and whites. In fact, most of the earliest European arrivals to America came under this system. For instance, a white Englishwoman named Molly Welsh was forced into seven years of servitude in Maryland for allegedly stealing a pail of milk. Welsh was the grandmother of the mulatto surveyor and astronomer Benjamin Banneker. Upon completion of their terms of servitude, indentured servants were free to find other work or set up their own plantations; this was probably the course taken by the first twenty Africans in America.

The Negroes, like the monks of the Dark Ages, engross all the knowledge of the place, and being infinitely more adventurous and more knowing than their masters, carry on all the foreign trade; making frequent voyages in canoes, loaded with oysters, buttermilk and cabbages. They are great astrologers predicting the different changes of weather almost as accurately as an almanac.

—from a skit written by Washington Irving (1783–1859)

‹‹‹

AUGUST 21

This day in 1831 started as a typical antebellum Sunday. Planters in Southhampton County, Virginia, sat on their porches sipping apple brandy after attending Church, visiting with relatives and friends. Terror struck when a small band of slaves, led by Nat Turner, began killing all slave owners in their path—men, women, and children alike. "Remember," said Nat to his original band of men, "that ours is not a war for robbery, or to satisfy our passions; it is a struggle for freedom."

For three days the rebel slaves continued towards Jerusalem—the county seat, which they intended to seize—building support from fellow slaves along the way. Meanwhile, three thousand federal and state troops converged on Jerusalem, capturing and killing rebellious slaves, as well as innocent bystanders. All in all, over 120 blacks and 60 whites were killed. Turner was captured two months later and was hanged on November 11.

When Turner was born his mother was so distraught about bringing another child into slavery that she had to be restrained from killing him. But soon enough his mother was prophesying that her son was destined for greatness. By the 1820s Turner had become something of a local celebrity among both blacks and whites, with a reputation for extreme austerity. Turner knew that "to be great, [one] must appear so." Thus he kept largely to himself to help fire the mystery. He never smiled, never drank liquor, and never appeared to have any money. He became a Christian preacher and local prophet who had visions, such as seeing "drops of blood on the corn as though it were dew from heaven."

AUGUST 22

In August 1859, Captain Foster guided the slaver *Clotilde* into Mobile, Alabama, under a veil of secrecy. The vessel was laden with human cargo in violation of a ban on the international slave trade. To avoid being arrested by federal authorities, Captain Foster hid his African captives ashore and set fire to the ship. Foster and the ship's owner, Timothy Meaher, found it impossible to secure buyers for their contraband cargo and were forced to keep all the intended slaves themselves. Not long afterwards, at the outset of the Civil War, Meaher and Foster freed the *Clotilde* captives. The *Clotilde* was the last known slave ship to arrive in America.

Captain Foster had purchased the 130 slaves in West Africa from a Dahomey Prince who had raided an inland Tarkar village. One of the Tarkars, Ka Zoola, at one point apparently had an opportunity to escape

Slave ship

but opted to stay with the captives to remain with his wife. Ka Zoola (later called Cud-Joe Lewis) and his wife Celia kept the Tarkar villagers together after being freed and formed a village called Affriky Town, now Plateau, Alabama. The Tarkars maintained many of their African customs, their language, and traditional names.

Despite the fact that as of January 1, 1808, Congress had banned the international slave trade, it is believed that from 1808 to 1857 as many as 250,000 slaves arrived in the United States illegally.

> *The history of the world shows us, that the deliverance of the children of Israel from bondage is not the only instance, in which it has pleased God to appear in behalf of oppressed and distressed nations.*
>
> —from Absalom Jones's "A Thanksgiving Sermon," delivered on January 1, 1808, upon abolition of the slave trade

AUGUST 23

On August 23, 1923, a confident, young writer named Walter White penned a letter to a potential editor defending his novel *The Fire in the Flint*, which dealt with American race relations and southern violence. White wrote:

> *I was born in Georgia. For twenty-four years I lived there. Between my junior and senior years in college I sold life insurance in that state, spending nearly four months living in small towns of which Central City is typical. There I talked with and learned to know white and colored people of all classes, particularly the better type....since I have been in my present work I have personally investigated thirty-six lynchings and eight race riots. Because of the peculiar advantage I possess of being able to go either as a white man or a colored man I have talked on terms of intimacy with hundreds of white*

men as one of them *and to hundreds, nay thousands, of Negroes as one of them. I hope I am not too over confident when I say that this varied and intimate experience in garnering all shades of opinion should qualify me to speak with some degree of authority on this subject.*

Although this particular editor rejected White's book, another one picked it up. White wrote several other books after this, including another novel called *Flight* (1926) and the autobiographical *A Man Called White* (1969).

White is probably best known for his years as executive secretary of the NAACP. He joined the organization in 1918 as assistant secretary of the national office in New York City. Living in New York during the Roaring Twenties, he became one of the Harlem Renaissance *literati*, not only contributing his own innovative writings but also using his power and influence to help promote African-American artists.

White was awarded the NAACP's Spingarn Medal in 1937 for his investigations of lynchings and race riots, and for his "remarkable tact, skill and persuasiveness" in lobbying to enact a federal antilynching bill. During one investigation in Tulsa, Oklahoma, the light-skinned White "passed" so successfully that he was made deputy sheriff and told, "Now you can go out and shoot any nigger you see and the law'll be behind you." White died March 21, 1955.

AUGUST 24

Sir,

For three years I have toured the principle cities of Germany, Austria, Hungary, where my representations have been crowned with the greatest success. It is unheard of that a person of African nationality should play dramatic roles. The success I have had in the greatest theaters of Germany, has increased my desire to make an attempt in the French capital.

His Majesty, the King of Prussia, has condescended to honor me with the Large Gold Medal for Art and Sciences, the Emperor of Austria with the Medal of Ferdinand, and Switzerland with the White Cross.

My intention is to come to France with a troupe of English players to give the following: Othello, Macbeth, King Lear, Richard III, The Merchant of Venice. I ask for a guarantee to cover the expenses I will have to bring my troupe to Paris. For each performance I ask for half the net receipts or a fixed salary. Waiting for the favor of your prompt reply.

Ira Aldridge, African Tragedian

The great Shakespearean actor Ira Aldridge wrote this letter on August 24, 1854, to a theater manager in Paris. Aldridge did play in Paris, as well as virtually every other major European capital. He became known on the Continent as the African Roscius, after a slave-actor of ancient Rome. His crowning achievement was the role of Othello. Since Othello was a dark-skinned Moor, Aldridge was able to act without the white face paint that he normally donned for his other Shakespearean roles.

The grandson of a Senegalese chief, Aldridge was born on July 24, 1807, in New York City. He began acting as a teenager in New York, then went to Scotland to obtain a university education but ended up on the stage in London. He became a British subject in 1863, married first an Englishwoman, who died, and then the Countess Amanda Pauline Brandt, a Swedish opera singer.

After the slaves were emancipated in America, Aldridge began planning a triumphant tour of his native land. Unfortunately, he fell ill and died on August 7, 1867, in Lodz, Poland, before he could embark on his American tour.

~~~~~~

AUGUST 25

The following poem was written by the slave Lucy Terry (1730–1821) describing a massacre that occurred in her village, Deerfield, Massachusetts, on August 25, 1746. This is believed to be the best record of the incident.

BARS FIGHT

August 'twas the twenty-fifth
Seventeen hundred forty-six
The Indians did in ambush lay
Some very valiant men to slay
Twas nigh unto Sam Dickinson's mill,
The Indians there five men did kill
The names of whom I'll not leave out
Samuel Allen like a hero fout
And though he was so brave and bold
His face no more shall we behold
Eleazer Hawks was killed outright
Before he had time to fight
Before he did the Indians see
Was shot and killed immediately
Oliver Amsden he was slain
Which caused his friends much grief and pain
Simeon Amsden they found dead
Not many rods off from his head.
Adonijah Gillet, we do hear
Did lose his life which was so dear
John Saddler fled across the water
And so escaped the dreadful slaughter
Eunice Allen see the Indians comeing
And hoped to save herself by running
And had not her petticoats stopt her

The awful creatures had not cotched her
And tommyhawked her on the head
And left her on the ground for dead.
Young Samuel Allen, Oh! lack-a-day
Was taken and carried to Canada.

This is the first poem known to be written by an African-American. It was passed down in oral form through several generations, until 1855, when Josiah Gilbert Holland published it in his book *The History of Western Massachusetts*.

~~~~~~

AUGUST 26

Norbert Rillieux registered Patent No. 3,237 for a Vacuum-Pan Evaporator at the U.S. Patent Office on this day in 1843. The Rillieux Evaporator revolutionized the sugar industry worldwide. His system increased fuel efficiency and made possible the production of refined and granulated sugar. Previously the same work had been done by hand, resulting in a crude, caramel-colored form of sugar. The principles of the Rillieux system are incorporated in all modern industrial evaporation processes, such as making soap, gelatin, glue, and condensed milk.

An engineer and Egyptologist, Rillieux was the son of a slave and a French planter. As a resident of New Orleans, he was dogged by racial prejudice. He left the city in 1854 after a requirement that African-Americans carry passes pushed him over the limit. He died in Paris in 1894 at the age of 89.

In the early 1900s scientists and sugar industry organizations commissioned a commemorative bronze plaque to be made in his honor. The plaque, crafted in Amsterdam, was donated to the Louisiana State Museum in New Orleans.

I have always held that Rillieux's invention is the greatest in
the history of American chemical engineering and I know of

no other invention that has brought so great a saving to all branches of chemical engineering.

—Charles A. Brown, sugar chemist, U.S. Department of
Agriculture

~~~~~~

AUGUST 27

Today in 1975, the last episode of *Mannix* aired on CBS. The one-hour television drama featured the character Joe Mannix, a Los Angeles detective. Actress Gail Fisher costarred as Peggy Fair, Mannix's girl friday.

For her role in *Mannix*, Fisher won the 1969–1970 Emmy for Outstanding Performance by an Actress in a Supporting Role in Drama. She was the first African-American female to win an Emmy, television's best-known prize. Fisher was nominated for the same award for the following three years.

"Unfortunately," wrote the author of *Black Women in Television* (1990), "Fisher never had the opportunity to appear regularly on another series. This was a true waste of talent."

~~~~~~

AUGUST 28

It was a balmy eighty-four-degrees in Washington, D.C. on this Wednesday in 1963, when 250,000 people marched down Constitution and Independence Avenues to the Lincoln Memorial in the largest civil rights demonstration in U.S. history. Asa Philip Randolph had been threatening to march on Washington since 1941. Now in his seventies, he—along with colleagues and supporters of the NAACP, SCLC, SNICK, CORE, and the National Urban League—had arrived in force.

Americans of every color and persuasion, including 60,000 whites, came to D.C. They came from far and wide in support of more freedom and jobs for African-Americans, and to push Congress to pass the Civil Rights Bill. Marlon Brando and Harry Belafonte jetted in. David Parker, a pants presser from Los Angeles, drove across America to the nation's capital with five friends "because my people got troubles," he said. A Jewish rabbi and a Presbyterian leader were among the speakers.

When Mahalia Jackson sang, "I'm gonna tell my Lord, When I get home. I'm gonna tell my Lord, When I get home. Just how LONG you've been treating me wrong," the crowded roared with cheers and shouts. And they cried and cheered hysterically when Martin Luther King Jr. delivered one of the most famous and oft-quoted speeches of our century—"I Have a Dream."

> *I have a dream that my four little children will one day live in a nation where they will not be judged by the color of their skin, but by the content of their character. I have a dream that one day in Alabama, with this vicious racist, its Governor, having his lips dripping the words of interposition and nullification—one day right there in Alabama, little black boys and little black girls will be able to join hands with little white boys and little white girls as brothers and sisters.*
>
> *I have a dream that one day every valley shall be exalted, every hill and mountain shall be made low, the rough places will be made plane, the crooked places will be made straight and the glory of the Lord shall be revealed, and all flesh shall see it together....*

AUGUST 29

Two notable events occurred in the life of Gen. Daniel "Chappie" James on this day in 1975. He was appointed commander in chief of the North American Air Defense Command (NORAD) and of the Aerospace Defense Command, and he became the first African-American four-star general. James had been one of the first African-American pilots in the army air corps during World War II. The six-foot-five-inch Tuskegee Institute graduate also flew missions during the Korean and Vietnam Wars.

I have a deep and abiding belief in my country and her security.

—General "Chappie" James

On this same day in 1962, Malvin R. Goode became the first African-American newscaster on network television. The 54-year-old newsman was assigned to cover the United Nations for the American Broadcasting Company (ABC). He had formerly worked in newspaper, radio, and television in Pittsburgh, Pennsylvania, where he had his own radio news program.

~~~~~~

AUGUST 30

Today in 1983, the space shuttle Challenger blasted off in the dark from Kennedy Space Center in Florida, carrying the first African-American astronaut to go into space. Forty-year-old Col. Guion S. Bluford Jr., a mission specialist, tested the Challenger's mechanical arm, helped launch weather and communications satellites, and performed experiments in electrophoresis.

Born on November 22, 1942, in Philadelphia, Pennsylvania, "Guy" Bluford was always interested in flying. He had dreamed of becoming an aerospace engineer since junior high school. He began his flying career in the air force, executing 144 combat missions over Vietnam. He earned his Ph.D. in aerospace engineering from the Air Force Institute of Technology in 1978—the same year he was accepted into the National Aeronautics and Space Administration (NASA) astronaut program out of 8,078 candidates. In 1983 he became the first African-American astronaut to go into space,* and in 1985 he was on the crew of America's first spacelab mission, the Orbiter Challenger.

> *It really proved to be better than I expected. It gives me a chance to use all my skills and do something that is pretty exciting. The job is so fantastic, you don't need a hobby. The hobby is going to work.*
>
> —Bluford on his job at NASA

~~~~~~

AUGUST 31

On this day in 1921, Marcus Garvey was inaugurated provisional president of the "Republic of Africa." One year earlier, riding in an open-top touring car, Garvey led an extravagant parade through Harlem. As the president-general of the Universal Negro Improvement Association (UNIA), Garvey was dressed in full regalia and was accompanied by hundreds of black "soldiers" in crisp, colorful uniforms. The parade marked the opening of the first International Convention of the Negro Peoples of the World. Held at Liberty Hall, the convention lasted for thirty days.

Garvey had come to New York from Jamaica in 1916 looking for support for his UNIA, which encouraged blacks to return to Africa and wanted to see African states freed from colonialism.

The slogan of Garvey's nationalist and separatist movement was Africa for the Africans. This charismatic leader even raised funds to purchase a steamship to carry Africans back to Africa. The substance and tactics of Garvey's platform, however, were somewhat unclear; Garvey himself never set foot in Africa.

---

*Bluford was not the first person of African descent to go into space. Arnaldo Tamayo Méndez, a Cuban of African descent, was aboard the Soviet Union's Soyuz 38 in 1980.

Despite the fact that his detractors called him outlandish, misguided and a failure, he succeeded in raising black consciousness—and over $10 million in two years. He also organized the first grass-roots mass movement of blacks in America.

Garvey was convicted of mail fraud in 1923, for which he served time in Atlanta's federal prison before being deported to Jamaica.

We of the U.N.I.A. believe that what is good for other folks is good for us. If government is something that is appreciable and helpful and protective to others, then we also want to experiment in government. We do not mean a government that will make us citizens without rights or subjects without consideration. We mean a kind of government that will place our race in control, even as other races are in control of their own government....We should say to the millions who are in Africa to hold the fort, for we are coming 400,000,000 strong.

—Garvey speaking to the UNIA in 1922

SEPTEMBER 1

On the first day of September, 1871, four privates of the all-black Ninth Calvary attacked twenty-eight Native Americans to recover a stolen herd of cattle. They were led by their white lieutenant, John Lapham Bullis, and engaged in battle for half an hour.

After the Civil War, the U.S. Army was occupied primarily in the western frontier fighting hostile Indians, border bandits, and outlaws, as well as protecting settlers and pacifying rowdy frontier towns. There were ten calvary regiments and twenty-five infantry regiments stationed in the West. The Ninth and Tenth Calvary and the Twenty-fourth and Twenty-fifth Infantry were all-black units serving under white commanding officers. In the 25 years or so that the all-black outfits were stationed on the American frontier, they engaged in some 200 battles, several times coming to the rescue of white troops.

The most famous such incident occurred not on the western frontier, but in Cuba, in 1898, during the Spanish-American War. African-American soldiers of the Ninth and Tenth Calvary came to the rescue of Roosevelt's hemmed in Rough Riders during the battle of San Juan Hill. Several of these fighting men were awarded Medals of Honor for their bravery. Recalling the historic charge up San Juan Hill, one Rough Rider said:

> *I joined the troop of the Tenth Calvary and for a time fought with them shoulder to shoulder, and in justice to the colored race I must say I never saw braver men anywhere. Some of those who rushed up the hill will live in my memory forever.*

A white southerner agreed, remarking, "I've changed my opinion of the colored folks, for all of the men I saw fighting, there were none to beat the Tenth Calvary and the colored infantry at Santiago, and I don't mind saying so."

Native Americans were likewise impressed by the bravery and fighting skills of African-American military units. They called the black troops Buffalo Soldiers because their wooly hair was reminiscent of bison, an animal the Indians respected for their size and strength.

From 1870 to 1890, fourteen African-American soldiers received Medals of Honor for bravery, and many others won Certificates of Merit.

SEPTEMBER 2

The last episode of the television drama *I Spy* aired on this night in 1968. The show followed two undercover agents on their escapades around the world. Bill Cosby played Alexander Scott, or Scotty, a Rhodes Scholar who masqueraded as a trainer to a tennis pro. Robert Culp played his partner Kelly Robinson, the supposed tennis pro. When *I Spy* first aired in September 1965, Cosby became the first African-American actor to star in a network dramatic series. He won three Emmys for his role as Scotty.

Cosby went on to become one of America's most successful television and film stars. From 1984 to 1992 he starred as Dr. Heathcliff Huxtable on *The Cosby Show*, one of the highest rated sitcoms in history. *The Cosby Show* is credited with helping NBC rise to the number one spot in television ratings, and set the stage for a host of television sitcoms about family life.

> *People who live in glass houses shouldn't walk around in their underwear.*
>
> —from Cosby's "Fat Albert's Survival Kit" (1975)

> *If white America chooses to withhold equality from the black man, the result is going to be a disaster for this country. But if*

whites allow the black man the same civil rights they them-
selves take for granted, then they're really in store for a shock;
this country will turn into the coolest and grooviest society the
world has ever seen.

—Cosby in a *Playboy* interview, May 1969

SEPTEMBER 3

On this day in 1922, Bessie Coleman made her first flight in an American airplane at an exhibition honoring the all-black Fifteenth Infantry Regiment of the New York National Guard. An African-American parachutist was also featured in the show. Coleman had recently returned from France, where, in 1921, she had received a pilot's license from the Fédération Aéronautique International. She was the first black, as well as the first American woman, to get an international pilot's license.

Born in 1893 in Texas to sharecropper parents, Coleman was the twelfth of thirteen children. She was inspired to become a pilot by Eugene Jacques Bullard, an African-American who flew for the French during World War I. Coleman was refused admission to flight-training

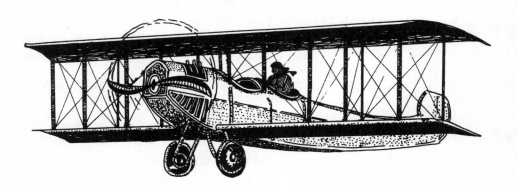

schools in America because of her color and sex. Undeterred, she learned to speak French while working as a manicurist. In 1920 she travelled to France, and in ten months acquired an airplane pilot's license.

After returning to America in August 1922—now a celebrity—she toured the country doing daredevil stunts at air shows. On April 30, 1926, she died when her plane crashed during a test flight in Jacksonville, Florida, dashing her plans to open a flight training school for African-Americans.

SEPTEMBER 4

On this day in 1781, forty-six settlers from Mexico founded Los Angeles, California. Twenty-six of these pioneers were recorded as being mulattos—of mixed African, Spanish, and Native American descent in varying amounts.

The first U.S. census in 1790 counted over 750,000 African-Americans, or about one-fifth of the total population of the country. Not surprisingly then, in nearly 200 years of history, Africans were one of the largest ethnic groups on America's western frontier, possibly outnumbering those inveterate frontier people, the Germans and the Scots-Irish.

Besides the many everyday, behind-the-scenes African-Americans on the frontier, such as trail cooks and cowboys, there was a host of legendary figures in the leagues of cowpuncher and marksman Nat Love (Deadwood Dick) and mountain man James Beckwourth. Other African-American characters of the Old West included: Aunt Sally Campbell, the first non–Native American woman to arrive in the Black Hills of South Dakota and a gold miner in Deadwood; mulatto Barney Ford, owner of restaurants and hotels in mining towns in Colorado and Wyoming, who both amassed and lost fortunes; and John Swain, one of the toughest citizens of Tombstone, Arizona, the town "too tough to die." Swain was a contender for the world heavyweight boxing championship in 1884.

There was also the six-foot tall, 200-pound mail carrier, Stagecoach Mary, who liked to smoke cigars and down shots of whiskey. She once knocked out a delinquent debtor with a single punch. And Annie Neal, sharpshooter and owner of the Mountain View Hotel in Oracle, Arizona, bragged that Buffalo Bill Cody was "the only hotel guest to whom I ever lost a shooting match."

~~~~~~

SEPTEMBER 5

Our Nig; or Sketches From the Life of a Free Black, in a Two-Story White House, North, Showing that Slavery's Shadows Fall Even There was self-published by author Harriet E. Adams Wilson on this day in 1859. This was the first novel written by an African-American to be published in the United States.

Wilson published the book in an effort to raise money to save her dying son. "Deserted by kindred," she wrote in the book's preface, "disabled by failing health, I am forced to some experiment which shall aid me in maintaining myself and child without extinguishing this feeble life." Wilson's son died at the age of eight, six months after publication of her book.

Despite its historical importance, the book remained in obscurity until 1983, when it was republished by Henry Louis Gates Jr.

> *Frado, under the instructions of Aunt Abby and the minister, became a believer in a future existence—one of happiness or misery. Her doubt was, is there a heaven for the black? She knew there was one for James, and Aunt Abby, and all good white people; but was there any for blacks? She had listened attentively to all the minister said, and all Aunt Abby had told her; but then it was all for white people.*
>
> —from *Our Nig*, Chapter 8, "Visitor and Departure"

SEPTEMBER 6

An intense twenty-two-hour operation to separate Siamese twins joined at the head concluded on this day in 1987. Ben Carson, Director of Pediatric Neurosurgery at John Hopkins Hospital in Baltimore, Maryland, led the team of more than seventy doctors and nurses who performed the operation. Carson noted that the team "did everything humanly possible" to carry out the first successful separation of this kind. Although the complicated procedure took at least five months to plan and cost hundreds of thousands of dollars, none of the surgeons accepted payment for the operation.

Carson grew up in a lower-class neighborhood in Detroit, Michigan. He received a scholarship from Yale University and also attended the University of Michigan Medical School. In 1984, at the age of 33, he became head of the pediatric neurosurgery unit at Johns Hopkins. Called the "most celebrated pediatric neurosurgeon in the world," Carson has written an autobiography, *Gifted Hands*, and a motivational book called *Think Big*.

From my mother I learned about being nice to other people—regardless of who they are or what they have achieved (or haven't achieved!). Mother used to say, "Be nice to everybody. You meet the same people going up as you meet going down.

"We cannot overload the human brain. This divinely created brain has fourteen billion cells. If used to the maximum, this human computer inside our heads could contain all the knowledge of humanity from the beginning of the world to the present and still have room left over.

—from *Think Big* (1992)

SEPTEMBER 7

John Minton's "Reminiscences of Experiences on the Oregon Trail in 1844" appeared in the September 1901 issue of the *Quarterly of the Oregon Historical Society*. In the article, Minton, a white pioneer, recalled meeting the free Negro George Bush along the Oregon Trail in early September 1844:

> *Bush was a mulatto, but had means, and also a white woman for a wife, and a family of five children. Not many men of color left a slave state so well to do, and so generally respected; but it was not in the nature of things that he should be permitted to forget his color. As we went along together, he riding a mule and I on foot, he led the conversation to this subject. He told me he should watch, when we got to Oregon, what usuage was awarded to people of color, and if he could not have a free man's rights he would seek the protection of the Mexican Government in California or New Mexico. He said there were few in that train he would say as much to as he had just said to me.*

Bush was believed to be the son of a slave father and Irish maid mother. He led a party of six wagons, in which there were three white families, to the Oregon Territory, where he established the first settlement north of the Columbia River. The Bush party settled in the Puget Sound area near Fort Nisqually, a Hudson Bay Company post. There they built the first sawmill and gristmill, and introduced the mower and the reaper to America.

Bush became a prosperous farmer—as he had been in Missouri—this time on 640 acres. A patriarchal figure in the region, he assisted new arrivals with accommodation and food, and gave aid to the needy. Today Bush Prairie bears this brave, industrious, and charitable pioneer's name.

SEPTEMBER 8

On September 8, 1981, President Reagan ordered the American flag to be flown at half-mast at all government properties in honor of Roy Wilkins, who had died that day at the age of 80. Wilkins served as executive director of the NAACP for twenty-two years—until he physically couldn't work anymore. He had also edited the NAACP's magazine the *Crisis* for about fifteen years.

Wilkins has been described as "courtly, gracious, gentle, quiet, effective and wise." He has also been criticized for being too conservative. Nonetheless, under his leadership the NAACP was successful in effecting many institutional changes for the benefit of African-Americans.

> *He was among the last of a generation of civil rights leaders who pulled and tugged and cajoled the nation through decades of change so profound that many Americans cannot imagine, still less remember, what segregation was like.*

> —*Newsweek* magazine

SEPTEMBER 9

On this day in 1739, the bloodiest slave rebellion of the century ignited at Stono, South Carolina, outside of Charleston. Twenty Angolans, led by a slave named Cato, seized weapons from a storehouse and began marching toward Florida, gathering support from other slaves along the way. Planters soon suppressed the runaways and slaughtered them in a field where they had been drinking and dancing in premature celebration. The planters "cut off their heads and set them up at every Mile Post they came to." Twenty-one whites and at least forty-four blacks were killed in the uprising.

South Carolina—at the time America's southern frontier—was repeatedly rocked by slave rebellions and acts of discontent during the eighteenth century. To list a few:

1720: *A plot to kill the whites and take over the town was uncovered in Goose Creek quarters.*

1730: *An uprising was planned for August 30 in Charleston.*

1733: *Large slave meetings were reported.*

1737: *Three Africans were arrested for conspiracy.*

1766: *107 slaves were reported "to have left masters and...fled to join runaways already in Colleton County swamps."*

One historian noted, "What visions of expansion and greater wealth the planters had were clouded by the danger of insurrection by the new and half-savage slaves. Formerly the problem of defense had been largely external, represented by the Spaniard and Indian, but by 1729 there had come about a fundamental change."

SEPTEMBER 10

This is the time of year when students are registering in colleges and universities across America. Below is a reminder of the historic trials and tribulations of one African-American student, James H. Meredith, when trying to register for school in 1962.

September 10: The U.S. Supreme Court ordered the University of Mississippi to admit James H. Meredith, a 29-year-old air force veteran. Meredith's application had been on file for fourteen months.

September 20: The governor of Mississippi, Ross R. Barnett, physically blocked Meredith from entering "Ole Miss." The Governor claimed he would rather die first.

September 24: The U.S. Circuit Court of Appeals ordered the Mississippi Board of Higher Education to allow Meredith into the school or face contempt of court charges. The board agreed to comply.

September 25: Again Governor Barnett personally stopped Meredith from registering at the university.

September 30: Meredith was escorted to the University of Mississippi campus by 15,000 federal marshals and soldiers. Rioting broke out on campus and in the town of Oxford, during which two people were killed and many others were injured.

October 1: Federal troops restored calm on the campus and in town. Finally, Meredith was able to register for classes. "It's more for America than for me," said Meredith.

Contrary to popular belief, Meredith was not the first American of African descent to attend the University of Mississippi. Harry Murphy of Atlanta, who successfully passed as a white student, was actually the first.

~~~~~~

SEPTEMBER 11

Time and trial, and anxiety, have made a wreck of Abraham. Yet he is straight, and active, and looks more intelligent out of one eye than many people look out of two. He is in full costume of the Seminoles. Turban, a la Turk, and hunting shirt, leggins, etc.

The national press was abuzz over the Negro interpreter accompanying a government delegation that arrived at the American Hotel in New York City on September 11, 1852. Over a decade earlier, Abraham had been one of the major players in the notorious Seminole Wars. This distinguished Seminole Negro had been living for years in relative obscurity, raising cattle along the Little River in Indian territory, when he was called out of semi-retirement by the U.S. government. His country had enlisted his aid to convince Chief Billy Bowlegs—the leader of renegade Seminoles still living in Florida—to surrender and move west into Indian territories. Bowlegs promised to comply but reneged, igniting the third Seminole War.

Abraham first attracted public attention in 1825–1826, when he accompanied the Seminole chief Mikonopi to Washington, D.C. as an interpreter. He was described by one observer as the "sense-bearer to the King." The U.S. government recognized Abraham's "sense-bearing" role and tried to court Abraham in the 1830s, hoping he would influence the Seminoles to quit Florida and move to designated Indian territories further west. Instead, Abraham was the main force behind preparing the Seminoles for resistance. He also led many battles in the early stages of the Seminole Wars.

Born a slave in the late 1700s, Abraham ran away to the Seminole nation, where "slaves" were treated largely as equals, though they were required to pay an annual tribute in the form of agricultural produce.

SEPTEMBER 12

On this day in 1992, Mae Jemison became the first African-American woman to go into space. "I'm extremely excited to be on the flight," said Jemison before the space shuttle Endeavor blasted off from Cape Canaveral, Florida, "because it's something that I wanted to do since I was a small child."

The 35-year-old Chicago native did experiments in weightlessness and motion sickness during the seven-day flight. Accompanying the first African-American woman in space were the first married couple and the first Japanese astronaut on board an American space mission.

Four African-American men preceded Jemison into space, beginning with Guion S. Bluford Jr. in 1983.

Jemison got an early start in life, at the age of 16 enrolling in Stanford University, where she studied chemical engineering and Afro-American studies. She then attended the Cornell University Medical College, after which she worked for a few years as a Peace Corps doctor in West Africa. Jemison was accepted into the NASA program as a science specialist in 1987. This physician and chemical engineer believes that space "is a birthright of everyone who is on this planet."

It's important not only for a little black girl growing up to know, yeah, you can become an astronaut because here's Mae Jemison. But it's important for older white males who sometimes make decisions on those careers of those little black girls.

—Jemison speaking to The Associated Press

SEPTEMBER 13

On this day in 1971, five days of rioting at the maximum-security prison in Attica, New York, came to a dramatic conclusion. "The rebellion at the Attica Correctional Facility ended this morning in a bloody clash and mass deaths that four days of taut negotiations had sought to avert," wrote the *New York Times*. "1,000 state troopers, sheriff's deputies and prison guards stormed the prison under a low-flying pall of tear gas dropped by helicopters."

The majority of the security guards at Attica were white, while 85 percent of the inmates were African-American and Puerto Rican. The inmates had become increasingly politically aware and had expressed grievances over poor conditions, as well as more explosive race issues. Inmates took control of cellblock D after tensions reached the boiling point. Forty-three inmates and hostages died at Attica, making it the second deadliest prison riot in U.S. history.*

---

*On April 21, 1930, at Ohio State Penitentiary, rioting inmates started a fire which trapped 317 prisoners in their cells, killing them all.

Four years earlier, President Lyndon B. Johnson had assembled the Kerner Commission to examine the underlying causes of the over 160 violent protests that rocked America that year. According to the commission, America's criminal justice system was one factor. Chapter 11 of their report noted "shortcomings throughout the system," such as, "assembly-line justice in teeming lower courts...wide disparities in sentences...antiquated corrections facilities...inequities imposed by the system on the poor—who, for example, the option of bail only means jail."

According to the book *Songs of My People*, a 1990 survey found that one out of every four black men were either in prison or under court supervision.

~~~~~~

SEPTEMBER 14

On this day in 1929, Speckled Red recorded the song "The Dirty Dozen" on the Brunswick Label in Memphis, Tennessee. It included the phrases:

I like your mama, I like your sister too,
I liked your daddy, but your daddy wouldn't do...

Slip you in the "Dozens," your pappy is your cousin,
And your mama do the Lordy-Lord...

Your face is all hid now your back's all bare,
If you ain't doin' the bobo, what's your head doin' down there?

Speckled Red had recorded classic examples of the uniquely African-American comedy form called Playing the Dozens. The Dozens involves flinging one-line insults at one another, often attacking the other's mother, and the meaner the better. The name comes from the dice game craps, in which twelve is the worst throw.

Called the blues of comedy, the Dozens is believed to have its roots in slavery, when slaves weaved insults and scandal into songs as a way of venting anger against an oppressive system. By the late 1800s, Putting in the Dozens had become a folk game in which players hurled nasty insults at each other until someone lost their temper. For a while the Dozens was a fringe form of blues music, like Speckled Red's tune. Bo Diddley's 1960 hit song "Say Man" was basically a recording of Diddley and his old friend and maracas player Jerome Green playing the Dozens. In this tune, Diddley recalls a gal so ugly she had to sneak up on a glass of water to get a drink. More recently the Dozens has become a spoken comedy form, as with the examples below:

Your mother is so old, she can read the Bible and reminisce. (Hugh Moore)

You're so ugly, your family sent you to the store for bread, and then moved.

Your brother is so stupid, he thought Boyz II Men was a daycare center.

~~~~~~

SEPTEMBER 15

On Sunday, September 15, 1963, a stick of dynamite was thrown into the basement of the 16th Street Baptist Church in Birmingham, Alabama. The blast killed four African-American girls who were attending Sunday school—Addie Mae Collins, Denise McNair, Carol Robertson, and Cynthia Wesley. The day of worship turned into a day of rioting between protestors and Birmingham's all-white police force.

This event marked an abrupt turn in race relations in the city. A horrified populace had had enough of a year of violence and accepted desegregation of the city.

And it [1963] ended in the bombing of a church in Alabama where four little girls, Christians, sitting in Sunday school, singing about Jesus, were blown apart by people who claim to be Christians. And this happened in the year 1963, the year that they said in that country would mark a hundred years of good relations between the races.

—Malcolm X speech at the London School of Economics, February 11, 1965

The 16th Street Baptist Church

SEPTEMBER 16

William Whipper's "An Address on Non-resistance to Offensive Aggression" appeared on September 16, 1837, in the *Colored American.*

Whipper was one of the first persons in the world to theorize on nonviolence. Whipper's landmark essay was published twelve years before American author and poet Henry David Thoreau wrote his famous treatise on the same subject.

Whipper was the darling of the abolitionists. His colleague William Still, the "president" of the Underground Railroad, explained that "in the more important conventions which have been held among the colored people for the last thirty years, perhaps no other colored man has been so often called on to draft resolutions and prepare addresses, as the modest and earnest William Whipper."

In addition to being an activist, Whipper owned, with his cousin Stephen Smith, a prosperous lumber yard in Columbia, Pennsylvania. This enterprise doubled as an important station on the Underground Railroad.

The following are excerpts from Whipper's tract on nonviolence:

The practice of non-resistance to physical aggression is not only consistent with reason, but the surest method of obtaining a speedy triumph of the principle of universal peace.

The love of power is one of the greatest human infirmities, and with it comes the usurping influence of despotism, the mother of slavery.

There is scarcely a single fact more worthy of indelible record than the utter inefficiency of human punishments to cure human evils.

SEPTEMBER 17

On this day in 1983, in Atlantic City, New Jersey, the first African-American Miss America was crowned. At the age of 20, Vanessa Williams of New York had won America's foremost beauty pageant.

Williams's crown was stripped from her ten months later after photos in which she posed nude were published in *Penthouse* magazine. The title went to runner-up Suzette Charles of New Jersey, also an African-American. Williams then embarked on a successful acting and singing career.

I've been "not Black enough." When I became the first Black Miss America, there was feedback that I wasn't representative of Black America because I didn't have true African-American features—my eyes are green, I have lighter skin.

—Vanessa Williams in *USA Weekend*, June 28, 1991

~~~~~~

SEPTEMBER 18

Today in 1895, Booker T. Washington delivered his famous speech at the Cotton States and International Exposition in Atlanta, Georgia. Known as the Atlanta Compromise, he proposed vocational education as opposed to academics as the way forward for African-Americans:

> ...*To those of my race who depend on bettering their condition in a foreign land, or who underestimate the importance of cultivating friendly relations with the Southern white man, who is their next door neighbor, I would say: "Cast down your bucket where you are"—cast it down in making friends in every manly way of the people of all races by whom we are surrounded. Cast it down in agriculture, mechanics, in commerce, in domestic service, and in the professions....No race can prosper till it learns there is as much dignity in tilling a field as in writing a poem. It is at the bottom of life we must begin, and not at the top. Nor shall we permit our grievances to overshadow our opportunities.*

The mostly white audience received his speech with great applause, as did much of the rest of America. Soon voices of dissent began to surface. Many African-Americans viewed Washington's platform as accepting second-class citizenship.

"I regard it as cowardly and dishonest for any of our colored men to tell white people or colored people that we are not struggling for equality," commented John Hope, a prominent educator of the day and future president of Atlanta University, "If money, education, and honesty will not bring to me as much privilege, as much equality as they bring to any American citizen, then they are to me a curse, and not a blessing."

Another rebuttal came from African Methodist Episcopal bishop Henry McNeal Turner, who said, "the colored man who will stand up and in one breath say that the Negroid race does not want social equality and in the next predict a great future in the face of all the proscription of which the colored man is a victim, is either an ignoramus, or is an advocate of the perpetual servility and degradation of his race."

SEPTEMBER 19

"I just run," said Wilma Rudolph in the September 19, 1960 issue of *Sports Illustrated*, "I don't know why I run so fast." Rudolph had just become the first American woman to win three gold medals in one Olympic meet, in Rome, Italy. She won the 100-meter dash with a time of 11 seconds flat, the 200-meter dash in 24 seconds, and was on the winning 400-meter relay team—clocked at 44.5 seconds.

An exceptionally graceful and elegant runner, Rudolph became the darling of the European public and press. The French called her the *Gazelle Noire* (black gazelle). One French photographer dubbed her *La Chattanooga choo-choo*. An English writer noted she had the carriage "a queen should have," and she was immortalized in Madame Tussaud's wax museum in London. She was named European Sportswriters' Sportswoman of the Year for 1960 and was the first American woman to win Italy's Christopher Columbus Award for outstanding international sportsperson.

The "world's fastest woman" was likewise adored back in the United States. October 4, 1960, was proclaimed Wilma Rudolph Day in her hometown of Clarksville, Tennessee. She appeared on the *Ed Sullivan Show* and met President John F. Kennedy at the White House. United Press International chose her Athlete of the Year for 1960, and the Associated Press named her Female Athlete of the Year in 1961. She served as U.S. goodwill ambassador to French West Africa in the early 1960s. In 1980 she was inducted into the Women's Sports Hall of Fame.

Hometown friends called Rudolph Skeeter, a nickname given to her by a high school basketball coach because of the way she buzzed around the court. Born into a family of nineteen children, her athletic success was made all the more poignant by the fact that she had suffered from scarlet fever and double pneumonia as a child and had been unable to walk from the age of four until she was eight years old. Rudolph died on November 12, 1994.

SEPTEMBER 20

On this day in 1664, Maryland passed the first antiamalgamation law. This was intended to prevent English women from marrying African men. Interracial marriage was a fairly common practice during the colonial era among white indentured servants and black slaves—as well as in more aristocratic circles.

The puritan law did not deter many colonialists, however. One colonial writer observed that mulatto children "swarmed" in Virginia. Benjamin Franklin had a reputation for fraternizing with African women, as did Patrick Henry, Alexander Hamilton, Daniel Boone, and vice president Col. Richard Johnson. Thomas Jefferson was also believed to have taken slaves as mistresses. One in particular, Sally Hemings, was the subject of a colonists' ditty:

> *Of all the damsels on the green,*
> *On mountains or in valley,*
> *A lass so luscious ne'er was seen*
> *As Monticellan Sally.*

After independence, race mixing shifted more towards slave owners having relations with slave women. A popular saying went: "The best blood of the South runs in the veins of the slaves." During these antebellum days some theorists contended that mixed marriage was the answer to improved race relations. A white Methodist bishop described mulattos as "the coming race in all its virile perfection...exquisite tints of delicate brown...handsome features...beautiful eyes...graceful forms."

Intermarriage bans were lifted during Reconstruction in the early 1870s, but by the end of the decade mixed marriages were declared void. It wasn't until the 1950s and 1960s that these laws were again lifted.

Statistics reveal that in 1970 there were 65,000 blacks married to whites, or 0.1 percent of the total number of married couples in America; by 1991 that number had risen to 231,000, or 0.4 percent. Studies have shown that up to 80 percent of African-Americans have either white or Native American blood. And about 21 percent of European-Americans are believed to have some African blood.

SEPTEMBER 21

Today in 1832, Maria W. Stewart delivered an address at Franklin Hall in Boston. Stewart was a women's and civil rights pioneer, and the first American-born woman to give public speeches. Below are excerpts from Stewart's speech.

Tell us no more of southern slavery; for with few exceptions, although I may be very erroneous in my opinion, yet I consider our condition but little better than that. Yet, after all, methinks there are no chains so galling ...as those that bind the soul....

It was asserted that we were "a ragged set, crying out for liberty." I reply to it, the whites have so long and so loudly proclaimed the theme of equal rights and privileges, that our souls have caught the flame also, ragged as we are....

And were it not that the king eternal has declared that Ethiopia shall stretch forth her hands unto God, I should indeed despair....

On this same day in 1833, Stewart delivered a farewell address to Boston before moving to Washington, D.C., in which she said:

...it is not the color of the skin that makes the man or the woman, but the principle formed in the soul. Brilliant wit will shine, come from whence it will; and genius and talent will not hide the brightness of its luster.

SEPTEMBER 22

Ralph J. Bunche was awarded the Nobel Peace Prize on this day in 1950 for his role as mediator in the Palestinian conflict. Bunche was the first African-American Nobel Peace Prize recipient. He won the NAACP's Spingarn Medal a year earlier for both his assistance in settling the armed conflict in the Middle East and for his work on the Myrdal Study.

The son of an impoverished Detroit barber, in 1934 Bunche became the first African-American to graduate with a doctorate degree in political science from Harvard University. He taught political science at Howard University and continued his postgraduate studies in anthropology. From 1938 to 1940 he worked with Swedish sociologist Gunnar Myrdal to prepare the celebrated study on race relations, *An American Dilemma: The Negro Problem and Modern Democracy.*

Bunche became a specialist on Africa in the State Department and at the end of World War II assisted in the creation of the charter for the United Nations. Bunche dedicated his later career to the United Nations, rising to the rank of Under Secretary General in 1967. He died on December 9, 1971, in New York City, one year after retiring from the United Nations.

To make our way, we must have firm resolve, persistence, tenacity. We must gear ourselves to work hard all the way. We can never let up. We can never have too much preparation and training. We must be a strong competitor. We must adhere

*staunchly to the basic principle that anything less than full
equality is not enough. If we compromise on that principle our
soul is dead.*

—Bunche from the July 1935 *Journal of Negro Education*

~~~~~~

SEPTEMBER 23

On this day in 1957, President Dwight D. Eisenhower issued Executive
Order No. 10730, forcing the integration of Central High School in Little
Rock, Arkansas. This order was necessary despite *Brown v. the Board of
Education*, which three years earlier had outlawed segregation in
American public schools. Section 2 reads:

*The Secretary of Defense is authorized and directed to take all
appropriate steps to enforce any orders of the United States
District Court for the Eastern District of Arkansas for the
removal of obstruction of justice in the State of Arkansas with
respect to matters relating to enrollment and attendance at
public schools in the Little Rock School District, Little Rock,
Arkansas.*

Two days later federal troops restrained a mob as nine African-
American children walked into the school for the first time. The Little
Rock Nine, as they became known, were awarded the NAACP's Spin-
garn Medal in 1958 for "their pioneer role in upholding the basic ideal of
American democracy in the face of continuing harassment and constant
threat of bodily harm."

*This may be looked back upon by future historians as the
turning point—for good—of race relations in this country.*

—Reverend Dunbar H. Ogden, president of the Greater Little Rock
Ministerial Association

SEPTEMBER 24

The first episode of *The Mod Squad* aired on this day in 1968. This action series featured a black man, white man, and white woman as a Los Angeles Police Department undercover cop team. *The Mod Squad* series drew a large audience during its five years on television. The last episode aired on August 23, 1973.

Twenty-nine-year-old actor Clarence Williams III starred as *The Mod Squad*'s Linc Hayes, a black-militant hero distinguished by his extra-large Afro hairstyle. Williams had been recommended by Bill Cosby, who—after seeing Williams in a Broadway play—referred to him as "the best young black actor." Producer Aaron Spelling agreed with Cosby, observing that Williams could "explode like charged lightening. Clarence is not a black actor, not a white actor, not a colored actor; he's an actor, the most professional I've worked with in my life."

In their book *Ethnic and Racial Images in American Film and Television*, authors Allen L. Woll and Randall M. Miller discuss the representation of African-Americans on television during this period. They recalled that "the late 1960s failed to realize the diversity of black images and voices available. Blacks found places in television series almost wholly in so-called salt and pepper combinations with blacks invariably in subordinate roles. Most of the black characters were bland and integrated into the white worlds in which they worked; they rarely threatened the dominant white culture. The 'hip' counterculture language and dress and the full 'Afroed' hair of Linc Hayes (Clarence Williams, III) in *The Mod Squad*, for example, could not disguise the fact for viewers that the black undercover policeman worked 'for the system.'"

Williams himself lamented the lack of representation of African-Americans on television, telling *TV Guide* in 1970, "A lot of people have died, bled, suffered and gone into poor states of mental health over this problem. You see, the cultural acceptance of black people has not happened yet. The black person's culture has not been put on television."

~~~~~~

SEPTEMBER 25

On this day in 1965—using a rocking chair and with a nurse waiting in the bullpen to massage his pitching arm—Satchel Paige pitched three innings for the Kansas City A's as the oldest player in major league history. Known for his wit, he titled his autobiography *Maybe I'll Pitch Forever*. Paige had an incredibly long career in baseball. He chalked up twenty-two years in the Negro Leagues and played over eighteen years in the major leagues, beginning in 1948 with the Cleveland Indians.

Paige was renowned for his fastball and showmanship. This athlete and country philosopher often cited the following as his secrets to longevity:

1. Avoid fried meats, which angry up the blood.
2. If your stomach disputes you, lie down and pacify it with cool thoughts.
3. Keep the juices flowing by jangling around gently as you move.
4. Go very light on the vices, such as carrying on in society. The social rumble ain't restful.
5. Avoid running at all times.
6. Don't look back. Something might be gaining on you.

~~~~~~

SEPTEMBER 26

Bessie Smith died this day in 1937 in Mississippi from injuries sustained in an automobile accident. Smith was the top blues singer of the post–World War I era and is widely regarded as the dean of female blues singers. This exceptional vocalist started out as a teenage performer on tent-tours with Ma Rainey and other traveling minstrel shows. By the 1920s the "Empress of the Blues" was playing music halls to popular acclaim. In 1923 she recorded her first hit, "Down Hearted Blues," which sold over half a million copies in six months.

By the time of the Great Depression Bessie Smith's fame—as well as the popularity of blues music—had waned and she took to the bottle. Smith made a comeback in 1933, recording with popular jazz artists. One of her songs, "Nobody Knows You When You're Down and Out," reflected the theme of her later life.

Nobody in town can bake a sweet jelly roll like mine.

—Bessie Smith in the 1920s

SEPTEMBER 27

On this day in 1912, "Memphis Blues" became the first blues song to be published. W. C. Handy wrote the tune for Edward H. Crump's mayoral campaign. A composer, pianist, and horn player, Handy is known as the Father of the Blues. Handy succeeded in making the blues a respectable art form, raising it from its humble origins in the brothels, saloons, train yards and back streets of the Mississippi Delta. From 1896 to 1903 Handy toured the country playing this uniquely African-American music and in 1926 he performed at Carnegie Hall.

One of Handy's most popular tunes, "St. Louis Blues," published in 1914, begins:

> *I hate to see de ev'nin' sun go down,*
> *Hate to see de ev'nin' sun go down,*
> *'Cause my baby, he done lef dis town.*
>
> *Feelin' tomorrow lak ah feel today,*
> *Feel tomorrow lak ah feel today,*
> *I'll pack my trunk, make ma git away.*
>
> *St. Louis woman wid her diamon' rings,*
> *Pulls dat man roun' by her apron strings.*
> *'Twant for powder an' for store-bought hair,*
> *De man ah love would not gone no where, no where.*

Got de St. Louis Blues jes as blue as ah can be,
Dat man got a heart lak a rock cast in the sea,
Or else he wouldn't have gone so far from me.

SEPTEMBER 28

On this balmy day in 1811, 20,000 people gathered at Thistleton Gap, England, to view a rematch between the English world heavyweight champion Tom Crib and the African-American contender Tom Molineaux. Having undergone rigorous training since his first match with Molineaux, on December 18 of the previous year, the Englishman solidly defeated the out-of-shape American in twenty minutes.

This rematch was a very different story from the first Crib-Molineaux fight, held at Copthall Common before a crowd of 5,000. Unquestionably superior, Molineaux had pummelled Crib in the twenty-eighth round. Crib couldn't stand up after the thirty-second break, but the referees refused to call the fight. Crib's handlers bought some time by charging that Molineaux had musket balls in his fists. When the hubbub had settled, Crib got back on his feet. After forty rounds the Englishman finally beat a dejected Molineaux.

Crib never stepped into the ring again after defeating Molineaux in the rematch at Thistleton Gap. Molineaux, on other hand, continued to earn good money in exhibition matches held throughout Great Britain— much of which he squandered on liquor, women and fast living. In 1815 a crushing defeat in Scotland marked the beginning of his decline. From that point on he continued to box but gave shoddy performances. He died not too long afterwards, on August 4, 1818.

Tom Molineaux, a former Virginia slave, was the first American heavyweight boxing champion. He declared himself champion in 1809, and nobody disputed it.

SEPTEMBER 29

When Union general Benjamin Franklin Butler planned an attack on Chaffin's Farm, he had two things to prove: He wanted to vindicate the Union Army's African-American soldiers who had largely been relegated to supporting roles during the Civil War; and he was determined to change his reputation of not being able to "fight his way out of a paper bag." He told Gen. Ulysses S. Grant that "the Negro troops had had no chance to show their valor or staying qualities in action" on the Virginia front. So, General Butler devised a surprise attack on Chaffin's Farm, the "impregnable fortifications" protecting the approach to Richmond, Virginia, the Confederate capital.

On September 29 and 30, 1864, the all-black Third Division of the Eighteenth Corps led the assault on the heavily fortified New Market Heights. As the African-American soldiers charged, Confederate soldiers taunted, "Come on, darkies, we want your muskets!" The Union soldiers eventually captured New Market Heights. But the victory was not without a heavy price—543 of the black soldiers in the advance regiments and all of the white officers were killed or wounded, leaving black officers in charge. One of them, Cpl. Miles James of the Thirty-sixth USCT, took a bullet in the arm, requiring amputation. Corporal James grabbed his gun with his remaining arm and continued to lead his men into battle. African-American soldiers earned thirteen Congressional Medals of Honor for bravery in the conflict.

Meanwhile, Richmond went into a panic "with orders to arrest every male person between the ages of 17 and 50 and send them to Cary Street for service," recalled a war clerk. The successful attack on New Market Heights and Fort Harrison was viewed as the beginning of the end of the Confederacy.

SEPTEMBER 30

General Colin L. Powell retired from military service on this day in 1993. Powell was the youngest and first African-American chairman of the Joint Chiefs of Staff. According to the *New York Times*, Powell "defined the United States' post–cold-war military doctrine. He talked tough to troops in the Saudi desert. He left skeptical lawmakers spellbound. He oozed self-confidence to millions of Americans when leading the United States into a Mideast war."

The son of Jamaican immigrants, Powell was raised in the Bronx, New York, in the 1950s. He joined the Reserve Officers Training Corps (ROTC) in college, and earned a master's degree in business administration. A career military man, in 1987 Powell was appointed national security advisor by President Ronald Reagan. Two years later he attained the rank of four-star general. In October 1989, President George Bush appointed him chairman of the Joint Chiefs of Staff—the principal military advisor to the president, secretary of defense, and the National Security Council.

Following his retirement from the military, the 56-year-old general pursued a career as a writer and public speaker, earning $60,000 per speech and signing a $6 million book contract. Powell often takes time to speak to young Americans. He encourages kids to get an education, saying to one audience, "If you get your diploma, you are on your way to somewhere. I am giving you an order—I'm a general you know—I order you to stick with it and get that diploma and stay off drugs."

Speculation as to whether this former soldier and statesman will run for presidential office is a frequent topic in the press. "Colin Powell is the ideal candidate," wrote *Time* magazine in March 1995, "Nearly 90 percent of the voters familiar with him across the political spectrum have a favorable impression of him."

OCTOBER 1

On the first day of October 1975, in the bout dubbed "The Thrilla in Manila," Muhammad Ali successfully defended his heavyweight title by defeating Joe Frazier in fourteen rounds.

The former Olympic gold medalist and world-renowned boxer won the heavyweight title three times—1964, 1974, and 1978. Born Cassius Marcellus Clay Jr., he adopted the name Muhammad Ali upon converting to Islam. Ali's first heavyweight title was suspended after he refused to enlist in the draft for the Vietnam War, having claimed "conscientious objection" as a minister of Islam. He argued, "You won't even stand up for me in America for my religious beliefs and you want me to go somewhere and fight, while you won't even stand up for me here at home." His title was restored in 1970 by a Supreme Court ruling.

Ali is known for his self-praising quips, such as the trademark "Float like a butterfly, sting like a bee" and "When you are as great as I am, it's hard to be humble." He titled his autobiography *The Greatest: My Own Story*. By the age of 50, Ali was diagnosed with Parkinson's Syndrome.

People say I had a full life, but I ain't dead yet. I'm just getting started. All of my boxing, all of my running around, all of my publicity, was just the start of my life. Now my life is really starting. Fighting injustice, fighting racism, fighting crime, fighting illiteracy, fighting poverty, using this face the world knows so well, and going out and fighting for truth and different causes.

—Ali quoted in Columbus Salley's *The Black 100* (1993)

OCTOBER 2

African-American painter Romare Bearden authored an article in the October 2, 1983 *New York Times Magazine* subtitled "When Manhattan's fast pace catches up with him, Romare Bearden escapes to the quiet of St. Martin island." In it he wrote:

> I remember one day in St. Martin I watched some workmen building a stone wall. Each time they needed stones for the wall, they went to a huge pile of rocks. Instead of breaking the rocks with powerful swings of their hammers, the men tapped the sides of the rocks, and at a certain point the rocks would crack into smaller pieces. I asked one of the men how this was done, and he explained that by tapping the rock the men were listening for its truth. When they discovered the vein of truth, only a few firm taps were needed. In our own soundings, I suppose, we find the truths and the real abilities we have to learn and relate.

Born in Charlotte, North Carolina, and raised in New York City, Bearden is considered one of the most admired artists of the twentieth century. He was particularly noted for his mastery of collage art. Bearden won numerous awards during his career that spanned nearly thirty years, including the National Medal of Arts, presented by President Ronald Reagan. The artist who once claimed, "painting is like...being in love—an adventure you plunge into without knowing how you will fare," died in 1988 at the age of 75.

> We look too much to museums. The sun coming up in the morning is enough.

> —Bearden interviewed in *Ebony*, November 1975

265

OCTOBER 3

On this day in 1949, WEDR—the first African-American radio station in America—began operating in Atlanta, Georgia. The station was originally scheduled to begin broadcasting in mid-August, but racially-motivated vandalism of a new $5,000 steel tower delayed the opening. WEDR was managed by Magic City Broadcasting Company and was "operated by Negro personnel for Negro patronage." According to the *New York Times* it was, "devoted to education, music and religious programs, with nothing of a 'controversial nature' on the air."

Today African-American radio programs are less likely to balk at controversial issues. For instance, in the final days of April 1992, KJLH-FM Los Angeles, California, ceased playing their usual R&B and pop mixes to air nonstop coverage of the South Central L.A. riots. "That was our opportunity to be the voice of the community....We did not shy away or run to music," said the station's general manager, Karen Slade, in an article in *Black Enterprise*.

The day after Magic Johnson's November 7, 1991 announcement that he had contracted the AIDS virus, urban radio stations filled their morning schedules with discussions about the disease. Many stations stepped up their AIDS awareness and safe-sex campaigns. "When somebody's singing about being down with O. P. P. and you're thinking about what happened to Magic, it's not fun anymore," said Mike Saunders of WPEG Charlotte, North Carolina, to *Billboard* magazine, "We will definitely think twice about this type of record."

According to *Black-Formatted Radio*'s 1993 report, African-Americans listen to the radio on average about three and one-quarter hours per week more than the average American. Over 50 percent of these listeners tune in to urban radio which often serves a dual role as both entertainer and community voice.

Heritage is our birthright. It is our responsibility to reach out and touch our market, to uphold our heritage. We have to do more than just play beats.

—Paul Major, owner of WTMP Tampa, Florida, speaking at the
  fifteenth annual Black Radio Exclusive Conference in 1991

OCTOBER 4

Today in 1962 Ermer Robinson was appointed coach of the American Basketball League's Oakland club, becoming one of the first African-Americans to coach a major professional sports team. Robinson began his basketball career touring in the 1960s with the talented and amusing Harlem Globetrotters.

The Globetrotters are an African-American exhibition team known for their trademark pregame circle routine and captivating comic stunts. The Globetrotters, who played their first game in Chicago in 1928, "are hard to beat as Americana," said *People Weekly* in November 1988. "They combine sports, show business, astonishing success and a not-insignificant historical role as products, victims and frequently conquerors of American racism." Today, the "Clown Princes of Basketball" continue to perform around the world for sold-out crowds.

Everyone has a gift, you let it take you as far as it can.

—Lynette Woodard, the first female Harlem Globetrotter, in *People Weekly*, March 7, 1994

OCTOBER 5

Charlie Smith died of natural causes on this day in 1979 in a nursing home in Bartow, Florida. He was believed to be 137 years old, making him the oldest person in the United States.

Smith was born with the name Mitchell Watkins in Liberia, West Africa, in 1842. He came to America as a child slave, claiming he was lured aboard a slave ship by promises of "fritter trees on board with lots of syrup." He arrived in New Orleans in 1854 and was given the name of his owner, a Texas rancher, as well as a new birth date—July 4th. Smith gained his freedom when President Lincoln signed the Emancipation Proclamation on January 1, 1863.

In his waning years Smith had both legs amputated because of circulatory problems. This impetuous character smoked cigarettes, drank whiskey, and washed down his vitamins with a shot of rum. The *Guiness Book of World Records* excluded Smith from their 1980 edition because they disputed his age, claiming he was only 104 years old based on a marriage certificate.

~~~~~~

OCTOBER 6

On October 6, 1871, the Fisk Jubilee Singers set out on their first national tour, making their initial stop in Cincinnati, Ohio. This ensemble of six female and five male students from Fisk University continued to tour the world for seven years, raising over $150,000 to help support their university. The funds were contributed toward the construction of the school's first brick building, Jubilee Hall. The Fisk Jubilee Singers brought African-American spirituals, such as "Go Tell It On the Mountain," to international audiences who had never before heard such music. The world responded by saying that the United States had finally created something culturally unique. In his book *The Souls of Black Folk*, W. E. B. DuBois remarked that Negro spirituals are "the singular spiritual heritage of the nation and the greatest gift of the Negro people."

The Fisk Jubilee Singers performed at the White House for President Chester A. Arthur on February 17, 1882, about which the *Washington Post* wrote:

> By appointment the colored Fisk Jubilee Singers accompanied by Rev. Dr. Rankin, called yesterday to pay their respects to President Arthur, and while there sang several melodies among them "Safe in the Arms of Jesus," which actually moved the President to tears. "I never saw a man so deeply moved," said Rev. Rankin, speaking of the incident last night, "and I shall always believe President Arthur to be a truly good man." The President frankly informed his visitors after hearing them that he had never before been guilty of so impulsive an exhibition of his feelings.

OCTOBER 7

On this day in 1821, William Still was born in New Jersey, a free man. Still was known as the "president of the Underground Railroad," and was the main strategist and leading spokesperson of the organization. His classic work, *Underground Railroad*, was published in 1872. Besides his humanitarian work, Still owned a prosperous coal stove business and lumber yard. He also founded the first YMCA for African-Americans.

    Still made his home in Philadelphia, Pennsylvania, where he personally greeted many passengers arriving from the South on the Under-

Runaway slave

ground Railroad. When runaways passed through his station, Still aided them with food, clothing, and money, and sent them "on their way rejoicing." He kept detailed records of those passing through. Below is an excerpt of an "examination" record dated December 29, 1854:

> *Jane, aged twenty-two, instead of regretting that she had unadvisedly left a kind mistress and indulgent master, who had afforded her necessary comforts, affirmed that her master "Rash Jones, was the worst man in the country." The Committee were at first disposed to doubt her sweeping statement, but when they heard particularly how she had been treated, they thought Catherine had good ground for all that she said. Personal abuse and hard usage were the common lot of the poor slave girls.*

Some of the legendary fugitives that Still assisted include William and Ellen Craft, Henry "Box" Brown, and Harriet Tubman. Tubman was regarded by Still as the greatest American heroine; he called her "an adventurous spirit wholly without fear." Still claimed that Tubman used to tell weak or faint-hearted escapees that a live runaway would do great harm by turning back, but a dead one would tell no secrets.

OCTOBER 8

On this day in 1831, Maria W. Stewart's pamphlet, *Religion and the Pure Principles of Morality, The Sure Foundation On Which We Must Build*, went on sale at the offices of the *Liberator* newspaper. Stewart—the first African-American female political writer and first American-born woman to give public speeches—was a regular contributor to the *Liberator*, a major abolitionist voice of the times. The following are excerpts from her pamphlet:

> *Charity begins at home, and those that provide not for their own are worse than infidels. . . .*

Possess the spirit of men, bold and enterprising, fearless and undaunted. Sue for your rights and privileges. Know the reason you cannot attain them. Weary them with your importunities. You can but die if you make the attempt; and we shall certainly die if you do not...

...why have not Africa's sons the rights to feel the same? Are not their wives, their sons, and their daughters, as dear to them as those of the white man's? Certainly God has not deprived them of the divine influences of his Holy Spirit, which is the greatest of all blessings, if they ask him. Then why should man any longer deprive his fellow-man of equal rights and privileges?

OCTOBER 9

Benjamin Banneker died on this day in 1806 at the age of 74 in Baltimore, Maryland. Banneker was a noted mathematician, surveyor, and astronomer, and was the most famous African-American of the colonial era.

Banneker was born in Ellicot Mills in 1731, the son of a free mother who purchased a slave and then married him—just as her white English servant mother had done. While still in his 20s, Banneker built the first clock made in America. People traveled long distances to see his famous clock, made entirely of wood using only a pen knife, and which worked accurately for twenty years. He also wrote ten almanacs, the first of which was released in 1792, in which he wrote antiwar, antislavery, anticapital punishment, and pro–free schooling articles.

Banneker was one of three men assigned by President George Washington to design the nation's new capital city. When the chief designer, Pierre Charles L'Enfant, packed up his plans and maps and returned to France in a huff before completing the project, Banneker and Andrew Ellicot were left to complete the work. This was possible because the brilliant Banneker had memorized L'Enfant's plans and in two days was able to redraw them. To this day, Washington, D.C. is considered one of the most accomplished urban planning efforts ever.

...one universal Father hath given being to us all; and he hath not only made us all of one flesh, but he hath also, without partiality, afforded us all the same sensations and endowed us with the same facilities; and that however variable we may be in society or religion, however diversified in situation or color, we are all in the same family and stand in the same relation to Him.

—excerpt from the first in a series of letters Banneker exchanged with then—Secretary of State Thomas Jefferson on the issue of slavery

OCTOBER 10

On this day in 1699, the Spanish kingdom issued a royal decree which stated that any Africans who came to St. Augustine, Florida, and adopted Catholicism would be protected from the English. This decree was repeated several times over the next forty-two years.

In 1738 the Spanish governor of Florida promised slaves from South Carolina freedom upon arrival, as well as land to cultivate. The Governor also encouraged them to take up arms against the British in the impending war. The Proclamation of 1738 drew large numbers of slaves to St. Augustine. They escaped by land and sea, sometimes stealing their owner's boats and horses, sometimes killing their owners, to join others who had already arrived over the years.

In one case, by December of 1738, the slave owner Captain Davis lost nineteen slaves to the lure of Florida. He verified his loss by traveling to St. Augustine, where he saw all of his former slaves, who reportedly laughed at him.

OCTOBER 11

The Supreme Court is not worth it. No job is worth it.... I think something is dreadfully wrong with this country when any person, any person in this free country would be subjected to this.... This is a circus. It's a national disgrace.

And from my standpoint, as a black American, it is a high-tech lynching for uppity blacks who in any way deign to think for themselves, to do for themselves, to have different ideas, and it is a message that unless you kow-tow to an old order, this is what will happen to you. You will be lynched, destroyed, caricatured by a committee of the U.S. Senate rather than hung from a tree.

These are the words then—appeals court judge Clarence Thomas, delivered on October 11, 1991, to the Senate Judiciary Committee during his reopened confirmation hearings. President George Bush had recently nominated Thomas to be the 106th Supreme Court justice, filling Thurgood Marshall's vacancy. Because Thomas's credentials were arguable and he held conservative views—particularly in regards to civil rights programs—support from the African-American community was mixed. The National Urban League and the Southern Christian Leadership Conference supported his nomination, while the NAACP and the Congressional Black Caucus opposed it.

After the initial hearings, despite any shortcomings he might have had, Thomas appeared to be a shoe-in. However, sexual harassment charges made public on October 6, 1991, by his former colleague, law professor Anita Hill, caused the hearings to be reopened. Aired on prime-time television, the hearings were transformed from a hashing over of credentials and measuring degrees of conservatism to a national spectacle, pitting man against woman and loyalty to race against loyalty to gender. On October 16, Thomas was confirmed by the Senate by four votes, beginning his term, as a *New York Times* article called him, as the "youngest and cruelest judge."

Toni Morrison summed up the significance of the Thomas hearings, stating, "It is clear to the most reductionist intellect that black people think differently from one another; it is also clear that the time for undiscriminating racial unity has passed. A conversation, a serious exchange between black men and women, has begun in a new arena, and the contestants defy the mold."

I resent the idea that people would blame the messenger for the message, rather than looking at the content of the message itself.

—Anita Hill

~~~~~~

OCTOBER 12

...after very well written and executed opening sequences relating to her impoverished, brothel-oriented early days, the script suggests that Miss Holiday somehow became a public name (she never was that in the usual sense of the word; she was however known to all musicians of the period)...

—*Variety* review of the film *Lady Sings the Blues* which was viewed on October 12, 1972, at the Directors Guild of America in Los Angeles

Billy Holiday's tragic life story was captured in the 1972 film *Lady Sings the Blues*, starring Diana Ross. The title of the movie came from Holiday's autobiography of the same name.

Although the exact date is uncertain, Billy Holiday was believed to be born on April 7, 1915, in Baltimore, Maryland. The daughter of a maid, her name at birth was Eleanor Gough McKay. Holiday became a successful jazz and blues songstress of the 1930s, '40s, and '50s. Nicknamed Lady Day, she recorded many hit songs, such as "God Bless the Child" (1941):

> *Mama may have*
> *Papa may have*
> *But God bless the child that's got his own*
> *That's got his own....*

"She was the greatest of all pure jazz singers," wrote author Barry McRae in *The Jazz Handbook*, "a superb artist whose career was inexplicably tainted by the word 'loser.' Her greatest gifts were a unique and intuitive sense of timing and her ability to lend credibility to even the most banal Tin Pan Alley tune."

The beautiful Holiday was troubled by racial prejudice. She became addicted to alcohol and drugs, for which she was arrested four times. Also a heroine addict, Holiday died in 1959, in her mid-40s.

> *You can be up to your boobies in white satin, with gardenias in your hair and no sugar cane for miles, but you can still be working on a plantation.*
>
> *You've got to have something to eat and a little love in your life before you can hold still for any-damn-body's sermon on how to behave.*
>
> —excerpt from the book *Lady Sings the Blues.*

OCTOBER 13

The gas mask was patented on this day in 1914 by an African-American inventor from Cleveland, Ohio. Calling it a Breathing Device, Garret A. Morgan wrote in his patent application No. 1,113,675:

> *The object of the invention is to provide a portable attachment which will enable a fireman to enter a house filled with thick*

suffocating gases and smoke and to breathe freely for some time therein, and thereby enable him to perform his duties of saving life and valuables without danger to himself from suffocation. The device is also useful for protection of engineers, chemists and working men who are obliged to breath noxious fumes or dust derived from the materials in which they are obliged to work.

Morgan became a national hero when, on July 24, 1916, he and his brother donned gas masks and personally led a rescue team in pulling out over thirty workers who had been trapped after an explosion in Tunnel No. 5 at the Cleveland Water Works. Morgan's gas mask—at the time called the Morgan Safety Hood—was also used during World War I.

In 1923 Morgan also invented the first automatic stoplight. Prior to his invention, policemen sat in towers overlooking intersections and manually changed signals. His earliest invention was a human-hair straightener, or refining cream. Today the G. A. Morgan Refining Company is still operating in Cleveland, Ohio.

Morgan was an active member of the NAACP. He founded a newspaper titled the *Call*, later called the *Call and Post*, which addressed African-American issues and circulated in Cleveland, Columbus, and Cincinnati, Ohio.

~~~~~~

OCTOBER 14

On October 14, 1971, the Pittsburgh Pirates defeated the Baltimore Orioles in the fifth game of the Sixty-eighth World Series. One of the keys to Pittsburgh's success was a Puerto Rican of African descent, Roberto Walker Clemente.

Commenting on the upcoming sixth game, Clemente said, "The Orioles are the best, and we want to beat them in competition. I'm thirty-seven and may not play in another Series. Money means nothing to me, but I love competition—and to me to compete is to compare, and that's everything." The Pirates went on to win the World Series. Clemente was named Outstanding Player, prompting teammate Charlie Sands to call him "the greatest ballplayer in the whole damn world."

Clemente was widely recognized as baseball's "best defensive right fielder." His accomplishments include: attaining a career batting average of .318; becoming the league's Most Valuable Player in 1966; and being named to the All-Star team twelve times. On September 30, 1972, in his eighteenth season, Clemente smacked his 3,000th hit, becoming only the eleventh player in major league history to do so.

Three months after leading the Pirates to the new world-series victory, on December 31, 1972, Clemente's exceptional career was abruptly and tragically cut short. A cargo plane in which he was riding crashed in the sea off the coast of Puerto Rico. Clemente had been spearheading Puerto Rico's relief efforts for the victims of an earthquake in Managua, Nicaragua, and was accompanying relief supplies being delivered to that Central American nation. The governor of Puerto Rico declared three days of national mourning for this son of a sugarcane plantation foreman—and the island's most famous sports hero ever.

If you have to die, how better could your death be exemplified than by being on a mission of mercy? It was so typical of the man. Every time I was down there, someone was always saying how he contributed to the youth and needy of his island; how he was going to make that his life's work. He did these things without fanfare or anything—just what he thought was right to help somebody else.

—John Galbreath, chairman of the board of the Pittsburgh Pirates, commenting on Clemente's death

~~~~~~

OCTOBER 15

Jelly Roll Morton, self-proclaimed "inventor of jazz," wrote his first jazz composition, "New Orleans Blues," on this day in 1902.

Jelly Roll was born in New Orleans during its waning days of glory. A Creole of mixed French and African blood, he bore the Christian name Ferdinand after the king of Spain. By the time the Depression rolled around, Jelly Roll went from being the King of Jazz in the 1920s to a forgotten man playing a forgotten music. In 1938 the "Father of Hot Piano" was spotted "playing for coffee and cakes in an obscure Washington nightspot." Jelly Roll did, however, participate in some fairly successful recording sessions from 1939 until his death in the summer of 1941.

In the words of Alan Lomaz, author of the biography *Mister Jelly Roll*, jazz is "the most original thing America has contributed to the arts of mankind" and is the "first international music." Although Jelly Roll Morton may not necessarily have invented jazz, he was certainly the first important composer of the music. "If you never heard Jelly Roll at his best," claimed critic Bud Scott, "you ain't never heard jazz piano...."

> *I'm Alabama bound,*
> *Alabama bound,*
> *If you like me, honey babe,*
> *You've got to leave this town.*
>
> *She said, "Doncha leave me here,*
> *Doncha leave me here,*
> *But, sweet papa, if you must go,*
> *Leave a dime for beer...."*

—"Alabama Bound," written by Morton in 1905

OCTOBER 16

On this day in 1968, during medal presentations at the Olympics in Mexico City, sprinters Tommie Smith and John Carlos bowed their heads and raised clenched-fists skyward while the "Star Spangled Banner" played. Smith wore a black glove on his right hand, while Carlos wore a black glove on his left, symbolizing racial unity. Smith and Carlos had won gold and bronze medals, respectively, in the 200-meter dash. The athletes gave the black power salute to protest racial discrimination in the United States.

"We are black," said Smith according to the *New York Times*, "and we are proud to be black. White America will only give us credit for an Olympic victory. They'll say I'm an American, but if I did something bad, they'd say a Negro. Black America was with us all the way through." Peter Norman of Australia, who stood beside them on the podium as the silver medal winner, told the press he supported their protest.

Smith and Carlos were allowed to keep their medals, but they were suspended from the U.S. team and prohibited from further competition.

OCTOBER 17

Capitol Savings Bank—the first African-American owned bank "independent of fraternal connections"—opened on this day in 1888. Located on F Street in Washington, D.C., the bank had an initial capital of $6,000, which increased to $50,000 over its sixteen years of operation.

The first independent African-American bank in the Deep South was the Alabama Penny Savings Bank, established on October 15, 1890. A year later, the short-lived Mutual Bank and Trust Company was formed in Chattanooga, Tennessee.

By 1993, African-American–owned banks, savings and loans, and insurance companies showed $4.2 billion in total assets. "Approximately 6% of the total commercial banking activity in the United States is conducted by black-owned institutions," noted an article in the June 1994 issue of *Black Enterprise*. "Of further import, the U.S. Census Bureau reports that African-Americans made up 12.5% of U.S. population at the end of 1993 and had a total pre-tax income of $284 billion."

In the 1990s, most minority-owned banks are located in inner cities and have strong links to the local community. "Survival is a tough thing for a minority banker," Louis Prezeau, president of City National Bank of New Jersey in Newark, explained in *Black Enterprise*, "But survive is what we have done in the past. We have done it through depressions and recessions. And we have done it clearly demonstrating our knowledge of the industry and by acknowledging that we continually have to do more with less."

Money is a great dignifier.

—Paul Lawrence Dunbar

~~~~~~

OCTOBER 18

The headline of a *New York Times* article dated October 18, 1964, read, "Negro Community Shrinks in West." The article was referring to Nicodemus, Kansas, the last remaining Exoduster community. Exodusters was the name African-Americans who migrated west in the late 1800s called themselves. The westward expansion of railway lines and the Homestead Act of 1862 inspired many Americans to move out to the prairies of the central plains. Many of these settlers constructed their homes from dirt blocks, and soon the region became known as the Sodhouse Frontier.

Following the abrupt end of Reconstruction, thousands of southern African-Americans joined the westward migration. African-Americans fled the South to escape increasing discrimination and to enjoy the full freedoms afforded by the Sodhouse Frontier. A large number of Exodusters were led west, mainly to Kansas, by Benjamin "Pap" Singleton, a modern Moses figure. Freedom came at a price, however, as life on the plains was extremely harsh. Relatively few of the African-American settlers lasted on frontier farms; many moved into towns and cities, and some even returned to the South. The most famous of the groups that weathered the hardships was the Nicodemus farm community in Kansas. Established on June 8, 1877, Nicodemus had its own school and post office and by 1878 boasted a population of 600–700.

Many good people in the East have probably heard of a "Kansas dugout" and have thought of it as a sort of human habitation peculiar to partial civilization and frontier barbarity. This is by no means a fair conclusion. "Dugouts" are not simply holes in the ground. They are generally dug into a side hill. They have two or more sides, with windows and doors. The floor and the roof are of earth. They are warmer than most of the more pretentious dwellings. They are as comfortable as they are cheap, and in nearly every place they protect a happy and prosperous family. Though comparatively few in number at the present time, they are still foremost among the best devices for building a fortune from the ground up. "Despise not the day of small things" is the motto of those who would dwell in the dugouts.

—the *Kansas Herald*, Topeka, Kansas, February 6, 1880

OCTOBER 19

Othello opened on this day in 1943 at New York's Shubert Theater, with Paul Robeson in the title role. Its 296 performances made it the longest running Shakespearean play in Broadway history. Robeson won critical acclaim for his role as Othello and was also highly-praised for his stage and film role as Emperor Jones. This bass-baritone will long be remembered for his rendition of "Ol' Man River" from the Hollywood production of *Showboat*. Critic George Jean Nathan called Robeson "one of the most thoroughly eloquent, impressive and convincing actors."

A Presbyterian minister's son, Robeson first entered the spotlight while at Rutgers University, where he was a two-time all-American football player. He worked briefly as a lawyer, but quit due to prejudice in the profession. Turning to theater, he proved to be an exceptionally talented actor. His rise to international fame began in the 1920s during the Harlem Renaissance.

Robeson and his wife lived in London for twelve years. He learned to speak over twenty languages and made several visits to the Soviet Union. There he felt "for the first time like a full human being," referring to the Soviet Union's apparent lack of racial prejudice. After returning to the United States, his liberal views, pro-Soviet statements, and opposition to the cold war led to his being branded a communist. These accusations sent his career on a tragic downward spiral. Despite never having joined the Communist Party, Robeson was blacklisted; his records were removed from shelves, and his personal appearances were halted by rioting. He was banned from television, radio, and the stage, and in 1950 his passport was revoked. Despite the suspended passport, in 1958 he returned to Europe, where he lived for five years. In weakened health, Robeson returned to America and lived in relative obscurity until his death in 1976.

> It is a sad and bitter commentary on the state of civil liberties in America that the very forces of reaction, typified by Representative Francis Walter and his Senate counterparts, who have denied me access to the lecture podium, the concert hall, the opera house, and the dramatic stage, now have me before a committee of inquisition in order to hear what I have to say. It is obvious that those who are trying to gag me here and abroad will scarcely grant me the freedom to express myself fully in a hearing controlled by them.
>
> ...my father was a slave, and my people died to build this country, and I am going to stay here and have a part of it just

like you. And no Fascist-minded people will drive me from it. Is that clear?"

—from Robeson's statements to the House Un-American Activities Committee on July 13 and July 23, 1956, respectively

~~~~~~

OCTOBER 20

On this day in 1898, the North Carolina Mutual and Provident Insurance Company was founded by John Merrick and Associates in Durhman, North Carolina. By 1992 Merrick's business—now called North Carolina Mutual Life Insurance Company—had become the largest African-American owned insurance company in America, with $8.8 billion dollars of insurance policies and $214 million in assets. It is lauded as the "greatest monument to Negroes' business enterprise."

North Carolina Mutual and Provident opened the same year that participants in the fourth annual Atlanta University Conference resolved to urge African-Americans "to enter into business life in increasing numbers."

Herdon [founder of Atlanta Life] and Merrick were obviously exceptional men, but the same wind blew, at lesser velocity, on other black main streets. In 1898, according to an Atlanta University study, there were 1900 black businesses in America. Most of these were small retail outlets, but some were of substantial size.

—historian Lerone Bennett Jr. in a December 1973 *Ebony* article

OCTOBER 21

The week of October 21, 1972, Chuck Berry's single "My Ding-a-Ling" hit number one on *Billboard*'s chart. Although this playful tune was his first number one single, he had previously written and performed many early rock 'n' roll classics, like "Maybelline," "Johnny B. Goode," "Roll Over Beethoven (and Dig These Rhythm and Blues)," and "Reelin' and Rockin'."

Called the Black Prince of Rock, Berry was one of the original rock 'n' rollers. He helped integrate pop music in the 1950s and was a major creative influence on contemporary pop music. Famed for his showmanship, Berry's trademark was the duck walk, in which he appeared to float across the stage, knees bent, all the while playing guitar. Through his stage antics, sleek appearance, and outlandish personal life, "he fixed the image of the rock artist as outlaw," wrote *Time* magazine.

I like to play music, softball, twenty questions, chess, croquet, house, and around.

—Chuck Berry in his 1987 autobiography

OCTOBER 22

James Bland, a mulatto of mixed African, Native American and European blood, was born on this day in 1854 in Flushing, New York. His father, Allen M. Bland, was one of the first African-Americans to graduate from college in America. The boy's first instrument was a banjo and soon he was earning a living singing, playing instruments, and composing songs. Like his more famous contemporary, the white composer Stephen Foster, Bland wrote sentimental ballads glorifying pre–Civil War plantation life in the South. Strangely, neither Foster nor Bland were southerners.

Bland travelled throughout the East Coast working in minstrel shows from 1875 until 1881, when his minstrel troop embarked on a European tour. Called the Prince of Negro Performers, he became the show's star attraction with his ballad "O Dem Golden Slippers." He remained in Europe—which he felt was less racist than his home country—for over a decade. There he was known as the idol of the music halls, reputedly earning over $10,000 per year for his shows and song royalties. It was also reported that he spent much of his large earnings on fine clothes and travel.

By the time Bland returned to the United States in the early 1900s, vaudeville had replaced minstrel shows as the new craze, leaving an aging minstrel in little demand. Soon the Ethiopian Songwriter, as he called himself, was lonely and broke—his royalties fading "to a trickle." He died of pneumonia in 1911 in Philadelphia at the age of 56.

Bland wrote over 600 songs during his lifetime. In his prime, in Europe, he averaged one song a week. Perhaps one of the best remembered Bland tunes is "Carry Me Back to Old Virginny," which became the state song of Virginia in 1940.

Carry me back to old Virginny,
There's where the cotton and the corn and the tatoes grow,
There's where the birds warble sweet in the springtime...

OCTOBER 23

On October 23, 1947, the NAACP filed formal charges with the United Nations accusing the United States of racial discrimination. The NAACP's 155-page "Appeal to the World" internationalized America's race problem and spurred President Harry Truman to create a Civil Rights Committee. The committee, however, was largely ineffective.

The document was presented to the U.N.'s assistant secretary general for social affairs by Dr. W. E. B. DuBois, then director of special research

W. E. B. DuBois

for the NAACP. DuBois claimed to speak on behalf of "fourteen million citizens of the United States, or twice as many persons as there are in the Kingdom of Greece," and added, "Nothing that the United States is, was or shall be is without the help of our toil, our feelings, our thought."

The petition's complaints included: segregation and inequities in public education; the national government's failure to make poll taxes illegal and to declare lynching a federal crime; discriminatory real estate covenants; and civil rights violations in the nation's capital.

Walter F. White, executive secretary of the NAACP, noted on the occasion that "two-thirds of the people of the earth are black, brown or yellow of skin and have been denied economic opportunity and justice for that reason."

~~~~~~

OCTOBER 24

On October 24, 1923, the U.S. Department of Labor estimated that in the previous twelve months approximately 500,000 African-Americans had migrated from the South. Lured by the possibilities of jobs and opportunities in the industrialized North, an estimated 5,600,000 people moved north between 1910 and 1950. Called the Great Migration, this was the largest wave of migration in America ever.

African-American newspapers played a major role in influencing black Americans to undertake the northward journey. Most notable of these was Robert Abbott's *Chicago Defender*. The *Defender* called out to the "unknown and unseen fellows" of the South, and promoted northern states as being full of opportunity for African-Americans. At the height of the exodus, the *Defender* had a circulation of almost a quarter of a million copies.

African-Americans moved primarily into the cities of Chicago, New York, Detroit, Pittsburgh, Philadelphia, and Gary, Indiana, where wartime industries offered an abundance of jobs. Southern African-Americans brought their politics, traditions, and music with them, an example of this being the migration of jazz musicians from New Orleans to Chicago.

> *They're leaving Memphis in droves*
> *Some are coming on the passenger,*
> *Some are coming on the freight,*
> *Others will be found walking,*
> *For none have time to wait.*
>
> —poem in the *Chicago Defender*

OCTOBER 25

On this day in 1976, Alabama governor George Wallace granted a full pardon to Clarence Norris, who had been sentenced to death on a rape charge forty-five years earlier. Norris's saga began on March 25, 1931, when, as a young man, he and eight other African-American boys were pulled off a westbound train at Paint Rock depot near Scottsboro, Alabama, taken to jail, and accused of raping two white women. The boys were convicted of rape by the all-white Alabama courts, even though doctors who examined the women testified that they had not been raped. All but one of the defendants were sentenced to death during what was called a "legal lynching."

The Scottsboro Trial, as it became known, was the most notorious legal case of the 1930s and involved a series of trials that went on for years. The nine young men were supported in their defense by northern liberals and radicals who recognized that they had been victims of racial bias.

The Scottsboro Trial resulted in two landmark Supreme Court decisions. In *Powell v. Alabama* (1932), the U.S. Supreme Court ruled that denying the defendants legal counsel had been a violation of the due process clause of the Fourteenth Amendment. This ruling set a legal precedent which states that indigent defendants in capital (death penalty) cases are entitled to representation; this was later expanded to other major noncapital criminal cases. In *Norris v. Alabama* (1935), the Court found that the defendants were denied equal protection of the law under the Fourteenth Amendment because African-Americans had been excluded from the Alabama juries.

In 1937, four of the Scottsboro nine were released from prison. The others were released over the next decade, with Norris finally being set free in 1946.

It touched black Americans as mothers and fathers and sisters and brothers, for they knew that the blight that had struck those boys could just as easily have struck their kin. They celebrated the decision as if it had been their own boys the Court had spared and given another shot at justice.

—James Goodman, author of *Stories of Scottsboro*, referring to *Norris v. Alabama*

~~~~~~

OCTOBER 26

The following pledge appeared in the *Black Panther* newspaper on October 26, 1968.

BLACK CHILD'S PLEDGE
by Shirley Williams
(Richmond Black Belt)

I pledge allegiance to my Black People.

I pledge to develop my mind and body to the greatest extent possible.

I will learn all that I can in order to give my best to my People in their struggle for liberation.

I will keep myself physically fit, building a strong body free from drugs and other substances which weaken me and make me less capable of protecting myself, my family and my Black brothers and sisters.

I will unselfishly share my knowledge and understanding with them in order to bring about change more quickly.

I will discipline myself to direct my energies thoughtfully and constructively rather than wasting them in idle hatred.

I will train myself never to hurt or allow others to harm my Black brothers and sisters for I recognize we need every Black man, Woman and child to be physically, mentally and psychologically strong. These principles I pledge to practice daily and to teach them to others in order to unite my People.

OCTOBER 27

Today in 1954 Benjamin Oliver Davis Jr. was appointed lieutenant general of the U.S. Air Force, becoming the first African-American of this rank. He was also the first African-American to command an air base. During World War I, Davis commanded the first all-black fighter pilot unit, the Ninety-ninth Pursuit Squadron, composed of Tuskegee-trained flyers.

Davis's father, Benjamin O. Davis Sr., had been the first African-American general in the regular army. On October 16, 1940, Davis Sr. was made brigadier general in the U.S. Army. A veteran of the Spanish-American War, World Wars I and II, the elder Davis received a Bronze Star and Distinguished Service Medal, among other honors. Like his son after him, Davis Sr. helped to desegregate the armed services.

Children have never been good at listening to their elders, but they have never failed to imitate them.

—James Baldwin

OCTOBER 28

The producer of Florence Mills's shows in London, England, told the British Broadcasting Corporation (BBC) on this day in 1926 that his star dancer and singer was not "for sale like a pound of tea." The BBC had planned to enlist Mills—who was enjoying great success on the London theater scene—to sing for fifteen minutes every night. "A broadcasting company cannot buy a big artist like that," continued the incensed producer, "any more than you or I can buy an old master by the yard."

The top African-American performer of her day, "Baby" Florence Mills debuted at the age of six in the musical *Sons of Ham*. By 15, she had formed the Mills Trio, a singing and dancing act. In 1920 she played a lead role in the classic African-American Broadway Revue *Shuffle Along* and in 1924 starred in *From Dixie to Broadway*.

Her signature tune, "I'm Just a Little Blackbird Lookin' for a Bluebird," was known to make audiences cry. The Prince of Wales reportedly attended her London musical *Blackbirds* sixteen times. One critic described her voice as beguiling, adding, "She never performs— she merely reacts to the delight of making a joyful sound."

Soon after she returned from Europe, in September 1929, the Little Blackbird's life was cut short. That November she died from complications of an appendectomy. In a fairy tale conclusion to this beloved performer's life, thousands of mourners followed her funeral procession through Harlem while an airplane flew overhead, releasing a flock of blackbirds. Upon arriving at Woodlawn Cemetery, the procession was greeted by a column of red roses piled eight-feet-high, accompanied by a card that read, "From a friend." Many believe that the anonymous friend was the Prince of Wales.

OCTOBER 29

The collapse of the stock market on October 29, 1929, heralded the beginning of the Great Depression. The Depression was especially hard on African-Americans—the first to be fired and last to be hired, many of whom were already experiencing economic hardship. Urban League director Lester Granger noted that black America "almost fell apart." By 1937 there was a 32 percent unemployment rate for African-American women and a 26 percent unemployment rate for African-American men. Urban areas were the hardest hit. In Atlanta, Georgia, 65 percent of African-Americans were on welfare; in Norfolk, Virginia, the rate was 81 percent.

Clifford Burke lived through the Great Depression. In an interview with Studs Terkel recorded in the book *Hard Times: An Oral History of the Great Depression* (1970), Burke said:

The Negro was born in depression. It didn't mean too much to him, The Great Depression, as you call it. There was no such thing. The best he could be is a janitor or a porter or a shoeshine boy. It only became official when it hit the white man. If you can tell me the difference between the depression today and the Depression of 1932 for a black man, I'd like to know it. Now, it's worse, because of the prices. Know the rents they're payin' out here? I hate to tell ya.

OCTOBER 30

Today in 1974, fifty million people across the world watched as Muhammad Ali regained the heavyweight boxing title from current world champion George Foreman. Held in Kinshasa, Zaire, this was the first heavyweight title bout held in an African country. "In perhaps the most dramatic scenario in boxing history," wrote the *New York Times*, "Ali had regained the heavyweight title at the age of 32 by out-punching a 25-year-old puncher who had recorded 24 consecutive knockouts in a previously unbeaten career. And he had accomplished it here before nearly 60,000 Zairians...in a spectacle that began at 4 o'clock in the morning."

Despite his prefight rantings about floating like a butterfly, Ali did not dance in the ring during the fight. Instead he pounded Foreman with stinging punches. "That was the surprise. That was the trick," claimed Ali after the match. "What you saw was the power of Allah in helping me win. That must have been Allah in there because I can't punch. My hands were so sore for Frazier and Norton, I needed Novocain. But they were good this time. I'm not known for being a hitter. Can you picture me making George Foreman helpless?" That he did, knocking out Foreman in the eighth round. *Sports Illustrated* named Ali the 1974 Sportsman of the Year. Four years later, Ali defeated Leon Spinks, becoming the first boxer in history to regain the heavyweight title two times.

The man who views the world at fifty the same as he did at twenty has wasted thirty years of his life.

—Muhammad Ali

~~~~~~

OCTOBER 31

Ethel Waters was born on this day in 1896. Waters began her career as a nightclub singer, using the stage name Sweet Mama Stringbean. This steamy songstress of the 1920s and 1930s recorded numerous hits, including "Stormy Weather," "Am I Blue?," "Dinah," "The Saint Louis Blues," and "Oh, Daddy." In 1939 she starred as Hagar in *Mamba's Daughters* on Broadway, becoming the first African-American female lead in a Broadway play.

During the war years, Waters appeared in such Hollywood films, as *Cairo* (1942), *Stage Door Canteen* (1943), and *Cabin in the Sky* (1943). She was nominated for an Oscar in 1949 for her role as Grandmother in the film *Pinky*. In 1955 she was nominated for an Academy Award as the cook in the film *The Member of the Wedding*; she won the New York Drama Critics Award for the same role in the stage version. It was in *The Member of the Wedding* that she first sang her signature tune, "His Eye Is on the Sparrow."

I sing because I'm happy,
I sing because I'm free,
For His eye is on the sparrow,
And I know He watches me.

After attending a Billy Graham crusade in 1957, Waters devoted the remaining years of her life to Christianity. This much-loved entertainer was called "a great soul" by Gloria Gaither, a Christian recording artist. Langston Hughes called her "that grand comedienne of song."

More than anyone in our business you are the most universally admired and respected person I can think of. More, you are the most cared about, and the most loved. When I think of you it is almost as a symbol—except that no symbol can evoke the humanness and warmth that you always represented.

—a message from Water's friend Art Linkletter, written on the occasion of her 80th birthday

NOVEMBER 1

In November 1900, brothers James Weldon Johnson, author, educator, and general secretary of the NAACP for a decade (1920–1930), and John Rosamond Johnson composed the song "Lift Ev'ry Voice and Sing." Commonly referred to as the black national anthem, the song begins:

> *Lift ev'ry voice and sing*
> *Till earth and heaven ring,*
> *Ring with the harmonies of Liberty;*
> *Let our rejoicing rise*
> *High as the list'ning skies,*
> *Let it resound loud as the rolling sea.*
> *Sing a song full of the faith that the dark past*
>   *has taught us,*
> *Sing a song full of the hope that the present has*
>   *brought us,*
> *Facing the rising sun of our new day begun,*
> *Let us march on till victory is won.*

NOVEMBER 2

St. Luke Penny Savings Bank opened its doors on this day in 1903 in Richmond, Virginia. Opening day receipts totalled $9,430.44. Patrons from around the region deposited hard-earned savings—often in denominations of nickels and pennies—into Christmas savings accounts. Today called Consolidated Bank and Trust Company, it holds the distinction of being the tenth largest African-American owned bank, as well as being America's oldest continually-operated minority-owned bank.

St. Luke Bank was founded and operated by Maggie Lena Walker, making it the first bank in America to be run by a woman. Author Martha Ward Plowden described Walker as "a tall, heavy, buxom woman, with a deep, mellow voice. Her ability to speak with confidence, knowledge, and charm became her trademark." Walker also owned a printing plant, office building, and other businesses, as well as edited a newspaper. Locals reportedly enjoyed watching this successful African-American female entrepreneur tooling about town in her chauffeur-driven limousine.

Walker died in 1934 at the age of 69. Her house at 110A East Leigh Street in Richmond, Virginia, was designated a national historic landmark in 1975.

NOVEMBER 3

On this day in 1920, Eugene O'Neill's play *Emperor Jones* opened at the Provincetown Theater in New York. Charles S. Gilpin—the dean of America's black dramatic actors—played the title role. Although it is difficult to pinpoint a single event, some historians cite the opening of this play as the beginning of the Harlem Renaissance.

Gilpin was a member of several of the first African-American stock theater companies, including the Pekin Players and Williams and Walker. Gilpin supplemented his income in turns as a printer, elevator operator, and switchboard operator. He claimed that his draw to acting, "was not due to any dreams of a stage career, but simply because I was trying to earn my bread and butter. I drifted into it because I had taken part in little plays and entertainments at school, where one of the teachers had given me some training in speaking and acting."

In 1921 Gilpin was awarded the NAACP's Spingarn Medal for his outstanding work in theater. He was forced to quit acting in 1926 after losing his voice and died four years later. Gilpin has been referred to as "the first modern American Negro to establish himself as a serious actor of first quality."

The play [Emperor Jones] and Gilpin—linked together forever in theater history—became famous practically overnight. Critics compared the play to Othello; *they didn't know to whom to compare Gilpin. There was no one else with that kind of power on stage. As the ill-fated emperor, Gilpin reached the highest point of achievement on the legitimate American stage that had ever been reached by a black.*

—James Haskins's *Black Theater in America*

NOVEMBER 4

Today in 1988, Bill Cosby and his wife Camille presented a gift of $20 million to Spelman College. One of the Cosbys' daughters had attended this prestigious women's college in Atlanta, Georgia. At the time this was the largest single donation made to an African-American college, as well as the largest single charitable donation ever made by an African-American. "I think we all understand that schools need money," Cosby said about the donation, "but I think we accepted that white folk were going to keep them alive."

There are 100 or so predominantly African-American colleges and universities in America. From 1944 to 1995 the United Negro College Fund raised approximately $1 billion for forty-four of these historically black institutions. In 1970 federal aid to these schools was $125 million; by 1992 federal aid had increased to over $633 million. Private organizations have also contributed funding over the years. For example, the Ford Foundation granted $100 million to African-American colleges in 1970 and has since continued to provide grants to these schools.

How important is the survival of black colleges? Statistics provide the answer: Even though black colleges enroll only 28 percent of all black students, they account for 40 percent of blacks receiving bachelor's degrees.

—*U.S. News & World Report*, November 21, 1988

NOVEMBER 5

On November 5, 1968, Shirley Chisholm became the first African-American woman to serve in the U.S. Congress. A Democrat, she represented the Bedford-Stuyvesant section of Brooklyn. In 1972 she became the first African-American and the first woman to run for president with a major political party. Aware that she would not win the nomination, Chisholm explained her motivation for entering the race:

The next time a woman of whatever color, or a dark-skinned person of whatever sex aspires to be President, the way should be a little smoother because I helped pave it.

Born in New York to West Indian parents, this charismatic educator and politician served in Congress for fourteen years. She was an outspoken champion of minority and poverty issues, fought to raise the minimum wage and to obtain federal funding for day care centers, advocated women's rights, and opposed defense spending. Chisholm wrote two autobiographies, *Unbought and Unbossed* (1970) and *The Good Fight* (1973), the latter of which tells the story of her presidential campaign.

We Americans have a chance to become someday a nation in which all racial stocks and classes can exist in their own selfhoods, but meet on a basis of respect and equality and live together, socially, economically, and politically. We can become a dynamic equilibrium, a harmony of many different elements, in which the whole will be greater than any society the world has seen before. It can still happen.

—Chapter 14 it *The Good Fight*

~~~~~~

NOVEMBER 6

On this day in 1920, James Weldon Johnson became the first African-American executive secretary of the NAACP. Johnson served in this post until resigning in 1930 to teach creative literature at Fisk University.

Johnson was truly a Renaissance man. He was a lawyer, diplomat (U.S. consul to Venezuela and Nicaragua), educator, civil rights activist, poet, editor, literary critic, and author. As a critic and author, he had a major influence on African-American literature in the early 1900s and was a primary figure during the Harlem Renaissance. His books include *The Autobiography of an Ex-Colored Man* (1912), *The Book of American Negro Spirituals* (1925), and *Black Manhattan* (1930).

For his multiple achievements, Johnson was awarded the NAACP's Spingarn Medal in 1925. He died in 1938 in an automobile accident in Maine. His epitaph, which he wrote himself, says:

I will not allow one prejudiced person or one million or one hundred million to blight my life, I will not let prejudice or any of its attendant humiliations and injustices bear me down to spiritual defeat. My inner life is mine, and I shall defend and maintain its integrity against all the powers of hell.

~~~~~~

NOVEMBER 7

On November 7, 1967, Carl B. Stokes was elected the fiftieth mayor of Cleveland, Ohio, then America's eighth largest city. Stokes is considered the first African-American mayor of a major American city.* He wrote a political biography of his four years in office called *Promises of Power* (1973). In it he explained:

> *For a brief time in Cleveland, I was the man in power. I had what no black man in this country had before: direct control of the government of a predominantly white population. That power came to me because I seized a situation that had made me like a savior to men who ordinarily look on blacks as an alien and vaguely dangerous force.*

Stokes swam in turbulent waters during his mayoral years; attempts at reform pitted him against Cleveland power brokers, such as city councilors and the police department. He contemplated the process of change in the last chapter of *Promises of Power*:

> *When you start dealing with real change you are talking about interfering with those who are in possession of something. Power never gives up anything without a struggle....Out of that struggle the cutting edge has to be blunted, dulled and even sacrificed. That's what happened to Carl Stokes in Cleveland. I accept it. I'll go on to the next thing and let someone else who is constituted differently from me come back one day and begin the process again. Someone will come. I don't know who it will be. But someone will come.*

A lawyer by profession, Stokes had been elected to the Ohio House of Representatives in 1962, becoming the first African-American Democrat in Ohio's legislature. After leaving political office in 1971, Stokes became coanchor along with Paul Udell of a New York City news program. Featured as a political commentator, he reportedly earned $100,000 per year. Two decades later, in the fall of 1994, he was appointed American ambassador to the Seychelles, an Indian Ocean island nation located off the east coast of Africa.

---

*Walter E. Washington became mayor of Washington, D.C. and Richard G. Hatcher was elected mayor of Gary, Indiana, in the same year.

NOVEMBER 8

On this day in 1938, Crystal Bird Fauset was elected to the Pennsylvania House of Representatives, becoming the first African-American female to serve in a U.S. state legislature.

Fauset was born in Princess Anne, Maryland, and raised in Boston. She attended Teachers College, Columbia University. After serving one term in the Pennsylvania House, she was appointed racial advisor in the Office of Civilian Defense. In this position she worked under the supervision of the assistant director of the office, Mrs. Franklin D. Roosevelt.

> *If white people will permit the President and Mrs. Roosevelt to work out their plans, not calculated to hurt anyone's feelings, but to give consideration to race problems not as a philanthropic gesture but as a great aid to national unity, then America will take her place and make democracy a reality in all the world.*

—Fauset quoted in the *New York Times*, February 10, 1942

NOVEMBER 9

Today in 1901, William Monroe Trotter founded the *Guardian* newspaper in Boston, Massachusetts. At the time of its inception some 150 African-American newspapers were being published in the United States.

As editor of the *Guardian*, Trotter was one of the few Negro newspapermen willing to publicly oppose the celebrated and powerful African-American social theorist Booker T. Washington. Trotter agreed wholeheartedly with W. E. B. DuBois's opinion that Washington was "leading the way backward" and became one of the harshest critics of his "sub-class" rhetoric.

Along with W. E. B. DuBois, Trotter was one of the leading figures of the Niagara Movement. Among the Niagara's demands were "justice even for criminals and outlaws," strict enforcement of the constitution, and a safeguarding of the right to vote for African-Americans. Their proposed methods for achieving these demands were "unceasing agitation" and "hammering at the truth."

However, because he distrusted "white folks," Trotter was conspicuously absent from the founding of the NAACP in 1909. This Harvard graduate and outspoken radical is considered a forefather of black militants.

NOVEMBER 10

The Centennial Exposition, held in Philadelphia, Pennsylvania, honoring one hundred years of America's independence, closed on this day in 1876. "As the exhibitors go away," wrote the *New York Times*, "whether they go with a sense of regret, or a relief from vexation, they certainly may carry with them the reflection that they have severally contributed to the achievements of one of the greatest of world shows."

African-American landscape and seascape painter Edward M. Bannister was one of the exhibitors who went away with pride. Bannister, from Providence, Rhode Island, had won a medal in the Plastic and Graphic Arts category for his oil painting. Some tried to discriminate against Bannister by denying him this award, but fellow artists insisted it be given to him.

The popularity of the visual art exhibits was mentioned on several occasions in the *New York Times*. "At the Philadelphia Exhibition," said one article,"the art galleries are so crowded that it is difficult to get from one room to another, and this has not been merely of late, but from the first." Over eight million people from many countries attended the Exposition, at the time the largest attendance for a World's Fair.

Edmonia Lewis, the first successful African-American sculptor, also exhibited at the Centennial Exhibition. By 1876 this "peculiar" and "intense" artist had already established herself as a talented neo-classical sculptor. Lewis, who dressed in masculine clothing and had an East Indian look, a result of her half Chippewa, half African parentage, she created the critically-admired busts of Col. Robert Gould Shaw, Henry Wadsworth Longfellow, Abraham Lincoln, and Senator Charles Sumner.

NOVEMBER 11

Louis Armstrong recorded the first of his "Hot Five and Hot Seven" songs on this day in 1925, forever altering jazz music. "The whole of jazz music," asserts jazz expert Hugues Panassie, "was transformed by Louis, overthrown by his genius."

Born in New Orleans on July 4, 1900, Armstrong grew up amidst the formation of jazz. Local musicians were combining blues, gospel, and other traditional music styles into what was then called "jass." This slang term for making love was adopted because, in its early years, jazz was performed in the brothels of Storyville, the section of New Orleans where prostitution had been legalized.

As a cornet player and vocalist in the 1920s, Armstrong hit the jazz world by storm with masterpieces such as "How Come You Do Me," "TNT," "Cold In Hand," and "Livin' High." By the 1930s he was the front man in jazz orchestras. Along with Duke Ellington, he helped popularize jazz throughout the world as an expression of the African-American experience.

Armstrong earned the nickname Satchmo in 1932, when he played at the London Palladium; an English pundit referred to him as "satchel mouth." Armstrong is considered by many to be the greatest jazz musician of all time. When asked the meaning of jazz, Armstrong replied, "If you have to ask, man, you'll never know."

NOVEMBER 12

The Paris Exposition closed its gates on this day in 1900. According to the *New York Times*, the show was a "gigantic success from the point of view of attendance," with fifty million visitors. African-American painter Henry O. Tanner was one of the 6,916 American exhibitors. Tanner won a silver medal for his entry.

Born on June 21, 1859, Tanner became one of the most famous African-American artists of his era and is considered the first internationally recognized African-American artist. Tanner's early works, such as his famous The *Banjo Lesson* (1893), depicted the everyday life of African-Americans. His later works tended to revolve around religious themes. Tanner's major works include *The Thankful Poor* (1984), *Daniel in the Lion's Den* (1896), *Flight Into Egypt* (1898), *He Healed the Sick*, and *The Raising of Lazarus*. He was awarded the Lippincott Prize in 1900 and the French Legion of Honor in 1923. During the height of his career, Tanner moved to Paris and remained in the City of Lights until his death in 1937.

NOVEMBER 13

On this day in 1985, New York Mets pitcher Dwight Gooden won the Cy Young Award. Just a few days shy of his 21st birthday, and after playing only two seasons in the major leagues, Gooden was the youngest pitcher ever to win this prestigious award. The Cy Young Award is decided by a panel of twenty-four baseball writers; in Gooden's case, all twenty-four judges selected him as their first choice.

In the same year, "Doctor K" was also the youngest pitcher and only the seventh in history to sweep baseball's coveted Triple Crown—highest number of wins (24 games), strikeouts (268), and lowest earned run average (1.53).

Born November 16, 1964, in Tampa, Florida, this African-American baseball prodigy was also the youngest player selected as National League Rookie of the Year, in 1984, and the youngest to be chosen for the All-Star Game. The Doctor's earnings skyrocketed from $40,000 as a rookie to $500,000 in 1985, and to over $5 million per year in the 1990s, making him one of the highest paid players in major league baseball. Gooden was suspended in 1994 for violating major league baseball's antidrug policy.

Everybody raves about Dwight's fastball, but at his peak, he also had the best curveball in the national league.

— Mark "the Shark" Howell, radio sports commentator

The most remarkable thing about him is that he seems to come up with something new every start. Just when you think you might have seen it all, he amazes you again.

— Mets manager Dave Johnson

NOVEMBER 14

"The singers were warmly congratulated by President Hayes, Mrs. Hayes and their guests," reported the *National Republican* on November 14, 1878. The article was referring to opera singer Marie Selika and her husband, the baritone Sampson Williams, who had performed a private concert in the Green Room at the White House. The young coloratura soprano, known as the Queen of Staccato, is believed to be the first African-American to perform at the White House.

James Henry Mapleson, an English impresario, wrote the following in his memoirs about a Selika concert he attended in Philadelphia's "extreme quarters":

On entering, I was quite surprised to find an audience of some 1,500 or 2,000 who were all black, I being the only white man present. *I must say I was amply repaid for the trouble I had taken, as the music was all of the first order.*

In the course of the concert, the prima donna appeared, gorgeously attired in a white satin dress, with feathers in her hair, and a magnificent diamond necklace and earrings....She sang the Shadow Song from Dinorah delightfully, and in reply to a general encore, gave the valse from the Romeo and Juliet of Gounod. In fact, no better singing have I heard.

NOVEMBER 15

On this night in November 1928, New York's Carnegie Hall was packed with admirers of Roland Hayes at the opening of his fifth American tour. His songs "clutched at the throats of enthralled hearers and drew their tears," wrote the *New York Times*. He sang Handel "in the poetic perfection of Milton's English" and Schubert "in limpid tone and crystal diction." Hayes's program closed with a set of Negro spirituals, and it was late in the evening when "an applauding cosmopolitan throng of every complexion and degree of connoisseurship slowly left the hall."

A regular soloist with the Boston Symphony Orchestra and other prominent orchestras, this African-American tenor was popular in both Europe and America in the 1920s. He gave sixty-eight performances in fifty-four cities in one season alone (1924–25). On July 1, 1924, he was awarded the NAACP's Spingarn Medal because he "so finely interpreted the beauty and charm of the Negro folk song."

There is nobody at all who can sing Schubert with such absolute sincerity, with the certainty that his songs are the most beautiful things on earth.

* * *

Art leaves the lowlands of mere polished excellence and rises towards the peaks of greatness, it appeals to something universal, and something far beyond the intellect, something

*you may be pleased to call the soul. And somewhere, con-
cealed, oddly enough nearly everybody has one.*

—critics waxing poetic about Hayes's singing

~~~~~~

NOVEMBER 16

An article in the November 16, 1991 edition of the *New York Times*
reported that basketball superstar Magic Johnson had accepted an
invitation from President George Bush to join the National Commission
on AIDS. Only one week earlier, the 32-year-old had stunned the world
by announcing that he had contracted HIV, the virus that causes AIDS,
and would retire from the Los Angeles Lakers. "The further I go on with
this," commented Magic in a *Sports Illustrated* article, "the more I
believe God picked me. If I didn't believe that, I'm not sure how I could
go on the way I have."

Magic is regarded as one of the greatest basketball players of all time.
He was also one of basketball's highest paid and most likeable characters. The six-foot-nine-inch point guard was the NBA's Most Valuable
Player three times and led the Los Angeles Lakers to five NBA
championships.

Magic and his inveterate rival Larry Bird are often credited with
rejuvenating the sport of professional basketball. Calling them "Ebony
and Ivory, Left Coast and East Coast, the Prince of Hollywood Showtime
and the Lord of the Blue-collar Masses," the September 1994 *Sports
Illustrated* placed Johnson and Bird at number eight on their list of the
most important sports stars of the last forty years.

Before retiring as a player, Magic gave an outstanding performance in
the 1992 NBA All-Star game and was a member of the U.S. Olympic
"Dream Team" in Barcelona, Spain. He then became a coach and part
owner of the Lakers. Johnson has since written a book, *What You Can Do
to Avoid AIDS*. By November 1994, the Magic Johnson Foundation had
raised $7 million in grants and funds for HIV and AIDS organizations in
America.

I want kids to understand that safe sex is the way to go. Sometimes we think that only gay people can get it [HIV], or that it's not going to happen to me. Here I am. And I'm saying it can happen to anybody, even Magic Johnson.

NOVEMBER 17

On this day in 1972, with the help of friend and ex-president Lyndon Baines Johnson, Barbara Jordan of Texas won a seat in the U.S. House of Representatives. This was the first of her three consecutive terms in the House. Jordan was the first African-American female from the Deep South to be elected to Congress and, along with Andrew Young of Atlanta, one of the first African-Americans from the Deep South to be elected to Congress since Reconstruction.

Jordan won a seat in the Texas State Senate in 1966 at the age of 31, making her the first African-American since Reconstruction to sit on the state senate. This Baptist minister's daughter and lawyer soon earned a reputation as an excellent legislator, for which the mayor of Houston proclaimed October 1, 1971, Barbara Jordan Day. The following year she was elected president pro tempore of the state senate. In this capacity she was sworn in as governor one day when both the governor and lieutenant governor were out of state—technically making her the first African-American female governor in America.

Jordan gained national exposure when serving on the House Judiciary Committee, which was considering impeaching President Nixon because of the Watergate scandal. She was selected Woman of the Year in politics in both *Time* and *Ladies Home Journal*, and a *Redbook* survey found that she was the Woman Who Could be President of the United States. She delivered a show-stopping keynote address to the 1976 Democratic National Convention in New York, securing her place in the Orators Hall of Fame. "I never intended to be a run-of-the-mill person," Jordan once said.

NOVEMBER 18

One Sunday in November 1787, Absalom Jones and Richard Allen, along with other free parishioners, attended church at their regular place of worship—St. George's Methodist Episcopal on 4th Street in Philadelphia, Pennsylvania. When the elder called the worshipers to prayer, in the words of Richard Allen:

> *We had not been long on our knees before I heard considerable scuffling and low talking. I raised my head up and saw one of the trustees...having hold of the Rev. Absalom Jones, pulling him up off his knees, and saying, "You must get up—you must not kneel here." Mr. Jones replied, "Wait until prayer is over." Mr.——said, "No, you must get up now, or I will call aid and force you away." Mr. Jones said, "Wait until prayer is over, and I will get up and trouble you no more."*

After prayer the colored parishioners left en masse, never to return. By 1794 Allen had formed the African Methodist Episcopal Church of Philadelphia, the first church in America controlled by African-Americans, and Jones had founded the African Church of St. Thomas, the first African Episcopal church in the United States. An inscription in the vestibule of St. Thomas reads: "The People Who Walked in Darkness Have Seen a Great Light."

NOVEMBER 19

"Stepin Fetchit Dead at 83; Comic Actor in Over 40 Films" read the obituary in *Variety* on this day in 1985. "The son of a Jamaican cigarmaker," said the article, "he was born Lincoln Theodore Monroe

Andrew Perry and was considered the father of black film stars and claimed to be the first black entertainer to become a millionaire." Stepin Fetchit had died of pneumonia and congestive heart failure in Woodland Hills, California.

This talented actor began his career working with partner Ed Lee as the vaudeville team Step'n'Fetchit: Two Dancing Fools from Dixie. The duo took their name from a horse that Perry had won a bet on in Oklahoma in the 1920s. When Perry went solo he kept the name. In 1929 Stepin Fetchit was featured as Gummy in the Hollywood film *Hearts in Dixie*. The first African-American to get feature billing in Hollywood, he went on to appear in some fifty films.

Stepin Fetchit's stereotypical characters—often lazy, dumb, klutzy, no-good, stammering, and shuffling—won him stardom; but they generated ample criticism as well, especially in his later years. His well-publicized personal life, including brawls and spending sprees (he was bankrupt by 1945), added to the rancor over him. Stepin Fetchit's last film was *Won Ton Ton, The Dog Who Saved Hollywood*, in 1976.

Of course, entirely outside the main story (what there is of it) is the amazing personality of Stepin Fetchit. I see no reason for even hesitating in saying he is the best actor that the talking movies have produced. His voice, his manner, his timing, everything that he does, is as near to perfection as one could hope to get....When Stepin Fetchit speaks, you are there beside him, one of the great comedians of the screen.

—a critic's review of Stepin Fetchit's performance in *Hearts in Dixie*

NOVEMBER 20

The Howard Theological Seminary was founded this day in 1866 by Union general Oliver O. Howard, commissioner of the Freedman's Bureau. Howard Seminary was established in an abandoned dancehall and beer saloon "for the education of youth in the liberal arts and social sciences."

Today called Howard University, it has become the nation's largest predominantly African-American university, with a campus covering eighty-nine acres in urban northwest Washington, D.C. Currently, more than 10,000 students are enrolled, 88 percent of whom are African-American.

The first African-American president of Howard University was Mordecai Wyatt Johnson. Johnson is credited with transforming the university "from a cluster of second-rate departments to an institution of national distinction."

> *Howard University has a reputation as being the nation's top predominantly black institution....Its purpose is not to produce more African-American studies majors. Rather, the administration explains, the school is a traditional institution where the African-American perspective is incorporated into the University's curriculum. Chemistry is chemistry, and zoology is zoology. The difference at Howard is that the contributions of African-American scientists such as George Washington Carver or Charles Drew are studied along with those of Jonas Salk or Edward Teller.*
>
> —from Edward B. Fiske's *The Fiske Guide to Colleges* (1994)

NOVEMBER 21

Washington, D.C. resident Alice Frazier once again made international news when she visited Buckingham Palace on this day in 1991. Frazier was the African-American grandmother who topped world news a year earlier when she hugged the queen of England.

In May 1990, during a state visit to the United States, Queen Elizabeth II made a trip to one of Washington D.C.'s poorest neighborhoods, Drake Place in Southeast. Upon entering the government-subsidized house of Alice Frazier, the queen received a bear hug and a spontaneous "How are you doin'?" from the 67-year-old woman.

It is against protocol to touch the queen of England, and shaking hands is only acceptable if the royal monarch has extended her hand first. Frazier is believed to be the first person in history to hug a British queen in public. Nothing but good came of Frazier's breach of protocol, however. Jack Kemp, then secretary of Housing and Urban Development, who was present during the queen's tour, remarked, "What a beautiful sight it was. God bless Mrs. Frazier." In honor of the news-making royal visit, Drake Place was renamed Queen's Stroll in November of 1991.

> *The next split second was one of those incredibly awkward moments the British are so good at. Here was an ordinary American insisting on being herself. The queen froze up. Frazier recoiled. Luckily, Barbara Bush was right behind to share a warm hug with Frazier.*
>
> —an account of the post-hug moment, from the *Washington Post*, May 16, 1991

NOVEMBER 22

Dan "Daddy" Rice performed his Jim Crow routine for the first time in November 1832 at the Bowery Theater in New York City. This white minstrel artist is believed to have modelled his plantation slave character after a crippled, elderly African-American he had seen doing a peculiar song and dance while working in a stable behind a theater. Rice adopted the man's song and odd manner of dancing and soon became famous across America for his Jim Crow minstrel act. His song "Jim Crow" became the first American song to enjoy international success.

> *Turn about an' wheel about an' do jes so*
> *An' ebery time I turn about, I jump Jim Crow.*

The precise origin of the name Jim Crow is uncertain. One source says the disfigured stable hand was himself named Jim Crow; others believe the name is derived from the saying "black as a crow." Yet another theory claims the term originated from a slave owner named Crow, or may have been the name of a soldier and former slave. Whatever its origin, the term later became synonymous with racial discrimination. Jim Crow laws, which prevailed in many southern states from Reconstruction to the 1950s, involved systematic discrimination against African-Americans.

NOVEMBER 23

Patent No. 594,059 was awarded on this day in 1897 to Andrew J. Beard, an African-American inventor. Despite having no formal education in engineering or metalwork, Beard had invented an automatic railroad car coupling device called the Jenny Coupler. Prior to the Jenny Coupler, train cars were joined together manually, causing thousands of railroad workers to lose their hands, arms, and even their lives.

Born in Eastlake, Alabama, in 1850, Beard labored for years in railroad yards, where he personally witnessed horrific accidents when workers tried to execute the rapid procedure of manually coupling train cars with a pin. Beard sold his lifesaving invention to a New York company for $50,000.

NOVEMBER 24

Scott Joplin, the King of Ragtime, was born on this day in 1868 in Texarkana, Texas. A skilled pianist and composer, Joplin started a twenty-year ragtime craze with the release of his composition "Maple Leaf Rag" in 1897, during the Gay Nineties.

Ragtime—scored piano music—at the time was considered Negro tavern and brothel music. Its tinny sound was the source of the name Tin Pan Alley, the center of ragtime in New York City. The lack of recognition of ragtime as a serious African-American musical art form plagued Joplin throughout his life. In his later years, Joplin spent all of his savings producing the ragtime opera *Treemonisha*, which he never saw fully staged. He died in an asylum in New York City on April 1, 1917, at the age of 49.

"The Entertainer," first released by Joplin in 1902, was revived seventy-six years later in the film *The Sting*, landing it on the top-forty charts. The movie's soundtrack, using mostly Joplin's music, sold over two million copies by the end of 1974. The opera *Treemonisha* was also revived and staged in various venues during the 1970s, including a short but successful run on Broadway.

"If you want to criticize *Treemonisha* from a cold academic point of view," said Gunther Schuller, who orchestrated the Houston Grand Opera's production, "you can find plenty of weaknesses....But...it has a period charm that's indestructible." Joplin was posthumously awarded a Pulitzer Prize in 1976 for *Treemonisha* as well as his other works. The Scott Joplin Ragtime Festival is held the first week of June each year in Sedalia, Missouri.

> *You might say he died of disappointments, his health broken mentally and physically. But he was a great man, a great man! He wanted to be a real leader. He wanted to free his people from poverty and ignorance, and superstition, just like the heroine of his ragtime opera, "Treemonisha." That's why he was so ambitious; that's why he tackled major projects. In fact, that's why he was so far ahead of his time....You know, he would often say that he'd never be appreciated until after he was dead.*
>
> —Joplin's wife, Lottie, from Jim Haskin's book *Scott Joplin, The Man Who Made Ragtime*

~~~~~~

NOVEMBER 25

On November 25, 1859, Frances Ellen Watkins Harper wrote a letter of support to John Brown, who was in prison after his unsuccessful raid on Harpers Ferry on October 16 of the same year. Harper had met Brown's wife in Philadelphia when she was staying at the home of abolitionist William Still while awaiting her husband's execution. The letter reads, in part:

Dear Friend:

Although the Hands of Slavery throw a barrier between you and me, and it may not be my privilege to see you in your prison-house, Virginia has not bolts or bars through which I dread to send you my sympathy. In the name of the young girl sold from the warm clasp of a mother's arms to the clutches of a libertine or a profligate,—in the name of the slave mother, her heart rocked to and fro by the agony of her mournful separations,—I thank you, that you have been brave enough to reach out your hands to the crushed and blighted of my race. You have rocked the bloody Bastille; and I hope that from your sad fate great good may arise to the cause of freedom. Already from your prison has come a shout of triumph against the great sin of our country....

...I have written to your dear wife, and sent her a few dollars, and I pledge myself to you that I will continue to assist her....

NOVEMBER 26

At 3:00 P.M. on this day in 1883, in Battle Creek, Michigan, Sojourner Truth passed into the Kingdom of Heaven. Born a slave in Ulster County, New York, Truth freed herself and became a self-styled minister and outstanding orator. She was an outspoken defender of both the abolitionist and feminist movements. Her "Ain't I a Woman" speech, delivered in 1852 in Akron, Ohio, to the second National Women's Suffrage Convention, earned her respect in her own day and secured her place in history.

Sojourner Truth

That man over there says that women have to be helped into carriages and lifted over ditches and to have the best places everywhere. Nobody ever helped me into carriages or over mud puddles or gave me any best place. And ain't I a woman?

Look at me! Look at my arm! I have plowed and planted and gathered into barns and no man could beat me—and ain't I a woman? I could work as much and eat as much as a man— when I could get it—and bear the lash as well, and ain't I a woman?

I have borne thirteen children and seen most of them sold off into slavery and when I cried out with a mother's grief none but Jesus heard—and ain't I a woman?

NOVEMBER 27

The performer of classic psychedelic rock songs, such as "Hey Joe," "Purple Haze," and "The Wind Cries Mary," was born on this day in 1942 in Seattle, Washington. Jimi Hendrix was a talented guitarist and vocalist known for his destructive stage shows during which he smashed guitars, used raw language, and made suggestive gestures. His band was called the Experience and was composed of Hendrix, Mitch Mitchell, and Noel Redding. Jimi Hendrix and the Experience played together from 1966 to 1969. In September 1970 in London, England, Hendrix died of a drug overdose, only one year after being named *Playboy* Artist of the Year.

> *Hendrix's music was perfectly tied to the times. It was a troubled, violent, confused, searching music on the one hand, an assertive, demanding, triumphant, sensual music on the other. Though it was often lost beneath the theatrics, Hendrix was a superb guitarist. His special attraction, however, was his masterful use of feedback. He got sounds out of the guitar that most people didn't imagine ever were there.*
>
> —the *Los Angeles Times*, October 4, 1970

NOVEMBER 28

On this day in 1960, African-American novelist Richard Wright died at the age of 52 in Paris, his adopted home. This self-exiled author wrote such acclaimed books as *Uncle Tom's Children* (1938), *I Tried to Be A Communist* (1944), and *Black Boy* (1945). His works shed new light on the experience of being black in America. In *Native Son* (1940), his most popular book, Wright addresses racism in the northern United States. This was the first book written by an African-American to become a huge mainstream success. It was also the first African-American title to be in the Book-of-the-Month Club, as well as the first in the Modern Library series.

Wright began his literary career in the 1930s. He initially espoused communism, but later moved away from that position. Despite being tagged a "protest novel" writer, his works were much more highly refined than that label might imply, and Wright was highly regarded in literary circles. He was awarded the NAACP's Spingarn Medal in 1941 for "his powerful depiction in his books, *Uncle Tom's Children* and *Native Son*, of the effect of proscription, segregation, and denial of opportunities to the American Negro."

> *He leaped up and opened the can of glue, then broke the seals on all the wads of money. I'm going to have some wallpaper, he said with a luxurious, physical laugh that made him bend at the knees. He took the towel with which he had tied the sack and balled it into a swab and dipped it into the can of glue and dabbed glue on the wall; then he pasted one green bill by the side of another. He stepped back and cocked his head. Jesus! That's funny....He slapped his thighs and guffawed. He had triumphed over the world above ground! He was free!*
>
> —excerpt from Wright's short story "The Man Who Lived Underground," written in the 1940s

NOVEMBER 29

Granville T. Woods patented his most famous invention, the Railway Induction Telegraph System, on this day in 1887. The Induction Telegraph helped reduce train collisions. An article in Cincinnati, Ohio's *Catholic Tribune* remarked on his new invention:

> *Mr. Woods, who is the greatest electrician in the world, still continues to add to his long list of electrical inventions. The*

latest device he invented is the Synchronous Multiplex Railway Telegraph. By means of this system, the railway dispatcher can note the position of any train on the route at a glance. The system also provides means for telegraphing to and from the train while in motion.

Called the Black Edison, Woods registered over fifty patents for electrical devices. His other inventions include a steam boiler furnace, an incubator, automatic air breaks, and an electric motor regulator that reduced loss of electricity and the chances of overheating. Woods was born in Columbus, Ohio, in 1856. He died on January 30, 1910, in New York City.

In the early stages of his career, Woods organized the Woods Electric Company of Cincinnati, Ohio. This company took over by assignment many of his early patents, but as inventions began to multiply and his fame increased, some of the largest and most prosperous technical and scientific corporations in the United States sought his patents. A perusal of the records of the U.S. Patent Office indicates that many of Woods' inventions were assigned to the General Electric Company of New York, Westinghouse Airbrake Company of Pennsylvania, the American Bell Telephone Company of Boston, and the American Engineering Company.

—from Romeo B. Garrett's *Famous First Facts About Negroes*

NOVEMBER 30

On November 30, 1830, the American Society of Free Persons of Colour met for the first time in Philadelphia, Pennsylvania. This permanent society was presided over by Richard Allen, AME bishop and the leading African-American of his day, with William Whipper as secretary.

The American Society of Free Persons of Colour was an outgrowth of the first national convention of African-Americans that had been held in September of the same year at the Bethel AME church in Philadelphia. Forty delegates from nine states, all legally freemen, attended this historic convention. One historian called them "the 40 immortals in our Valhalla."

Conference participants were all abolitionists, but with varying views on nonviolence versus self-defense. The delegates almost unanimously rejected attempts by the American Colonization Society to send African-Americans back to Africa; instead they urged African-American refugees to settle in Canada.

This pioneer convention laid the groundwork for future African-American national gatherings and organizations. In the words of historian Lerone Bennett Jr., the assembly "gave blacks a new conception of themselves and their possibilities" and "expanded the channels of communication."

According to the U.S. Bureau of Census, at the time of the convention of 1830 there were 319,000 free men of color and 2,009,034 enslaved African-Americans. Of the free African-Americans, 3,777 families owned slaves, mainly in Maryland, Louisiana, Virginia, North Carolina, and South Carolina.

This is our home and this is our country. Beneath its sod lies the bones of our fathers; for it, some of them fought, bled, and, died. Here we were born and here we will die.

—excerpt from the report of a local convention, held in New York around the same time as the national convention in Philadelphia

DECEMBER 1

On this day in 1955 in Montgomery, Alabama, after a long day of work as a seamstress, Rosa Parks refused to relinquish her bus seat to a white man. This was in defiance of a local Jim Crow law which allowed black passengers to sit only if no whites had to stand. Parks said, "My only concern was to get home after a hard day's work," but she set off a 381-day bus boycott, led by a young and relatively unknown preacher named Martin Luther King Jr. Addressing a community gathering on the first night of the boycott, Reverend King explained:

> There comes a time that people get tired. We are here this evening to say to those who have mistreated us for so long that we are tired—tired of being segregated and humiliated; tired of being kicked about by the brutal feet of oppression. We had no alternative but protest.

The boycott ended successfully in December 1956. King later called Parks "the great fuse that led to the modern stride toward freedom." In June 1973 Parks was awarded an honorary L.H.D. (Doctor of Humanities) from Columbia College in Chicago. The award citation said, "Truly, when you sat down in a Montgomery, Alabama bus, all men and women were free to stand more humanly erect."

DECEMBER 2

On this day in 1859 John Brown was hanged for treason in Charles Town. On October 16 of the same year, Brown had led a band of twenty-one men, including two of his sons and five African-Americans, in an attack on Harpers Ferry, West Virginia—then located in the southern slave-holding state of Virginia. Brown's band easily took control of the town's federal armory and arsenal, and then stationed themselves inside an engine house, holding eleven hostages. Instead of sparking a local slave uprising, as Brown had confidently anticipated, residents attacked him and his men and held them under siege for two days until federal troops arrived from Washington, D.C. Under command of Col. Robert E. Lee, the troops stormed the fort and captured Brown.

The son of an Underground Railroad stationmaster, Brown had organized an antislavery convention in Chatham, Canada in May 1858, attended by about sixty blacks and a dozen whites. At the convention, Brown revealed his plan to establish a stronghold for runaway slaves en route to the North closer to the Mason-Dixon line—thus the attack on Harpers Ferry. In December 1958, he had successfully carried out a practice raid in which he freed eleven slaves in Missouri and sent them to Canada.

According to author Langston Hughes, "The Civil War that freed the slaves began with John Brown's raid on Harpers Ferry in 1859." W. E. B. DuBois echoed this sentiment, contending that Brown's attack "did more to shake the foundation of slavery than any single thing that happened in America." A monument to John Brown in Akron, Ohio, reads, "He died to set his brothers free and his soul goes marching on." One of the five African-Americans present at the raid, Osborne Perry Anderson, escaped and two years later wrote the book *A Voice From Harper's Ferry*.

> *You may dispose of me very easily. I am nearly disposed of now, but this question is still to be settled—this Negro question, I mean—the end of that is not yet.*
>
> —John Brown after being captured at Harpers Ferry

DECEMBER 3

The *North Star* newspaper was founded by Frederick Douglass on this day in 1847 in Rochester, New York. The paper's slogan was: Right is of no sex—Truth is of no color—God is the father of us all, and all we are Brethren.

Douglass had recently returned from England, where he lectured on such subjects as slavery and women's rights for two years. Overseas he had accumulated enough money to purchase his own freedom and to establish the newspaper.

Frederick Douglass

A principal spokesperson of the abolition movement, Douglass felt that "the man *struck*" should be "the man to *cry out*." His first editorial read:

To Our Oppressed Countrymen:

We solemnly dedicate the North Star to the cause of our long oppressed and plundered fellow countrymen....Giving no quarter to slavery at the South, it will hold no truce with oppressors at the North. While it shall boldly advocate emancipation for our enslaved brethren, it will omit no opportunity to gain for the nominally free, complete enfranchisement. Every effort to injure or degrade you or your cause...shall find in it a constant, unswerving and inflexible foe.

DECEMBER 4

The first African-American Greek letter society was founded on this day in 1906. The fraternity Alpha Phi Alpha was organized as a literary and study group at New York's Cornell University, a predominantly white school.

The first African-American sorority, Alpha Kappa Alpha, was founded in January 1908 at Howard University in Washington, D.C. Some three years later, Omega Psi Phi was also founded at Howard University, becoming the first fraternity established on an all-black college campus.

The majority of African-American letter societies emerged around this same time, including the fraternities Kappa Alpha Psi (1911) and Phi Beta Sigma (1914), and the sororities Delta Sigma Theta (1913) and Zeta Phi Beta (1920).

Today Delta Sigma Theta, with some 125,000 members, is one of the world's largest black women's groups. Prominent members have included Mary Church Terrell, Mary McLeod Bethune, Patricia Roberts Harris, Lena Horne, Leontyne Price, and Roberta Flack.

Omega Psi Phi boasts over 100,000 members. Its ranks have included, Carter G. Woodson, Dr. Percy Julian, Langston Hughes, Bill Cosby, Michael Jordan, and Jesse Jackson. Like other African-American fraternities and sororities, Omega Psi Phi raises considerable funds each year for donation to charitable and community projects, such as adopt-a-school programs and literacy training. The fraternity donated $50,000 dollars in 1990, $100,000 in 1991, and $150,000 in 1992 to the United Negro College Fund. They have undertaken historical restoration projects, awarded college scholarships, sponsored historical exhibits, held youth leadership conferences, and organized talent searches.

We have to move down the economic avenue as contributors, producers, and managers of finance. We have to address the Black male youth in this country. Both are a vital link to our future.

—Omega Psi Phi's Grand Basileus C. Tyrone Gilmore in *Ebony*,
September 1993

DECEMBER 5

On this day in 1946, President Harry S. Truman signed Executive Order No. 9808. This landmark order established the first President's Committee on Civil Rights, charged with examining law enforcement agencies and government systems to determine how their means of safeguarding the civil rights of Americans could be improved and strengthened. The committee was ordered to report their findings to the president in writing. The order reads:

Whereas the preservation of civil rights guaranteed by the Constitution is essential to domestic tranquility, national security, the general welfare, and the continued existence of our free institutions; and
Whereas the action of individuals who take the law into their own hands and inflict summary punishment and weak

personal vengeance is subversive of our democratic system of law enforcement and public criminal justice, and gravely threatens our form of government; and

Whereas it is essential that all possible steps be taken to safeguard our civil rights...
[Creation of the committee is then outlined.]

The committee's report, titled "To Secure These Rights," noted that American democracy suffered from "a moral dry rot." The report went largely unheeded by lawmakers.

DECEMBER 6

Thomas Barber, an African-American pioneer of the American West, was murdered on this day in 1855 in Lawrence, Kansas. The following are excerpts of a poem written in his memory which appeared in Whittier's *The Anti-Slavery Poems:*

> *Bear him, comrades, to his grave;*
> *Never over one more brave*
>   *Shall the prairie grasses weep,*
> *In the ages yet to come,*
> *When the millions in our room,*
>   *What we sow in tears, shall reap.*

> *Bear him up the icy hill,*
> *With the Kansas, frozen still*
>   *As his noble heart, below,*
> *And the land he came to till*
> *With a freeman's thews and will,*
>   *And his poor hut roofed with snow!...*

> *While the flag with stars bedecked*
> *Threatens where it should protect,*

And the Law shakes hands with Crime,
What is left us but to wait,
Match our patience to our fate,
    And abide the better time? ...

Plant the Buckeye on his grave,
For the hunter of the slave,
    In its shadow cannot rest;
And let martyr mound and tree
Be our pledge and guaranty
    Of the freedom of the West!

DECEMBER 7

Doris "Dorie" Miller, a navy mess attendant, was going about his daily chores of gathering laundry on the USS *Arizona* on this day in 1941 when Japanese war planes attacked Pearl Harbor. Miller ran on deck and manned a machine gun. With no previous gun training, he shot down four enemy planes before being ordered to abandon ship. Miller was awarded the Navy Cross for his extraordinary courage.

The 24-year-old black hero was then sent on a tour of African-American communities to help sell war bonds. He went back into the navy, again as a mess attendant, and was stationed on an aircraft carrier in the Pacific. In 1943 the *Liscombe Bay* was hit by a Japanese torpedo killing all on board—including the first hero of World War II, Dorie Miller.

I turned on my radio and I heard Mr. Roosevelt say,
I turned on my radio and I heard Mr. Roosevelt say,
"We want to stay out of Europe and Asia but now we all got
    a debt to pay."
We even sold the Japanese brass and scrap-iron and it makes
    my blood boil in the vein,

We even sold the Japanese brass and scrap-iron and it makes
   my blood boil in the vein,
'Cause they made bombs and shells out of it and dropped
   them on Pearl Harbor just like rain.

—"Pearl Harbor Blues," recorded by "Doctor" Clayton in March 1942 in
Chicago

DECEMBER 8

On this day in 1967, Maj. Robert H. Lawrence Jr., the first African-American astronaut, was killed when his F-104 Starfighter crashed at Edwards Air Force Base in California's Mojave Desert. The crash occurred only six months after the 31-year-old air force major had been appointed to the NASA space program.

A native of Chicago, Illinois, Lawrence worked his way through high school and college, earning a B.S. in chemistry from Bradley University and a Ph.D. in physical chemistry from Ohio State University. He was the only astronaut at the time who held a doctorate degree.

Asked by journalists if his selection to the space program was a "tremendous step forward in race relations," Lawrence replied he thought it was "just another of the things we look forward to in the normal progression of civil rights in this country."

Lawrence was the ninth astronaut to have died in an accident. It wasn't until 1983 that an African-American astronaut—Guion S. Bluford Jr. of the crew of the space shuttle Challenger—actually traveled into space.

DECEMBER 9

On December 9, 1872, Pinckney Benton Stewart Pinchback was sworn in as governor of Louisiana. A former riverboat hand, P. B. S. Pinchback was a major Reconstruction politician. He held more high-level government offices than any African-American in history. He was the first African-American president pro tempore of a state senate; for a short time in 1871–72 he served as lieutenant governor and acting governor of Louisiana; in 1872 he was elected to the U.S. House of Representatives; in 1873 he was elected to the U.S. Senate.

A well-dressed, daring, and handsome man with "Brazilian" good looks, Pinchback was a popular national figure. His arrival in Washington D.C. was reported to thrill the capital's high-society women, who apparently jockeyed to get the opportunity to meet him. Upon arrival at the Senate, Pinch, as he was known, stated:

> I am not here as a beggar. I do not care so far as I am personally concerned whether you give me my seat or not. I will go back to my people and come here again; but I tell you to preserve your own consistency. Do not make fish of me while you make flesh of everybody else.

Pinchback was denied his seat in the Senate on March 8, 1876.

DECEMBER 10

Today in 1967, the Lost Genius of Soul died along with six others when his private airplane crashed into Lake Monona in Madison, Wisconsin. Just three days earlier, the 26-year-old Otis Redding had recorded his most memorable hit "(Sittin' on) the Dock of the Bay." This classic tune shot to number one on the *Billboard* chart and stayed there for four weeks, selling over one million copies. Redding's earlier hits included "My Girl," "Satisfaction," "Try a Little Tenderness," "Day Tripper," "Shake," and "Let Me Come on Home."

> *Otis Redding had one of the most honest, heartfelt and emotional voices in soul music history and thoroughly deserves all the recognition he has acquired over the years. He was a visionary who sang about life and the human condition with deep understanding and knowledge but without being bombastic or preaching. His voice was gentle yet confident, it could sing the ultimate love song and very often did.*

—author Ralph Tee in *The Best of Soul: The Essential CD Guide*

DECEMBER 11

'Dr. King Accepts Nobel Peace Prize as 'Trustee'" read the front page of the *New York Times* on this day in 1964. Dr. Martin Luther King Jr. had accepted the Nobel Peace Prize in Oslo, Norway, "on behalf of the civil rights movement and 'all men who love peace and brotherhood.'"

At a ceremony in a marble hall at Oslo University attended by the king of Norway and other world leaders and diplomats, the 35-year-old Baptist minister and civil rights leader said:

> *We feel that we are the conscience of America—we are its troubled souls—we will continue to insist that right be done because both God's will and the heritage of our nation speak through our echoing demands.*

Malcolm X, a contemporary of King's but with a different approach to civil rights, was skeptical of the occasion. "He got the prize, we got the problem," said Malcolm. "If I'm following a general, and he's leading me into battle, and the enemy tends to give him rewards, or awards, I get suspicious of him. Especially if he gets a peace award before the war is over."

King himself questioned the notion of receiving an award for a cause that had not yet won its goal of peace and brotherhood and that was "beleaguered and committed to unrelenting struggle." After contemplation, King concluded that the award was given as "a profound recognition that nonviolence is the answer to the crucial political and moral questions of our time—the need for man to overcome oppression and violence without resorting to violence and oppression." King donated the prize of about $54,600 to the civil rights movement.

Non-violence is a powerful and just weapon. It is a weapon unique in history, which cuts without wounding and ennobles the man who wields it. It is a sword that heals.

—Martin Luther King Jr.

DECEMBER 12

Several major events took place on this landmark day for African-Americans and the sport of golf:

- On December 12, 1899, Dr. George F. Grant, a Harvard-educated African-American dentist, patented the wooden golf tee. Prior to Grant's invention, mounds of dirt were used by golfers to elevate the ball.
- On this day in 1969, African-American golfer Charlie Sifford of North Carolina won the Los Angeles Open, helping to break professional golf's color line. "All I had was a stupid head, a raggedy golf game, and determination to be a golfer, one of the best in the world, not a black golfer," said Sifford, according to the *Black Athlete*.
- On this same day in 1974, Lee Elder also won the Los Angeles Open. During his thirty years of play in the PGA, Lee Elder was the first African-American professional golfer to earn over $1 million. On the

heels of Lee Elder came Calvin Peete, "the best black golfer to date," who won some $2 million in PGA play.

African-Americans had been barred from playing professional golf up to the middle of this century. Because the PGA's 1916 constitution prohibited nonwhites, the United Golf Association (UGA) was formed in 1928. The UGA held regional tournaments and national opens. Presenting only a $100 first prize at its first national open, the UGA soon became known as the Peanut Circuit. With prizes this meager, players had trouble sustaining golf as a hobby, let alone a career. In 1948 three African-American golfers sued the PGA for denying them places in a tournament for which they qualified, finally forcing the PGA to drop their caucasians-only rule.

DECEMBER 13

On this day in 1944, African-American women were sworn in for the first time to the Women Accepted for Volunteer Emergency Services (WAVES), a women's naval reserve. The WAVES were the first women's branch of the U.S. armed forces to achieve full racial integration of companies and duties. However, by 1945 there were not yet fifty African-American WAVES.

The majority of African-American females who served during World War II enlisted in the Women's Army Corps (WACs). Of the estimated 350,000 women in the armed forces during World War II, about 4,000 were African-American. "World War II provided the first opportunity for significant numbers of black women to serve in the American military," states a Department of Defense publication.

> As a direct result of pressure from the American black community, 800 black women from the Army Air Forces and the Army Services Forces were organized into the 6888th Postal Battalion and sent to England and later to the European

mainland where they performed a commendable service by unraveling the gigantic snag that had developed with regard to the delivery of mail to servicemen.

—excerpt from the Department of Defense publication *Black Americans in Defense of Our Nation*

By the war's end, over one million African-Americans, both male and female, had entered the U.S. military. This represented about 6 percent of the total number of Americans who served. (By comparison, in 1992 African-Americans composed over 30 percent of the U.S. armed forces.)

~~~~~~

DECEMBER 14

On December 14, 1964, the U.S. Supreme Court ruled unanimously against an Atlanta hotel owner who refused service to African-Americans. The hotel owner challenged the Civil Rights Act, which had become law in July, claiming Congress did not have the right to regulate discrimination in private accommodations.

The Civil Rights Act of 1964 was the most comprehensive antibias statute ever written and employed federal means to prevent private discrimination. The act prohibited discrimination on the basis of race, sex, religion, or nation of origin in public facilities such as schools, as well as in private facilities including hotels, restaurants, and pools. The act also prohibited discrimination in employment and federally-funded programs. With this act the Equal Employment Opportunity Commission was formed.

In *Heart of Atlanta Motel, Inc. v. United States*, the Supreme Court found that racial discrimination by private businesses did, in fact, violate the Thirteenth and Fourteenth Amendments. This decision overturned an October 15, 1883, Supreme Court ruling. At that time the Court declared that Congress did not have authority to make laws regarding racial discrimination by privately-owned businesses, as conservatives considered this to be an infringement on personal freedom of choice. The 1883 ruling itself overturned the Civil Rights Act of 1875.

~~~~~~

DECEMBER 15

Today in 1761, Jupiter Hammon published the broadside poem "An Evening Thought: Salvation by Christ with Penitential Cries." This was the first single poem published by an African-American. (Phillis Wheatley published the first volume of poetry in 1773.) In 1778 Hammon released "An Address to Miss Phillis Wheatley, Ethiopian Poetess," in Boston, the second of his several broadside poems. Broadside meant that the works were printed on one side of a large sheet of paper.

Hammon was born in Africa in 1720. He became a house slave of the Lloyd family of Queens Village on Long Island, New York, where he was encouraged to learn to read and write. Hammon is generally considered the first African-American man of letters.

> Salvation comes by Christ alone,
>   The only Son of God;
> Redemption now to every one,
>   That loves his holy Word.
>
> Dear Jesus, give thy Spirit now,
>   Thy grace to every Nation,
> That han't the Lord to whom we bow,
>   The Author of Salvation.
>
> Dear Jesus, unto Thee we cry,
>   Give us the Preparation;
> Turn not away thy tender Eye;
>   We seek thy true Salvation.

> Lord, hear our penitential Cry;
> Salvation from above;
> It is the Lord that doth supply,
> With his Redeeming Love.
>
> Dear Jesus, by thy precious Blood,
> The World Redemption have;
> Salvation now comes from the Lord,
> He being thy captive slave....

—the first five stanzas of An Evening Thought: Salvation by Christ with Penitential Cries

DECEMBER 16

On this day in 1976, Andrew Young was named ambassador to the United Nations, a cabinet-level post under the Carter Administration. He was the first African-American to hold this position. Young was later pressured into resigning from his U.N. assignment because of a secret meeting he held with the Palestinian Liberation Organization in violation of U.S. policy.

An ordained minister and promotor of nonviolent change, Young was active in the civil rights movement of the 1950s and 1960s, and was a chief associate of Dr. Martin Luther King Jr. From 1972 to 1977 he served in the U.S. House of Representatives for Georgia, one of the Deep South's first African-American congress members since Reconstruction. Young was mayor of Atlanta from 1982 until 1990. His 1990 bid for governor of Georgia was unsuccessful.

> After all, in our prisons too there are hundreds, perhaps even thousands, of people I would call political prisoners. Ten years

ago in Atlanta I myself was tried for having organized a protest movement.

—Andrew Young quoted in *U.S. News & World Report* on July 28, 1978, after President Carter had just condemned the USSR for trials of Soviet dissidents. This statement was construed as undercutting Carter's human rights campaign.

Nothing is illegal if one hundred businessmen decide to do it, and that's true anywhere in the world.

—Andrew Young

DECEMBER 17

Maria W. Stewart, the first American-born woman to give public lectures in America, was buried this day in 1879 at Graceland Cemetery in Washington, D.C. She died at the age of 76. The *People's Advocate*, a Washington D.C. newspaper, remembered Stewart in an article dated February 28, 1880:

> *Few, very few know of the remarkable career of this woman whose life has just drawn to a close. For half a century she was engaged in the work of elevating her race by lectures, teaching and various missionary and benevolent labors.*

Stewart delivered four public lectures in Boston in 1832 and 1833, speaking on issues of education, political rights, and public recognition for African-Americans. She also wrote essays for the *Liberator* newspaper, making her the first African-American woman to write on political subjects. She was opposed to the "back to Africa" colonization movement.

A pioneer in women's rights, civil rights, and the abolitionist movement, Stewart's style has been called "challenging," "unsparing," and "militant." She wove deep religious convictions into her speeches and writings, giving them an almost evangelical flare. Like many of today's evangelical preachers, she used "call and response" techniques and rhetorical questions to captivate audiences.

O, ye daughters of Africa awake! awake! arise! no longer sleep nor slumber, but distinguish yourselves. Show forth to the world that ye are endowed with noble and exalted faculties.

—from her pamphlet *Productions of Mrs. Maria W. Stewart,* printed in 1835

DECEMBER 18

Andrew Jackson issued the following proclamation on December 18, 1814, in New Orleans to the African-American soldiers who fought with him in the War of 1812:

TO THE MEN OF COLOR.—Soldiers! From the shores of Mobile I collected you to arms; I invited you to share in the perils and to divide the glory of your white countrymen. I expected much from you, for I was not uninformed of those qualities which must render you so formidable to an invading foe. I knew that you could endure hunger and thirst and all the hardships of war. I knew that you loved the land of your nativity, and that like ourselves, you had to defend all that is most dear to you. But you surpass my hopes. I have found in you, united to these qualities, that noble enthusiasm which impels to great deeds.

On this same day in 1865, it was announced that the Thirteenth Amendment, abolishing slavery, had been ratified by the required number of states. The following is the first verse of a celebration poem written for the occasion.

It is done!
Clang of bell and roar of gun
Send the tidings up and down.
How the belfries rock and reel!
How the great guns, peal on peal,
Fling the joy from town to town!

DECEMBER 19

Carter G. Woodson was born on this day in 1875 in New Canton, Virginia. The son of former slaves, Woodson is known as the Father of Black History. A Harvard-educated historiographer, he founded the Association for Negro Life and History, and in 1916 began publishing the *Journal of Negro History.* As an educator in Washington, D.C., Woodson became aware that history textbooks glossed over the role of African-Americans. Thus, in 1937 he began producing the *Negro History Bulletin* for elementary and secondary school teachers.

Woodson advocated the establishment of a Black History Week each February to coincide with the birthdays of President Lincoln and abolitionist Frederick Douglass. The first Black History Week was held in 1926. The celebration now spans the entire month of February as Black History Month.

Woodson wrote numerous books, including *A Century of Negro Migration* (1918), *Negro Orators and Their Orations* (1925), *The Miseducation of the Negro* (1933), and *African Heroes and Heroines* (1939). He was awarded the NAACP's Spingarn Medal in 1926 for his pioneering achievements in African-American history. Through his work, both black and white communities were encouraged to reexamine African-American history, as well as African history.

Woodson died in 1950 at the age of 74 in Washington, D.C. His home at 1538 Ninth Street, N.W., is a national historic landmark.

We have a wonderful history behind us....It reads like the
history of people in an heroic age....If you read the history of

Africa, the history of your ancestors—people of whom you should feel proud—you will realize that they have a history that is worthwhile. They have traditions that have value of which you can boast and upon which you can base a claim for the right to share in the blessings of democracy. We are going back to that beautiful history and it is going to inspire us to greater achievements.

—Woodson from *The Black 100*

DECEMBER 20

A *Variety* film review, dated December 20, 1939, after applauding the performances of Vivien Leigh (as Scarlett O'Hara) and Clark Gable (as Rhett Butler), read:

On the heels of these two, Hattie McDaniel, as Mammy, comes closest with a bid for top position as a trooper. It is she who contributes the most moving scene in the film, her plea with Melanie that the latter should persuade Rhett to permit burial of his baby daughter. Time will set a mark on this moment in the picture as one of those inspirational bits of histrionics long remembered.

Hattie McDaniel won an Oscar for Best Supporting Actress for her portrayal of Mammy in the classic *Gone With the Wind*. She was the first African-American to win an Academy Award.

McDaniel began her career on the vaudeville circuit. An excellent blues singer, she was the first African-American woman to sing on radio. She starred in the *Beulah* series on both radio and television.

During the 1930s and 1940s McDaniel acted in over seventy films. Her roles were nearly all the same, playing the supportive, but independent and outspoken Mammy-type, which she had perfected in *Gone With the Wind*. Asked about her restricted movie roles, she replied, "I would rather play a maid than be one."

339

DECEMBER 21

Today in 1767, Phillis Wheatley's first poem, titled "On Messrs. Hussey and Coffin," was published in the *Newport Mercury*. Upon publishing *Poems on Various Subjects, Religious and Moral* in January 1773, Wheatley became the first African-American and second American woman to publish a volume of poetry.

Born in Senegal and brought to Boston, Massachusetts, as a slave, this child prodigy became the most famous eighteenth-century black poet in America and Europe. Her writings, in conforming to the style of the colonial era, tended to be puritanical and unemotional; the main themes were education, virtue, and religion. Although her poetry may not have been exceedingly masterful, the poetess impressed all those she met with her wit, poise, and modesty, not to mention her attractiveness. She was well received by prominent Americans like Thomas Jefferson, John Hancock, and George Washington, as well as by British high society during a trip to England.

Always in fragile health, Wheatley's physical state declined even further after her runabout husband abandoned her and their children. One evening, after she returned home after working twelve hours as a housekeeper, an exhausted Wheatley laid on the bed beside her youngest child—the last surviving of three—until their hearth fire burned out. That night mother and child died of malnutrition, fatigue, and cold. Wheatley was 31 years old. Friends and fans learned of her death four days later, when it was announced on December 9, 1784, in Boston's *Independent Chronicle*.

> *But when these shades of time are chased away,*
> *And darkness ends in everlasting day,*
> *On what seraphic pinions shall we move,*
> *And view the landscapes in the realms above?*
> *There shall my tongue in heav'nly transport glow;*
> *No more to tell of Damon's tender sighs,*
> *Or rising radiance of Aurora's eyes,*

For nobler themes demand a nobler strain,
And purer language on th' ethereal plane.
Cease, gentle music! the solemn gloom of night
Now seals the fair creation from my sight.

—Wheatley poem about death

~~~~~~

DECEMBER 22

On this day in 1939 the "Mother of the Blues" died of heart disease at the age of 53 in Columbus, Georgia. Ma Rainey was the first of the legendary blues singers. Bedecked in glittery jewelry and fancy dresses, and belting out the blues in her dramatic, melancholic style, Rainey came into fame and fortune during the classic blues period of the pre-Depression.era.

She was born Gertrude Malissa Nix Pridgett on April 26, 1886. As a child she worked in the Negro vaudeville shows in the South, singing and dancing with the Rabbit Foot Minstrels. By the 1920s she was touring America with her Georgia Jazz Band making a respectable living as a headliner act on the Theatre Owners' Booking Association circuit. Rainey's folk-blues held a special appeal for the mainly working-class vaudeville audiences in the South and Midwest.

The "Black Nightingale" signed with Paramount Records in 1923, and within five years she had recorded ninety-two records earning another nickname—the "Paramount Wildcat." Now that Ma's hits like "Bad Luck Blues" and "Moonshine Blues" were on vinyl, African-Americans who had recently migrated to northern cities could reminisce about home at will.

Train's at the station, I heard the whistle blow,
Train's at the station, I heard the whistle blow,
I done bought my ticket but I don't know where I'll go.

—Ma Rainey's "Traveling Blues"

341

Many days of sorrow, many nights of woe,
Many days of sorrow, many nights of woe,
And a ball and chain, everywhere I go.

Chains on my feet, padlocks on my hands,
Chains on my feet, padlocks on my hands,
It's all on account of stealing a woman's man.

—Ma Rainey's "Chain Gang Blues" (1925)

DECEMBER 23

Sarah Breedlove was born in Louisiana on this day in 1867 to former slave parents. Orphaned as a young girl, married at the age of 14, and widowed by 20, Breedlove went on to become the first African-American female millionaire.

Madame C. J. Walker, as she became known after her second marriage to newspaperman Charles J. Walker, invented a hair conditioning and straightening formula and enlisted "home visiting agents" to sell her products, opening the door to the world of cosmetics, hair products, and toiletries for African-American women. Walker also established beauty salons in the United States, the Caribbean, and Europe. Josephine Baker, an African-American cabaret star residing in France, was known to be a fan of Walker's products.

This former washerwoman was a generous philanthropist. She made donations to the NAACP, Bethune-Cookman College, the Tuskegee Institute, and other African-American educational establishments.

There was some debate over Madame C. J. Walker's beauty products, in particular the hot comb and conditioner for straightening hair. Several contemporaries, such as Marcus Garvey, felt these beauty techniques were an attempt to make black women look more like whites. Others, like James Weldon Johnson, felt the products were simply a means to enhance a black woman's natural beauty. Explained Johnson:

She taught the masses of coloured women a secret age-old, but lost to them—the secret every woman ought to know. She taught them the secret of feminine beauty.

∿∿∿∿∿∿∿∿∿∿∿∿∿∿∿∿∿∿∿∿∿∿∿∿∿∿∿∿∿∿∿∿∿∿∿

DECEMBER 24

Last Christmas was my most memorable one. Everything seemed to work out right. The farmhouse was finally finished and we decorated with real evergreen garlands and holly boughs...the whole setting was perfect—a snowy Christmas Eve with my family and many of the people I love most. Even the dogs were decked out in red bows. We opened gifts by the fireside and drank hot cider.

Oprah Winfrey, America's richest female entertainer, was responding to the query "What Was the Best Christmas You Ever Had?" in an article in the December 1991 *Ebony* magazine.

The mega-star had reason to feel warmly reminiscent of her most recent years: A 1990 Gallup Poll had listed her among the people most admired by Americans; her combined earnings from 1990 and 1991 bolstered her to number three on the *Forbes* list of the forty richest entertainers; and *The Oprah Winfrey Show*, her popular daytime television talk show had brought in $157 million in 1991.

Winfrey's phenomenal success may be attributed to her charismatic personality, franktalking style, and an endless ability to sympathize, and in many cases empathize, with her audience. She herself struggled with sexual abuse as a child and weight problems as an adult.

A former beauty contest winner, Oprah began her television career at the age of 19 as a news anchor in Nashville, Tennessee. She then cohosted a talk show in Baltimore, Maryland, and later hosted a morning talk show in Chicago. She first gained national recognition when she appeared in the 1985 Steven Spielburg film *The Color Purple*, for which she was nominated for an Academy Award. The popularity of her Chicago talk show eventually forced the *Phil Donahue Show* to transfer from Chicago to New York. By 1989 *TV Guide* claimed she was the richest woman on television.

~~~~~~

DECEMBER 25

Cabell Calloway Jr. was born on Christmas Day in 1907 in Rochester, New York. "Cab" Calloway rose to stardom during the big-band era of the 1930s. He first entered the limelight as leader of the Missourians, the house band at Harlem's Cotton Club. Calloway became known for his scat singing—a style using nonsense syllables—on songs like "St. Louis Blues" and "Minnie the Moocher." His trademark "Hi-de-Ho" shout was repeated across America, becoming part of the lexicon of the era. Not strictly a great musician, Calloway's fame stemmed from a flamboyant and upbeat stage personality and his knack for leading talent-filled big bands.

Throughout Calloway's long career he appeared in several films, such as *Big Broadcast* (1932), *The Cincinnati Kid* (1965), and *The Blues Brothers* (1980). He also played roles in the stage productions of *Porgy and Bess* and *Hello Dolly*. Calloway died on November 18, 1984, in White Plains, New York, at the age of 87.

My audience is my life. What I did and how I did it, was all for my audience.

Clean living. I don't do anything that would injure my health. That's why I'm eighty-one years old and I've been able to work this long.

—Calloway, quoted in 1988

DECEMBER 26

Today marks the first day of Kwanzaa. Kwanzaa is a uniquely African-American holiday that was conceived in the 1960s by Dr. Maulana Ron Karenga, a professor at the University of California.

The name Kwanzaa is derived from the Kiswahili phrase *Matunda Ya Kwanzaa*, which means first fruits and is used to refer to harvest celebrations in Africa. Kwanzaa lasts for seven days, each day designed around *Nguzo Saba*, or seven principles, based on African values. They are:

Umoja: unity
Kujichagulia: self-determination
Ujima: cooperative work and responsibility
Ujamaa: cooperative economics
Nia: purpose
Kuumba: creativity
Imani: faith

This nonreligious holiday has gained popularity in communities, homes, and schools in America's major cities, as well as being celebrated

Kwanzaa

345

throughout the African diaspora—including Canada, the Caribbean, and parts of Africa and Europe. It is estimated that as many as thirteen million Americans celebrate Kwanzaa.

> *Kwanzaa brings families and communities together to cele-brate the "fruits" of their year's labors, to give thanks (asante), to evaluate their achievments and contributions to family and community, and to lay plans and set goals for the year ahead.*

> —from David A. Anderson's *Kwanzaa: An Everyday Resource and Instructional Guide*

> *The fact that we are black is our ultimate reality.*

> —Maulana Ron Karenga

DECEMBER 27

On December 27, 1919, twelve African-American men were condemned to die for the killings of whites during rioting in Elaine, Arkansas, in November of the same year. It all began when African-American tenant farmers who were attempting to organize a union held a meeting on September 30, 1919. The meeting was attacked by suspicious whites, and in a confusing firefight a white man was shot. The next day rumors spread that the tenant farmers intended to revolt, kill landowners, and steal their property. Riots broke out, with some whites and many blacks losing their lives.

Scipio Africanus Jones, a respected African-American lawyer from Little Rock, and Colonel Murphy, an elderly ex-Confederate soldier, took up the defense of the condemned men. The two lawyers appealed to the state supreme court for a new trial, which was granted. However, the colonel died during the appeal trial, leaving Jones to fight the case alone. A persistent and courageous Jones ventured into the courtroom in virulently racist Helena, the seat of Phillips County. During the trials, for his safety, he slept at a different African-American family's house each night, knocking on their door without prior notice and being received without question.

After repeated appeals by Jones, the case was finally brought to the Supreme Court in 1922. On February 13, 1923, the Supreme Court agreed a fair trial was not possible in the heated environment of Helena and called for a retrial. By this time six of the defendants had already been discharged by the Arkansas Supreme Court. The Arkansas governor reduced the sentences of the remaining six men to twenty years in jail. By January 14, 1924, Jones had convinced the governor to grant the men pardons—four years and one month after they had been sentenced to death.

DECEMBER 28

Today in 1835, the first battle of the second Seminole War was fought. A Seminole and Seminole Negro force attacked a column of 100 soldiers under the command of Maj. Francis L. Dade, who had been sent to reinforce Fort King. Led by Alligator, Jumper, and Micanopy, the warriors wiped out Dade's column near Wahoo Swamp, beginning seven more years of fighting.

The United States had acquired Florida from Spain in 1819, after which the U.S. government attempted to forcibly remove Native Americans from Florida to Indian territory west of the Mississippi. The Seminole Indians and Seminole Negroes put up violent resistance to being relocated to a foreign land, where hostile Indian tribes and harsh weather threatened their survival.

The precise incident which sparked the brewing second Seminole War was the seizure of the half-Indian, half-black wife of Osceola, the Seminole leader. Osceola was thrown in jail for his violent protests to her capture. However, the Seminole chief got his revenge when his men defeated General Dade's column.

The second Seminole War was the most intense Indian war in U.S. history. It cost $32 million dollars, as well as the lives of 600 soldiers, 30 officers, and hundreds of Seminole Indians and Seminole Negroes.

...the Indians themselves are determined to hold out, and are encouraged and sustained by the gang of sable banditti nominally their slaves, but who are really their chief counsellors, and in effect their masters. It is a negro, not an Indian war.

—excerpt from an article in the *New Orleans Bulletin*, January 7, 1837; at the start of the war there were about 1,800 Seminole forces, of which some 250 were Negroes

DECEMBER 29

The Cleveland Browns played their last game of the season against the Detroit Lions on this day in 1957. Although the Browns were solidly defeated in their bid for the NFL title, it wrapped up an incredible season for rookie fullback Jimmy Brown. The Cleveland Brown's first-year sensation led the league in rushing, with 942 yards, and broke the NFL record for most yards rushing in one game (237 against the Los Angeles Rams).

Known for his aggressive running style, Brown broke almost all existing rushing records during his career. In Brown's nine seasons in the NFL, he led the league in rushing eight times. He is the only running back in NFL history to average more than five yards per carry and remains the standard against which all modern running backs are measured. Other NFL records broken by Brown included rushing yards in a single season (1,863), total career rushing yards (12,312), and career touchdowns (126).

In the 1960s there was no debating that Jim Brown was the greatest running back in football history. Despite more recent all-star backs—like O. J. Simpson, who surpassed Brown's season rushing record, and Walter Payton, who eventually scored more rushing touchdowns—many contend that Brown remains the greatest running back of all time. He was inducted into the Pro Football Hall of Fame in 1971.

"What he could not run past he would try to run through," wrote author Morris Eckhouse in *Day by Day in Cleveland Browns History*

Jim Brown

(1984), "and he kept coming year after year. Fans still see glimpses of Brown's amazing runs, dragging tacklers, spinning away from defenders, outracing defensive backs...."

Brown retired from football to pursue a career on the big screen, starring in such movies as *Rio Conchos* (1964), *The Dirty Dozen* (1967), and *Three the Hard Way* (1974). Brown went on to establish the national Amer-I-Can Foundation, an organization that targets inner-city African-American youth, gang members in particular. He also returned to the Cleveland Browns as a team consultant.

349

DECEMBER 30

On December 30, 1952, the Tuskegee Institute reported that 1952 was the first year in seventy-one years of record keeping that no one was lynched in the United States. This was not to last, however. On August 28, 1955, 14-year-old Emmett Till was kidnapped and lynched in Money, Mississippi.

The Tuskegee Institute had begun keeping lynching records in 1882. Examples of previous totals include 211 killed in 1884, 235 in 1892, and 200 in 1900. By the turn of the century the total number of recorded lynchings was 3,011; and in every year until 1900, a minimum of 100 persons—mainly African-Americans—were shot, hung, burned, tortured, or beaten to death.

In 1929 Will W. Alexander, Director of the Commission of Interracial Co-operation, somewhat incorrectly predicted that "lynching will be a lost crime by 1940—something for scientists to study and the rest of us to remember with unbelief." Horace B. Davis of Southwestern College in Memphis may have been more accurate with his statement that, "figures for reduced numbers of lynchings are not satisfactory so long as they merely cover up a change in style, from rope to gun."

DECEMBER 31

On the last day of the year in 1980, the *New York Times* announced that African-American country-and-western singer Charley Pride would be among the entertainers at President Ronald Reagan's Inaugural Gala early the next year. One of the best-selling songsters in America, Mississippi-born Charley Pride is the first African-American country music star.

A former baseball player in the professional Negro Leagues, Pride recorded his first album *The Snakes Crawl at Night*, in 1965 on the RCA label. In 1967 he became the first African-American to appear at

Nashville, Tennessee's Grand Ole Opry. By 1969 he had released his first number-one hit on the country music single's chart, "All I Have to Offer You (Is Me)." At the fifth annual Country Music Awards at the Grand Ole Opry in 1971 he won country music's top award, Entertainer of the Year, as well as Male Vocalist of the Year. "I'm shaking again," said the star upon receiving the entertainer of the year award, "but I'm just happy." He then performed his hit song "Kiss an Angel Good Morning," for which the Grand Ole Opry crowd gave him a standing ovation.

BIBLIOGRAPHY

Adams, Russell L. *Great Negroes Past and Present*. Chicago: Afro-American Publishing Company Inc., 1963.

Bennett, Lerone, Jr. *Before the Mayflower, A History of Black America*. New York: Penguin Books, 1988.

Bennett, Lerone, Jr. *Wade in the Water: Great Moments in Black History*. Chicago: Johnson Publishing Company Inc., 1979.

Blanco, Richard L. *The American Revolution 1775–1783, An Encyclopedia*. 1993.

Blockson, Charles L. *Hippocrene Guide to the Underground Railroad*. New York: Hippocrene Books, 1994.

Bogle, Donald. *Blacks in American Films and Television*. New York: Garland Publishing, Inc., 1988.

Bontemps, Arna. *The Harlem Renaissance Remembered*. New York: Dodd, Mead and Company, 1975.

Brown, Sterling A., Davis, Arthur P. and Lee, Ulysses, eds. *The Negro Caravan*. New York: The Citadel Press, 1941.

Busby, Margaret, ed. *Daughters of Africa*. New York: Pantheon Books, 1992.

Byrd, Rudolph P., ed. *Generations in Black and White*. Athens, Geo: University of Georgia Press, 1993.

Cantor, George. *Historic Black Landmarks, A Traveler's Guide*. Detroit: Visible Ink Press, 1991.

Carruth, Gorton. *The Encyclopedia of American Facts & Dates*. New York: Harper and Row, 1990.

Foley, Albert S. *God's Men of Color*. Salem, New Hampshire: Ayer Company Publishers Inc., 1955.

Gale Research Co. *Dictionary of Literary Biographies* Afro-American Writers and Poets Series, Detroit.

Garrett, Romeo B., *Famous First Facts About Negroes*. New York: Arno Press, 1972.

Gross, Ernie. *This Day in American History*. New York: Neal-Schuman Publishers, 1990.

Haber, Louis. *Black Pioneers of Science & Invention*. New York: Harcourt Brace Jovanovich, 1970.

Haglund, Elaine J., and Harris, Marcia L. *On This Day*. Littleton Colorado: Libraries Unlimited Inc., 1983.

Harrison, Paul Carter. *Black Light, the African-American Hero*. New York: Thunder's Mouth Press, 1993.

Haskins, James. *Black Music in America*. New York: Thomas Y. Crowell, 1987.

Hughes, Langston; Meltzer, Milton; and Lincoln, C. Eric. *A Pictorial History of Blackamericans*, New York: Crown Publishers, 1983.

Katz, William Loren. *Eyewitness, The Negro in American History*. New York: Pitman Publishing Corp., 1967.

Kirk, Elise K. *Musical Highlights From the White House*. Florida: Kreiger Publishing Co., 1992.

Knaack, Twila. *Ethel Waters, I Touched a Sparrow*. Waco, Texas: Word Books, 1978.

Lomax, Alan, *Mister Jelly Roll*. Berkeley: University of California Press, 1950.

McNeil, Alex. *Total Television, A Comprehensive Guide to Programming from 1948 to the Present*. New York: Penguin Books, 1991.

McRae, Barry. *The Jazz Handbook*. Boston: G. K. Hall and Co., 1987.

Meltzer, Milton. *In Their Own Words, A History of the American Negro 1865–1916*. New York: Thomas Y. Crowell Co., 1965.

Mullane, Deirdre. *Crossing the Danger Water, Three Hundred Years of African-American Writing*. New York: Doubleday, 1993.

Oliver, Paul. *Blues Fell This Morning, Meaning in the Blues*. Cambridge, England: Cambridge University Press, 1960.

Ovington, Mary White. *Portraits in Color*. New York: Books for Libraries Press, 1927.

Packwood, Cyril Outerbridge. *Detour—Bermuda, Destination—U.S. House of Representatives: The Life of Joseph Rainey*. Bermuda: Baxter's Limited, 1977.

Ploski, Harry A., and Williams, James, eds. *The Negro Almanac: A Reference Work on the Afro American*. 4th ed. New York: John Wiley & Sons, 1983.

Plowden, Martha Ward. *Famous Firsts of Black Women*. Gretna: Pelican Publishing Co., 1993.

Porter, Kenneth W. *The Negro of the American Frontier*. New York: Arno Press and the *New York Times*, 1971.

Richardson, Marilyn, ed. *Maria W. Stewart, America's First Black Woman Political Writer*. Bloomington: Indiana University Press, 1987.

Riley, Dorothy Winbush, ed. *My Soul Looks Black, 'Less I Forget, A Collection of Quotations by People of Color*. New York: Harper Collins Publishers, 1991.

Salley, Columbus. *The Black 100*. New York: Carol Publishing Group, 1993.

Sharp, Saundra. *Black Women for Beginners*. New York: Writers and Readers, 1993.

Sloan, Irving J. *The Blacks in America 1492–1977*. New York: Oceana Publications Inc., 1977.

Stambler, Irwin. *The Encyclopedia of Pop, Rock & Soul*. New York: St. Martin's Press, 1989.

BIBLIOGRAPHY

Stevens, Peter F. *The Mayflower Murderer and Other Forgotten Firsts in American History.* New York: William Morrow and Co. Inc., 1993.

Studio Museum in Harlem, New York. *Harlem Renaissance, Art of Black America.* New York: Harry N. Abrams Inc. Publishers, 1987.

Tee, Ralph. *The Best of Soul: The Essential CD Guide.* San Francisco: Collins Publishers, 1993.

The Schomburg Library of Nineteenth-Century Black Women Writers. *Two Biographies of African-American Women.* New York: Oxford University Press, 1991.

Vecchione, Joseph J., ed. *New York Times Book of Sports Legends.* New York: *Times* Books and Random House, 1991.

Yates, Elizabeth. *Amos Fortune Free Man.* New York: E. P. Dutton and Co. Inc., 1950.

Yount, Lisa. *Black Scientists.* New York: Facts on File, 1991.

INDEX

Subjects are indexed by date.

INDEX

Convention of 1830 (November 30)
Cooper, Ralph (August 10)
Cornish, Samuel E. (March 16)
Cosby, Bill (September 2, November 4, December 4)
Cotton Club (June 30, December 25)
Counter, Dr. S. Allen (April 6)
Craft, William and Ellen (October 7)
Crazy Snake Uprising (March 28)
Crib, Tom (September 28)
Crisis magazine (January 12, May 26, July 23)
Crocker, Sergeant (May 13)
Crummell, Alexander (April 1)
Crump, Edward H. (September 27)
Cuffe, Paul (February 9)
Cullen, Countee (January 9, March 1)
Culp, Robert (September 2)
Custer's Last Stand (June 25)

D

Dade, Maj. Francis L. (December 28)
Dart, Isom (August 5)
Davis, Angela (March 29, June 4)
Davis, Benjamin O., Jr. and Sr. (October 27)
Davis, Miles (January 11)
Davis, Sammy, Jr. (March 8, May 25)
Deadwood Dick (February 10)
Delany, Dr. Martin R. (February 6, April 1, August 19)
DeLarge, Robert C. (March 4)
DePriest, Oscar (June 24)

Democratic National Convention (Chicago, 1968) (July 14) New York, 1976 (November 17)
Desegregation of Washington, D.C. restaurants (June 8, July 21)
Detroit riots (July 25)
Diddley, Bo (September 14)
Diggs, Charles C. (January 22)
Dinkins, David (January 2, July 5)
"The Dirty Dozen" (September 14)
Dorman, Isaiah (June 25)
Douglas, Aaron (March 1, May 26, June 9, July 8)
Douglass, Frederick (February 6, 20, March 14, April 12, July 25, August 15, 19, December 3, 19)
Downing, Al (April 8)
Drew, Charles R. (July 16, August 14)
DuBois, W. E. B. (January 8, February 12, 19, 23, March 1, April 5, May 5, 13, June 26, July 11, August 18, October 6, 23, November 9, December 2)
Dunbar, Paul Laurence (June 27, August 4, October 17)
DuSable, Jean Baptist Point (March 13)
Dyer Anti-Lynching Bill (July 29)
Dyson, Michael Eric (April 4)

E

Eatonville, Florida (January 28)
Ebony (January 19)
Eckstine, Billy (March 27)
Eisenhower, Dwight D. (January 4, September 23)

INDEX

Elaine, Arkansas riots (December 27)

Elder, Lee (December 12)

Elizabeth II (Queen of England) (November 21)

Ellicot, Andrew (October 9)

Ellington, Duke (March 1, May 24, 28, November 11)

Elliot, Robert Brown (January 6, March 4)

Ellis, Jimmy (February 16)

Ellison, Ralph (May 31)

Emancipation Proclamation (January 1)

Emporer Jones (May 23, October 19, November 3)

Estabrook, Prince (April 19)

Estavanico (March 7)

Ethnic names (July 24)

Evers, Medgar W. (June 12)

Exodusters (February 7, October 18)

F

Fard, W. D. (August 13)

Farrakhan, Louis (August 13)

Faulkner, William (May 31)

Fauset, Crystal Bird (November 8)

Fetchit, Stepin (November 19)

Fields, Jackie (May 9)

Fifteenth Amendment (February 3, March 30)

Fifty-fourth Massachusetts Volunteers (January 26, April 12, July 18)

First African settlers in America (August 20)

First Church of Christ, Farmington, Connecticut (March 9)

First Church of Christ, Lynn, Massachusetts (March 20)

First South Carolina Volunteers (April 12)

Fisher, Gail (August 27)

Fisk Jubilee Singers (October 6)

Fitzgerald, Ella (August 10)

Flack, Roberta (February 24, December 4)

For Colored Girls Who Have Considered Suicide When the Rainbow Isn't Enough (July 7)

Ford, Barney (September 4)

Ford, Wallace L., II (July 24)

Foreman, George (October 30)

Fort Des Moines Provisional Army Officer Training School (June 15)

Fort Wagner (January 26, July 18)

Forten, James (March 18, August 17)

Fortune, Amos (April 22)

Foster, Stephen (October 22)

Founders of Los Angeles (September 4)

Four Tops (April 14)

Fourteenth Amendment (July 9, December 14)

Franklin, Benjamin (February 18, September 20)

Frazier, Alice (November 21)

Frazier, Joe (February 16, October 1)

Free Speech and Headlight (March 25)

Freedman's Bureau (March 3)

Freedom Riders (May 4)

Freedom's Journal (March 14, 16)

Fuller, Henrietta (March 18)

Fuller, Meta Vaux Warrick (June 9)

359

INDEX

INDEX

N

Napier, Sam (April 17)

Nashville Student Movement (May 4)

Nation of Islam (May 19, August 13)

National Association for the Advancement of Colored People, (NAACP) (February 12, 13, 23, May 4, 17, June 8, July 11, 21, 25, August 23, 28, October 11, 13, 23, November 6, December 23)

National Association of Colored Graduate Nurses (June 29)

National Association of Colored Women (February 22, July 21)

National Convention of Colored Men (August 15)

National Council of Negro Women (June 28)

National Liberty Congress of Colored Americans (July 29)

National Press Club (February 5)

National Urban League (January 12, February 13, July 31, August 28, October 11)

Native Americans (February 17, March 12, 13, 28, June 25, September 11, 20, December 28)

Neal, Annie (September 4)

Negro Digest (January 19)

New Negro (March 1)

New Orleans Riots of 1866 (July 30)

Newman, Lyda D. (July 17)

Newton, Huey P. (March 29)

Niagara Movement (July 11, 21, August 18, November 9)

Nicodemus, Kansas (February 7, October 18)

Ninth Calvary (September 1)

Nixon, Richard (January 22, June 17)

Nobel Prizes (March 31, September 22, December 11)

Norman, Peter (October 16)

Norris, Clarence (October 25)

North Carolina Mutual and Provident (October 20)

North Star (February 6, 20 December 3)

Northwest Ordinance (July 13)

O

Oberlin College (June 19)

Ogden, Dunbar H. (September 23)

Okker, Tom (July 5)

Opportunity magazine (January 12, May 26)

Our Nig (September 5)

Owens, Jesse (August 3)

P

Paige, Satchel (September 25)

Palmer, Arnold (July 15)

Pan-African Congress (February 19)

Paris Exposition of 1900 (November 12)

Parker, Alice H. (July 17)

Parker, Charlie (March 27)

Parker, David (August 28)

Parks, Gordon Sr. and Jr. (June 16)

Parks, Rosa (December 1)

Payton, Walter (December 29)

Peary, Adm. Robert E. (April 6)

Peete, Calvin (December 12)

Perry, Jim (May 30)

Peterson, Thomas (March 30)

INDEX

INDEX

S

St. Augustine, Florida (October 10)

St. Luke Penny Savings Bank (November 2)

Salem, Peter (August 16)

Salem Witchcraft Trials (February 29)

San Juan Hill (September 1)

Saunders, George W. (May 30)

Saunders, Wallace (April 30)

Schaap, Dick (March 8)

Schmeling, Max (June 22)

Schwerner, Michael (June 21)

Scott, Dred (March 6)

Scottsboro Trial (October 25)

Seale, Bobby (March 29)

Searles, Joseph L. (January 30)

Selika, Marie (November 14)

Selma to Montgomery March (March 21)

Seminole Wars (March 28, May 27, September 11, December 28)

Shange, Ntozake (July 7)

Shaw, Robert Gould (April 12, July 18, November 10)

Sheridan, General (July 30)

Shoe Lasting Machine (March 20)

Shuffle Along (May 23 October 28)

Sierra Leone (May 8)

Sifford, Charlie (December 12)

Simpson, O. J. (December 29)

Sinatra, Frank (June 26)

Singleton, Benjamin "Pap" (February 7, October 18)

Sirhan, Sirhan (June 5)

Sissle, Noble (May 23, June 30)

Sitting Bull (June 25)

16th-Street Baptist Church (September 15)

Smalls, Robert (April 12, May 13)

Smith, Bessie (March 1, September 26)

Smith, Charlie (October 5)

Smith, Tommie (October 16)

Smokey Robinson and the Miracles (April 14)

South Carolina Constitutional Convention (January 14)

South Carolina Slave Rebellions (September 9)

South Central Los Angeles riots (April 29)

South Pacific (April 7)

Southern Christian Leadership Conference, (SCLC) (February 13, May 4, August 28, October 11)

Spanish-American War (September 1)

Speckled Red (September 14)

Spelman College (November 4)

Spingarn, Joel E. (February 12)

Spinks, Leon (October 30)

Stagecoach Mary (September 4)

Staupers, Mable Keaton (June 29)

Stephens, Alexander H. (January 6)

Stevens, Thaddeus (March 3)

Stewart, Maria W. (February 27, September 21, October 8, December 17)

Still, William (September 16, October 7, November 25)

Stock exchange (January 30)

Stokes, Carl B. (November 7)

Stono Slave Rebellion (September 9)

Vesey, Denmark (July 2)
Vietnam War (March 24)
Villa Lewaro (May 11)
Voodoo Queen (June 23)
Voting Rights Act of 1965 (February 3, March 15, 21)

W

WACs (December 13)
Walker, A'Lelia (March 1, May 11)
Walker, Alice (January 28)
Walker, David (*Walker's Appeal*) (January 18)
Walker, Madame C. J. (May 11, December 23)
Walker, Maggie Lena (November 2)
Walker, Moses Fleetwood (January 24)
Wallace, George (March 21, October 25)
Walls, Josiah T. (March 4)
War of 1812 (December 18)
Warren, Earl B. (May 17)
Washington, Booker T. (April 5, June 27, July 11, 17, 28, August 18, September 18, November 9)
Washington, George (April 19, 25, October 9)
Washington (Walter E., November 7)
Watergate (June 17)
Waters, Ethel (March 1, May 28, October 31)
Waters, Maxine (April 29)
Watson, J. B. (August 18)
Watts Riots (April 29, July 25, August 11, 12)

WAVES, (December 13)
"We Shall Overcome" (March 15, 21)
Weaver, Dr. Robert (January 13)
WEDR, (October 3)
Wells, Ida B. (March 25, July 21)
Wheatley, Phillis (April 25, July 24, December 15, 21)
Whipper, William (September 16, November 30)
White, Walter (March 1, August 23, October 23)
Wilkins, Roy (July 25, September 8)
Williams, Clarence, III (September 24)
Williams, Daniel Hale (August 4)
Williams, Paul R. (June 26)
Williams, Sampson (November 14)
Williams, Shirley (October 26)
Williams, Vanessa (September 17)
Wills, Frank (June 17)
Wilson, Flip (March 23)
Wilson, Harriet E. Adams (September 5)
Wilson, Jackie (January 21)
Winfrey, Oprah (December 24)
Witt, Katarina (February 8)
Wonder, Stevie (April 14)
Woodard, Lynette (October 4)
Woods, Granville T. (November 29)
Woodson, Carter G. (June 29, December 4, 19)
World War I (June 15)
World War II (June 6, December 7, 13)
Wright, Fanny (February 27)
Wright, Orville and Wilbur (June 27)